A HORROR BEYOND DESCRIPTION

He heard the other men of the so-called search party singing and fighting and cursing behind him, and he couldn't understand how they could be so callous about it.

Then he saw something caught in the glare of his flashlight.

·Something appeared to be—bending, if that was the word—over the remains of a human body. He saw other figures lying there, too, just on the edges of the circle of light, their bloodied and mutilated forms covered by shadows. The lips of the thing—if you could say it had lips—were eating something: a piece of meat, a morsel, no longer recognizable as part of a leg or an arm. Blood dripped down from the chewing orifice. He stepped back, too shocked to scream, and his light shined over the other bodies which had been formerly hidden by the dark. His eyes widened in pain and disbelief, his worst fears realized . . .

SPAWN OF HELL

William Schoell

LEISURE BOOKS ❧ NEW YORK CITY

A LEISURE BOOK

Published by

Dorchester Publishing Co., Inc.
6 East 39th Street
New York, NY 10016

Printed in the United States of America

Prologue

Hillsboro, Vermont—Summer, 1983

Violet Harper wasn't sleeping very well.

She would have been surprised to know that out of the six hours since she'd gone to bed, she'd actually been asleep for a full hour. It seemed to her as if she had spent the entire night tossing and turning, practically delirious, odd thoughts and pictures entering her head, keeping her from getting her rest. No one could have convinced her that in between these frequent spells of restlessness she was indeed held tight in the arms of slumber; not deeply, but enough for her to dream, and in those dreams, to see the same images, hear the same words she had been tormented by while awake. To her the night had been one long uninterrupted bout with insomnia.

That's why she was surprised when she looked over to the other side of the bed and saw that her husband was gone. How the hell had he sneaked out of there without her even hearing? She was startled by a footfall, and then the sight of her husband re-entering the bedroom. She expected to see a glass of milk or a sandwich in his hand, and was prepared to scold him—he'd stay on his diet if it killed her—but if Robert had eaten he had done so in the kitchen in private.

"What you up for?" she asked. Her hair was in

curlers and there was cold cream on her face, and she looked a fright, but they'd been married much too long for her to care at this point. At forty-five she had other things to worry about. She had the kind of homely face that on women often develops character and dignity with age. Not that she looked dignified right now.

"Couldn't you hear the dog yammering?" her husband whined. "She's been hollering on and off for the past hour and a half." Robert was three years older than Violet, slightly plump around the middle, with thick reddish hair above a broad and pleasant face. He sat down on the edge of the bed and let out a long, low sigh of exasperation.

"What's the matter with her? Did she have to go?"

"She did and she's done it. Maybe now we'll have some peace."

That was not to be the case.

Both of the Harpers were fluffing up their pillows, straightening the blanket, when suddenly they heard it. An odd sound. A strange sound. Something like a kiddie car—one of those little autos children could sit and drive in—pulled over concrete, its small plastic wheels stumbling over the cracks in the sidewalk.

Only there was no sidewalk. And neither of their children had a kiddie car to play with.

Then the dog started to bark again, as if she too had been alerted to some threat. And worst of all, little Bobby began to cry.

"Oh dear," Violet complained. "Won't I ever get any sleep tonight?"

"Stay here, honey," her husband instructed. "I'll see what the matter is." He got back out of bed, put on his bathrobe, and walked out into the hall. Violet couldn't help but smile. Robert doted on that son of theirs—only three years old and such a doll. He didn't pay as much attention to their daughter Lucy, who was seven, but he still loved her, she was sure, and didn't mean to ignore her. Besides, Violet made up for it by giving Lucy that much extra time. Violet saw the bright moonlight streaming in through the bedroom windows and idly wondered if it was the cause of her insomnia.

She couldn't hear that odd sound anymore, not over the barks of the dog and Bobby's crying.

Robert Harper walked down the hallway to the children's room. Someday they'd both be yammering for their own room and he'd have to build an addition onto the house. If he could afford it. He spent most of his waking hours wondering where he'd get the money for this and that. There was never enough, although they got by better than most. He wondered if it were the dog that had awakened his boy.

He opened the door of the nursery and stepped inside. The room was slightly illuminated by a glow from the window. Lucy was wide awake, sitting up in bed, her blanket pulled up and wrapped around her, her little fists holding onto it as if it were all that stood between her and the frigid arctic winds. Robert Harper could see horror in her face.

"What's goin' on in here?" he said in a cheery voice, his hand inching up towards the light switch, trying to find it, but missing. He looked over at Bobby's bed. The little fellow was really wailing now, frozen on top of the mattress, his tiny eyes fastened on some form—hidden in the shadows—that was sitting by the side of the bed. Unable to find the light switch quickly enough, Harper swore and moved forward while the room was still dark.

"What the Hell—!" For just a moment Harper was convinced that the *dog* had somehow gotten into the house, and he moved angrily over towards her. Then he stopped short. There was something wrong. For one thing, he could still hear the animal hollering out in the garage. For another, the children would never have been scared of her, not even if she had crawled unbidden into the blackness of their bedroom.

"Daddy! Daddy!" Bobby cried. "It's on my leg! It's on my leg!"

Lucy screamed in empathy.

Harper saw that the black shape had indeed moved up to the mattress, part of it covering the lower portion of Bobby's body. There was a disgusting, slurping sound and the child screamed out in pain. Lucy stood up straight on her mattress, still clutching the blanket. Harper ran the few steps between him and the bed, and began to beat at the form covering Bobby's legs. "Lucy. Turn on the light. For God's sake, go and turn on the light!"

Lucy was too stricken with terror to do anything but watch her father battle with the thing in the corner by Bobby's bed. Harper felt something sharp insert itself into his arm, felt the bulk of the beast as it threw itself against his body. He nearly tumbled to the floor. His hands tried to grab the thing, but slid off as if it were coated with grease. A slimy substance dripped onto his fingers and his clothes, and an overpowering odor filled the room. Something like a needle, only thicker, punctured his right leg, and he dropped to his knees in agony. He heard the sound again, like the one before, only louder, closer. He screamed.

Lucy saw the two shapes twisting together in the darkness, and even if she could have turned on the light she would not have. The forms rose, then fell, then rose again, neither seeming to have the advantage. One figure —she could tell if was her father—collapsed onto the ground and didn't get up. She waited and waited but he did not rise. She heard horrible noises, like chewing sounds.

Then she heard another kind of noise. Something was clambering in through the open window. Another one of *those*. It dropped to the ground with a thud, then climbed up the bed and onto her brother. Plop. Another

8

one dropped in. Then another. They all climbed on top of Bobby.

And then they came for her.

She wondered all that time where her mother was, and why she did not come to help them.

In the bedroom down the hall, Violet Harper was recoiling from the sight of something that had smashed in through the window a few minutes before. She could not take her eyes off it. She was simply too shocked to call for help. She was dimly aware of the screams of her husband and children from the nursery, but she was quite incapable of reacting to them—and would never be able to again.

The thing on the floor made its way across the thick blue carpet towards the double bed. Its eyes glared back into Violet's horror-twisted countenance. It moved past the door to the bathroom, blocking the view of tiled floor; gleaming chrome and porcelain; yellow shower curtain. It moved past the dresser, with its collection of music and jewelry boxes and pictures of the long-ago honeymoon. Past the ottoman at the end of the bed, where Violet often sat to remove her stockings at the end of a weary day. Violet thought of the most mundane things as her death slowly approached her: an extravagance, Robert had said of the ottoman, but she had liked it.

No one could have said that the thing on the floor was even remotely human. It had no arms or legs, but rather patchwork parts that seemed more common to other species, other animals. It was quite large and lumbering. But the worst thing, the absolutely worst thing, the thing that kept Violet paralyzed on her bed, the thing that almost made her welcome death as an alternative to madness—was the *head*.

The head wasn't quite human, either. It had unusual features, a foreign look about it, indicating different ways of . . . eating. But it had a face. Oh yes, it had a face.

It was the face of someone who'd been dead for six months.

It was the face of Violet's mother.

Part One

Birth

Chapter One

New York City—Spring, 1983

David Hammond was being released.

After a lengthy stay in an antiseptic place filled with crisp-looking nurses, efficient doctors and desperate patients, there was nothing more they could do for him. Nothing more they could say. He was finally going home.

He changed from his hospital gown into his clothes. Faded blue jeans. A pale blue shirt with what appeared to be a mustard stain on the front of it. Green wool socks. Brown shoes. A thin gray jacket with a zipper that only worked half the time. He waited for the nurse to come.

While he waited he looked around the room and studied for the final time the place that had been his home these past few weeks. The floor was a collection of dirty yellow tiles, each perfectly square and of similar size, except for those near the walls which were cut by the room dividers into fractions. His bed was higher off the floor than a normal one would be, and had a thick, hard mattress that was good for his back, but not especially comfortable. The sheets were brilliantly white. Only on closer inspection could one see the assorted stains that the Clorox couldn't get out. Those stains always disgusted him. They were other people's stains half the time, he thought, not his. It made no difference now. He was leaving.

The walls, too, were yellow. Painted only a year or so ago. They would have captured the sunlight from the big long windows over the radiator had any managed to cut through the billowing clouds outside. There were no paintings or posters of pictures on the walls. Nothing.

Next to the bed was a night table within which was the usual assortment of hospital giveaways. A small container of mouthwash, a small tube of toothpaste, a tiny little toothbrush, some deodorant and extra soap. Things like that. David stuffed it all in his jacket pocket; he could use it.

There were some old papers, magazines and dog-eared paperbacks lying on top of the table. He looked through them but saw nothing he wanted to keep, nothing he'd need to read again. He picked up a large white cup full of water and drained it. It was warm and tasteless, but he was thirsty.

He stepped into the bathroom and stared at himself in the mirror. His blue eyes were still the same. He still had that waif-like look, that quiet despondency in his eyes, intensified by his loss of weight and the other debilitating effects of a hospital stay; the after-effects of the accident. His face was somewhat pale and gaunt. He didn't look healthy, but they said he was. He needed to get out in the sun.

His thick black hair needed a good combing. If he was the type he would have planned on getting it attractively styled, but he couldn't afford it even if he wanted to. Besides, keeping it short the way he usually did (although it needed trimming now) left it looking nice enough for him. Cheap, too.

His deep-set eyes, strong nose and chin, not-quite-full lips made a nice-looking face, if not a handsome one. Thirty-three. Thirty-three years old. God—he couldn't believe it. Just yesterday he was fresh out of college,

14

looking for work, planning a career. He had worked out his whole life ahead of time, each tomorrow building into an even better one, a fabulous future full of enough money, some fame, lots of friends.

Instead he was broke, struggling along, virtually friendless, his career going nowhere. The accident had been the topper. What a way to begin the Eighties. Everything had been bruised and battered, except, luckily, his face, which wouldn't have mattered that much as he wasn't a beauty to begin with—no modeling or movie career for him. Yet he was still relieved. There was already enough stress in his life.

Perhaps this depressing stay in the hospital was exactly what he'd needed. Lots of rest. Fairly good food, three times a day. (Did people still eat three meals a day?) A healthy doctor-approved diet instead of one forced on him by poverty. Time off from his worries and woes. Except that worrying about his legs kept him from relaxing very much, aside from when they gave him medication, in which case sleep would come no matter what. He had substituted the tension of surviving day to day with the strain of wondering if he would walk like everyone else did, or come out of the accident with a permanent disorder.

Well, now he knew. He would limp the rest of his days. Noticeably. His right leg just wouldn't do what it should. Oh, it got by. He didn't need crutches; nothing like that. An operation—a costly one—might improve it a bit, but not much, and it wasn't all that bad to begin with. He had practiced walking up and down the hospital halls, and discovered that if he put his mind to it and walked fast enough, people might not even realize that he was mildly crippled. Dancing? Out of the question. Running? Not for long. Swimming? No problem. Standing? Not for lengthy periods if it could be avoided. He had a right to those subway seats marked: PLEASE SAVE FOR THE HANDICAPPED.

He kept telling himself that he was lucky. It hadn't been worse. It could have been. He could have been dead, like . . . like . . . no, he couldn't say the name, couldn't think of—of her—just now. Too early for that. Much too early.

He put his hair in place with a little institutional comb, pocketed it and left the bathroom. He sat back down on the bed.

He should consider himself lucky.

But one he left the hospital, it would be back to the same desperate life of trying to get ahead while getting nowhere. Spaghetti six days a week, chicken on Sundays. One meal a day. Lots of old pictures on TV instead of going to the movies. No luxuries—what most people considered necessities. Struggling, struggling, struggling. No sex, no romance. Back to that? He'd rather stay in the hospital. Put it off awhile. Once he was out he'd have to think about the bill. Not that it mattered. He had lots of bills, none of them paid. It was a good thing debtors weren't jailed these days. He would have declared bankruptcy if he could have afforded it.

The nurse came in.

"How are you today, Mr. Hammond? Glad to be getting out?" A burly elderly wheeled a chair into the room. David smiled but did not reply.

"Is this necessary. I can walk."

"Rules are rules," she said. Small face, stringy hair. About forty-five. He had liked her. She was motherly.

They helped him into the wheelchair and rolled him out of the room and onto the elevator. In a few minutes, he would be free.

And trapped again.

Home looked the same as when he had left it. He hadn't been here since before the accident, before he took that fateful ride with . . . it all came back to him in a flood as soon as he opened the door to his apartment

16

and saw the pad lying on the floor next to the couch which served as his bed. *Not now! Not yet!*

He had been sketching a drawing of her when the call came. He'd been down on his knees working on the floor as he preferred, busy shaping her mouth, her eyes, her lovely cheeks, trying to capture her just so. He didn't want to look at that sketch. Not now. He bent down, picked it up, flipped it over and threw it onto the kitchen table. The "kitchen" was really just a corner with a refrigerator, small stove and sink.

For ten years he had lived in this studio in a brownstone near Riverside Drive. During that time he had worked at dozens of odd jobs, trying to feed himself and pay the rent, which was low once and higher now, while building a career as a commercial artist and cartoonist. He had once come close to getting a deal with a syndicate for a series in a daily paper, many papers around the country. But it fell through. That was another thing he didn't want to think about. It had been tough going ever since.

He went over to his file cabinet, actually a box on top of a chair at the table. Full of thousands of papers full of sketches, rejected drawings, ideas, concepts, doodles. He had sold a few things over the years, but not enough to support himself. His last odd job as a clerk in a greeting-card firm (he'd tried countless times to show someone his drawings, to no avail) had ended with him being laid off and going on unemployment. He'd made up his mind that he would "make it" during those few months when he got those small, but functional checks from the city. But by the time his unemployment was up, he was still nowhere. He'd done a lot of work without reward.

He'd lived on his savings, watching them dwindle dangerously. Still working, working, working, pursuing the odd job now and then without conviction. Then came the accident.

It changed everything. It changed nothing.

Now he was back to square one. Minus one friend. *Friend?* She's been much more than a friend. And now she was dead. He began to wonder if he had really been the lucky one.

He could still hear her voice. Light. Musical. Perfect diction. Her lips crafting words instead of speaking them. "Let's go out to the country this afternoon, okay?"

"I can't. I'm busy," he had said.

"I know I promised never to disturb you when you were working. But it's such a beautiful day. Are you sure you want to be cooped up like that? It's so hot and stuffy in that apartment."

Oh, how she could work on him. So hard to resist. He was naturally lazy. "It's not that bad. I've got the window open. There's a breeze from the river."

"Watch out some burglar doesn't come up the fire escape and crawl into your window." A persistent fear.

"What would he get?" A dollar in change?

"Look, I'll leave you alone. I don't want to be selfish. But if you change your mind I'll be home until three."

"What's happening at three?"

"If you don't want to go for a drive, *I'm* going to the movies."

"What's playing?"

He didn't remember what her answer had been. Had she answered? Maybe she had not had a specific picture in mind. Then he had said:

"Give me half an hour to finish."

"I'll pick you up in an hour."

He *had* finished in half an hour. Then, while waiting for her to buzz him over the intercom in the downstairs hallway, he had idly doodled, then worked seriously on a sketch of her. *That* sketch of her, on the table. The last thing he had ever done. Before . . .

But why think of it? Time to wipe away the cobwebs.

Time to get what was left of his life back in order.

He wondered: Did anyone know he was alive? A few people—*her* friends—had wanted to see him in the hospital, but he had instructed the nurse to tell the front desk that he wanted no visitors. In time they gave up trying. Of course, his father was sick himself and couldn't make it, and David had told him not to worry. His father was lots worse off than he was, recovering from a stroke; the man would probably never be the same. David would have to call him later, tell him he was out of the hospital.

His legs started throbbing as he went around the small studio apartment looking things over. They had said that that would happen occasionally; he would get used to it. But it made it hard to concentrate.

The bed was a mess, just as he'd left it. One of the cupboard doors above the sink was wide open, revealing a few supplies of canned goods and detergent. The tattered blue rug that covered only half the floor looked worse than ever. The plaster on the walls was peeling.

It was worse in the bathroom, which was so small he could barely turn around without bumping into something. Mildew had conquered and crowned itself king, and some of the tiles in the shower had fallen out of the wall and into the tub. It was impossible to see out of the grimy yellow window set high in the wall. He splashed some cold water on his face. He looked different in this mirror, because of its oddly curved and cracked glass which distorted his image, and the low light in the room, which created attractive shadows on his features. He didn't look so pale.

The phone rang. He went to the night table next to the sofa-bed and picked up the receiver in the middle of the third ring. He recognized the craggy voice on the other end of the line immediately. It was his father. He could picture him sitting up in bed, one of those cigars of his in his mouth—of course they wouldn't let him smoke in the hospital—jowly and red-faced, with small black eyes peering out intensely from a field of flesh. How old now —sixty? Sixty-one? Forcibly retired from his job with a pharmaceutical company by illness.

"I called the hospital," his father said. "They told me you had been released."

"Ah, so that's how you knew." David sat down on the bed, wondering what they'd say to each other. Five minutes at least.

"How are you feeling? I'm glad you're out."

"Yeah—me, too. I'm okay. My leg hurts, but that's life."

"Is it very bad?"

"No. I won't be able to jitterbug, but I was never much for that." He let out a feeble laugh. His father did not respond. He sounded worried. Very worried.

"You must need money."

"No, no," David said quickly. "I'll be all right. Don't worry."

"I don't have much, but if you need—"

"No. No really. That's okay. Now that I'm out of the hospital, I should be able to find work in a few days. And I've still got money in the bank." He knew his father didn't have much money. And his *own* hospital bills were tremendous.

"Well, if you're sure. Look, did you ever think about coming up here to live? The house is empty now, you could stay there. You could look for work in Hillsboro. Did you ever think about that?"

"Dad, there are very few opportunities for artists in Hillsboro; *this* is the place—"

"Are you still on that 'artist' kick?" Kick. It would always be a "kick" to his father, even when David was fifty years old. A kick.

"I'm talking about real work," the old man continued. "There are jobs up here. Hell, maybe you could even get work as an artist. There's a lot less competition up in this neck of the woods for that sort of thing, y' know."

"Yes, I'm sure there is." Oh boy, how he didn't want the conversation to go in this direction.

"It's just a thought, y' know. If you have problems, you know you can come home."

"I know that, Dad. Thanks. But I'd rather take my chances down here; at least for a while." Now it was coming, David thought in an instant, now he'd say: *You've had ten years already.*

But he didn't. Instead he said. "So, how was it in the hospital? Did they feed you properly?"

They talked for several minutes on David's stay in the sick ward, the food, the nurses, the care he'd received. And so on. *Her* name was never mentioned. David realized how much he needed someone to talk to, about her, about himself, about everything. But his father wasn't the one. His father had his own worries, his own humiliations and defeats to nurse. Near the end of his life, he couldn't worry that much about David's, which was just beginning in comparison.

"Well, time for me to take my medicine." His father ended every conversation by saying "time to take my medicine," regardless of the hour.

"Thanks for calling, Dad."

"You'll be okay?"

"Yeah. I'll be all right. Don't worry."

"Okay then. I'll speak to you again next week some time." His father started to say something else, then paused, leaving the words hanging in the gap between them. David waited for him to continue. A few seconds later, the old man said, "I'm glad you're going to stick it out down there. Y'know you're always welcome, but— well, things are going kinda funny up here."

"What do you mean?"

"Oh, nothing. It's just that—" He stopped suddenly. David could hear a woman's voice through the phone, probably a nurse, walking over towards his father's bed. She sounded as if she were scolding him. He heard a squeaking noise. She was wheeling in a tray, a lunch tray probably.

"I've got to go now," his father said. "I'll call you next week just to see how you are."

"Next week. Fine. It was nice talking to you."

"Okay. Goodbye now."

"So long, Dad."

They both hung up.

The walls of his apartment seemed to close in and David felt an almost physical loneliness surrounding him.

He went out that night with a dollar in his pocket that he had found tucked in the top drawer of the bureau. He had planned on going to the bank until he realized that it was already past three and his branch didn't stay open any later. A look in his bankbook had told a depressing story. He had about seven days of living—not very comfortably—before he would begin to starve.

A dollar would enable him to buy about three glasses of beer if he stuck to the Blarney Stones or similar Irish bars where the stuff was on tap. The singles bars offered big mugs for about seventy-five cents. There were few places where he could get a bottle of beer for a dollar or under.

He wandered into a Blarney Castle on Seventy-ninth street and walked way down to the far end of the counter, past dozens of drunken old men, guzzling teen-agers and dissipated middle-aged ladies whose noses were as red as the rouge on their cheeks. He hadn't been in this place for over a year. He saw that a younger crowd was beginning to make its presence known, edging out the older alcoholics who spent nearly every waking hour hunched over a shot glass. The jukebox reflected this. There were fewer Irish standards and Frank

Sinatra tunes and more disco numbers. He imagined that the younger people came in from the singles bars in the area for a respite, as well as for cheaper booze.

He sat down on a stool that had seen better days; the red vinyl cover was ripped and oozing patches of white stuff. The seat to his left was empty. On the right was a woman of about forty-five, drinking herself straight down towards the floor. Her hair was the kind of red that one's hair could be naturally. Her cheeks and eyes were puffy. She wore enough makeup to last most women a year. She looked at David while he waited for the bartender to notice him. David looked back, briefly. He hoped she wasn't the talkative kind. He was not in a mood for conversation.

The bartender sauntered down to where David sat and took his order for a glass of beer. The man was around David's age, with a thick Irish brogue and a face that smiled even though there was nothing to laugh about. His hair was as dark as David's. His mood couldn't possibly have been.

David waited for the man to bring him his beer. The lady beside him leaned over and said in a gravelly voice, "Got a cigarette, hon?"

David patted his shirt pocket. He smoked occasionally, usually bumming from other people, now and then buying his own pack. "Sorry. None on me tonight."

"Oh," she said, a glaze in her watery eyes. She turned away, then back. "Thank you anyway. I 'preciate it."

"That's all right."

"You're a nice fellow. You know that? A nice man. Anybody ever tell you that?"

The bartender came with the beer and David gave him a quarter and a nickel he had found in his back pocket, saving the dollar for later.

The bartender counted the change. "It's thirty-*five* cents," he said.

David should have known. He took back the money,

23

pulled the bill out of his pocket and handed it over. The bartender took off for the cash register.

"Anybody ever tell ya? That you're a nice man?"

He figured it might be worse if he ignored her. "No. Nobody ever has. Why do you think I'm nice? I didn't *have* a cigarette."

She had to think that one over. The bartender came back with the change before she had a chance to reply. "Here you go. Thank you, sir."

"You're welcome."

"How's it goin', Jeannie?" the bartender asked the woman. "You feelin' good today?"

"Stick it right in here," she said, pointing her thumb down towards and nearly into her half-filled scotch glass. "Then I'll feel good. Stick it right in. I'll lick it off for ya."

The bartender howled, delighted at her crudity. David suspected that they went through the same vulgar routine every evening like clockwork.

"Just stick it right in there. It'll feel good. It'll make me feel good, too."

The barman looked down towards the front of the counter, capturing the attention of a pair of men holding court near the television set. "Jeannie's making passes again, boys."

One of them hollered back: "Hey, Jeannie! Can I stick it in, too?"

She leaned back for a better look at the guy, nearly falling off the stool in the process. "Awww you! What do I want with an asshole like you?"

That drew guffaws from the rest of the patrons in the bar. David couldn't help but smile, but he knew that he'd need at least ten beers before this place amused him. It was like a collection of the doomed, and he fit in perfectly. He raised the glass of beer to his lips and tasted it, cold and sharp and clear, while the man behind the counter and the woman next to him traded quips. He gulped down the whole glass and asked for another.

A young lady pressed a button on the jukebox and soul music came on. Shaking her body to the beat of the song, the woman made her way to the booth in back where her friends were sitting. Friends. It had been a long time since David knew what it was like to have some.

"Stick it in right there," Jeannie continued. "All your two inches will fit right in there."

The barman doubled over with laughter again. "What's the matter?" she said, scrunching up her face in mock puzzlement. "Don't tell me you've only got one and a half?"

This put the bar in an uproar again, temporarily drowning out the sound of the music. Jeannie began to wiggle to the beat—or at least tried to—and sang along with the vocalist. She turned to David. "I've heard this song a hunnert times and I still don't know what she's singin'. Do you?"

David sipped the second beer, which the bartender had handed him. "Haven't the slightest."

She squinted her eyes and leaned over towards him. If she had blown on a match it would have burned like a blowtorch. "Whatzat?"

"I said I don't know what she's saying, either." It was something about "My man done lost me," or left me, or loves me, or something like that, over and over and over again. David didn't object to disco, but he didn't go out of his way to listen to it either.

"Ah," Jeannie said, waving her arm at him and turning away in disgust. "You can go to Hell."

David wondered what he'd said to offend her. Not that it mattered. She was in a half-fantasy land now, and any real or imagined slight was enough to turn her off. Who knows what she had imagined him saying to her; for that matter, who knows who she might have imagined him to be. An ex-husband, a dead paramour, a childhood friend from finishing school. Sure, she had gone to

25

finishing school and it had finished her off.

David finished the glass of beer quickly, then left the bar. He just wasn't up to people like Jeannie tonight, or any other night for that matter. Maybe he'd have better luck at some other place. Maybe he'd be left alone. He wanted to sit in darkness, in shadows. The Irish bars were too well-lit, everything and everyone exposed, naked, sitting there at the mercy of anyone who wanted to put them under close scrutiny. David just wanted a beer, plain and simple. No company, no conversation, no drunkards breathing in his ear.

He left the bar and walked over to Amsterdam Avenue. There was a little hole-in-the-wall a couple of blocks away, where the lights were kept low, and the bar emptied out when the late supper crowd went home. It was called Peg O' Hearts. He'd been in there several times, whenever he wanted to be by himself, to think things over. He should have gone there earlier. He had enough left to get a small mug of beer.

As he stepped inside, he was relieved to see that the bartender he liked was working that evening—the quiet one. They had another night barman who was more talkative than a parrot in heat. This guy tonight was a tall, good-looking fellow with longish blond hair. His routine never changed. He would come over, take your order, deliver it and make change, then retreat to the other end of the bar, where he would stand looking sullenly over the diminishing crowd in the restaurant section, or else watch something on the television set directly above his head. Tonight he seemed glummer and more listless than usual. Good; he'd be sure to leave David alone with his thoughts.

The bar was an attractive place with a low wooden railing that separated the booze area from a room full of round wooden tables covered by red-and-white table-cloths. The bar counter was a deep rich brown. A low lavender glow bathed everything in a pinkish hue. Old-fashioned lamp lights hung over either end of the bar, and a huge mirror took up most of the space behind it, which was full of neatly stacked and organized liquor supplies.

David got his beer and paid for it. Some fool put on a dreadful country-and-western tune in the jukebox which he managed to ignore. He sat there, sipping his drink, trying to figure out what to do with his life. He was crippled now. No use denying it. At least his hands hadn't been affected. Although they might as well have been, as he wasn't making any money with them. If only that greeting-card firm had looked at his work, or had at least accepted free-lance submissions through the mail. He sent out his stuff regularly to other firms, and had managed to get a few assignments, but his style usually didn't "suit their present needs." The problem was, he had no connections. No uncle to introduce him to the right people. No cousin on the staff of *The New Yorker*. His father wasn't on the board of directors at Hallmark. It left him feeling bitter and untalented, although he knew he wasn't.

He was nearly at the bottom of his mug, and no closer to finding solutions to his problems, when he heard someone pulling one of the wooden chairs away from the counter. He turned and saw a statuesque brunette sitting down three chairs to the left, a tall, handsome man pushing the chair closer to the bar once she was firmly planted in its seat. They were a very well-dressed pair, looking as if they'd just come from the theater or a formal reception. Both had faces that could have easily graced the covers of fashion magazines. The man looked like the stereotypical male model. Granite jaw, sunken cheeks, Colgate teeth, formidable black eyes, straight, sleek nose, a mouth set in a brooding, almost petulant, sneer. The woman leaned in towards him as he took the chair next to hers, and he laughed, becoming more human as a smile lit up his face. He brushed a hand through wavy brown locks as the bartender approached, then lowered it to straighten his tie with a glimpse in the mirror.

The woman was a stunner in any language. A small shred of humanity seemed to leak out from the carefully manipulated shell of her luxurious makeup job. Glossy lips caught the pink light of the bar, reflecting crimson. Her long hair glistened as it hung down and covered her bare shoulders. Creamy skin. She wore a pale blue evening gown. Her mink stole had been piled on top of her lap; no way would she let it out of her sight. It was clearly for show only, as the weather was not quite cold enough to indicate its use. She was near thirty, at least. So was the man. If they were models, as young as they were, their careers would soon be coming to a close.

They talked in quiet, sophisticated tones as they each sipped what appeared to be a gin and tonic. David tried to look away, to ignore them, but found himself unable to tear his eyes away from the woman. He had seen her before, somewhere, although he didn't remember when. He knew he had never met her. She was too classy to travel in his circle, and he too poor to travel in hers. Perhaps he had seen her on television, or in a magazine ad. Surely anyone who looked as good as she did would have to make a living off her looks. If only he could remember where he had seen her before. Did she do commercials? It seemed to him that he had seen someone like her hawking some kind of product.

If they noticed him staring in their direction, neither of those handsome people made it known. Absentmindedly, David drained his beer mug, then panicked, digging his hand into his pockets, trying to find enough change to get another. He was ten cents short. He would just have to sit there with an empty glass until the bartender asked him—meaningfully—if he wanted another. He turned back to the woman.

It wasn't just her looks, her way of laughing, her trim

and lovely figure. There was something else about her. She was entirely different from Janice, and perhaps that's what he found so attractive about her. Normally David wasn't at all interested in the glossy, made-up type of woman, but this one was special. However, if the hunk next to her was an example of what she went for, then David was clearly way out of his league. Janice used to tell him that he was "cute," even good-looking, but he was no matinee idol and he knew it.

The bartender was looking in his direction, strolling down the bar towards him. Any moment now he would notice that David's glass was empty and would politely ask him if he wanted another. David could stall by saying "not just yet" with enough conviction to imply that he would indeed order another in a few minutes. Still, he hated that cheap, naked feeling one got by doing that, like telling a waitress in a busy greasy spoon that you weren't ready yet for another cup of her lousy coffee. He could read the look in their eyes: Don't Park It Here, Buster. Or was he being paranoid?

Bless the hunk. The man with the woman of his dreams stopped the bartender in mid-passage and ordered another round for him and the lady. David had at least a few more minutes to stare. Then, while business was transacted, the woman rose to her feet, excused herself, and walked up the bar towards the ladies' room. She would have to pass right by him.

David swiveled slowly in his seat, trying not to call attention to himself too soon. He simply had to do it. Now facing in her direction, he stamped what he hoped was a pleasant, non-committal grin on his face, and stared off into the space above her head. When she was nearly in front of him, he turned nonchalantly towards her, enlarging his grin.

Much to his surprise, she smiled back.

He had walked slowly around the Upper West Side of

the city for an hour and a half before going home, giving his leg exercise and his mind time to think. That smile had made his evening, made his week, hell—it had made his year. He knew he was giving it too much importance. He was not in love, or even pretending to be, and he had no need or desire for any attachments at this point in his life. He had had one already, of sorts, and look where that had gone.

What were his priorities? Money, a career, security. Learning to deal with the almost constant, steady pain in his right leg. Those were his priorities. After that, he could think about getting a lover. He had already learned what it was like to have somebody love him. Perhaps someday he would learn what it was like to have somebody like *her* love him. What would it be like, to live with her day after day after day? And would he care about her when her face was put away in the assorted tubes and jars and bottles on the dressing table?

What did it matter? He'd never see her again, and he had much more important things to worry about. Like getting up in time to make it to the bank before it closed.

He turned onto his block, entered the foyer of his building, and started to climb up the dark, winding stairs to his apartment. He was on the landing directly below when he stopped short, suddenly sensing that he was being watched.

There was something in the shadows up ahead. The light had gone out during his hospital stay and had not yet been replaced, leaving the whole corridor in darkness. But there was something up there, standing just out of range of the light shining up from the floor below.

David heard a labored, wheezing sound, like a dying dog trying to catch its last breath, a sound like a cough from the depths of a body wracked with high fever, collapsing from chills. Then the thud of a step, an ominous footfall, as the thing in the shadows slowly advanced towards the edge of the stairs.

"David Hammond," someone said.

And the thing started walking right down the stairs towards David.

Chapter Two

David had started to back down the stairs, planning to run towards the front door and the safety of the night, away from what undoubtedly was a mugger, a junkie, lying in wait for the unsuspecting, when he realized—*he knows my name!*

"David," the thing's voice said again, stepping out into the light, a dirt-encrusted boot hovering above the first step, stamping down upon it, almost losing its balance.

He had heard that voice before. In childhood. Or even later. But when?

He tried to recognize the man as he walked down the stairs, tried to remember who he was. What he saw gave him no clue. The man looked like a bum who spent all his time sleeping in alleyways; he smelled of fish and dog feces and a strong, almost overpowering body odor. He looked like a lunatic, long hair flying in a thousand directions, a thick black beard matted with spit and other foul substances. The clothes were more like rags. A smelly gray suit jacket with gaping wounds in the cloth. An undershirt underneath, full of holes like a wedge of swiss cheese. Baggy black trousers, the knees worn away, and the cuffs hanging heavy with repulsive pieces of lint.

Wild black eyes stared out atop a broad brown nose.

Whoever it was was olive-complexioned and big, once muscular. An urban Robinson Crusoe was camping out at David's doorsteps and he didn't know who he was or what he was doing there. He could only stare back, wondering how anyone he might have known in his thirty-three years could have turned into *this*.

The man had an awful-looking cut—a slice, really—on his forehead. It looked comparatively recent, just starting to heal. It would leave a wicked scar.

"David. I've got to talk to you."

And then it happened. The man was nearly at the landing where David stood stock-still. David was backing away, about to ask the man who he was and how he knew him. But then—he recognized him. He recognized the eyes, those sad, pathetic eyes. Could it be? Yes, it was.

"George Bartley. My God—is that you?"

"It's me, David. George."

David didn't know what to say.

"David. I've got to talk to you."

The voice was different. The same deep, crude tone, but none of the swaggering confidence of before, none of the machismo. David mentally computed how many years it had been since he had seen him. Ten. Maybe more. But no, he had seen him once or twice on his visits back home. Maybe five years then. Was five years enough to do this to a person?

He remembered George Bartley as a tough, ebullient personality. Nice-looking, strong. He came on dumb and beefy, but was not as stupid as people thought he was. He and David had grown up together in Hillsboro. George had been transplanted there from Brooklyn when he was around ten, but he never quite lost the accent, the street savvy that distinguished him from the other Vermont children. He and David had been, if not best friends, then pretty good buddies when nobody else was around to play with.

George and his parents had lived in a white cottage near the Illian River. His father and David's father had worked for the same firm. They all went to company picnics together. The Hammonds and the Bartleys. Although David's mom and Mrs. Bartley never really hit it off that well. They didn't fight or anything like that, they just never became very close.

And here was his childhood friend, someone he hadn't spoken to in at least five years. And for a good five years before that their conversations, when they bumped into each other in town, had been strained and brief. George must have been in big trouble to come to David for help. How long had he been living off the streets of New York, literally?

"Come on inside," David instructed, sensing that George was weak and could use help up the stairs, but not wanting to touch him, lest something crawl out of the seams of his jacket and enter his own skin. He climbed up ahead of him and opened the door, turned on the light.

George came in and David locked the door behind him. He would have to overcome his repulsion long enough to show this man some compassion. Probably he hadn't eaten in days. Boy, did he pick a loser, David thought. *I'm almost as bad off as he is.*

George sat down on the floor, threw his head back, and breathed in and out for several moments, the wheezing so pronounced that for a second David was afraid the man was having an attack. Then he stopped and leaned his head against the wall. David was about to offer him the bed, if he could make it over there, but decided to wait until after he had a nice, long, hot bath.

"I have to talk with you, David," George repeated. "I have to talk to you."

David squatted down before him. "I know. Listen, don't strain yourself. Why don't I make you something to eat, okay? Then when you feel a little better you can

34

tell me what's on your mind. All right?"

George nodded feebly.

David got up, went to the cupboard, and pulled out a can of mixed vegetables. Probably the healthiest thing he had in the place. He opened it, poured the contents into a saucepan, and put it over a flame on the stove. He didn't bother with a dish. He just brought the heated vegetables, plus a spoon, over to George and let him eat it right out of the pot.

George ate in spurts. He would shovel in spoonful after spoonful, spilling juice all over his beard and jacket, then lie back, exhausted with the effort. Then start up all over again. He went through the routine six times until he was finished.

"Something to drink?" David said from the bed where he was trying not to watch.

George nodded again.

David got him some water. There was nothing else.

George managed to get about one-quarter cup of the glass of water into his mouth. The rest trickled down over his face and clothes.

"Do you want to wash up?' That got no reaction. "Would you like to rest a while, go to sleep?" David asked.

"I've got to talk to you."

"Go ahead," David said. "I'll listen." He didn't bother asking him the usual questions, or try to deal with him on a normal level. George was working now on that most primitive plane, incapable of engaging in awkward small talk. David wondered if the man were even sane. What did he have to tell him? The story of how he came down from a middle-class existence in a small Vermont town to barely surviving in a metropolitan city? It made no sense. George had friends, family. In any case, he had been too gutsy, too smart to stay out on the street for long. How had he come to this? Unbathed, unshaven, practically unclothed. How does it happen to anyone? If it could happen to George, could it happen to him?

"I've got to talk to you."

"Go ahead, George. I'm listening. Tell me what's wrong. I'm your friend."

"Got to talk to you."

He seemed unable to say anything else. "Talk to me about what?"

"Talk to you."

"Shall I call your family, George? Shall I tell them where you are?"

That got a reaction. George managed to get to his feet, a horror-stricken expression on his hairy face, panic in his eyes. He began to whimper. "No. No. NO!"

"All right. Calm down. I won't call them. Okay? I won't call them."

George seemed to believe him, but David's words had not quite the tranquil effect he might have hoped for. George started to walk back and forth, back and forth, across the apartment, shaking his head, muttering under his breath. David could pick out only one word. "Unbelievable. Unbelievable."

"What is it, George? Why don't you tell me? *What's* unbelievable?"

George's behavior was getting more frenetic by the moment. David was afraid of what he might do, to himself, to the apartment. He reached out both hands and grabbed the man firmly by the shoulders, exerting what he thought was just enough pressure to keep his friend's burly frame from moving.

But his hands met no resistence! Gripping the shoulders and pressing inwards, they *kept on going,* as if George's body was just a big, man-shaped piece of sponge, as if it were composed only of flesh and muscle, but no bones. With hardly an effort, David's hands had squeezed George's shoulders practically in to the neck!

"My God!"

David let go and stepped back, horrified. There was

36

only, could only be, one explanation. George had lost an incredible amount of weight. The jacket was several sizes too big for him, and it had been the jacket—not the man's shoulders—that had crumpled in under the force of David's grip. Even now as he looked the shoulders were resuming their former width. David looked to George for some sort of comment, some reaction, but he was only still and blank-eyed, as if nothing had happened.

David backed away steadily from George until he finally bumped up against the kitchen table. There was a clattering noise that seemed to snap George out of his spell. David looked up from the table, having checked to make sure nothing had fallen to the floor, and waited for George to say or do something.

"I've got to talk to you."

"Tell me, George. Tell me what's wrong. What's happened to you? For God's sake—"

"Unbelievable."

"Yes. Yes. What's unbelievable?"

"You won't believe me." George took a step towards David, his eyes ablaze with a mad mental electricity, an emotional lightning.

"What won't I believe? You must tell me. I'll help you if I can. I promise."

"What they did to me!"

"What, George? What did they do to you?"

"They—" He bent his head down and covered his face with his large and trembling hands. David could see the calluses, a working man's hands. How come his hands were so large and strong, his wrists so thick, when all the rest of him was so dissipated? George's body heaved while he sobbed. Tears flooded out from between the fingers over his eyes.

George Bartley was crying. David never thought he would see the day.

And David thought—if whatever had happened did

this to George Bartley, what on earth would it do to me?

It was bright and sunny the following day, as if denying all that had transpired the night before. He had not been able to get any more information out of George; he was simply too incoherent and too depressed to speak. David had pulled out a sleeping bag for the big man to lie down on during the night. Then he had gone to bed himself, hoping that in the morning the mystery of George's appearance would be resolved.

It didn't look that way. At least not now, with George still fast asleep and snoring on the sleeping bag, still wearing all his clothes (which David simply could not bring himself to touch). With the daylight from the window shining all over him, he looked even worse than he had at night, sheathed in shadows. There was no shade for his ugliness to hide in. And once he had been an attractive man, might still be, under the dirt and the hair and the odor.

David debated whether he should wake him, get a straight story (or send him to some institution), or simply let him sleep while he went off to the bank and a few job agencies. David didn't like the idea of the man being left alone. He was clearly unstable, and there was no telling what he might do, or for that matter, what aid he might require in David's absence. He might wake up and not know where he was. Then again, he *had* been lucid enough to look up David in the phone book. He didn't know how else he might have gotten his address, unless somebody in Hillsboro gave it to him. Who? His father?

He would have to chance it. The bank wouldn't be very crowded now and he needed the money, might even have to give some to George. Besides, he'd rather leave George alone in his apartment while the man was sleeping than while he was awake. Sleeping dogs do little damage.

He washed up quickly with a wet cloth (not wanting to

38

shower while an emotionally disturbed person was in his apartment—shades of *Psycho*), changed into fresh clothes, and got his bankbook out of the night table drawer. George was still snoring blissfully as David went out the door.

The spring weather was getting warmer today. Many people went without jackets, although David still felt enough of a chill to keep his on. It was that bright sun up there, so unusual coming among so many smog-filled days, that made it seem deceptively hotter outside. He withdrew most of his "savings" from the bank without a hitch (except for the condescending look from the teller which was meant to pass for pity), did some grocery shopping, and went back to his studio. George was still fast asleep.

There was no way David could concentrate on interviews, not to mention arithmetic, typing and filing tests, while the man was still at large in his apartment. He hoped the smell of fresh coffee would wake him up. If drugs or alcohol had been responsible for his condition last night, perhaps their effect would have worn off by now, and the java couldn't hurt. He wanted to find out what was on George's mind, and thereafter get him back to wherever he belonged, or needed to be, as quickly as possible. David deliberately did not think about the incident with the man's sponge-like shoulders. There had to be a logical explanation, and he would not let it bother him, no matter how odd and disturbing it had seemed. He had already convinced himself that it had not been as bad as he had imagined. If George was wasting away, it was up to his family to put the meat back on his bones, get him in a hospital, or whatever. David thought again of calling George's father, but George had been so adamantly opposed to it last night that David decided to put it off until he heard just what it was his old chum had to say. If anything.

The coffee worked. George turned around on his

back, and lifted himself up by the elbows, looking around the apartment with a mildly perplexed grin on his face. He spotted David just as his friend said, "Good morning." He did not reply. David was afraid that any second he would start up again with "I've got to talk to you," over and over again, like a foreigner who only knew one phrase of English.

"Want some coffee?"

The man's mouth worked, but no sound came out at first. His lips formed the word, his voice stuttered, "Y—Yes. P-p-please."

David sat down on the bed while the coffee perked, filling the room with a brisk, delicious aroma. "Look, George. I gather you're in some kind of trouble. If I can help you, I'll be glad to. But you have to spell it out. Level with me. Or there's nothing I can do. Now I want you to have some coffee—and I've got some donuts, too —and then you're going to take a nice hot bath because frankly," he smiled briefly to take the sting out of his words, "you need one. Maybe I can even rustle up some clothes that'll fit you, although you're a lot bigger than I am. Okay? Do you understand what I'm saying?"

George nodded several times. His eyes seemed clearer. David hoped he'd be more communicative this morning. He got up and poured them both a cup of coffee. George nodded again—not a man of many words—when David asked if he wanted milk and sugar. He handed the cup to him, making sure he had a firm grip on it before releasing it. George bit hungrily into the donut, blew on the coffee to cool it, slurped it down eagerly. It seemed to have a good effect on him.

David sat down again on the edge of the bed. "Well. Why don't you tell me why you came here last night. Not that I'm not glad to see you. But—I think you've got something on your mind."

"They—they tried to kill me," George said promptly.

"Who?"

"My father's—friends. They tried to kill me."

40

"George! What are you talking about—"

"They said it would be safe. Said they took good care of their guinea pigs," he laughed bitterly. "Sure they do. Just look at me."

"I don't understand."

"Dad 'volunteered' me for one of their experiments. But it didn't work out right. When I tried to get away they said I couldn't go; the experiment wasn't over and I'd ruin everything. But I broke out one night. I broke out, and I've been running ever since. I hitched down to New York. Had to hang out in the street. Afraid they'd track me down. Had no money or nothin'."

"How long have you been running around like this?"

"A week. Two. I don't know. And David—the worst thing—the worst thing is—" He got up off his feet and walked over to David's side. "I think it's affecting my mind, too. God, it's affecting my mind." He pushed his hand back through his tangled, greasy hair, pulling it off his forehead. David got a better look at the awful red scar on his brow.

"Who did that to you?" he asked as gently as possible.

George touched his other hand to the scar, but did not answer. A look like a frightened animal came into his eyes. David assumed he had received the injury in the act of "breaking out."

"Don't worry about your mind," David said. "Anybody would feel upset if they were in your condition. If only you'd tell me what this is all about. Just who was experimenting on you? What did they do to you?"

That blank look came over him again and David knew he had said the magic words, the words that made George retreat back into a fantasy land of his own devising. Whatever they had done must have been pretty horrible.

If "they" had done anything at all.

George walked listlessly over to the window and stared out over the rooftops of the smaller buildings beyond. David decided to call the man's parents at the earliest

41

opportunity. There was a distinct possibility that George had simply run away from home—an odd term to use in regards to a thirty-four-year-old—because of some trouble or something like that. As a kid he had always been getting into fights. Sooner or later he was bound to crack up over the frustrations of small-town life and a small-town job, taking out his anger on some poor slob in Joey's Bar and Grille. Maybe he'd even killed somebody, or at least busted them up pretty bad. That might have been enough to make him run, unprepared. He had always basically been a moral, if rambunctious sort; the thought of what he'd done might eventually unhinge him. Coupled with the fact that he was suddenly thrust out alone into the world, it would clearly affect him adversely.

David didn't want to rat on an old friend, but his parents were probably frantic, wondering where he'd gone. There was no way David could take care of him, not in these troubled days ahead; that responsibility had to be his folks'. And it was becoming increasingly clear that he would never be able to get a straight story out of George, that George was incapable of giving one. He would have to wait until George was sleeping again, then would sneak out and call his parents from a pay phone.

"George, you still look a little tired. You can sleep a while longer if you like. Then we can figure out what to do. Okay?"

George turned from the window to look at him. He nodded, finally.

David didn't want to wait until he fell asleep. "You lie down. I have to go out again."

George went over to the sleeping bag, and began to lower himself on top of it. He stopped suddenly and looked at David. "Don't call my father," he said piteously. "Don't call him."

"No. I won't. I just have to take care of some things. I'll be back in a little while." He put on his jacket, waited until George's head hit the small pillow at the top of the sleeping bag, and left the apartment again. He did not remember the Bartleys' number and did not have it written down anywhere. He would have to call information; another good reason to call from outside. He would have to distinctly say the name "Bartley" when he spoke to the operator, and the sound of it might make George go absolutely berserk.

There was a phone at the corner across from the entrance to Riverside Park. Two little girls were skipping rope near a huge marble statue depicting a man astride a horse, sword upraised in the air. Classical music played sweetly from somebody's window. David could not tell if it was live or recorded.

He got the number from information. He dug out the change he would need for the call, wishing he had the nerve to call collect; it was not inexpensive. Three rings and someone picked up. "Bartley residence." A woman's voice. French. Since when had the Bartleys had a maid? Apparently Ted Bartley had come up in the world in the past ten years.

"May I speak to Mr. Bartley, please?"

A pause. "May I ask who is calling?" Jeez, he was getting the full treatment. He gave her his name.

"Mr. Hammond. I'm afraid Mr. Bartley isn't in." She hadn't even taken the time to check.

"Then can I speak to *Mrs.* Bartley?"

"I'm afraid that both Mr. and Mrs. Bartley are out of town for the week."

"Well, when will they be back?"

"Not for a few days, I'm afraid. Could I take a message?"

David explained the situation as clearly and concisely as possible. When he was through, he heard the maid exhaling dramatically, pausing as if for effect. When she finally spoke, she sounded flabbergasted. "I had thought that George had accompanied his parents. I

43

guess I must have been mistaken."

"Perhaps they went to look for him. Did you know where they were off to?"

"Something about a conference, or a convention, in Lancaster. I'm not sure."

"Surely they left a number where they could be reached."

"Yes, yes . . ."

"Well, could you call them for me? Explain the situation? I don't know what to do with him."

"Are you sure it's George?"

"Yes. I'm afraid it is."

"All right. I'll get in touch with them. May I have your number so I can call you back?"

David didn't like the idea of them calling his apartment, but liked the idea of waiting for their call at the phone booth even less. He gave the woman his number. "When do you think they'll call me? I'd hate to have to sit by the phone all day."

"That I couldn't say, sir. I'll try and get in touch with them right now."

"All right. Thank you very much."

She hung up.

He replaced the receiver on the hook, staring out at the park and the little girls, hearing but not listening to the music, not knowing quite what to do. How long would he have to sit up there, playing nursemaid? He felt terribly sorry for George, but there was nothing he could do to help him. He was shaken out of his reverie by a middle-aged woman tapping him on the shoulder. He made way for her so she could use the phone.

Back at the apartment, he settled into the business of waiting.

Three hours later, he was still waiting.

He had made lunch, had two more cups of coffee, read four or five different art magazines for the fiftieth time,

44

tried to start a paperback novel three times, all the while watching the steady rise and fall of George's chest as he slept. But the phone, that damnable phone, never rang.

And to think that he could have gone out, could have applied at several agencies, bought some new supplies. What wasted time! He had debated whether or not to call the Bartleys back, but figured that if the maid had reached them they would have rung him up by now. It was all very frustrating.

He waited another hour. George began to toss and turn in his sleep, but showed no signs of waking. The man probably needed medical care. Perhaps it would be better to forget all about the Bartleys and their convention and take George to the nearest hospital. Assuming George would go of his own free will, which was unlikely. This whole business was a hot potato and was the last thing David needed right now.

He dialed the Bartleys' number again. This time there was no answer. What had the maid done—driven to Lancaster after them? He hung up, waited ten minutes, then called again. Still no answer. He let it ring a full twenty times in case the woman was hard of hearing. The Bartley cottage wasn't all that big, assuming they still lived there. If they had hired a maid they might have been able to afford a new house, too. George had never seemed foolhardy enough to run from affluence, though.

He was hungry again. He made himself a light supper of canned peas and corned beef hash. He thought of waking George, but wasn't in the mood for his company, the soulful stares, the cryptic words, the haunted eyes. He already felt guilty about calling his parents. But what else could he have done?

He turned on the TV set, keeping the volume low so as not to disturb his visitor. The *I Love Lucy* rerun was half over when the commercial came on. *The* commercial. The one that had eluded him last night. He had wondered where he'd seen that woman before—the one at

45

Peg O' Hearts—and now he knew.

It was a commercial for Exclusiva Cosmetics. She was the Exclusiva woman! She looked different in this particular ad—there was a whole series of them—with her hair done up, and her body tucked into tight-fitting jeans and a white blouse; an odd combination of tomboy and glamor girl. "I wear Exclusiva—and nothing else," she purred, looking at the camera with a combination of arrogance and sensuality. There were shots of her dancing at a disco, dining in a fancy restaurant, walking down the city streets hand in hand with a male model, wearing her Exclusiva wherever she went. That certain quality she had, a humanity beneath the artifice, came through even in her ads. As the music came up, the screen showed a closeup of her beautiful face. Creamy, flawless cheeks, full lips, large blue eyes, a slightly turned-up nose. Her head was not exactly round, but not narrow either. She did not have the gaunt look of other models. "In my Exclusiva," she said confidently (the camera pulled in for a tight closeup now, her lips shining provocatively), "I'm exclusively yours."

How many men—and quite a few women—wished she was saying those very same words to them? David laughed. He felt like a kid again, getting crushes on beautiful movie stars. But the woman had that effect on him. Momentarily, he felt thrilled that he had been *that close* to her in the bar, that she had smiled at him, had been near enough to touch. Then he snickered, and said out loud, though softly: "She has to take a shit just like everyone else does. Don't get hung up on images, Davey boy."

He looked over to the sleeping bag to make sure that he hadn't disturbed George. No, he was still fast asleep, snoring again, a slight whistling sound coming from between his parted lips. David wished that he had made the man take a bath. The odor was beginning to permeate the room, and it was bound to get worse.

He tried the Bartleys' number again. No answer. He did not want to sit here and keep George company all evening. Then again, what else did he have to do? If he couldn't watch over a friend—a former friend, at least—for a few hours of his life, what kind of person was he? Still, George's presence didn't make it any less lonely.

He watched some more TV, then rang the Bartleys' number again. This time it was picked up on the first ring. He heard the French woman's voice again, informing him whose resident it was.

"Yes. This is David Hammond again. I—"

"Ah, yes, Mr. Hammond. I've reached the Bartleys and they left a message for you in case you should call again."

"I've been calling and calling all afternoon." He wondered why she didn't get in touch with him.

"They wish me to tell you that their son George is with them in Lancaster, and that they have no patience with practical jokers. And neither, I assure you, do I!" She hung up again, emphatically.

"But, but," David stammered into the silent receiver. He had wanted to tell her who he was, to tell her that the Bartleys had known him for years, that he had grown up with George, that he ought to be able to recognize their son, that they couldn't do this to him. That he would have no reason to make up such a story, no reason to play such an absurd and sick and pointless practical joke.

But all he could do was look over toward the figure sleeping in the bag over in the corner.

For if that wasn't George Bartley . . .

Who—or what—was it?

Chapter Three

"Get up!"

The sleeping figure groaned, stirred, then turned over, pushing his face down sloppily into the pillow. A drop of spittle fell from his mouth.

"I said Get Up!"

Careful not to hurt him, David nudged George's body with the tip of his shoe. He didn't want to use his hands on him again, couldn't bare to touch him after that one time last evening.

George only dug his head further into the pillow, shimmied his body deeper into the sleeping bag.

David crouched down beside him and peered into his face, trying to imagine what he would look like if the beard was gone, if the skin weren't quite so mottled, the eyes open and clear. Last night he had been sure that this man before him was George Bartley, but now he had no choice but to assume that it was someone else. This person was in such sad shape that he probably wouldn't recognize his real name anyway.

And yet? What if there were some other explanation for what the Bartleys' maid had said, her denial of David's allegations? Perhaps George *had* been running from some crime, perhaps his parents had disowned him, no longer concerned about his welfare. It wouldn't be the first time that a mother and father felt that way about a child who disappointed or disobeyed them, and it wouldn't be the last. Yet the maid had seemed to be telling the truth when she had said that she had thought George was with his parents.

And what about this man's strange story about experiments, running away, the implications he'd been held against his will? Who in Hillsboro would do a thing like that to someone? Where was he being "experimented" on? Bellevue's psycho ward, probably.

David looked closer at the man. That was George's nose, George's eyes, all right. But could he be positive? He searched his memory, straining to recall if he were remembering the features of someone other than George Bartley, some other friend or acquaintance. But no—if it wasn't George, then it was nobody he had ever met.

He had called the Bartleys' house back since the last brief conversation, but the woman wasn't answering.

"Get up! I've got to talk to you, George. Or whoever you are."

Finally the man woke up with a start, turning over to face David, rubbing his eyes to see more clearly. David had prepared a cup of instant coffee, and handed it to him when he seemed awake enough. "Drink this up. It's time we had a little talk. I want some satisfactory answers, or I'm throwing you out right now.

"First," David continued, squatting in front of the man, "what is your name?"

"George. George Bartley."

"Really? Isn't that interesting? According to the maid at your house in Hillsboro, George Bartley is on a trip with his parents at this very minute. George Bartley is several hundred miles away. How do you explain that?"

The man's eyes widened with fear. "You didn't—call them? Did you?"

"Yes I did."

"No, no." He was so startled that he spilled some of the coffee into his lap. "You mustn't get in touch with them."

"I can see why. You were afraid they'd give you away, weren't you? Come on—tell me who the hell you really are."

"I *am* George. I swear. They have their reasons for lying. They don't want anyone to know about me."

"You're not making any sense. Why would they lie about something like that?"

"I can't explain. You wouldn't believe me."

"Look. George, or whatever your name is, you came here last night for help of some sort. What did you want? A free meal? A place to sleep? Is that all? I gave you that, but I can't give you anymore. I think you should either go home—if you are George—or go back to wherever you came from. I have enough troubles right now without—"

"I AM GEORGE!" The violence of the man's outburst was alarming, to say the least. "God, I won't let them take away my identity!" He grabbed David by his shirt front with such force that David nearly toppled over onto the sleeping bag. "Listen to me! You must believe me!"

"Let me go!"

"Do you remember the swimming hole, near Patter's apple orchard? We used to go there instead of the quarry sometimes. Remember Crazyman Patter, we used to call him Crazyman Patter. Do you remember? He had big ears that stuck out, and he was always blowing his nose. You've gotta remember. One night we took Sue—Sue Elliot and her friend, her friend Betty—we took them up there, and the deputy drove by and shined his light on the four of us, and you said, you said we were inspectors from the Johnny Appleseed Society. Do you remember? Tell me, you remember!

"You've got to remember!"

That was the way it had been, all right. The deputy had not found David's wisecrack very amusing. He'd come after them with his flashlight, and they quickly took off. Sue Elliot screamed as she stepped into a load of dog shit, and David had tripped over a devilish piece of root. But they'd all gotten away. They laughed about it all the way home, running through fields and across rutted country lanes, glad to be out of Deputy Forster's clutches.

"I remember." He stared into the man's face, wondering how someone could share George Bartley's memories, wondering if it were a trick. But he saw the desperation in the eyes, the anguish in the voice. This *was* George Bartley. He didn't know why anyone would want to lie to him about his identity, why the maid had done what she'd done. Why his parents had told her what they'd told her, assuming she had spoken to them at all.

"All right, George. I believe you. But I don't understand any of this. Are you on the outs with your folks? Is that it?"

"Yeah. That's it. You didn't tell them where I was, did you?"

"Yes. I didn't know what else to do. You weren't talking. You were just staring out the window, muttering. I didn't know what to do."

"I'm better now. My—my head is clearer."

"Clear enough to tell me what this is about, I hope."

George turned away, heaving with a sigh. "I'm not sure I should. I came here because I had no place else to go. Looked you up in the phone book. Thought I might be able to talk things over with you. But there's nothing you can do, nothing anyone can do." His eyes were fogging up again. David was losing him.

"Trust me," he said. "If you had anyone else to turn to you would have done it by now. Tell me what kind of trouble you're in." David wasn't sure that he wanted to know. He did not feel like harboring a fugitive from justice. And he was much too poor to convince anyone that he hadn't been aware of the situation.

"No. You'll never believe me. You'll just call them and they'll come and get me. They're probably on their way now."

"Who? Your folks? I thought they weren't even talking to you?"

"They'll send somebody to get me. And they'll take me back up there and put me away for good." George was starting to cry now. God! He must have escaped from some kind of institution. This was getting worse and worse every minute.

"Maybe that would be for the best," David said softly. "I can't do anything for you here, George. You need help."

George stared at David, a hopeless look on his face. "Nobody can help me now."

"Let me try calling your parents again later, okay? Maybe they'll reconsider."

"No. No. I've got to get out of here. Before they get here."

"They're not coming, George. They would have said so."

"You might be in danger. Don't stay in the house tonight. Go out. Stay out. Until morning. Don't come back until morning." He said it with such conviction that it chilled David down to his bone marrow.

"What about you?"

"I'm going to leave." He got up on his feet.

"Wait," David protested. "You can't walk off like this. Let me give you a little money. I don't have much but—"

"Don't want your money."

"Please. Let me give you some clothes. At least wash up before you go." David tried to keep him away from the door.

Suddenly George reached out and hit him across the head, knocking him across the room and onto the bed. David sat up stunned, his head still ringing. He resisted an urge to go after George, to hurt him in kind. "Goodbye to bad rubbish," he muttered, as the sound of the man's footsteps receded down the stairs.

He'd had more than enough of Crazy George Bartley.

David had a lump on his head just above the right eyebrow. Aside from that, there were no ill effects. Muttering under his breath the entire time, he made himself dessert, ate it quickly, and gulped down another cup of coffee. He kept watching the clock. How long would it take someone to drive down from Vermont? Five hours? What if they came by plane? In either case, they would already have arrived by now. It was seven o'clock. They could get his address out of the phonebook like George had done.

He tried to forget about what George had said, about how he should vacate the premises until morning. Surely he was in no danger. Bartley was only suffering from paranoid delusions, thinking the whole world was out to get him. David still couldn't figure out why his parents could be so callous in regards to the welfare of their only son, but there was nothing he could do about that. He didn't want to call George's folks up again, only to have that old hag hang up on him. But what if it were all a misunderstanding? What if there had been some perfectly reasonable explanation for the maid's reaction? Maybe there was a good reason for her not to believe David's story; maybe they'd received other crank calls about George. It was all so confusing.

He dialed the Bartleys' number again, but there was no answer. Along with the pain, his anger towards George's last action before leaving the apartment had subsided. He had concluded long ago that George had only wanted to prevent him from following, that in his sick, troubled mind he was doing what he had to do. Surely had had not meant to injure David, or kill him— he could have done a lot worse than simply deliver a back-handed slap; there was still strength in those limbs. Whether it was true strength or just manic energy remained to be seen. David was in no hurry to find out.

David decided to forget all about it until morning. He would have to try to reach the Bartleys again. They should be made to accept the fact that their son needed help badly, and that they had to do something about him wandering the streets of Manhattan alone with no one to turn to. David thought of going out and looking for him, but George could have gone anywhere, and David was afraid to confront him again, the bump on his head testifying to the man's deadly capabilities if pushed to the edge. Still, he was haunted by the image of the man out there alone, indistinguishable from all the rest of the pathetic tramps and bums and derelicts. It horrified David to think that a friend of his—even one from long ago—should be in such a position. As long as there was anything he could do about it, he wouldn't rest. If the Bartleys refused to speak to him in the morning, he would call his own father, ask him what could be done.

It was creeping toward eight o'clock now. He'd sat and mulled the whole mess over for an hour. Didn't realize how long it had been. He had an urge to get out of the apartment, to get out fast, and he felt frightened suddenly, wondering why the place seemed small and shadowy. Not a safe haven anymore, but a place of dread. He didn't know why his apartment had taken on this new coloration, so dark and gray. Had it to do with George's warning? David thought of himself as a rational man and dismissed the idea from his head. Yet he virtually ran from the apartment only a few minutes later, denying that his friend's words had had anything whatsoever to do with it. All he knew was, he did not want to be in that apartment alone.

While he walked up the block, he told himself over and over again that he was simply lonely, as he had been the night before. Maybe he hadn't been aware of how comforting George's—another human being's—presence had actually been. Wasn't it natural for him to go out and seek company? But, he wondered, if anyone asked to come home with him, would he agree? Or would not even someone else's being there with him erase the ominous feeling, that strange sense of being in the wrong place at the wrong time? He didn't know.

He had been walking for about twenty minutes when he suddenly realized where he was. Subconsciously (or was it all that subconscious?) he had been heading towards Peg O' Hearts. Come on, Davey, he thought. You're overdoing it. How obvious can you get. The chances of her being there two nights in a row are not very good. Then again, for all he knew she might have decided to make the place her regular watering hole. Everybody had a favorite spot, one they went to a few nights a week. Why would she be different? He had not seen her in there before, true, but he hadn't been in there for quite a while, since before the accident. She might have only recently relocated to the neighborhood.

But she wasn't there.

The place was not as empty as it had been the night before because it was the middle of the late supper hour, and most of the tables were taken. The bar was full of people waiting for a table, or neighborhood residents having an early drink. David found an empty chair, luckily enough, and looked about to see if *she* were present. From what he could tell from his vantage point, she was not.

He ordered a martini and sipped it slowly. Very slowly. He did not want to get so drunk that he would have to go home to pass out. He did not want to go home. Even the thought of being there chilled him. He felt safe and secure now, surrounded by all these people.

It was going to be a long night.

He knew it was foolish of him to go out drinking when he had so little money and didn't know when there'd be more coming in, but he couldn't help it. He could always go home to Vermont for a week or two instead of starving, but even there his food and funds would be limited. His father would insist on giving him some money, but he didn't have much to give, as he had admitted on the phone. Besides, Vermont was not the place to be when one was trying to find work in New York.

He sat back in his seat, sipped his drink—it was deliciously dry, cool and perfect, with a twist—and listened to the sounds all around him: the clink of glasses, idle conversation, spirited, boozy debates on life and love, the clatter of forks on plates, the rustle of menus, the rattle of ice cubes, the soft whine of the blender in the corner. The TV was off at this hour. It would have been gauche to leave it on. If the diners wanted to watch television they could have stayed at home hunched over a TV dinner, which, incidentally, had comprised hundred of David's meals for the past few years. He hated to cook.

David had always been a private child, a quiet man. He had never been lonely—particularly in his youth, although he had not been very popular—because he had always been able to amuse himself, to create an elaborate fantasy land full of playthings which were preferable to whining children and breakable toys. He managed to find adventure in the most mundane places, the most undistinguished objects. He retained this gift as he grew older, this ability to create a whole world of entertainment inside his head, so that whereas most people in his situation would have been lonely, he simply shrugged it off—if he were aware of it at all—by concentrating on the solitary things that brought him pleasure.

Unfortunately, all that was changing. As he grew older, he realized how much he craved companionship, new friends, new surroundings. He would find them, and lose them, then find still more, then lose them again.

And then he had met Janice.

It would be simplistic to say that his life had been revitalized by love. For he did not love her. And maybe that's what hurt the most about her death. He could not sit for hours staring at her picture, would not be haunted by what might have been, for there would have been nothing. He felt guilty that he did not care more. Although he had been shattered by her death, he had not been emotionally paralyzed, as he would have been had she been a lover.

He had, however, loved Janice Foster platonically—more than platonically—and when she died he had lost his only friend and he still grieved over that loss bitterly. But he hadn't been *in* love with her, and for some strange reason it left him feeling empty and sorrowful that she would not be mourned the way someone as wonderful as she had been should have been mourned. Janice had deserved someone who would have felt passion and all-consuming grief and rage at her untimely passing for the rest of his life, for always.

They found her head ten feet away. . . . He blinked his eyes rapidly, chasing away the bad thought.

He was working himself into a deep depression now, a whopper. He tried to snap himself out of it, hoping no one had been watching him do the sad-sack routine. He was surprised to realize that he had been thinking all this over for quite some time. The restaurant was practically empty, and even the bar had cleared out except for four or five hardcore cases.

He was feeling giddy enough to be daring. He waited until someone played the jukebox—the noise would cover up what he was about to say from those at the end of the bar—and signaled the bartender. It was the same fellow who'd been on the night before.

As the man placed the third drink on a napkin in front

57

of him, David said, "You probably don't remember, but I was in here last night around this time."

The man shrugged. "I think I remember you. Just hanging out tonight?"

"Yeah. The reason I mentioned it is that there was this woman here last night, too. Maybe you know her. She does those Exclusiva makeup ads on television." From the look on the barman's face, David knew he wouldn't have to nudge the man's memory any further.

"You mean Anna Braddon?"

"What's her name?"

"Anna Braddon, the model. Sure, she does those commercials. She comes in here all the time."

"You know her? I mean, personally?"

"Well, I've never talked to her at length—"

"I mean you knew her name and all."

"I read an article about her in *People* magazine. She's making big bucks. Used to do fashion photography, then moved up in the world, went on to better things."

"And she comes in here a lot?"

"Yep. She and her husband."

David tried not to look too surprised. "You mean that guy who looks like a model himself?"

"Yeah. Derek Bishop. He *is* a model. Big bucks, too. There was a big spread on them a few weeks ago. I read in some gossip column a few days ago that they're separating. They still seem to get along fine when I see them."

"People must bother them all the time when they come in here."

"Not really. They always come in pretty late, and most people here are pretty together. They smile, say hello, but otherwise leave 'em alone. That's the way it should be." Was that a hint?

"Well," David said, "I was just curious. I thought she looked familiar. I figured you would know if she was who I thought she was."

"Well, she is."

"Thanks." The bartender went off to see to some other customers.

David felt pretty stupid now. Surely the bartender would figure out why he was going to sit here for the rest of the night. His motives were strictly see-through. What did he hope to gain anyway? She'd come in again with her husband, and maybe she'd give David another smile, and that was that.

Still, he had no intention of going back to his apartment until it was as close to dawn as possible. He decided he would finish this drink—very slowly—then go to another bar that stayed open later. What he would do from four a.m. until approximately six was another story altogether. He would have to sit in an all-night coffee shop, reading the paper and nursing a cup of coffee. He felt, once more, like an idiot. What he really wanted to do was go home and sleep.

At least he didn't feel depressed any longer. The liquor had taken care of that. He sat back in his chair with a feeling of deceptive tranquility and contentment. Brain cells being destroyed, he supposed. In the bloodsteam. Through the circulatory system. Instant nirvana.

And then she walked in. Sans husband.

Hmmm. Liza or Suzanne or whoever the gossipmonger was had been right. Splitsville. Of course, in the back of his mind David knew that just because Ms. Braddon came into the bar by herself one evening did not necessarily mean that there was any truth to the rumor of her impending divorce from her husband. But he took solace in the fact of her solitude anyway. What did he care if she was married or separated or whatnot? He wasn't in love. He just wanted an affair. A one-night affair, if need be. Hell, one hour would do. Or would it? His feelings towards her seemed to go beyond lust.

She was wearing a jumpsuit, a blue jumpsuit, and her hair was in a ponytail. She didn't look younger; perhaps because she still wore makeup, perhaps because she'd look too sophisticated in *any* outfit, *any* hairstyle, to ever be girlish. And hadn't that been the main problem?

Her head was found ten feet away. . . .

He shook himself, making the bad thought go away again.

Anna Braddon sat down two seats away from him, and he could smell her, a lovely scent, and he didn't care if it was too powerful or if she wore too much of it. He looked over at her—discreetly, he hoped, although after three martinis there was no telling what he might consider discreet—and studied her, the cool way she sat awaiting her drink, her composure. That was it! A cool composure coupled with sex appeal. Devastating sex appeal. What on earth made him think she could ever see anything in him? Next to her husband, he was a schmoe. God, she knew how to carry herself. It was hopeless, hopeless.

So he sat there and wondered how he could start up a conversation with her.

It had not been a good evening for Anna Braddon Bishop.

She knew it was going to be a disaster when Derek called at six o'clock and said that he'd be late getting home. They were due at the party at seven sharp and there'd be no way they could get there on time if they didn't leave within forty minutes. She knew how long it would take Derek to get home—at least twenty minutes from the midtown office of the Longton Agency—and then another half hour for him to shower, shave and change into formal clothes. Ten minutes late wouldn't matter for most occasions, but Miriam Hunter meant it when she said, "Be on time." To walk in ten minutes after everyone else would be embarrassing, to say the least. Miriam allowed time for one drink before dinner, along with the de rigueur hors d'oeuvres, but few people managed to finish their cocktails before they were ushered into the dining room. Mrs. Hunter did not approve much of drinking, social or otherwise. And Anna loved a drink before dinner, especially this kind of dinner, sitting right next to two film stars, three producers and a director, along with other society types. She'd need something to calm her nerves, and she didn't want to take another Valium. But if they were late—too late to be offered a drink—she'd *have* to. Damn Derek.

She knew that he'd been in a meeting with the head of the Longton Modeling Agency since two p.m., discussing new projects, tossing around the idea of Derek doing the Sexton Men's Jeans campaign, which would take him to Europe at just the time he needed to be in New York to record his first album. Derek hadn't much of a voice, but record producer Lydia Allstedder had taken quite a fancy to him. Anna was no fool. She knew exactly what Derek's audition for the old battle-axe had entailed. She wondered idly while she dressed if the meeting with Sam Longton had actually run overtime, or if Derek had been calling from Mrs. Allstedder's—or some other woman's—apartment. Did it really matter?

And then to make matters worse, Tallulah, her Irish setter, came running in, anxious to frolic with her mistress.

"I'm in a hurry, Tallulah," Anna said, "and I don't have time to play with you this evening." She looked through her jewelry case for her earrings. Damn—she'd seen them only a minute ago. "Why don't you go downstairs and see if Clara had made your dinner yet?"

But Tallullah could not be gotten rid of so easily. The setter grabbed hold of one of Anna's brand new shoes and began to chomp on it delightedly.

"No, Tallulah!" Anna screamed. "Give me my shoe!" She managed to pull the shoe out of the dog's mouth before too much damage had been done, but it wasn't exactly in great condition, either.

Looking for new amusement, the setter jumped up on Anna's lap and started lovingly licking her freshly made-up face.

"No, no! Get away! Tallulah! Get away from me!"

The dog fell to all fours dejectedly. "I've had enough," Anna scolded. "I have to do my face all over again, pick out a new pair of shoes, and brush the red hair off my dress. Now get out of here!"

Bored and annoyed, Tallulah turned on her heels and went downstairs to terrorize the maid.

Surveying the damage in the mirror, Anna could only think that things would get worse.

They did.

Anna and Derek arrived at the Hunter dinner party at exactly 7:15. Not only did they not get a cocktail, but they were told to wait in the living room until dinner was over and dessert was served. Derek helped himself to a drink, ignoring the dirty look from the butler, while Anna fumed. She held her tongue, though; she didn't want that ugly, dour-eyed manservant to overhear their quarrel. And it would be quite a quarrel. Finally, the man left to attend to some other business.

"Aren't you humiliated?" Anna hissed.

"No." He smiled, sipping his martini. "I had a bite to eat just before the meeting broke up. Sam had sandwiches sent up from the deli."

"Wonderful. Well, I'm starving."

"You'll get dessert."

"That's not what I had in mind. Mrs. Hunter has her own chef. I wanted some of his French cuisine. He's famous for it."

"Pour some wine over your chocolate cake and you'll have French food, all right?"

"Derek, sometimes you make me want to scream."

"I can't put up with all this 'society' jazz. The only reason we ever get invited to these silly functions is because half the people want your body and the other half want mine. They don't invite us for our brains, darling."

"Maybe in your case they know better than to expect something 'upstairs.' Couldn't you have tried a little harder to get home on time? You knew I was counting on you."

"I feel real sorry for you, Anna."

"Why is that?"

"Because you're trying too hard to be accepted. You won't face the fact that these people aren't interested in *you*, in Anna Braddon, the person. They're interested in the voluptuous model in the TV ads, the personality, the celebrity—to put it bluntly—the tits, baby, the tits."

"Do you have to be so crude?"

" 'Do you have to be so crude,' " he mimicked. "You don't even talk like the lady I married. You're letting the current American obsession with your looks go straight to your head."

"Oh! And what about you?—God's gift to women. Are you supposed to be a shrinking violet? You've used your looks to get into every bedroom in town, not to mention a record contract."

"That's because I'm smart enough to know what people want of me. Nobody cares if either of us know how to use the finger bowl, or if we know the difference between the salad fork and the one you use for the main course. We're here tonight strictly as window dressing, and frankly, I'm getting bored with it. At least I know where to go when I feel like being useful."

"Mrs. Allstedder's, I suppose. There's nothing more useful than screwing your way into a second career."

"A most lucrative one, I might add. You know, your holier-than-thou attitude is beginning to bug me. You weren't exactly little Miss Goody Two Shoes during your long climb up the ladder of success."

"I know that. I'm not saying either of us should be

ashamed of using our looks to get ahead. Anyone would if they were able to. I'm not blaming you for that. I've had plenty of male Mrs. Allstedders in my life. It's just that—I want something more. I don't know."

Derek looked at her and said very softly, almost sweetly, "I'm sorry, honey. I love you, but I don't want to live like this, worrying about impressing people who are no better than I am. I grew up in the Bronx. I wanted money and success all my life, just like you did. But I don't want a wife like Billie Burke in *Dinner At Eight.*"

"I never saw that picture."

"Pity. We don't even like the same movies."

And then the butler came out and told them that dessert was being served. They were ushered into the next room, a huge dining room with a long table covered with a gold and white cloth. The supper dishes had been taken away, and all eyes of the ten or so guests looked up and over to the door as the handsome duo walked in. Anna felt her face turn hot and red and sweaty with embarrassment. Derek was, as usual, the epitome of cool, so self-assured in his staggering sex appeal and its effect that he was totally unconcerned with the stares.

Mrs. Hunter got up to greet them. She was fortyish, plump, with a wavy black hairdo streaked with sections of white. "So sorry you missed dinner," she cooed, pressing her cheek against Anna's, and then Derek's.

"If you're sorry, why didn't you let us in here?" Derek said smoothly, not blinking an eye.

Anna cut into the awkward silence which followed as gracefully as possible. "I know it's terrible when your guests don't show up on time," she said, her smile too big, her laugh too strained, "and interrupt everything. All we're in the mood for anyway is some nice cake and coffee; right, dear?" She patted Derek's cheek with more force than necessary.

Mrs. Hunter showed them to their chairs and introductions were made all around. They sat across from each other, at the head of the table, right next to the hostess. The film stars were no-shows and had been replaced by an obscure senator and his wife. A heavy-set film producer with bulldog jowls sat on Anna's right, his wife on Derek's left. She looked like a female version of her husband. Within ten minutes the producer's hand was on Anna's knee; his wife's hand was practically in Derek's lap. There was no subtle way of removing it.

The cake was served, along with several delicious pastry selections, hot coffee, spicy tea and liquor. Derek spilled half a glass of creme de menthe on his shirt (he flicked it off with his fingertips, hoping no one would notice), when the producer's wife's fingertips crept over spiderlike to the lump inside his trousers.

After coffee they all went back into the living room, where Derek tried to disengage himself from the woman. Anna was having no better luck trying to get rid of *Mr.* Bulldog. The man blabbered on about a picture deal of some sort, although she doubted if he had any intention of putting her in movies.

Anna looked over at her husband. She could read the look on his face easily: "So *this* is 'society,' " it said.

The fight on the way home in the cab was even worse than the minor spat they'd had in Mrs. Hunter's living room. It was somewhere between Park and Fifth Avenues that Anna finally realized that their marriage was over, and there was no chance left to save it. They *had* decided almost a week earlier (as the gossip columns had accurately reported) to have a trial separation beginning the next month, for Anna had hoped that some time away from each other would help strengthen their relationship in the long run. But she knew that she had been fooling herself.

She believed in open marriage, she knew that she and Derek might have to engage in extramarital episodes in order to get ahead, she recognized that she was more concerned with upward progression among the upper classes than Derek was. For all his beauty and sophistication, Derek was still "just plain folks" and always would be. She thought she could accept his quiet mockery of her hopes and dreams of traveling in better circles now than she had traveled in her youth.

But she couldn't. Open marriage was fine for other people, but Derek's indiscreet playing around was getting to her ego, and the fact that she was desired by thousands of men she'd never even met or seen didn't help to take away any of the hurt and loneliness. Derek seemed to take his infidelities much more seriously than she ever could; he went into it with a relish far surpassing any feelings she could generate for some rich TV executive who promised her a juicy contract for one night in the hay. He seemed to need these episodes. Did he need constant reaffirmation of his attractiveness; was he a repressed, unliberated bisexual with a Don Juan complex, bedding women when he really wanted men? Did it matter? No. In any case, Anna simply couldn't take it any longer.

There was a lot of shouting and screaming and crying, and the cabbie had an earful. It was nothing they hadn't said a million times before, and they decided to go for the Big D. Divorce. Anna rushed into the house leaving him to pay the driver. She stormed into her bedroom and slammed the door so hard the whole house shook. She flopped onto the bed and had a good cry. Derek was wise enough to stay out, out of the room, out of her way. Half an hour later, in casual clothes and her hair pulled back, she had stormed out the door and into the night.

So here she was in Peg O' Hearts again—where she and Derek had shared a drink only the night before, had laughed, and reminisced and enjoyed each other's company—trying to think things over by herself, away from the house, *his* house. She had to face it. She was just another date as far as he was concerned.

And just when she'd decided that she'd had her fill of handsome models and playboys and jetsetters, she looked up from her martini and saw this sort of disheveled-looking character, a half-inebriated sad sack, attractive in a waning sort of way, sitting farther down the bar, almost the complete opposite of her husband in style and demeanor. She remembered that she had seen him the night before. What was he—a wacko? A sex-starved Jack the Ripper? A groupie? Another "television producer"?

Or better yet, a perfectly nice guy who found her attractive and wanted some fun. A real lamb. A pussy-cat. Somebody who could take her mind off Derek. Somebody who was nothing like Derek. Or were "all men the same?" *No.*

She ordered another martini. And then another.

What *was* there about that fellow? He was kinda cute and lovable, one of those people you could tell was *nice* just by looking at them.

So she finally motioned the bartender over and told him to buy the gentleman a drink, on her. She watched as the barman placed the martini in front of the man, saw the astonished look on his face as he was told who'd bought it for him.

Anna, she thought, *you're drunk*.

And as he started to open his mouth, started to say *thank you* and *hello*, Anna was part relieved, part glad—and part afraid that she had just made the worst mistake of her not very long or satisfying life.

Chapter Four

They woke several hours later in the Belaire Hotel, fourteenth floor, room 1408.

David was wide awake while Anna was still yawning and stretching her arms. He took a look around the room —it was nearly a suite, actually—and couldn't believe it. Then he took a look down at Anna and couldn't believe it even more. He, David Hammond, in one of the city's ritziest hotels, in bed with one of the world's ritziest women. He vaguely remembered what had transpired during the night—before they'd come to the hotel, that is —the rest he would *never* forget.

She had stunned him by making the first move in the bar, by buying him a drink. He'd said "thank you" and she took off with it, inviting him to sit next to her, engaging him in small talk that seemed stimulating and witty coming from her lovely lips. They had one or two more drinks—he was lucky he hadn't passed out—and then she asked him if he'd like to spend the night with her. It was that simple.

She took charge right away, which was lucky, considering that David could not have spared the money for the cab and then the hotel room. He remembered sitting on one of the sofas in the stadium-sized lounge, while Anna went over to the desk clerk and began expressing "dismay" over losing her luggage. Chances are in this day and age that even the finest hotels wouldn't raise an eyebrow, but perhaps she was thinking of her image. A twenty-dollar bill in the clerk's palm helped to get them a good room at that hour without luggage or reservation, and they had made their way up to 1408 posthaste. David was quite flattered—imagine her spending so much money just so she could have a one-night stand with the likes of him. Not that it would make much of a dent in her income. Still . . . it was nice.

He went into the bathroom and washed up a bit, sloshing around toothpaste in his mouth with his finger. Like the hospital, the hotel supplied small little tubes and bottles of assorted toiletries. He was splashing water on his face when he saw her in the mirror, standing by the door, absolutely naked and beautiful. She smiled when she saw that he had seen her.

"Good morning," she said, one hand on her hip. "When you're through, we'll go down for breakfast."

A momentary panic seized David in its grip. Breakfast in this joint would cost a pretty penny, and he didn't have much on him, and couldn't spare any of it to begin with. How much longer could he mooch off her? If only she had added "on me." Maybe he should just tell her that he had an early appointment and had to split. He dried his face with a towel and went back into the bedroom. No. He wanted to spend more time with her, to get to know her better. He would order coffee (probably $2.50 per cup in this place) and hope that breakfast was dutch.

"I'll only be a minute," she said, stepping into the bathroom and closing the door. She kept her word. She came out only minutes later and went to the chair where they had piled their clothes. She slipped into her jumpsuit while David checked how he looked in his wrinkled outfit in the large mirror over the dresser. It would have to do.

He noticed that she was wearing none of her Exclusiva

cosmetics and she looked just as lovely without them. He saw a small patch of freckles under her eyes, barely visible on the pale skin. Her eyes were a magnificent shade of blue. Her body—now covered—had been breathtaking. He had felt positively ugly next to her. Stone-cold sober he would never have been able to make love to her. He would have felt like the beast molesting beauty, Quasimodo ravaging Esmeralda. He knew he wasn't unattractive, but he also knew that she had made love regularly to a husband who was built like a Greek god. Yet, she had seemed to enjoy his ministrations during the evening; he knew he had enjoyed hers.

"Ready?" she said. He nodded and they stepped out into the corridor. David realized that neither of them was saying very much, but somehow it seemed perfectly natural and comfortable, at least to him, as if they were old friends who didn't find it necessary to converse every single second. He liked that.

Waiting for the elevator, she turned to him, and brushed a piece of hair back up off his forehead. "Do you have a busy day ahead?" she asked.

"Not really. I have a few things to do."

She consulted her wristwatch. "Well, it's 10:30. I hope you didn't miss anything."

He couldn't help but laugh. "It wouldn't have mattered if I had. I've been having a wonderful time."

"Me, too." She kissed him lightly on the mouth. "David."

He smiled. It was nice that she had remembered his name.

"Do *you* have a busy day?" he asked.

She bit her lip and thought for a moment. "Nothing today, really. An appointment at three." Before she could continue, the elevator came. They got on, managing to stay together despite the fact that the car was packed. David noticed a few people staring at Anna,

70

having recognized her. Two middle-aged women began whispering.

The car opened again at the lobby floor, and they disembarked; Anna led him to a small coffee shop located at one end of the lounge. A waitress showed them to a table, and handed them menus. "This is on me," Anna said. "Have anything you like."

"Well—that's very nice of you," he said, feeling relief. He was very hungry, but didn't want to take advantage. He decided on some bacon and eggs and coffee, which was reasonably priced, if nowhere near as cheap as in most restaurants.

Anna had the same. As she sipped her grapefruit juice, which the waitress had brought immediately, she asked: "Going job hunting today?"

"Why—how did you know that?"

"You mentioned it last night." That's right, he had forgotten. "I've been unemployed myself. I know how it is."

He felt a trifle embarrassed. The meal, the room, the cab, even the drinks last night. She had paid because she knew how poor he must have been. He hoped he hadn't sounded desperate about it, although he was certainly in a desperate position.

"Well, you certainly don't have to worry about that now," he said. "I see your commercials all the time."

She laughed. "Yes. Last night you went over each commercial with me, analyzing each shot practically."

"Really? I must have been a big bore."

"Not at all. I was flattered that you took such an interest."

"I recall you telling me how they managed to get a shot of you dangling from a helicopter. Didn't you say it was a double in the long shots—"

"And back projection in the closeups, yes. You remembered."

"Where will you be wearing your Exclusiva next? Flying over a bullring? Skiing down Mount Everest? Floating on the Hudson?"

She giggled and dug into her bag for a cigarette. She offered him one, but he declined. "Sometimes I wonder myself. I have to admit that those ads are pretty silly. But I have fun doing them. Except it's much more tedious than one would imagine. A lot of waiting around. Endless hours in the chair being made up, having your hair styled. Not that I'm complaining. Exclusiva has revitalized my life. Took me out of the struggling model category, not that I was doing all that badly before. But now I have the freedom to do just about anything I want." She sipped her coffee. "That's what money does for you."

"Yeah," he nodded. He was aware that she was aware that she had been going on about money to a man who was out of work and who was more or less destitute. Her face reddened a bit. David spoke into the awkward silence quickly, hoping to save the situation. "Do you think you'll retire young in life?"

"Who knows? I can't model forever. I suppose it depends on my disposition in a few years. I can't imagine doing *nothing* all day long. I'll just have to wait and see."

She paused, looked down at her fingernails, poking at a chip with another fingertip. "Besides, I've got a lot of readjusting to do. I think I mentioned my up-and-coming divorce last night, didn't I?"

"Yes. But you sounded as if nothing was definite about that."

"I must have been suddenly optimistic because of the liquor. No, I think it's over, all right. But I don't want to bore you with *that*."

"You won't bore me. I just don't want to pry into your personal life. If you want to talk about it, though, go right ahead. Sometimes it helps."

"There isn't much to say. I'm just going to have to find a new place to live. And I won't have to think about two people all the time like I used to. Only one. I guess I can manage. There are really simple solutions to everything, if one puts one's mind to it."

Their eggs came and they attacked the food hungrily, preferring nourishment to conversation for the nonce. They relaxed over a second cup of coffee afterwards. Anna finally said what David had been hoping to hear. "I'd like to see you again, if that's all right with you."

"Of course, it is. I'd love to see *you* again."

"Can I reach you by phone?"

He gave the number to her, and she took a pen out of her bag and wrote it down on a napkin. She handed him a small white business card with her name and a phone number, and the name of her agency, written on it. "I can be reached there. Or leave a message," she said. Obviously, she didn't want to give out her home phone, but this would do nicely.

They parted a few minutes later. On the front steps of the hotel, Anna suddenly grabbed his face in her hands and kissed him on the mouth long and voluptuously. She broke the embrace after awhile and said, "Can I take you anywhere?"

"Anywhere!"

"I mean by taxi," she laughed.

"No, thanks. I can walk home from here. It seems like a nice day."

"All right, then."

He watched her drive off in the cab, delirious from her kiss, from her lingering presence, but desolate from the knowledge that she was a woman who lived far, far above his means.

Anna sat back in the cab, and rubbed her arms, hugging herself, still thinking of the night she'd spent with that wonderful guy. Poor thing was as poor as a church mouse, but somehow she didn't care. She'd had enough of the idle rich. Derek with his inherited dough, Mrs. Hunter with her dull dinner parties. Was she slumming? She didn't care.

She had not given up her dreams of becoming part of "society," of being with a better class of people then the jerks and yokels she'd grown up with. But she needed somebody different in her life now, someone she could relax with, not bother to impress. The poor dear was so obviously impressed already, simply by who she was, that she wouldn't have to put on airs.

She realized that she had used him, that she would not have picked him up if she hadn't fought with Derek, hadn't needed the attentions of another man. David was attractive and virile, certainly, but what would she need with some poverty-row, unemployed bar fixture if her life were working the way she wanted it to? Yet, she did need him now; she was convinced of that. And he did know how to make love, of that there was no doubt.

She decided to put him out of her mind until she decided to see him again. Damn it—he was getting to her, and that just didn't make sense. He wasn't what she wanted, was he? Yes, he was different from Derek, but did she have to go to extremes?

The cab pulled up to the building which housed the Longton Agency. She paid the driver and stepped out onto the sidewalk. It was getting hot today. Lionel Hanson, the man who photographed her for a magazine layout, had promised to send copies of the shots to the agency for her to look over; she might want blowups made of some of the more interesting photos. She took the elevator to the eleventh floor and entered the agency's office. The receptionist smiled, said hello, and handed her a large brown envelope. It was Hanson's photographs.

She left the office before anyone could waylay her and took a cab back to the townhouse. She wanted to get in a few more hours' sleep before her session at three. She went straight to the bedroom, changed into a dressing gown, and tore open the package. She studied the pictures with a magnifying glass. Hanson had circled the ones to be used in the campaign; she would have chosen others, but who was she to argue? She had liked the male model she had worked with in this spread, a handsome, personable young fellow named Eric Marton. Eric was the man in the ads smitten with her because she was wearing new nine-hour Exclusiva eye shadow. Actually, Eric had a very good-looking male lover.

A shadow suddenly covered the bedspread where she lay. She looked up from the pictures and saw Derek glaring down at her. He looked angrier than she had ever seen him before. Something told her to stand up; she was in too vulnerable a position where she was. She was relieved to see that he had nothing in his hand that could have been used as a weapon.

"What do you want?" she said. "Why the nasty stare? Well, say something!"

He glared at her a few seconds more, then said, "Where were you last night?"

"Why is it any of your business?"

"I wanted to talk to you some more. And you ran out of her like a bat out of hell." She saw the fire in his eyes and couldn't help but think of that old cliche: *You're beautiful when you're angry.* And he was.

"Isn't that just like you," she argued. "You're never around when I need you, never on time when I want you to be. But when *you* want to talk, I don't dare leave the house. That's a lot of crap and you know it!"

"We came to an important decision last night. When all the screaming was over, I thought we could sit down and talk things over calmly."

"Do you mean to tell me that you *don't* want a divorce?"

"I didn't say that. But it's a big step, and should be

75

discussed carefully. We should take the time to think things through."

"We've had enough time. I'm sick of this relationship, Derek. I'm bored. I want to move on to something different, to something else. I don't want to wait on tenterhooks wondering in which direction our marriage will go. I want to settle things as quickly and as firmly as possible."

"You said you want 'something else.' Are you sure you don't mean some*one* else?"

"What if I do? Surely you're not going to give me grief on *that* point. After all the extramarital mischief you've been up to? Spare me the righteous anger of the bereaved husband. It's a role that simply doesn't suit you."

"I saw you coming out of Peg O' Hearts with some guy last night."

"What did you do, follow me? I suppose I should be flattered."

"I wasn't checking up on you, if that's what you were thinking. I just wanted to find you, so we could talk. I thought you might like some company."

"I had wonderful company, thank you."

"I'm sure. Is that what this is all about? Why didn't you come right out and admit it? You've found another man. Why blame me for this breakup when it has nothing to do with *my* 'extramarital mischief'?"

"Derek, you astonish me! Do you mean to tell me that your precious ego can't accept the fact that your wife might be up to some fun herself, that your wife might be fiddling around with something decidedly undecrepit. You amaze me, husband. But you're not getting away with it so easily."

"What do you mean?"

"I mean you're not going to blame this divorce on me. I only met that gentleman last evening, for your information. Derek, I don't need your money, if that's what

76

you're worried about. I won't be terrorized by you, afraid to have a possible affair because you'll be able to produce 'the other man.' You can keep your money, your alimony, the house, the maid. All I want is my freedom. That's all. I no longer want to be married to Derek Bishop. Period. End of sentence. This isn't a marriage, so why should either of us hang onto it? I just want out. That's all there is to it. This can be the easiest and fastest divorce on record."

"I'll believe that when I see it, bitch," he snapped. "I suggest you hire your *own* lawyer; I already have one." He walked out to the hall, slamming the door behind him.

"Derek," she whispered. "You always have to create melodrama, don't you?" She sat down on the bed, picked up the magnifying glass and looked over the photographs again, although her mind wasn't really on them.

The moment David put his key in his lock, he knew that something was wrong. The lock wasn't broken, luckily, but it seemed looser, easier to open than before, as if someone had jimmied it open, damaging it slightly in the process. Someone had been in the apartment.

He stood there, holding his breath, closing his eyes. There was so little inside to steal. Still, he was afraid to see the mess inside, to see what condition the burglars must have left the place in.

He pushed the door open, steeled himself, and took a good, long look.

Nothing seemed to have been disturbed.

He went through the drawers, checked the bathroom, but there was no indication that anyone had even been there, let alone lifted something. They didn't even take the TV set, which was probably the only thing of value in the apartment. Why the hell did they have to pick on *his* place?

Then he recalled George Bartley's final words. The same words that had convinced him not to spend the night in the apartment. He added up one and one and got two. Someone had come to the apartment to look for George. They had gone in, looked around, seen that he wasn't there. What would they have done to David if he had been at home? He didn't know. He was just doubly glad that he had gone out that night. It might have saved his life.

He took a shower and changed into a light suit and tie. He was going to make the rounds today, although he wasn't very hopeful. He needed quick cash, so a temporary job that paid on Friday would be his best bet. He'd go to several office temp agencies and hope that one of them could give him immediate work.

It was a depressing day. He had to take those idiotic tests to see how well he could type or file or add up figures. He saw few men his own age. Mostly college kids and older women. He felt very much like a loser. Even if they got him a job he wouldn't make much more in a week than Anna Braddon spent in one day. And this week he'd get only two days pay. Pitiful!

It wasn't until he got to his fourth agency, around four p.m., that he let himself even think of her. Had the night in bed with her satisfied his curiosity, his lust? Was she now out of his system for good? He didn't think so. But he also knew that he could only function with her on that one level, the plane where all class boundaries dissolved, the great equalizer known as flesh. He didn't have the money to take her out where she was accustomed to going. He was not a diehard chauvinist; clearly he didn't mind a woman picking up the check, especially if she had more money than he did. But how could he date anyone, even Little Orphan Annie, when he couldn't afford to pay his own way? He didn't mind being treated now and then, but there had to be a limit. He had to at least be able to return the favor sometime.

He had her number, but he knew he'd never call her. What would they talk about? In the glow of a good night's sleep and fresh sex, their conversation at breakfast had seemed stimulating, but it had only been vapid small talk. Anyway, he knew he did not want to be the shoulder she would cry on over her disintegrating marriage. But even while he thought all this, even while he recognized that Anna Braddon was not, when all was said and done, his type, he knew that he would be thinking of her often.

"Hammond? David Hammond?" The counselor's voice calling from the other side of the room woke him up from his daydream. It was time for his interview. A tall blond fellow with a bushy mustache stood at the end of the hall, holding a card and looking around.

David stood up. "Over here. Sorry." He followed the man down the hall and into his office. It was a mere cubbyhole. He sat in the seat in front of the man's desk, while the counselor sat down behind it. The man studied the form David had filled out earlier.

"I see you have some clerical experience," he said. "But your typing isn't too good. Let me see what I have here."

David sat back and tried to relax, while the man— who was at least five years younger than he was—went through an index-card holder, flipping each card in search of some elusive position. "Ah ha," he said, pulling one of them out with his fingers. "This might be for you. Let me make sure this isn't filled yet." He picked up the phone and dialed another extension in the same office. "Is the Belmont Cards job taken?" he asked. David heard a female voice respond. Moments later, the counselor hung up the phone and smiled.

"At least five days, 9:30 to 5:30. Minimum wage, I'm afraid. Starts tomorrow. How does that sound?"

"Better than nothing."

"I'll write down the information for you. You report

to Miss Chilton tomorrow morning. It's a nice place. Many of our employees have told me how much they enjoy working there."

"Uh, what exactly will I be doing?"

"Filing order forms, other clerical work. General stuff."

"I see."

The counselor handed him the slip, shook his hand, and ushered him out the door.

Belmont Cards. *Shit.* Just what he needed, another greeting-card firm. By hook or by crook he'd get somebody to look at his sketches if he had to steamroll his way into the art department.

Thirty-three, he thought as he walked towards the subway. Thirty-three years old and I'm a temporary file clerk. And last night I made love to a woman who must make $500,000 a year.

As the train came roaring into the station he contemplated jumping in front of its path, ending it all quickly: the humiliation, the frustration, the bitter sense of defeat.

But he didn't jump. With his luck, he figured, he would probably only maim himself for life.

Miss Chilton turned out to be a stern, no-nonsense old bitch who practically snarled at David when he walked into her office at quarter of ten.

"You're late," she snapped.

"I'm sorry, the train—"

"Never mind." She got up and instructed him to follow her down the hall. She was about fifty-five, with puffy cheeks and small eyes and gray hair pulled back in a bun. She wore a blue pants suit that looked absolutely ridiculous on her.

As they waited for the elevator, she looked David up and down with obvious distaste and said: "Tomorrow wear a tie."

A tie? For this shit job? Minimum wage? David held his tongue but wanted to spit on her.

"You'll be working in the order department," she said, once they'd boarded the elevator. "With Peggy Cummins. She'll be your supervisor."

If he thought Miss Chilton was bad, Miss Cummins was even worse. After Chilton left to make somebody else's life miserable, Peggy took him down a dingy hallway, into an ugly green filing room with harsh fluorescent lighting. A long wooden table was situated right smack in the middle of the room. Peggy was in her late twenties, and seemed incapable of getting out of bed in the morning, let alone running a department. Her face was bland and baggy, and she wore a perpetually pained look that made her resemble an abandoned basset hound. She was too old for acne, but her skin hadn't been told that, for reddish patches inflamed the areas around her nose and chin. Somehow one could feel sympathetic towards her, although her complete lack of a personality made it hard to even think of her as a living person.

David was getting more depressed and horrified every second, and when he met his coworkers for the first time, he knew that things were bound to get worse. They sat around the table drinking coffee, waiting for someone to tell them what to do. They were all much, much younger than he was, and he felt even more humiliated than he had up in Chilton's office. One was a young woman whose eyes were nearly closed; not from fatigue, he discovered momentarily, but from the fact that she was almost always stoned on grass. She giggled when David was introduced, and looked as if she was about to slide right off her chair and onto the dirty tiled floor. A male Oriental-American of high school age sat next to her, a transister radio attached to his ear. He bounced up and down to the song. What was worse, he sang along with the music, seemingly unaware that he was practically tone deaf. The third was another young lady—Maritza, she was called—who sat popping her gum and drawing doodles on the bag which had once held her morning donut.

The room looked as if it had been filled according to some sort of quota system. The two young women were black and Puerto Rican, respectively, the kid was Chinese, and David was the closest thing to a WASP they could probably find. He couldn't have cared less about his coworkers' races, sexes or ethnic backgrounds. But God—their ages! They were *children*, and he was doing children's work. He thought of that subway train again and wished he had jumped.

He spent most of the morning listening to Miss Cummins droning on about the peculiarities of the Belmont filing system, and learning what to do with the white, black and buff copies of the order forms which were delivered by dour-looking mailroom boys two times daily in large brown sacks. "It's the time when stores order their fall line of cards," Peggy explained, "which is why we have to hire extra help to take some of the weight off our regular file people."

"Where are they?" the Chinese kid inquired.

"Upstairs in another office."

"We temps get stuck down here in the black hole of Calcutta," Concetta, the black woman, explained. "And we get paid about half of what the permanent workers do."

"That's because the agency gets fifty percent of our salary, practically," the Puerto Rican lady added.

"And it's such shit work, too," Concetta groaned, not caring if Miss Cummins heard or not.

It was nearly lunchtime when Peggy finally finished explaining. (Like David, his three coworkers were pros —together they had managed to stretch out the training period to nearly four hours, playing dumb, asking questions over and over again. Peggy was too stupid to catch on. Or else unconcerned.) David was glad that they'd been given a brief reprieve before starting in proper on what promised to be some of the most boring work ever conceived for the hapless temporary worker. He went out and grabbed a slice of pizza for lunch. He was on a very tight budget until payday, and even after that, as his check would be pretty pathetic.

He spent the afternoon tearing carbons, and scribbling the names of stationery stores on pink slips, and going back and forth to the john to take up time. Concetta, Maritza, and Joe, the Oriental lad, all seemed to be nice enough, but they were still living with their folks, or just earning extra money, concerned with problems peculiar to their age, problems David could no longer relate to. Finally, it happened.

"How old are you?" Concetta asked, scrunching up her face quizzically.

David told them.

"Man, that old and working here. You must really need the money," she said mercilessly, though without any actual hostility.

"That's the way it is," he said, thinking: *I will not last another day on this job*.

At three o'clock they had a coffee break. Joe turned up his radio and resumed his excruciating vocal activities. Concetta slipped out to the ladies' room, smoked another joint, and came back even more blurry-eyed and silly than before. Maritza continued to draw her terrible sketches on every unused piece of paper. Any minute he expected her to pull a sanitary napkin out of her purse and doodle on that. What was worse, she insisted on showing everything she drew to David, who had to nod and pretend he liked it. He decided not to mention that he was "into" art; she would probably *never* let him be if he did.

He couldn't take much more of this. He went back to work, pulling off the carbons, scribbling the names, filing the white copies in the makeshift boxes which served as filing cabinets. Pulling carbons, scribbling names, filing white copies, pulling carbons, scribbling names, filing white copies, pulling carbons . . .

By four o'clock he was nearly half-crazed with boredom. He decided to find out where the art department was. He excused himself from the room, went to the elevator bank and went up to the main floor. He stepped out into the corridor, hoping Miss Chilton wasn't around. He went over to the receptionist, and asked where the art department was, hoping she'd assume he had to go there on some errand. She bought it. "It's on this floor, to your right. The third door."

He thanked her, and followed her directions. Right inside the third door was another receptionist, a pretty blonde woman with a short hairdo and long bangs. "Can I help you?" she asked.

"Could I speak to the art director?" he queried.

"Can I ask what this is in reference to?"

He decided to level with her. He was midway through his explanation, trying to be as charming and vulnerable as possible, when the receptionist's eyes whirled up towards an attractive, aggressive-looking brunette coming in from the hallway. "This is our art director," the blonde explained. "Ms. Morrison."

"Yes. Can I help you?" the brunette asked pleasantly.

David took the plunge. "Could I talk to you for a second? I'm a new employee. I work in the ordering department." That much was true. Morrison didn't ask him what it was "in reference to," thank goodness, but simply ushered him into her office.

David knew this was a golden opportunity and that he couldn't afford to blow it. This was one card company that rarely used the work of free-lancers, relying instead on a regular staff of artists. David had figured that without connections he'd never get on their staff, so he had never bothered sending them any material. Now, the art director was sitting right in front of him, waiting for him to speak. He did.

He told her that he thought his work was good, too good for him to be pulling carbons on the lower floor in a room without filing cabinets. He asked if he could show her some samples on the following day. She was decidedly noncommittal, but told him that he could. "I'll be in and out tomorrow, but keep trying. I can't promise anything. We don't use freelancers, and there aren't any openings right now. But . . . you never know."

David thanked her profusely and left. It had just been a freak chance that she'd walked in just when he was talking to the receptionist. Otherwise he might never have been granted an interview, which is what had happened at the other greeting-card firm he'd worked at. She had been kind enough to at least give him a chance. He had to go home, look over his portfolio, perhaps draw up some new stuff. He was really excited.

He was in such a happy mood that he threw himself into his work when he got back to his spot at the table. Said work had piled up. His coworkers had been careful to evenly distribute the workload, and his percentage of the order forms were waiting for him to process. He speeded up, trying to catch up with the others. The only way to survive work like this was to make a game of it.

They heard footsteps out in the hall. "Must be that Peggy creature," Concetta said.

It wasn't. It was dear Miss Chilton. She asked David to step out into the hall with her. Oh no, she couldn't fire him! Not now! What if he was unable to get in to see Morrison? He told himself to stop being silly. All he had to do was call the woman and make an official appointment.

"What were you doing upstairs?" Chilton asked.

"I—uh—had to see somebody."

"Who?"

"Someone in the art department. I'm an artist."

"Really?" She was unimpressed, a dried-up old witch who had to make everyone else miserable because she was. "The temporary workers are not supposed to go around bothering people. I'll be held accountable for your actions. Please stay down here. And remember. Tomorrow, a tie."

It was nearly five. The moment the ogress had gone up to her office in one elevator, David went down to the lobby in the other. He was anxious to get home and go through the sketches. Miss Chilton would not get in his way or he would run her over. He suddenly remembered that he had forgotten to say good night to the "children," but he didn't care.

Two good things happened when he got home.

He found a money order for 150 dollars from his father. Someone at the home must have taken care of it for him.

And Anna Braddon called at six on the dot.

"Did you have a nice day?" she asked.

"All right." He told her about finding work. He mentioned the part about seeing the art director, but intentionally left out all details of the carbon copies and the file room. He had to have *some* dignity, didn't he?

He wanted to ask her out for a drink, for dinner. For anything. But it was too late to cash the money order, and any restaurant she picked would probably eat up most of the money. He felt trapped. The conversation went on and on, small talk, lots of pauses, giggles over remarks that weren't funny. Both of them were waiting, waiting for the other to make the first move.

"Well, I just thought I'd call and see how things were going," Anna said, her voice weary, frustrated.

David took the plunge. "I'd like to see you again. Soon."

Anna didn't waste a moment. "My husband is out of town. Come to dinner this evening. My place."

86

She didn't have to ask him twice.

Derek Bishop's townhouse was most impressive. A strong black metal fence went around the building, which took up half a block, and there was a path up to the stoop with a small lawn and bushes on either side of it. David walked up and rang the bell. He was dressed casually, but handsomely. He smelled of a nice, fresh scent he'd found in the bathroom cabinet, but had only used twice before tonight. His leg was hurting like hell. Subconsciously he'd been trying to hide his impairment now that he was out among people again. He'd barely limped the whole time he was with Anna, or while he was at work. Now he was paying the piper with pain, baby, pain. He didn't want to come on like a cripple. But surely Anna must have noticed there was something wrong with his leg by now. He had no choice this evening but to limp quite noticeably. He hoped it wouldn't repel her.

The maid opened the door and David was ushered into a huge foyer.

"May I take your coat, sir?" the elderly woman asked. David handed over his jacket and she hung it up in a nearby closet. David looked up and saw Anna come rushing down the wide white stairs leading off from the hall. He was relieved to see that she, too, was dressed casually. Tight jeans, a pink blouse. She went straight over to David and gave him a big kiss. David licked his lips as she led him into the living room; she tasted like fresh strawberries.

She sat down next to him on a big couch, and asked him what he wished to drink. The maid went to get them the cocktails, and David wondered what he and his hostess would talk about. He didn't have long to wonder. Anna grabbed him and kissed him again, and didn't let go until Clara came back with the drinks. David washed down the strawberries with some scotch.

They resumed kissing, their mouths even tastier than before.

They went in for dinner a little while later. Anna seemed quite different tonight. While Clara served the chicken and vegetables, she asked him again about work, and what he hoped to do, and stuff like that, but she wasn't even bothering to pretend that she was actually interested. It was as if he were there to satisfy some sudden craving, nothing more. As if only his body interested her. He should have been flattered, happy. But he felt disillusioned. Anna made countless witticisms throughout dinner, acting like a frivolous schoolgirl determined to be light and bubbly and entertaining at all costs. And the cost was that what David had hoped would be an evening to bring them closer, to help them discover more about each other, was instead turning out to be a vapid disappointment.

"Will you do some cartoons for me later?" she purred in a mock seductive tone, her lips clamping down on a forkful of spinach. David felt like a ten-year-old whose interests were being humored by a sexy older cousin.

"If you'd like," he answered. He felt like adding that he'd do a caricature of her, but she was already making a caricature out of herself, wasn't she? David wanted to talk about something more serious, perhaps, but her mood was not conducive to anything other than silly remarks and giggles and cutesy-wutesy expressions that he could do little but respond to as best as he was able.

Clara was about to serve dessert when the phone rang in the kitchen. She went to answer it, then came back and told Anna it was for her. Anna excused herself and stepped into the next room. Clara cut him a big slice of chocolate cream pie which he dug into with relish.

He could hear Anna's voice turning more serious, starting to tremble, as she listened to the caller on the other end of the line. Had something happened to Derek?

A few minutes went by. "Thank you for calling," she said. A few moments later she walked back into the dining room, pale and dissipated, as if someone or something had taken all the energy from her, had sucked away the vigor and vitality that she'd been running on all evening, leaving her hollow and drained, too tired to stand.

"Is something wrong?" David asked.

She didn't answer at first, but sunk down into her chair and buried her face in her hands. He couldn't tell at first if she were laughing or crying, until she looked up and he saw the tears running down from her eyes.

"It's my brother," she said. "Jeffrey. He's dead."

She got up at the same time he did, then he held her as she collapsed into his arms, sobbing and shaking all at once. He didn't know what to say.

He wanted them to be closer. But not at such a price. She needed someone—needed *him*—now, and he was not going to leave her, would never leave her, if she didn't want him to.

He took her into the living room, and they sat on the same couch as before, and she told him all she knew about her brother Jeffrey's death.

Part Two

Containment

Chapter Five

Milbourne, Connecticut—Spring, 1983

Milbourne, Connecticut is a quiet farm community, population: 4,500. Harry London had lived there for the past twenty years, working diligently in the large sporting goods store he owned in the center of town. The shop was surrounded by a block or two of other stores, a bar and theater, which together made up the entire Milbourne commercial district; a quite respectable one for such a small town. At age forty-eight, London was looking forward to an early retirement—his store was doing marvelously, and had become *the* place to go to for sports and outdoor equipment, not only in his section of the state, but in nearby New York and Massachusetts communities, as well.

It was a Monday afternoon in the spring—too early in season to be really hot, too late to bother with jackets—that his world began to slowly crumble; to evolve, to *mutate*, into something vast and unusual, something unknown and frightening. London had always lived an extremely calm and conventional life, and had thought he was satisfied with that, but he was to discover that he secretly longed for something different and more exciting. At that time, however, he had not been aware of the price he would have to pay for misadventure.

His store had two floors, not including the basement

area, which was stocked with camping equipment and open tent displays. It was a handsome place, full of colorful arrangements of the items for sale, with light blue walls that were painted fresh every two years. The floors were washed and polished nightly. London was very proud of his "little" emporium.

He had moved to the town not long after his marriage, hoping that he could sustain a business successfully while raising children in fresh air and sunshine. His wife had been a lovely but frail little woman, and she had died before three years were up, and they had never had children. Harry threw himself into his business, hoping it would replace the loss of wife and family, knowing it never could. He'd still been a young man then, still was, depending on how you looked at it. He'd met and dated several women, but nothing had ever clicked. Perhaps he was too afraid to start a relationship again, to risk the pain of losing a loved one for a second time.

His two closest friendships were with the current assistant manager of the store, Jeffrey Braddon, and his head clerk, Paula Widdoes. They spent a great deal of time together, the three of them, and some suspected that London was "carrying on" with Paula. Actually, Paula was carrying on with Jeffrey, although it had never become serious in a romantic sense. They were both about the same age, mid-thirties, both attractive. Harry was a plain older man with a bald pate and graying sideburns. He kept himself in nice physical shape, but half the time felt like a protective father worrying over his two younger associates.

He was sitting in his office, eating a lunch of yogurt and half a swiss cheese sandwich, when Paula came in, a tense expression on her face. "I've been calling and calling his house," she said, "and there's no answer."

"Now don't worry," Harry said as soothingly as possible. "Are you sure he was due back *today*?" He dipped a plastic spoon into the yogurt, came up with a creamy dab of pink goo.

"Of course, I'm sure. You remember. He was going to spend a week in New York, and be back at work on the 12th." She tapped the calendar on the wall with her pencil. "That's today. I hope everything's all right."

"Jeffrey was probably having such a good time that he decided to stay a few more days."

"Without calling us? I don't believe that. He's not that irresponsible. I have three new clerks to train today. He promised to help."

"Well, I have his sister's number in New York. She might know what happened to him."

"He wasn't planning on staying with her. He wasn't even sure he was going to call her. She has such a busy schedule, no time for her family." Her words took on that familiar bitter tone he'd heard coming from Jeffrey himself time and time again.

"It's worth a try," Harry insisted.

"I'd be embarrassed. Suppose he *didn't* get in touch with her. It could make for an awkward situation."

"Well then, relax. He'll probably come strutting in here this afternoon, with a good, if maddening excuse. If I'm not worried, why should you be?"

She sat down on the edge of his cluttered desk and exhaled dramatically. "I guess you're right. I'm just so *tired* this morning. And those new people. Phew! Two of them act like they can't understand a word I say. The third is gonna be trouble, I can tell already. The thirty-minutes'-work-in-three-hours type. You wait and see."

"You've been wrong before." He scraped out the last of his yogurt. "This isn't enough for me," he whined, throwing the container and the spoon into the waste-basket at his feet. "Half a sandwich. I hate diets. I need something substantial."

"Me, too. To help me get through the day."

"Since when are you dieting? You don't need to." Her lovely slim figure was a constant source of admiration. Those beautiful green eyes and naturally long lashes. Black hair cut short, curling inwards at the chin-line. A very attractive woman. Damn Jeffrey.

"Neither do you," she countered. "But you struggle along on your half-assed diets anyway, year after year. Why? To *stay* slim, right? Me, too. I want to *stay* slim."

"Well, one good meal won't make us fat, will it? On me. How about it? Can I buy you lunch?"

She shot up and smiled down at him. "You certainly can. But I thought you've already eaten." She motioned towards the brown paper on the desk, the crumbs of bread and bits of cheese left over.

"A mere appetizer, I assure you."

They went out into the street, full of traffic and pedestrians shopping and carrying out other errands, pretending they were living an exciting life in a big city. Milbourne wasn't exciting, but it was clean and attractive. Most of the shops looked new, and those that didn't were quaint and charming. They walked past the deserted and shuttered building next door—the closest thing to an eyesore in the town—and went into a restaurant on the corner. They found an empty table immediately. When the waitress came, Paula ordered a cheeseburger deluxe, and Harry a banana split. Paula chuckled.

They said nothing until halfway through the meal. They were that close. Silences were not awkward or threatening.

"I'm still worried," she said, looking off into space somewhere to the right and above her lunch companion's head. "It's just so unthinkable for Jeffrey not to call, to do anything on impulse. Anybody else, I'd assume they did what you said. Decided to stay longer, the hell with work. Who wants to call work when you'd rather forget about it? But Jeffrey isn't like that."

No, Jeffrey wasn't like that. Jeffrey was an enigma. He was the forgotten, unknown, unrecognizable relative of an increasingly visible public figure. If anyone wondered what it was like to be the brother of a famous individual—or someone on the verge of being famous (big movie contracts and TV series deals were in the cards for model Anna Braddon, or so everyone said)— all they had to do was look at Jeffrey. He and his sister had never been that close, perhaps that was the problem. He could not bask in reflected glory, could not live among her circle of rich, successful friends. His ambition seemed to decrease as he got older.

While attractive, he was not beautiful like his sister was. He was quiet and likable, fast with a joke, easy to talk with. His qualities were unsensational and unexploitable. No one ever knew quite how he got to Milbourne, as he had not been born there and—being a bachelor—had not come there seeking peace and sunlight for his family. Whenever the subject came up, he would mutter some noncommittal, unintelligible phrase, shrug his big shoulders and cough to show his unease.

No one really knew why Jeffrey shut himself away in a small Connecticut town. No one ever knew what he wanted out of life. After a while, no one cared.

Harry and Paula sat there listening to the muted conversations of other diners in nearby booths, the clatter of plates and yelling from the kitchen, and for once in their lives, there was a void that needed to be filled. A pause that *was* awkward.

Harry wondered later why he said it. It just slipped out:

"You're very fond of him, aren't you?"

"Of course," she said, putting on a perplexed expression, as if she didn't know what he had really meant. "Aren't you?"

"Very much. He's a fine man. A good friend. But

97

your feelings for him go slightly deeper than that, don't they? I'm sorry." He shifted uncomfortably in his seat, wishing he were back at work. "I didn't mean to get so personal. It's none of my business."

"That's all right, Harry," Paula said, smiling a the-heck-with-it kind of smile. "I can't really answer your question, if you want to know the truth. I just don't know how I feel. You know that Jeff and I have been— intimate. But physical intimacy and emotional need are two different things entirely. I want his friendship. I have his friendship. Maybe that's all there is. All there needs to be. I don't know."

He patted her hand (a condescending if well-intentioned gesture, he thought later), then called for the waitress to bring the check. "Unless you want dessert?" he asked.

She declined. They walked back slowly to the store, discussing the new clerks, display plans, stuff that was important in regards to work, but trivial in terms of their friendship.

The afternoon was considerably more eventful than the morning had been.

At 2:30 Jeffrey had still not arrived. Paula called his house again and again, but got no answer. She wished that he had told her specifically where he was going to stay in Manhattan. She didn't like the idea of bothering his sister—although she had her number—and decided not to do so until absolutely necessary. Surely he would be back by tomorrow.

What bothered her was that she had not even had a chance to say goodbye. She had gone out to do some quick shopping late that afternoon—the last day before his vacation—and he'd been gone by the time she got back. She had called his house to wish him a happy trip, but there had been no answer then, either. Oh, she hoped he was all right.

The new trainees were not shaping up very well, although Paula rationalized that many slow learners blossomed into genuine treasures. Unfortunately, none of the three—all young people from the town wanting summer work—had very outgoing personalities, a must for a successful salesperson. She hoped she wouldn't have to let them go.

At 3:15, Harry asked to see her and inquired as to the whereabouts of some large posters they had used a year or two ago to advertise a sale on basketballs. "I asked Jeffrey where they were the day he left. He went off to find them, but I guess he had no luck. He left before I had a chance to check with him."

"Are you putting those old things on sale again?" she asked.

"They might go faster. I don't want to get stuck again."

"I think they might be in the cellar. I'll go and look."

"Why don't you send someone down there?" he suggested.

"No. They'd only have to come and get me. Better I look. I think I was the one who put them away in the first place."

The basement was empty except for the salesman and a family looking through the tent display over in the far corner. Paula walked past it—smiling at a small child who was lounging on the carpet of fake grass around the tent—and entered another chamber through a large metal door. She went down three concrete steps into what was usually referred to as the "sub-basement," although it was adjacent to the cellar, not really below it. She flipped on the light switch on the wall, illuminating a gray and dusty corridor leading into the far right side of the lower part of the building. She wished that someone would move the switch up to the metal door behind her. Someday someone would break their neck on those steps in the dark.

This storage area was used so infrequently that there were cobwebs lining the walls, hanging down from the low ceiling. Shuddering involuntarily, she pushed her way through them—thank goodness the webs were not large—and made her way down to another metal door at the very end of the hall. Unused items and boxes and assorted junk had been stored in this room as long as she had worked here, a good ten years, and if those posters were anywhere, they would be inside.

She opened the door and stepped inside, inhaling the disagreeable, musty odor of the chamber, and made the mistake of walking ahead briskly to the light cord hanging down in the middle of the fair-sized room. She had only a brief glimpse of the metal racks, laden with cartons and stacks of paper, before she felt herself falling into a crumpled section of the flooring. She heard a cracking sound, a splintering noise, and suddenly she was plunging into a dark hole underneath her, dropping through the jagged wood floor and down to an abrupt and painful halt on a mound of moist dirt.

Her ankle was killing her, but she seemed to be all right otherwise. She picked herself up from the ground, brushing dirt off her clothes, and looked around. She couldn't see much; the only light was the little bit from the corridor above that came down through the same hole she had fallen through. Her body felt sore, especially her rump. The drop was only a few feet, luckily, and she had landed on soft earth. Otherwise, it could have been a lot worse.

How could this have happened? What could have made the floor fall in like that? It had been cracked open before she'd stepped on it; she was sure of that. Her feet must have just touched the edges of the hole, making the floor directly below give way under her weight. Maybe somebody else had fallen through at some time.

She tried reaching the hanging wood beams above her head, but it was no use. There was nothing down there for her to stand on either, just blackness and more blackness on every side. She wondered how far she could walk before she hit a wall or foundation. The deserted building next door must begin somewhere at this point. The only thing separating it from the store was a very thin alleyway no fat person would ever dare to walk through.

She tried not to panic, keeping her screams for help urgent, but not hysterical. When nothing happened after a few minutes, she figured "the hell with propriety" and began to holler at the top of her lungs. Although the door to the store room was still open, the other door leading into the main part of the cellar was closed. And it was thick.

Ten minutes went by. Her throat was raw and hoarse, and she had begun to notice a sickening odor down in the hole, coming from a distance, coming closer all the time. Or perhaps she was just becoming more aware of it. The only word she could use to describe it would have been *stench*. A real, honest-to-goodness *stench*.

Then she heard footsteps. She wiped away the silent tears that had been running down her cheeks for the past few minutes, and began to yell again. "Help me. Help! I'm in the storeroom. Help me!"

She heard a voice, a man's voice. Roger, the clerk. He probably wasn't busy and, having noticed her enter the sub-cellar, had come in to see if he could help. "Don't step in the room," she warned. "The floor has fallen in. You'll have to get a ladder."

He must have heard her, because the footsteps stopped right outside the door. "Paula," he called. "What happened?"

"The floor. The floor fell in. I fell into a hole in the floor. Be *careful.*"

"Holy!" He had obviously peered in and seen the condition of the floor for himself. "How far down are you?"

"About three feet too far, I'm afraid. I must have

101

fallen about eight feet."

"Are you all right?"

"A little bruised and my ankle hurts, but I think I'll live."

"I'll get a ladder. And some of the fellows. We'll get you out of there."

"All right. But hurry, it's creepy down here. And it smells."

"Okay. Be right back."

"And Roger?"

"Yes, Paula?"

"Tell Harry about it. He'll need to know sometime."

Harry and Roger and two other clerks were there five minutes later. The whole staff would have been there, Paula suspected, had they not had customers to wait on.

"Jesus Christ!" Harry's familiar lament. "Are you okay?"

She assured him that she was. "You and your damn sale posters," she laughed.

"Get out of the way," someone yelled, "we're sending a ladder down."

"No, no," Harry said. "Get one of the rope ladders. That wooden thing is too heavy. This whole floor is about to go any minute."

There was another brief delay. And then an unraveling string rope came flying down into the darkness. Paula grabbed for it.

"Shall I come down and help you get up?" Harry called.

"No," she said, pulling herself onto the bottom rung. "I can make it."

"Watch out for the sharp ends of the broken wood," Harry cautioned.

"I will."

She was pulled up and out into the corridor a few moments later. "Boy, am I glad to be out of there. It *stinks!*"

She raced upstairs to take a valium.

"Hand me that light," Harry instructed. "I'm going to take a look around." He climbed down carefully into the dark hole below, followed gingerly by Roger. Harry told the other two men to stay put just in case.

"What could have caused this?" Roger asked. He was a bearded man of thirty-five, with a protruding pot belly and dark blue eyes. "It looks as if something *pushed* the floor upwards."

He was right. Harry looked up and saw that most of the cracked wood was pointing upwards, except for the pieces which had swung down when Paula crashed through. "That's odd. Come on. Let's look around."

This troubled Harry. Troubled him more than he let on. He hoped the whole structure of his building, his store, his *life*, had not somehow been damaged beyond repair. They walked to the right. "We should hit the foundation of the Forester Building soon," he said. The Forester Building, so called because it had been built by the prominent Forester family in the early 1900s, was the abandoned building next door.

They both shined their flashlights into the blackness before them.

"Look," Roger cried. "The wall's been eaten away. Must have collapsed." They were walking through a hole in the bottom wall of the Forester Building, apparently entering a kind of sub-basement. Only it wasn't a sub-basement any longer, assuming it ever had been.

"I didn't know the Forester Building had such a deep cellar, did you?" Harry asked.

Roger shook his head. "It seems to be a *cave* instead. I wonder how big this is."

It was becoming more apparent that they were walking in some sort of huge cavern, stretching out ahead of them endlessly, although they could see the

103

rocky sides of the enclosure at the far edges of their lights. The cavern was about fifteen feet across, eight feet high. There was no telling how long it might be. And Paula had been right; the odor was horrible and getting worse.

Roger began to shine his light all over, up and down, trying to figure out if the space was natural or man-made. He finally shined it straight up, almost as an afterthought, and let out with a low whistle. "Mr. London. Take a look! It's unbelievable!"

The light revealed *several floors* above them; it looked like a shaft had been ripped right out of the building—a shaft going from cellar to attic. At this point, the ceiling of the cavern did not exist. The light shined through the tattered, torn remnants of each floor above, clear up to the undisturbed roof of the Forester Building. The shaft was shaped in a rough circle, approximately ten feet in circumference.

"It looks like somebody dropped a safe down from the attic and it smashed through every floor," Roger said.

It did look that way. Several safes. Large ones.

"How come the floors collapsed in only one end of the building?" Harry wondered out loud. "Everything seems intact elsewhere. Besides, this building was being used only six months ago. Don't tell me this could have happened in so short a time."

"Maybe there was an explosion," Roger offered.

"An explosion that we didn't hear next door?"

"It could have happened at night."

Harry ignored the remark and pointed upward to the spot illuminated by his flashlight. "Look at the wood here. It hasn't been smashed upward like in the storage room. It hasn't been smashed downwards, either. It looks as if it's simply crumpled up and fell apart."

"Could termites do that?" Roger asked.

"Why would they concentrate only in one area? Why

104

not the whole house? Besides, that's almost a perfect circle!"

"We don't know about the upper floors," Roger said. "They might be in a similar state on the other side of the building."

Harry shrugged. "You've got a point. Let's get out of here. I want to go next door and take a look around."

"A look around the store?"

Harry laughed. "Confusing, isn't it? I should have said that I want to take a look upstairs. In the Forester Building."

Roger didn't say anything, but he didn't need to. From the look on his face Harry could tell that his portly employee wouldn't have stayed down there in that odorous pit any longer if he'd offered to triple his salary.

Harry called the Chief of Police and explained the situation. Chief Joe Walters was a heavy-set, punctual sort who stumbled about with a dumb expression on his roundish, balding countenance that belied his continued efficiency. "The Forester Building, hmmm?" he repeated over the phone. "That's been vacant for months now. Belongs to the township. I'll get the keys and bring 'em over and we'll have a look inside."

"Good!" Harry hung up and got himself a glass of water from the cooler outside his office door. He knew Joe would arrive within minutes, ever on time. He checked in to see how Paula was doing. She was on the phone in her office, but hung up when she saw Harry. He sensed that she didn't want him to know that she'd been ringing Jeffrey again. It might make her seem too possessive in his eyes. Clinging. He didn't know. But ever since she'd been rescued from the hole in the storage room floor, it was as if some horrible thought had seized her mind in a merciless grip, had seized it and refused to let go. She was more tense and nervous than ever.

Harry remembered that on the day of Jeffrey's departure, he had asked the man if he knew where the sales posters were—the same ones Paula had been trying to find downstairs—and Jeffrey had said that he would look for them before he left. Harry had assumed that he had simply forgotten all about it in the excitement over his trip. But now he wondered. Had Jeffrey also gone down to the storage room, fallen into the hole below? He had not seen any sign of him; if he'd been injured or killed the body would have been discovered immediately. Still, Harry couldn't help but worry.

He knew that Paula's thoughts were focused in the same direction. She couldn't keep herself from calling Jeffrey's number, over and over, until he answered, until she heard that cheerful voice of his, heard some excuse, some reason for his not coming to work that she'd gladly forgive and accept and understand. Harry wondered if a woman would ever again feel that way about Harry London.

"Chief Walters will be here any minute," he told Paula. "We're going to look around next door. See what we can discover."

"Creepy, isn't it?" she said. "That big abyss in the cellar. I wonder what could have caused it?"

"That's what I keep asking myself. Well, we'll find out. Want to come have a look?"

"I'll pass. I have to check up on my trainees. I've ignored them practically all afternoon."

"Not many customers anyway," he laughed. "Maybe this hole of ours will improve business."

"You could always put up signs and charge them for a look-see." She brushed her hair into place and added: "Speaking of signs, I never did get those sale posters for you."

"Forget about it. I'll have one of the high school boys make up some new ones. They're not worth a broken neck." He came closer and took her hand in his own, squeezed it gently, affectionately. "I'm sorry . . . about down there. I should have gone myself."

"Don't be silly. I'm fine."

He nodded, squeezed her hand again, then dropped it and stepped outside. Joe Walters was walking towards his office through the aisle packed with tennis equipment.

Walters was a man of few words, and the formalities were dispatched with swiftly. Harry called Roger, and the three of them went outside and walked up the steps of the Forester Building. It was getting hotter outside and a stale breeze blew low in the air.

"Who was renting this place last?" Harry queried as Walters fiddled with a huge set of keys of different shapes and sizes. One long silver job was shaped like a naked woman, but Harry didn't ask where it had come from.

"Some corporation. It'll be listed in the Hall of Records somewhere if you're interested," the Police Chief grumbled. He finally found the right key and inserted it in the lock. "They wanted to use this for research and storage. I think they had a few small labs built on the premises." The door swung open. Immediately Harry and Roger recognized the stench that came from within, the same odor they had smelled earlier in the cellar. Joe had not had occasion to encounter the smell, so he recoiled even more than his companions did. "Yuuch. We must have something dead in here."

"What did they need the laboratories for?" Harry asked as they stepped inside the foyer. Directly ahead was a thick double door made of wood. To their right was a wooden staircase which led to the upper floors. The chipped white walls had not been painted in years. This outer chamber was very bright, lit by sunlight coming in through the skylight, the only window that had not been boarded up. The foyer stuck out from the rest of the building and did not support anything heavier

107

than the air immediately above it.

Walters opened the inner door and the odor got stronger. "I don't know," he finally said in response to Harry's question. "But it better not have been to make explosives." The three of them stepped into a corridor tht ran through the back of the building; several rooms led off from it.

"Let's go to the back room and turn right," Harry instructed. "That should be where we'll find those shattered floors."

They started down the hall, alternately fanning the air with their hands and holding their noses. It got more breathable as they progressed, as they got used to the odor. It wasn't so much unbearable as it was *different*. "Didn't anybody check the place out after this corporation's lease was up?" Harry asked. "Somebody must have noticed the damage."

"It might be recent. Just like the damage to your cellar floor. When's the last time somebody went down there?"

Harry had to stop and think. "I'm not sure. Couldn't have been more than a month or so ago." He remembered the posters and Jeffrey again, and a new chill went all the way through him. His dismissed his grim thought quickly. Jeffrey was on vacation, that's all there was to it. *Somebody* must have said goodbye to him; he would check when he got back. "So someone did check this place out when it was vacated?"

"Sure. We had somebody here all the time. A superintendent. But when a couple of months went by and it didn't look as if anybody was going to rent it, we decided to close the place up and figure out what to do with it."

"I always wondered why the town didn't make it a landmark. It *is* a real old building," Roger said.

"That would be the smart way of doing things," Walters replied. "And this town doesn't work that way. That's one thing I know after twenty years of service."

Both Roger and Harry knew better than to encourage the man in one of his famous tirades against the town elders of Milbourne; they kept quiet and he ran his course pretty quickly this time. "Anyway," the Police Chief continued, "we wanted to put the janitor in another place—the school, I think—and shut this place up, but he decided to retire. There was nothing wrong with it then. Somebody would have said something if there had been. Except a few mice. And how much harm can a few mice do?"

"Lots," Harry said. "But nothing like *this.*" They turned into the last room on the right and walked through the portal in darkness. "Hold it!" The Police Chief turned on his flashlight and illuminated the floor —or rather the lack of a floor. Halfway across the room it had simply disintegrated. He shined the light up and saw that this was true of every floor in the building. The whole right side had practically been eaten away. "What the hell!" Walters exclaimed.

"Now you see," Harry said. "This whole place is falling apart."

"What happened?" Joe asked, rubbing the back of his head with his fingertips.

"I wish I knew, believe me," Harry replied. "Because whatever did this must have . . ." he fished in his mind for the proper word, " . . . *burrowed* under the foundation and gone underneath my place."

Walters peered down into the pit exposed by his light. "How many feet under your building does this go? Lengthwise."

"About five feet. Just underneath that one storage room."

"And in the other direction?"

"We saw no end. The cavern, or whatever it is, didn't appear to be any wider than the width of this building, but it stretched out farther than we could see lengthwise."

"I've gotta take a look at this," Walters said determinedly. Too determinedly, as if he really didn't want to go, but was trying to force himself to do so.

"I've brought along the rope ladder," Roger said. "If you don't mind, I'd rather stay up here this trip."

Harry smiled and took the ladder from him, then unfurled it into the hole. "Hold the fort," he said as he descended. He held the ladder while the rotund police chief lowered his bulk down after him. Roger squatted at the edge of the hole and watched their lights get dimmer and dimmer, and the sound of their voices receded under the building.

Down below, Harry and Walters had walked past the far boundary of the Forester Building and judged that they were now somewhere below the intersection of Charlton Street and Halsford Avenue. "How far does this go?" Walters asked no one, trying to catch a glimpse of some sort of barrier or ending at the edges of his light.

"Do you think this cavern has always been here?" Harry asked. "It's below cellar level. That would explain why it was never discovered before."

"I don't know. Somebody should have come across it while putting up the buildings over our heads. Who can tell. This could be man-made, but what purpose would it serve?"

"None that I can think of."

"What I'd like to know is, why does it stop under your storage room?"

"Maybe it was looking for something. And didn't find it."

"*What* was looking for something? You think some kind of animals did this?"

"I don't know what to think. No, I can't imagine what could burrow under the ground like this, but there has to be some explanation." He bent down and touched the dirt. "The ground is loose and wet. Look, it has lots of furrows, as if something—a lot of somethings—dragged themselves along the ground."

"You trying to scare me? I hate snakes."

"I never said it was snakes." The furrows were too wide, for one thing.

"Then *what*, for Christ's sake!"

"I don't know. Listen, how much farther should we go?"

"I'm getting tired, there doesn't seem to be an end to this, and my shoes are full of mud. Let's call it a day. I'll send my hardy young patrolmen down here with lots of rope and—"

"Wait a minute! Look at the end of your light. The cavern is branching out." The Chief realized what Harry was talking about. He walked forward and saw that the underground chamber now divided into four tunnels leading away in different directions.

"Tunnels. *Now* what?"

Harry sshed him. "Listen. Do you hear a noise?"

"What?"

"It sounds like a sort of snapping sound. Like somebody stepping on twigs."

"Christ. I hear it, but not too clearly."

"It's gone now. It came from one of those tunnels. I'm sure."

Harry went ahead rapidly, heading towards the tunnel on his far left, his light shining above waist level. Suddenly he tripped on something lying in his path. "Aghh. What did I hit?" He tried to stay upright, but tumbled down indelicately into the dirt.

Harry looked up and saw that Walters was staring at the object that Harry had tripped on. Harry would have to swivel his body and crane his neck to see exactly what it was.

"My Lord Oh My Lord Oh My Lord Oh My Lord Oh My Lord"

Harry had never seen Joe Walters in such a state; the

man *never* showed any emotion. Joe had seen it all: highway accidents, dead children, gunshot victims. What on Earth was he seeing now?

Harry got up and took a good look himself with the flashlight. It was—it was Jeffrey Braddon! Or rather, *half* of him. The other half, the back half, everything behind his sideburns on the head, halfway through the shoulders on the body, had simply been eaten away. His face, his chest, the front of his legs—including the clothes covering those areas—had been left intact. But something had gotten hold of everything else, chewed away whole chunks of him. One could almost see half-moon patterns, bite marks, all along the sides of the left-over corpse.

Harry had only a second to realize that the Chief of Police was off in a corner puking his guts out when he himself fainted and fell to the ground in a heap.

Chapter Six

"They wouldn't tell me much about it," Anna said through her tears. She kept pushing a Kleenex to her nose, wiping it dry, until the next fresh onslaught of sobs. "They said he had died under 'mysterious circumstances.' What the hell does that mean? He worked in a sporting goods store. What could have killed him there?"

They were sitting on the living room couch, David's hands holding hers. He delicately pushed a strand of hair off her forehead, and asked, "Who exactly did you speak to?"

"Something Walters. The Police Chief in Milbourne. He said they found Jeff's body this afternoon. He fell through a hole in the cellar floor, in this room hardly anybody ever went into. And everyone—God!—everyone thought he'd gone on his vacation. Nobody saw him leave, they all just assumed—" She threw her head down on David's chest, too overcome to continue speaking.

David was horrified by the whole affair. A week? Her brother must have starved to death. Or died of injuries he sustained in the fall. What was so "mysterious" about that? Why didn't they level with Anna? Accepting once and for all that her brother had died a horrible death, left alone for a week, his cries unheard, dying of injuries and lack of food, was better than imagining all kinds of even worse horrors, was better than having one's mind wander around in a state of unclarified unheaval. Why hadn't they just come out and told her exactly what had killed him?

Anna pulled herself together momentarily and rubbed her eyes. "I'm sorry to put you through all this. I'm not a very good date this evening."

"That's all right," David assured her. "You've nothing to apologize for. You've just received a terrible shock and you need to talk it over with someone. I don't mind. I'm glad I can help."

"Thanks. Thanks so much." She dabbed her eyes and nostrils with the tissue again. "I just can't believe it. But you're right. You are a help to me. There's nobody else I could talk to. No one. Clara can't cope with things like this any better than I can. And even if Derek weren't out of town he wouldn't be any use to me. He can't stand it when I cry."

She got up very suddenly and walked over to the fireplace. "Oh God, I thought I was strong enough to cope with things like this; I thought by *now* I could cope with life, deal with these things, these disasters. But I can't. I just can't. I can't believe he's gone. We had such little contact. We hardly knew each other. But I loved him anyway. Do you know how that is? You can love somebody without really knowing them, without really knowing, or caring, what goes on in their minds, what they want out of life, or even think about. I didn't understand him."

She sat down next to David again and continued. "We went our separate ways a long time ago. He went off on his own before our parents had died. We only heard from him now and then, on holidays, Christmas. He never forgot my birthday. Not ever. I don't know how he managed to get along sometimes. He drifted from place to place, job to job. A few years ago, when I was still a struggling young model with acting aspirations, we got together for lunch, and he told me that he'd been living in New York for eight months. Eight months, and I hadn't even known! He said he'd met a woman—at a bar? I don't remember—and she lived in this small town in Connecticut, and he was planning to move there. He didn't ask me for money, but I knew he needed it. I gave him what I could spare, and he went off to the country to be near his lover. Only she got married to someone else two months later."

"That must have been pretty awful for him."

"I still have the note he sent to me about it. Such a sad, pathetic letter. He said that he should have expected it, that he was a loser through and through. He wasn't a loser, not to me. I don't know why he stayed there. I guess he got tired of moving from place to place. And the worst thing is, I never offered to help him. I used to rationalize, tell myself, 'He has a steady job now, at that store, he must be happy, he must be solvent.' But I forgot about loneliness. I forgot about the other things that can hurt people, can kill people. I didn't want to think about them. I was on my way up; finally I had what I had always wanted. My career. A rich, handsome husband. What more was there to life? My brother reminded me of what I had come from and I didn't want him around."

She put her head down on David's shoulder. "He never even got his crummy vacation."

David hugged her, soothingly, and kissed her forehead and her eyes, which were moist again. He had finally seen the strength beneath the facade and he loved her for it.

"I have to speak to Derek eventually," she said. "He's so much better at things like this. He can help me make all the arrangements."

She got up again and walked over to the window. There was a breeze outside and it made the branches of a tree scrape against the pane of glass. It was an ominous sound. "Oh, Jeffrey," she said sadly, quietly. "I'm so, *so* sorry."

There was silence for a few minutes; she by the window, he on the sofa, wondering what he could do. He studied his fingertips, straightened his tie. He realized that he wanted the taste of strawberries again, and felt ashamed that he could think of something so—so earthy —at a time like this. She'd helped him feel sorry for Jeffrey, but after all, he had never even met the dead man, his grief could never cut as deeply as hers. Anyway, she was the one suffering now; her brother was beyond such feelings.

"Would you like me to leave?" he asked. "Maybe you'd like to be alone."

"I'm not very good company," she said. "I can't blame you if you're dying to get out of here."

"It's not that . . ."

"I know, I know. But this evening hasn't turned out the way either one of us would have liked it to. I had planned to seduce you."

"Again?"

She laughed. "I'm afraid I'm not in a very seductive mood."

"That's understandable. Look, why don't I go and give you a call tomorrow to see how you are? You should probably get a rest, have a good cry—without having to worry about what you look like."

He had meant that affectionately and she took it that way. He got up from the couch and she walked over to him. She kissed him rather chastely—for her—on the mouth, then backed away. "I guess I should be alone for awhile. I'm sorry. Sorry about tonight."

"I'm sorry about what happened."

She walked him to the door. They could hear Clara puttering around in the kitchen, probably wondering what to say to her employer besides the usual hasty condolences. Anna got David his jacket, kissed him again,

116

longer this time, and opened the door. David gave her a "be strong" smile and walked down the front steps. He turned to wave goodbye, but she had already closed the door.

Anna couldn't sleep, no matter what; not even a tranquilizer did the trick. Thoughts of Jeffrey kept coming into her mind. Thoughts of growing up with him, playing with him. Wondering where he was all the time after he had left home. Those cards and letters and birthday gifts sent in the mail. His sad eyes. It all came back and kept coming back and it seemed as if hours were going by.

She slept intermittently. Finally she saw the light coming in through the window, checked the clock, and discovered it was six a.m. For a second she wondered where David was—she had planned for him to sleep over —then realized that he had not spent the night, and worse, realized *why* he had not. Thoughts of Jeffrey came back to her again, leaving her hollowed and desolate with despair. Now that her marriage was breaking up, she had subconsciously been thinking more and more about her brother, her closest relative. He had always been there, a comforting presence, only a phonecall away. Someone to talk to. Now there really was no one she could talk to. Except maybe David.

She thought about David again, wishing he had been with her all night. Her fingers strayed down between her legs, and she imagined him beside her, inside her, all over her, kissing her neck, as he had done the first and only time, kissing her mouth, her face, his hands in her hair. She groaned aloud with pleasure, feeling his presence by proxy. She felt herself follow the twisting paths of her imaginary erotic journey until she reached its obvious conclusion.

She relaxed and thought about David in less sexual terms. Was he someone she could count on? She knew nothing about him. Last night in the living room he had been warm, comforting. Did that make him special? Was she maximizing his strengths and minimizing his weaknesses because she feared being alone, feared the loneliness her life might be plunged into once her break-up with Derek was finalized? *Loneliness can kill,* she remembered saying. But wasn't it preferable to plunging into another pointless relationship? Another Derek she didn't need. Although David was nothing like Derek, who knows what hidden flaws he might have.

Besides, it wasn't 1950 anymore. A woman didn't have to run from one man to another, as if she were somehow incomplete all by herself. She could go it on her own if she had to. There was no need to rush into anything.

Derek wasn't going to be back until the evening, if then. She wondered for a second how she could have been so bold, actually planning to screw another man in their very bedroom. What if Derek had come back early? Would it have made any difference? Would she have been glad to see the surprised look on his face? How *would* he have reacted?

That almost brought a smile to her lips. She got up out of bed, put on a bathrobe, and went down to have some breakfast. She put a pot of coffee on the stove. Clara was still sleeping; there was no reason to disturb her.

She was trying very hard not to dwell on Jeffrey's death. The Police Chief had said he would call today if they had any new information, new details. She was in part dreading the call. Details? What kind of details could there be to what was apparently some sort of horrible, tragic accident? She couldn't bare details. *Bad enough to know someone you loved had died in, say, an auto crash, without finding out how many pieces they'd been left in.* Although she had no reason to think that anything quite *that* awful had happened to her brother.

She remembered that the police chief had said some-

118

thing about the body being held for study beyond the initial autopsy. What were they doing to it? *Putting it together?* Stop that, she thought. Stop being more morbid than you have to be. He *only* fell through a hole.

And then what?

The coffee was ready. She drank the strong and tasty brew slowly, not sure if she *wanted* it to clear away the cobwebs, to perk her up and help her to face the unfaceable.

Perhaps oblivion was better.

So far this had been a very eventful week for David. First, he had gotten out of the hospital, then he'd run into George (or his clone), then he'd met and made love to *the* Anna Braddon, and now he was on his way to an interview with an art director at a prestigious greeting-card firm. Everything was so upbeat too, except for his encounter with George; and, of course, the news of Jeffrey Braddon's death. For the first time in a long time David felt like things might be swinging his way. It was a fabulous feeling.

He had had a good night's sleep and gotten up extra early. He put together what he hoped was an impressive portfolio, and went to the Post Office to cash the money order his father had sent. Then he took the subway to work.

He went straight to the ninth floor, bypassing the one with the stoned young lady and the kid with the radio stuck on his ear. He went down the hall and turned into the art department. The receptionist had not yet arrived. He sat down on the small sofa across from her desk and waited.

A few minutes later he heard the sharp *click click* of high heels and the woman he was waiting for rounded the corner. She was wearing an attractive blue dress that matched the color of her eyes. Her hair was short, but full and bouncy. David figured that she was around thirty-seven. He hadn't noticed much about her yesterday, he'd been so glad she had even deigned to speak with him.

Ms. Morrison took pity on him again and escorted him into her office. She took a canister of coffee out of a paper bag and sat down behind her desk. David opened up his case and removed the sketches. He realized that he was shaking a little, and he felt as if the temperature in there had risen to ninety degrees. Why did he have to get anxiety symptoms now, when he had been so calm and cool beforehand?

She was wonderful. She made him feel right at home, and showed genuine interest in his work. She particularly liked his drawings of cute little animals. He knew they'd look good on greeting cards. "You're very talented," she said.

She completely forgot about her coffee, concentrating instead on his assorted designs, done in ink or charcoal, on all kinds of backings, some in colored pastels, some black and white. "Yes, yes," she said, nodding her head. "This is good stuff." She looked up at him. "I like your work."

He sat down, wondering when the bubble would burst. Things were always most encouraging just before the final letdown.

But she did not let him down. "Look, we haven't any openings in our department this minute, but we will have in a month or so. Maybe two months. One of our senior designers is retiring this summer, definitely by September. We'll need extra help then. Would you be interested?"

He stammered. "W—would I? You bet."

"In the meantime, I could give you some free-lance assignments. We simply don't need a full-timer just yet —although we will—but we do need extra work done from time to time."

"That's okay with me."

"Good. You'll have to fill out some forms. Didn't you say you were working here already?"

"Temporarily—through an agency. But not anymore." He had just blurted it out. There was no way he could descend to the depths of clerical work now that he'd found a creative niche of sorts. He'd think of another way of surviving until September, at the latest, if the free-lance stuff didn't pay well enough, or if there wasn't enough of it.

"Well, come with me to personnel, and let's fill out some forms. Then we'll come back here and I'll give you some things to try out.

"Yes," she said with a smile. "I think you'll do nicely."

David beamed.

The Milbourne Police Chief had not yet called. Clara was busy fixing a delicious Spanish supper that she hoped might help to cheer up her employer. And Derek walked in at quarter of six, briefcase in hand, looking tense and, as usual, gorgeous in spite of it.

"What a fucking day this has been?" He threw his case onto the couch and went straight to the bar to fix himself a drink. "Can I make you one, Anna?"

She sat in a chair by the window, flipping through a fashion magazine. She had been home most of the day, except in the afternoon, when she'd taken a walk around the block. She had canceled the two appointments she'd had. "No, thank you," she replied. "Didn't things go well today?"

"I suppose so. It was just hectic, that's all. How about your day? You look awful, if I may be so blunt."

"You always are. I got bad news last night. My brother was killed."

Anna found herself still in the habit of making excuses for Derek. He did his best to look disturbed, but he had never met Jeffrey, and Anna probably looked so distant,

121

so untouchable, that he couldn't summon up enough energy to show concern. "Oh, Anna. That's too bad. How did it happen?"

She told him what she knew. "I've been waiting for the police to call, but . . ."

"Forget about waiting," Derek said. "Let me give this joker a ring right now." He headed towards the phone on the corner table.

Anna hated herself the most at times like this. She hated—yet loved—the way Derek (in fact everyone she knew, except herself) could instantly take charge of a situation, could in fact, take charge of *her life*, just like that, and do a better job than she would have. She'd been pampered and petted all her life, dressed in glamorous outfits, sculptured with cosmetics, told which lines to say and how to look and how to walk. She had taken on the role of mindless sex object gladly, anything to escape the drab existence of her youth, anything to ensure that she'd never have to live a life that didn't suit her. What a price she had paid. With a few drinks she could maneuver a man into bed, but she couldn't even make arrangements for her brother's burial. She was glad Derek would do it for her, although she wished that he wouldn't have had to bother with it. She wished she was stronger.

Derek got much more information than Anna had. Apparently the man in the police station gave her husband some of the grisly details about the condition of Jeffrey's body that he would never have given her. Before he was through, Derek had finished one martini and was motioning Anna to make him another: a double. Anna tried to decipher what he and the other person were talking about, but all she got from Derek's end were grunts and monosyllables and a troubled expression. When he finally hung up the phone, she handed him his drink, and clutched his shoulder with her tapering fingers. "What did he say?"

"Uh, the Chief of Police wasn't there, so I spoke to someone else."

"Yes?" She nodded impatiently while he took a healthy swallow from the cocktail glass.

"It isn't pleasant, Anna."

"I didn't think it would be."

"Ann, he's dead. There's no need to go into all this."

"I can handle it, Derek. He's my brother. I've got to know what really happened."

"Anna, are you sure? Sure you can handle it?"

"Tell me, Derek. Please."

"All right." He went over to the couch and sat down, then patted the cushion on his right. Anna came and sat beside him. "Well?" she said.

"He wasn't killed by the fall, assuming he really did fall through the floor in the store's cellar. They accidentally found him down below after another employee had fallen through. His body had . . . deteriorated. Anna, they think he was killed by some sort of animal or something. Nobody knows for sure. They're still investigating. His death is a bonafide mystery."

"Animals? What kind of animals? What did they do to him?"

"They'd been—they'd been *at* him. Maybe it was rats."

Anna grimaced and turned away, her hand to her mouth. "God. God. God."

"Now they didn't say it was rats. Something else may have happened. They just don't know yet. But they have to keep looking over the body for some clues. They're afraid what happened to Jeffrey might happen to others."

"*What* happened to him? What are they doing to him? Dissecting him, studying him like he was some piece of meat. They can't do that to his body, I won't let them."

Derek appeared to be afraid that she was going to get

hysterical. Perhaps he figured a good shock might serve to stun her into silence. "Anna, there wasn't much left of him to begin with."

It worked. She got up, and walked slowly to the window, muttering over and over again: "I don't understand. I just don't understand." Her fingers went into her mouth and she started chewing them nervously, all thought of her lacquered nails forgotten. "Oh, Derek, I've got to go up there and speak to someone. I have to know what happened."

"After what I've just told you, why would you want to know more? It happens, Anna. Bodies lie around in dark places for days and something happens to them. That's all there is to it. I can't understand why there's such a mystery about it myself. Look, if you're that interested why not call them back after dinner?"

"Dinner? I don't want dinner. I want to find out what happened to my brother."

"The Chief of Police will be back around eight p.m. the guy said. Why not give him a call? Look, if you want Jeffrey buried immediately you can have it done. They probably can't keep his body a day longer if you don't want them to. But what if it's important? You *do* want to know why he died, don't you?"

"Why did they tell you all that stuff, and not me? Did they think I couldn't take it because I'm a woman?"

"Because you're his *sister*. They don't give out details like that the same time you're notified of someone's death; and they don't give details to someone quite so close to the deceased."

The deceased. Jeffrey wasn't a person anymore. He was something to be studied. An enigmatic corpse.

"I don't want to talk about it over the phone," Anna said. "I want to go to Milbourne to find out what this is all about. I'll drive up there tomorrow. Will you come with me?"

"Anna, really. Let the experts handle this. They said

they'd call us when they had more information."

"I don't care about experts. I want to find out what happened to my brother once and for all. I'm not going to go to pieces over this. I'm not. I can do that much for him, at least."

"Jeffrey is dead. There's nothing you can do for him."

"Will you go with me?"

"To Milbourne? No. And I think you're crazy to waste your time that way."

"He was my brother. It's not a waste of time."

"They can't tell you anything more than they could say on the phone."

"You don't know that. I'll intimidate them if I have to. I'll threaten legal action. I'll—"

"Calm down."

Clara chose that moment to come in and announce that dinner was served. For Derek it was an easy way out of an awkward situation. He moved towards the dining room.

"What do you have to do tomorrow that's so important?" Anna accused. "I happen to know you don't have another photo session until Monday afternoon."

"I have things to do," he replied.

"More important than this?"

"Anna, you can be perfectly intimidating without my help."

"I suppose you're going to see your precious Mrs. Allstedder. What will she promise to get you *this* time, hmmm?"

He slammed his drink down on the glass table in front of the sofa. "Considering the fact that you plan to divorce me any day now, I think you have a hell of a lot of nerve ordering me around and asking me to change my plans at the drop of a hat. I'm sorry about your brother. The guy never did a thing to me. But I can't adjust my schedule because you suddenly have guilt feelings over a brother you never paid that much

125

attention to when he was alive. Suddenly you're the loving sibling, rushing off to defend his corpse. Well, I don't want any part of it. Why don't you ask your new boyfriend to drive up with you?" He stormed out of the room, flapping his arm at her in angry dismissal.

One thing for Derek, Anna thought bitterly, he knew just what to say to get her where it hurt the most. Maybe he was right; but that wouldn't deter her. Surely she could find someone to make the trip with her—or she'd do it on her own. The thought of facing the unknown all by herself left her feeling panicky. Who could she get to accompany her? She didn't have many friends; lots of hangers-on, attracted to the young and beautiful, but few real friends. She wondered if she should take Derek's advice and ask David to go with her. She dismissed the idea; she barely knew the man.

But while she sat there, wondering if she should go in and have some of that delicious-smelling Spanish supper —although she was not in the mood for Derek's company—the phone rang and she *found* her companion for the following day. She answered the phone with hesitation, afraid it might be more bad news.

It was David Hammond. She had given him her home number last evening. "Hi," he said cheerfully. "I meant to call earlier, but something exciting happened today and I got all caught up in it." Before she could find out what it was, he asked, "How are you feeling?"

"Not so good." She explained that she had heard nothing further about her brother; there was no need to mention the things Derek had told her. "I'm going to drive up there tomorrow and find out what I can."

"Not by yourself, I hope."

"Yes. Why?"

"Well, you should have somebody with you at a time like that."

She really hadn't planned on asking him, she told herself. It didn't matter, though, because he was offering to

126

go with her before she could say a word about it. "I'll try not to be as gloomy as I was last night," she assured him.

"You be in whatever mood you feel like," David said. "I'm not expecting a fun time. I just think you need somebody with you and I'd like to be that somebody."

They didn't talk much longer, just made arrangements for the drive. Anna had mixed emotions when their conversation ended. She was disturbed that once again she had to fall back on yet another person, another man, but glad that David Hammond was the one she was falling back on.

Chapter Seven

Doug felt as if his back was breaking, that his legs would fold under him at any moment. They'd been walking for two hours now and enough was enough. Had he not been afraid that his "manhood" would have been compromised, he would have called a halt to it right then and there. Jack showed no intention of slowing down or stopping. Doug brushed his right hand through his thick, sweat-matted hair, pulling away pieces of leaf that had lodged in the locks while walking. His broad, boyish features scrunched up as the last rays of the setting sun glared relentlessly into his eyes. The view was breathtaking from up here, but he didn't care.

He looked to his right and saw that Sue and Emily, though they must have been hurting as much as he was, were determined to see this through no matter what. Whose dumb idea had it been, this backpacking trip over Hunter's Mountain? His, probably, although his girlfriend Sue had been insistent on making the suggestion a reality. Of course she was tired. Emily was showing signs of strain, too. But neither of them would admit it, too afraid of being weak or inferior in the eyes of their men. If that was liberation, they could have it. Doug couldn't see how acting macho and dumb like boys was going to set women free. He figured it had nothing to do with sex as much as it did with that damnable peer pressure. Had it not been for his susceptibility to same he would not have been up here on this fool mountain when he could have been drinking beer in Joey's Bar and Grille, watching TV or sitting in a movie theater. He was not the outdoors type and never would be.

Finally Jack said the magic words: "Let's rest for a while and enjoy the view." Doug almost forgot himself and breathed a sigh of relief, but caught it just in time. He would be damned if he'd act worn-out while Jack just stood there radiating health. How sickening. Doug knew he was being childish, but the one thing he'd swore he'd never do was let Jack Potter get the better of him.

Jack was a handome boy of twenty, a year older than his best buddy, Doug Withers. While they both looked somewhat alike, only Jack had that certain charisma, a by-product of confidence, that enabled him to overcome all obstacles. Hence he stood taller, walked straighter, had a gleam in his eyes and a shine on his cheeks and stood out in a crowd. Both he and Doug were broad-shouldered and of medium height, but brown hair and blue eyes. Jack worked out and it showed. Doug's dour expression seemed to fit a body forever on the verge of ballooning. If he stayed slim it was only because of his metabolism.

Their girlfriends were quite the contrast. They looked nothing alike, yet had dispositions as similar as Doug's and Jack's were dissimilar. Sue had long, straight black hair and an elongated face that looked sexy depending on how much makeup she put on. She was skinny as a rail, but knew how to dress so that her thinness was an asset. Emily was short, almost squat, and had auburn hair and freckles. She never used makeup; her mother would have killed her, although she was, like Sue, eighteen. She had recently taken a bold step in cutting her hair short in a style she'd seen in a woman's magazine. "Practically to the scalp!" Sue had teased her, but Emily knew she looked good. Real good.

Finally.

Jack had taken the Thermos out of his backpack and was passing iced tea around to everyone. The girls sat down on a carpet of leaves, while Doug leaned against a tree and looked out on the horizon. The view *was* beautiful. In the distance they could see the whole town of Milbourne. Frutter's fruit market on Route 92. The old movie theater that had burned down in '73, now a blackened shell of a building where brave kids went to hunt ghosts. The Chartam River, which ran alongside the town two blocks from Main Street, then abruptly turned right and headed out of the state altogether. The air was fresh and clean, and for a moment he was glad that he had come.

"Do you think we'll get back before dark?" Emily asked, as nonchalantly as possible, though of course she was concerned. Doug looked at Jack, waiting for an answer, trying to look equally inscrutable.

"Sure we will. If we don't stay here too long. We'll have to keep up the same pace."

Oh Lord, Doug thought. This means we'll have to stomp down the mountains like stormtroopers again. Yet the thought of being in the woods after dark made him feel uncomfortable, though he didn't know why. He was not afraid of anything that flew or crawled through the forest. He'd seen it all when he was growing up. Yet, he had this feeling of foreboding that he simply couldn't shake. He drank the rest of the iced tea in the cup and decided to forget it. He would simply stormtroop along with the rest of them, and be snug and safe at home before nightfall. Nothing to worry about.

They stayed there a few more minutes, then collected themselves into a tight little group and started the descent, this time heading down the other side of the mountain. There was a trail to follow, a weak one, but passable, and Jack had assured them that he knew this way around irregardless. Doug would have preferred to cut the climbing time by simply going back the way they had come, but knew Jack would have none of that. He was determined to do the whole trip, showing off his expertise. "Why, I practically used to live up here when I was a kid," he had repeated over and over. Doug still didn't know why they all had to carry these heavy backpacks on their shoulders; half of the stuff they wouldn't use. They'd eaten the lunch up two hours ago, before the climb, and there was enough first-aid equipment to bandage an army if need be. Better safe than sorry, he supposed.

As they started down the trail, a faint breeze blew up over their heads, rustling the leaves and their hair, carrying a sweet fragrance of the earth and the air down into the valley towards which they were descending. They turned a corner and the view was gone, and once more they were surrounded by thick batches of trees cutting off any glimpse of the land below. Bird cries sang out clearly and melodiously deep in the woods. Oaks and redbuds and gooseberry shrubs were plentiful.

An hour passed and they still had almost half the trip ahead. They were all walking slower now, even Jack, in spite of the fact that it was all downhill and therefore easier to traverse. They were simply too tired to go any faster. The sun was low in the sky, almost touching the ground, and a bold pink stripe cut beautifully through the cloudy blue canvas above.

The four of them talked very little, commenting only occasionally on something or other which piqued their curiosity: an unusual growth, strange prints on the ground, tracks of animals, a colorful bird flying over-head. Another half hour had gone by when Jack said, "We're coming to the caves now."

Doug knew that Sue was glad to hear this. She had moved to town recently as compared to the others, and had never once been to the caves at the edge of the woods. At first she had planned to pester the rest of them until they agreed to begin the ascent at this end of the trail so that she could see the caves in the morning right away, but then had decided she'd rather wait until the end of the trip, nourishing her anticipation for it during the afternoon.

Doug, on the other hand, was less than overjoyed. He was really anxious to get home now. Not only was there a good twenty minutes to go until they got to the very end of the trail, but they had to walk all the way around the side of the mountain until they reached the starting point where they'd parked their cars; another forty-five minutes at least. And now Sue would want to poke around the entrances of the caverns for yet another half hour until her childlike curiosity had been abated. At least it would give him a chance to rest.

They turned another corner in the path and there they were, about twelve yards away, their ominous black maws clearly visible through the spindly trees of the area. There were times when one could almost walk right by the caves and practically miss them, but the vegetation was scarcer this time of the year and they stood out starkly in the darkening daylight.

"Oh wow," Sue shouted, running gleefully over to the cliffside. "I love caves. I love to explore."

"Watch it, Nancy Drew," Doug warned her. "Don't go in any of them too far or we'll never see you again."

"Sue," Emily whined. "It's getting late."

Doug didn't say anything, but he could tell that Sue was irritated that they didn't share her enthusiasm, or even want to let her look around for a moment, she knew they had all been here many times before, but surely they could give her "just a minute" to explore? Well, she'd have her minute, thought Doug as he lowered himself to sit at the bottom of a huge, spreading tree, its gnarled branches bereft of leaves.

Sue had been waiting all day for this, and she wasn't

about to let the others spoil her pleasure. She picked out the cave that seemed to be the largest and wandered into the entrance. She was a tall young woman, nearly five-eleven, and still didn't have to crouch to get in—in fact the rocky ceiling seemed to be at least three feet above her head. She couldn't see very far inside the cave and wished that she had brought the flashlight with her. She would definitely have to come back here some time when she was not in a rush.

"*Sue!*" Emily called impatiently.

"Just a minute," she yelled back. "I'll only be a second."

She advanced farther into the cave. There was a strong odor that she couldn't place, and her imagination began to play tricks on her. It was as if there were forms, shapes, turning and twisting in the darkness ahead. She glanced up and it looked as if the ceiling lowered the deeper one went into the cave, though when she raised her hand to check she could still feel nothing. She looked behind her and saw the comforting patch of light where the cave opened out into the woods, could hear the soothing voices of her friends, soothing even though they were yelling at her to come out.

But she had to go farther, had to see what was back there. She knew she was foolish, and she was even getting scared, but something Pandora-like in her nature refused to turn around and back out. The sensation that she wasn't alone was increasing. Along with the gyrating shapes she heard noises, odd noises, like something out of her childhood, but she just couldn't remember what they were. Where had she heard that sound before? The odor was thicker and stronger now, and for a moment she was afraid she was going to gag.

"Susan Benson, will you come out now?"

The spooky sensations were too much for her, and she turned, responding to the urgency in Emily's voice. She could always come back here some other day. She'd talk

Doug into taking her, and they'd bring flashlights and a picnic lunch and a blanket . . .

Something touched her leg. She froze, trying to see what it was. Then she felt something crawling over the one arm that still hung by her side, as the other had come up to cover her mouth. She opened her lips to let out a scream, but the sudden sharp pain that shot through her ankle, right down to the very bone, cut it off before it could sound. She felt something wet and slimy and smooth push against her, knocking her to the floor of the cave. Her ears and nose were filled with the sounds and smells of the creatures, but her eyes could still see nothing. Whatever it was, it was on top of her now, and she sensed that there was more than one of them surrounding her. She felt life rapidly draining away.

Outside in the woods her friends were losing patience. "Look how dark it's getting," Emily pouted, pointing to the sky with a needless gesture. *"Will you come on, Sue?"*

Jack looked disturbed. "She doesn't answer. She might be hurt," he said.

"Or maybe she's playing a joke on us," Doug snickered. "I'll go get her." He set off toward the cave, shaking his head with annoyance, his lips set in a grin which suggested that he was used to his girlfriend's behavior.

Jack and Emily went after him. It was so dark now that although the sun had not yet completely set, the moon stood out clearly in the sky. A full moon.

And when the horrible, agonized screams of the three youths rang out from the confines of the cave, the moon was the only one who heard them.

It was too early and too chilly that morning for David and Anna to say much of anything to each other. Upon

134

his arrival, Anna had simply thanked David again, invited him in for a quick cup of coffee—Derek was nowhere to be seen—and then led him to the garage where they kept their car. They were taking Derek's compact job, a smooth-riding and comfortable vehicle that, Anna claimed, got very good mileage. The man seemed to take forever until he drove the vehicle up the ramp. A lot of fussing with keys; Anna was nervous. Finally they pulled out into the early morning Manhattan traffic. Considering all, however, Anna seemed to be holding herself together pretty well. By 10:35 they were on the road to Milbourne.

David had had the good fortune to fall asleep quickly upon entering bed last night, and to sleep well and deeply, without any dreams, at least without any that he remembered. He hadn't had a chance to mull over the fact that this would be the first time he had been in an automobile since the day of the accident. For just a second, at the garage, he had panicked, afraid that Anna was going to ask him to drive. Luckily, she hadn't. He had to get used to simply being in a car before he could take over the wheel again. Not that he'd been driving *that* day, but the accident had left him with a fear of holding his—or anyone else's—life in his hands on the highway.

By the time they approached the bridge out of the city, David felt enough at ease to picture himself offering to drive on the way back. Or was it only an illusion he was perpetrating upon himself in order to keep from acting like a fool? He kept telling himself, *I'm in a car, I'm in a car, I can't believe I'm in a car,* but he knew that sooner or later it was something he would have had to face. He was glad this first time was with Anna, a nice way to end a kind of virginity. Still, she was an unknown factor, or at least her driving was. She *seemed* to handle the wheel nicely.

He tried to relax.

They made small talk for a while, but there was nothing much to say about the events ahead. Anna didn't really want to think about what might be facing her, about what the authorities might tell her, about whether or not this trip was just a waste of time. If she went along in that vein, it threatened to overwhelm her. She concentrated on the road.

Her thoughts kept coming back to the man sitting next to her, who now had his eyes closed (although the lids kept fluttering open as if he were trying to keep awake). She thought she might be in love with him. Already? That was unlikely. Yet, there *was* something there. She felt a stab of embarrassment as she recalled how she had acted the night he'd come for dinner, the night the police had called with the news of Jeffrey's death. She saw herself at the dinner table, making inane and silly remarks, confusing a combination of cuteness and petulance with sensuality. Had she really acted that way, like an intoxicated kewpie doll flirting with a good-looking nitwit, like a playboy bunny thrusting her boobs in some old man's leering face? Now she was going overboard. She had been *silly*, that was all. She always acted silly when she was nervous. He would forgive her. He *had* forgiven her, his presence in the car was ample proof of that.

"Sleepy?" she asked. "I don't blame you."

"I shouldn't be." He smiled. "I slept pretty good last night."

"Wish I could say the same."

"It's understandable."

David opened his mouth again, about to say something, and she hesitated, not knowing whether or not to speak. When he kept silent, she asked, "Were you about to say something?"

He had been wondering whether or not to tell her

136

about the accident. Surely she had noticed his limp; it had been rather pronounced this morning. She might feel more at ease if he offered an explanation for it. But this was the wrong time . . . in an automobile yet! He answered her question instead by saying, "Do you ever want to comment on something, then forget what it was?" She nodded. "It couldn't have been important," he said.

They talked for a while about t' emerging sun above their heads, the way the temperature was rising, the flat, ugly look of the topography around them. There were not many cars on the highway—another thing adding to David's comfort—and they were making good time.

They fell silent again, sharing each other's space comfortably and quietly, feeling no need to shatter the moment with idle, aimless chatter. They knew that was when two people felt good around each other; the silences were as important as the rest.

They stopped for coffee at one of the roadside restaurants—all of gray brick, and all with picnic areas—that dotted the highway every few miles. They got out and walked to the restaurant, passing only a few people: tourists, families, a businessman or two. A little kid stood in a patch of flowers by the restaurant's big window, crying for his mother. The woman came and carried him off angrily. A handsome young man with sad eyes licked an ice cream cone as he held the door for Anna.

Inside they sat at a booth in the back. If anyone recognized Anna, they kept it to themselves. Both of them were grateful for that. The waitress came over and they both ordered coffee. Anna also asked for a chocolate donut. "Won't you have breakfast?" Anna asked. "Eggs or something? My treat."

God, she was sweet. But he declined. He really wasn't that hungry. Did she realize just how poor he was? She lived in a world so far removed from financial stress and strain that it wouldn't have surprised him if she'd not given the matter any thought at all. We all assume everyone we meet is in the same social class we are, David thought.

Almost as if she could read his mind, Anna asked him about the job he had mentioned briefly earlier that morning.

"It doesn't really start for a few weeks yet. But they did give me some free-lance assignments."

"An artist," she sighed. "I'd love to see some of your work sometime."

"You will. Hopefully on a greeting card one of these days."

"Is that your specialty?"

"No. I've also dabbled in cartooning, commercial art —of a different type. Y'know, for ads and things."

"I once had a friend who drew comic books."

"Ah, a lucrative field. For the publishers, at least. I'm afraid my style isn't really suited for that kind of thing, although I admire their work. Some comic books and comic strips are beautifully done."

Their coffee came. Record time, thought David. The place was underpopulated and overstaffed this morning.

"Has your work appeared in magazines? Anything I might have seen?"

He paused for a moment, wondering how much humilation he was prepared to endure at this moment. "Uh, Anna, I'm an artist, but," he laughed without humor, "not a *successful* artist. I'm really just starting out. In fact, I've been 'starting out' for the last ten years. This job I've told you about is my first real break. My work has yet to grace a greeting card, but now . . . that might just change. Finally."

She smiled very warmly and understandingly, and put her hand over his. "It always takes time. Lots of people work hard all their lives, and boom—they're forty-five and famous. Look at it this way. You're a step ahead of them, you're still in your thirties."

"Forget famous, at this point I'll settle for being solvent." *Idiot! Why did you have to say that?*

"I think you'll be very successful." She raised her coffee cup, and prompted him to do the same. She clinked his cup with hers. "To the future."

The coffee was lukewarm, weak and bitter, but somehow he just didn't care. In fact, he barely noticed, so intent was he upon her smile.

It was a quiet day in the town of Milbourne, like every other day (except perhaps for the time when Jake Astor's convertible had crashed into the five-and-ten store on a drunken Saturday night). When things, bad things, happened, people usually *whispered* the news from family to family, nodding their heads in sympathy, calling the bereaved with kind words, calling on them with warm soup. That was how the news of Jeffrey Braddon's death got circulated.

But now something had happened which eclipsed the man's horrible death—the "full" facts of which were known to only a few—and that was the disappearance of four Milbourne youths who had been camping down by Hunter's Mountain.

Chief Walters had received a call from Sue Benson's mother the previous night after supper. She had called the parents of the other three children—two boys, one girl—who had accompanied her daughter, but none of them had known what might have been the cause of their delay. Jack Potter's father was half-drunk as usual; he neither knew nor cared where his son might be. Emily Silverstein's folks were worried, but had wanted to wait a while longer before pressing the panic button. After all, the children were only an hour or so overdue. Mrs. Benson couldn't believe that her daughter would stay out later than she had promised to unless something awful had happened. Taking the initiative, something she frequently did to her husband's regret, she called up Walters and demanded that he send out a search party.

In the city, the Police Chief thought, in the city they would have laughed at her. Four kids kicking around, not even a few hours late? Big deal. In the city they would have laughed at the woman and told her to call back in twenty-four, hell, forty-eight hours. But in a small town like this there was room for leeway. The Bensons were comparative newcomers to the town, and they were overprotective of their daughter, but Joe Walters knew what the mountains and the forest were like after dark, knew that four kids fooling around could get in serious trouble, and decided to get Patrolman Hanson and take a run up to the area himself.

They'd found the cars all right, but no sign of the kids. They'd poked and probed around with their flashlights, but there was nothing to indicate foul play or much of anything else. The kids could have gone anywhere, in any direction. All Chief Walters could do was notify the parents and hope the children came back to their cars from wherever they went and were back in their beds before midnight.

Doug Withers' parents called him almost every hour on the hour. Sam Withers drove up to the picnic area and looked around himself. They'd not spent all those years raising their beloved son, building their hopes for the boy's future, only to see him lost in the forest. By the time dawn came, all the parents—except for Jack's father—were there at the encampment, along with Patrolmen Hanson and Stevens. The brunt of the blame was placed squarely on Jack Potter, who had been doomed to pay for the "sins of the father" until his untimely death. "I know that damn kid is behind this," Sam Withers kept saying over and over, as if the boy's guilt would somehow bring his son back to him. By noontime, the wives had gone back home for sleep and consolation, while the men stayed out beating through the brush, struggling up and down little-used trails, up and down cowpaths, through fields and along streams, shouting out the names of four people who would never be able to answer.

Chief Walters was grabbing a quick bite at his desk when Anna Braddon—*the* Anna Braddon—walked in with a bright-faced young man he had never seen before.

They introduced themselves. Cecilia, the dispatcher, a tubby, middle-aged lady with shockingly bleached hair, was staring at them unabashedly, and Tony, the building's janitor, stopped his sweeping to survey that woman he swore he saw huckstering goods on the television set virtually every night. The police station, actually a substation since the town was so small, was just a big, square room with partitioned offices in the back, a lot of desks in the front, and the switchboard off to one side. The building was old. The floorboards creaked and the paint was peeling. The only thing modern about the room, the newly installed fluorescent lights overhead, seemed out of place, and lent the room a harsh glow that bathed everything in an ugly, eye-straining hue.

Before Anna could say anything more, Walters said, "You didn't have to come all the way up here, Mrs. Braddon. We could have handled everything over the phone. Shipping the body, everything. Of course, there are your brother's personal effects. But there's no—uh—hurry for that."

"We—I came here for information, Officer. There are a lot of things I don't understand about Jeffrey's death and . . ." She looked at the chair in front of Walter's desk. "May I sit down?"

He gestured. "Be my guest." David stood in back of Anna, as if hovering protectively. The Chief could have had one of the offices in back if he had so desired, but he had (although he would never admit it) a mild case of claustrophobia. It had never interfered with his work

141

and had not prevented him from going down in that hole in the Forester Building with Harry London, but he saw no need to sit in an enclosed space when it wasn't even necessary. So he sat at a big desk in the middle of the room, where he could keep an eye on everything, and everyone could keep an eye on him. He was always in and out, in and out all the time anyway, so the position of his desk had never been very important.

"You spoke to my husband yesterday," Anna continued. "And he—he told me that the details—surrounding Jeffrey's death were quite unpleasant. I know you're only trying to spare my feelings, but you see . . ." she almost started to cry, " . . . he was my brother. The least I can do it find out, is understand, what happened to him."

Police Chief Walters put down his sandwich and leaned back in his chair. He rubbed his eyes with his knuckles and exhaled dramtically. "Mrs. Braddon. I fully understand what you're going through. But to be perfectly honest with you, we don't *know* what killed your brother. His body was found in a state of deterioration. The coroner determined that he had been dead for at least a week, but that wouldn't have accounted for all his injuries."

As if sensing that Anna could use more than a little support, David said, "We heard he was killed falling through a broken floor . . ."

"The fall didn't kill him, as far as we can tell. The condition of his body was such that a lot of things we might have found out are now impossible to discern. The floor in the storeroom where he worked was broken. We assume he fell through to a sub-basement level, a cavern which appears to run underneath the street for several blocks. His body was found quite a distance away from the area where he fell. Like I said, we still don't know what killed him."

"He couldn't have starved to death?"

"If he had been down there alive for a week, maybe. With a broken leg, unable to yell for help. But the coroner says he was dead for a week, which means he probably died the same day he fell through the floor. The coroner's guess—and it is only a guess—is that he died from certain injuries which he sustained not from the fall, but from something else which he came into contact with in the cavern."

"What?"

"We don't know."

"Animals of some sort?" David suggested.

"That seems to be indicated." Walters looked quickly at Anna to see how she was taking it. *He was eaten, your brother was eaten.* He felt bile rising from the thought of what he had seen down in that cavern. *Your brother was eaten. Your brother is dead.*

"What's being done to find out, to find out what, or who, was responsible for Jeffrey's death?"

"The coroner is performing certain tests." He saw the grimace on her face. "I know it's unpleasant, but it has to be done. That's why we haven't released the body yet. I know you'd like to be able to make complete funeral arrangements. You should be able to by the end of the week, if not earlier. While you're up here you can drive over to Jeffrey's house, if you'd like, take a look at his belongings. We've gone though them, of course. Far as we can tell he didn't have a lawyer and he never made a will, so I assume the house will belong to you now. And everything in it. You might want to pack it all up and sell the place. But perhaps I'm being a bit premature."

"I hadn't even thought of that," Anna said, smiling tightly. "Is there—is there a lot?"

"I imagine so. Your brother lived here for several years. Things have a way of accumulating. It will probably take more than a day to get things in order."

"My brother and I lost contact over the years. Did he have any friends, close friends, up here I could talk to?"

"Why don't you talk to his employer, Harry London? He knew Jeffrey quite well. Was a good friend, too." He told her where the store and Jeffrey's house were located. "I believe Harry also had a set of keys to Jeffrey's place. I'm sure he'll be glad to give them to you."

"Thank you."

"Is there anything else, Miss Braddon?"

"No. You'll let me know if you find out anything more, won't you?" She rose from her chair and shook his hand.

"Of course," said the Chief as he rose, grasped first her hand, then David's. "I'm very sorry, Mrs. Braddon, I want you to know that. We all liked your brother very much here."

She thanked him, and walked silently and slowly toward the door, the young man holding onto her shoulder. Chief Walters stared after them long after they had gone out into the street.

Cecelia came over, her hand to her mouth, eyes aglow. "Isn't she beautiful?" she gushed. "I didn't dare ask for her autograph. Is she coming back?"

"No," Walters said, "I don't think we'll be seeing her here again."

Meanwhile the search continued for the four young people who had vanished overnight. By now many neighbors and friends of the youngsters' families had joined the search parties, spreading out over wider and wider areas of the woods surrounding the base of Hunter's Mountain. Unfortunately, the searchers focused their efforts almost exclusively on the southeast side, where the cars had been parked, assuming that the kids had stayed in that area. If the men and women combing the woods had all been trained in such endeavors, they might have noticed unmistakable, if subtle signs which would have indicated the direction taken by the four youths. Even the police officers, out-numbered ten to one by the civilians, weren't experts in the art of tracking. Someone suggested they go over and look in the old caves on the other side of the mountain, but the caves had been passe as meeting and making-out points for teenagers for so many years that no one thought anyone bothered going there anymore. The caves were like a "haunted house" that had been slept in overnight without any harm coming to the participants, demystified due to the lack of ghosts or demons. The dangerous, romantic aspect of the caves, too, had been challenged and found wanting. No one bothered with them now. Rumor had it that they all ended a few yards within the mountains, and had been thoroughly explored without ever revealing any secrets.

"Forget the caves," someone else muttered. "I still say the kids are somewhere in this area."

Many of the people in the impromptu search parties were participating only for the sake of the parents. Most of them firmly believed that the kids were playing a joke, or had gone off to another town on impulse, gone on a spree for a lark, without a care for how their parents might react, deliberately leaving the cars behind so that no one would suspect that they'd left the area. Maybe they'd been afraid people might spot the cars on the road as they traveled, so they'd walked or hitchhiked instead. Children never did things that made any sense.

That darn Jack Potter, son of a drunkard, could talk the teenagers into doing anything. That good-looking critter had the kind of matinee-idol features that could easily persuade schoolgirls to engage in unnatural acts. For the parent's sakes, the townspeople trudged through the woods calling out names, brushing past tree branches and spiny bushes, knowing all the while that the brats would show up before dark with some stupid excuse and a smirk on their foolhardy faces. Few took the search very seriously.

Still, a few of them started up the same path the teens had taken the previous morning. Emily's mother had been the only parent to see her child actually leave the house, and had finally remembered the backpack strapped to the girl's shoulders. "I wondered why she took that, instead of the cooler. She never mentioned doing any climbing."

On the chance that they were still up in the woods, at a campfire somewhere, a few men set out along the mountain trail, stocked up with a few six packs for aid and comfort. They would have cursed and muttered what everyone else was cursing and muttering, only Sam Withers was with them and they had to keep their mouths shut. They feared what would happen when he got his hands on Douglas. If the kid was alive he'd soon wish he wasn't. Each of them firmly believed they'd find the boy and his pals somewhere on the trail, puffing joints, maybe rollin' in the buff (most of them would have loved to see the girls in their birthday suits) in the manner of all wayward, rebellious youth. "He's gonna catch it but good, when his pa gets his hands on him," they whispered. "Mom's near worried out of her mind."

So no one went directly to the caves. It would be a few hours before the men on the trail would reach that particular point.

And down there in the darkness something waited.

The hardware store did a thriving business that day.

Harry London sat in his office and wondered if it had anything to do with Jeffrey Braddon's death. He concluded that it didn't. True, since Jeff had had no family in town, this was the only place where people could, in a sense, come and pay their respects, talk to other people who knew him. Some had asked morbid questions, as was to be expected. But most who had known the man simply muttered regrets. Some even went so far as to express sympathy for Paula; her feelings for Jeffrey had not been as secret as Harry had suspected. Everyone seemed to be buying things they would have needed and would have bought even had the tragedy not occurred. That was a small consolation. At least Harry could never say he had profited from someone else's death.

It would have been an easier day if Paula hadn't stayed out, although he understood what she was going through. He had sat with her at her house for a good part of the last two evenings, saying little, making her tea, holding her hand. How much he had wanted to comfort her, to tell her: You are *still* loved. But her mind had been on one man only, as was proper, and it might be some time before she could have room in her heart for another. What was that he had thought about never profiting from tragedy?

The trainees Paula had supervised the other day weren't working out very well, and for the first time in years, Harry found himself working a full shift behind the counter. Normally, he only stepped in for a while on special occasions with certain customers, usually spending his time on the books, huddled over order forms, arguing on the phone, supervising. He had worked long and hard and had earned the right to what basically amounted to semi-retirement. Still, he found that working as a clerk as he had in the old days was somewhat energizing. It was nice to be able to talk to the customers, to trade gossip, to ask how their kids were and how things were going in general.

The minute he saw Roger conferring with them and pointing in his direction, Harry knew that the couple walking towards him weren't customers, but rather were here to see him exclusively on a special matter; he could tell from the solemn look on their faces. Harry was not a great fan of television, therefore did not recognize Anna Braddon, and the man she was with was just as much a stranger. He didn't notice any family resemblance between the woman and his late employee until after she

147

had told him who she was.

"Mr. London?" the woman asked. He nodded affirmatively, giving his best professional smile. She said, "I'm Anna Braddon. Jeffrey's sister. Chief Walters suggested that I see you." He dropped his smile immediately and told her how sorry he was about her brother's tragic and pointless death. Anna looked momentarily embarrassed, almost self-conscious. She changed the subject abruptly by introducing David. The two men shook hands warmly.

Harry took the both of them into his private office. "I'm afraid there's not much I can add to what the Police Chief told you." He paused, contemplating the effect his words might have, and added, "Did Walters tell you what we found in the Forester Building next door?" He was glad to have something to say, anything to fill up the awkward space surrounding them, the atmosphere of gloom and regret.

"No," Anna replied. "Does it have to do with Jeffrey's . . ."

"I'm not sure." He told them about the hole in the building next door, how odd and inexplicable it had appeared.

"Is anyone looking into it?" David asked.

"Yes, I'm having some men look it over this afternoon. I think whatever happened in that building might be a key to what happened to Jeffrey, so it's more than worth checking into. And my building here was also affected. Something broke through the floor in that storage room, made it fall apart. It's a mystery that should be resolved."

David asked about the Forester Building, what it had last been used for and so on. Harry explained what he could, then added, "I've since found out that its former tenant was something called the Barrows Corporation, but that doesn't tell us much of anything. The Barrows Corporation is a huge conglomerate of various firms and

148

operations. One hand doesn't know what the other is doing. Chief Walters and I tried to find out what they had used the building for, but got nowhere. No one seems to know, no one has any records. Everyone passes the buck along to somebody else, some other executive or PR officer or division head. It's all very frustrating."

"You don't have any ideas?" Anna asked.

"No. And I could be barking up the wrong tree, altogether. I don't know for sure that the condition of the Forester Building is related to Jeffrey's death. The semi-collapse of the building might have been due to structural flaws. I don't know what to say. It seems to me that if anyone can ever determine the real cause of your brother's death, it's the coroner, or whomever he calls in for consultation. I'm afraid that's not very consoling or satisfying, but like the Chief must have told you, that's all there is right now."

Anna rose and thanked him for his time, then remembered to ask for the keys to Jeffrey's house. "Yes," Harry said. "We all had a pair of each other's keys, just in case. I remember he locked himself out one night," he chuckled, "after an office party." He handed her a metal key ring. "There you go. The door is easy to open, as I recall."

Harry sensed that Anna wanted to ask a lot of questions, that she wanted him to tell her *who* her brother had been. But she didn't come right out and ask, and what was there to *say*, really. "He was a nice guy"? As he watched the two of them leave the hardware store, Harry realized how grateful he was for their sudden appearance. It had barely been a couple of days since Jeffrey's horrible death, and he had already been growing complacent, going about his business, waiting for Walters and his staff, in their own slow, quiet way, to shed some light upon the mystery. But an employee— more, a *friend*—of his was dead and there was no reason for it, no rational explanation. He could have sought retreat and comfort in his day-to-day concerns, until time passed and Jeffrey's death had become just another memory. But he owed the man a lot more than that.

Something funny was going on in this town, and he swore he was going to find out what it was.

Jeffrey's house was on the outskirts of town, not far from the lake and the forest. It was a white, one-story clapboard structure, perfectly square and neat and clean. There was a tiny stoop one step above ground level in front of the white-painted door. A curtain hung over the window. There was another, larger window to the right of the door, looking into the living room. Anna felt a fresh flood of tears gathering in the corners of her eyes, but she held them back, not wanting to make a scene in front of David. He had been nice enough to come all the way up here with her. She would not make it any more uncomfortable for him than she had to.

They parked next to a blue station wagon which they assumed had been Jeffrey's car. The front lawn was brown and patchy, but he had made a game effort to keep it green and growing. There was a single, solitary tree a few yards from the house, a mere sapling struggling to survive in the drought-ridden atmosphere. They could see a laundry line strung up in the back. It ran at a diagonal from the house and over to a stake in the ground. There was a redwood picnic table, too. Both the line and the table were bare.

There was another car parked in back which they could not see. They could not have known it was *that* car which belonged to Jeffrey, and not the one in front.

Harry London had been right; there was no trouble with the lock. One swift jab with the key and the door swung open easily. Anna and David found themselves in a small foyer with a coat rack on their right. Several hats and a gray raincoat were on the rack, and a black umbrella stood in a wastebasket near the entrance to the living room. The kitchen was on the left.

Anna stiffened when she heard a noise from the bedroom in back. Was it possible? Had it all been a mistake? Had the awful, mutilated body they'd found belonged to somebody else? Was there still a chance, still time for her to tell her brother that she loved him, that she cared? Was it not too late? She heard a stifled cry, a gasp, then the sound of bedsprings squeaking as if someone had stood up from a mattress, and the soft approach of footsteps up the hall. Any second she imagined the owner of those footfalls would appear, and it would be— had to be—her brother.

But it wasn't.

It was a woman. In her mid-thirties. Very pale, very thin. Like someone who spent all her time in twilight and who shied away from sunshine. She looked quite ill and weak, like someone who'd been bedridden for some time, or someone shattered by grief. Her eyes were red and moist and it was obvious that she had been crying. Her hand went up to her mouth when she saw them, and her face turned red beneath the ghostly, unfading white, as if she had been expecting someone else. The blush in her cheeks stayed there for a few seconds, while she wiped her eyes in embarrassment and quickly extracted a handkerchief from her coat pocket to wipe her nose with. She wore a simple white blouse and a light brown skirt.

"I'm sorry," she said. Her mouth opened and closed, forming words, but no sound issued from her lips. Her eyes darted around the enclosure, as if checking the walls and ceiling for flies or spots of dust. She licked her mouth with a slim, supple tongue.

Anna moved a step closer, not sure herself of what to say. "I'm Anna Braddon."

Paula Widdoes relaxed a bit at that, managing a sincere, if nervous smile. "Hello." She held out her hand for Anna to take, then pulled it back suddenly, as if she had almost committed a nasty breach of etiquette. "I'm sorry. You must be wondering . . . My name is Paula Widdoes. I was a friend of your brother's. I had a key to the place. I came here to . . . to . . ."

She couldn't say any more. Suddenly she rushed at Anna and threw herself trembling and sobbing into her arms. "I'm so sorry," she said, over and over. "I loved him. I loved your brother. I can't believe . . . I just can't believe it. He's dead! Oh God, he's dead!"

Anna comforted the woman as well as she could, leading her slowly but firmly into the living room, sitting down on the couch with her, her arms still around her. David stood by the side, watching them, seemingly aware that there was nothing to say and nothing to do. Whoever this woman was, she had been more than fond of Jeffrey Braddon.

"I came here just to feel near him," Paula said, when she had recovered enough to speak. She pulled away slightly from Anna, apologizing again, dabbing at her eyes with the kerchief. "I can't accept it, you see. No matter how hard I try, I can't accept it. I was almost hoping I'd find him here, reading his magazines, sitting in front of the television, nibbling pretzels the way he used to. He didn't have very large dreams, you see, not like some people. But does that mean that he had to die? I don't understand, Anna. I don't understand."

Anna pulled her close and stroked her hair, and asked, "Is there something we can get you?"

"Some tea. Maybe some tea." She whimpered so softly it was hard to hear her. David saw Anna start to rise, but waved her back. "I'll get it," he said. Anna realized he probably had offered to make the tea more out of fear of being left alone with Paula than out of an effort to be helpful. He'd probably had his fill of weeping women.

"I'm so sorry," Paula said, trying to compose herself. "This is the last thing you need. It must be tough enough for you without having me around to complicate things."

It was quite the opposite. Anna was glad to know that Jeffrey was being properly mourned by someone who really knew him and needed him, although she was sorry for Paula, of course. She said, "You're not complicating things. I know Jeffrey meant something to you. I think his death has hurt you even more than it has me. I can't tell you how sorry I am. We lost contact some time ago, Jeffrey and I. I didn't know that he had someone . . ."

"We were just friends," Paula said quickly, too quickly. "Good friends." She paused a moment and looked out into space. *More* than friends. But we never decided to do anything about it. Nobody's fault." When Anna said nothing, she added, "I wasn't trying to imply that I was his girlfriend or anything like that. I mean, Jeffrey was a very private person. I mean I—" The words had come rushing out, filling the air, closing the gap between them. "I wasn't his fiancee or anything like that. I—" Paula put down her head and looked into her lap, brushing away some nonexistent piece of lint from her skirt. "I just loved him."

Anna wondered if Paula's love for her brother had been returned. She hoped so. If it hadn't, she thought morbidly, then Jeffrey's death might have been the best thing that could have happened as far as the woman was concerned. She would have been doomed to pine away for a man who lived, yet did not love her. Now Paula would be free to find someone else. Yet, what if she gave up the search altogether, and spent the rest of her life longing for the presence, the caress, of a corpse? Forever haunted by what might have been? Wouldn't that be even worse? Anna erased the train of thought from her mind. It was sick to think like that, sick to even suggest with unspoken words that her brother's death was for "the best" in any way, shape or manner.

"I'm very sorry I intruded here," Paula continued. "I hope you don't mind. I just wanted to sit here, to look at

153

his things, to feel him. To feel his presence. It's captured in everything he possessed, in everything he touched. It's almost as if he were still alive, about to come home any moment, to step in that front door. I know that won't happen. But I can sit here and pretend, can almost feel him all around me. I didn't mean to intrude."

"You didn't intrude." Anna squeezed Paula's hand gently with her own, again ashamed that she had barely known the man that this woman had felt, still felt, such passion for. This stranger had known her brother so much better than she had. She felt a stab of regret, of loss, aware too late of what she had missed. "Is there anything of Jeffrey's you'd like to keep? I thought I might go through his things while I was up here. I won't have any use for . . ." She regretted her words immediately, afraid that they'd sounded too harsh, to unfeeling. "Is there something that might mean something to you?"

Paula shook her head. "No. No, thank you. He gave me gifts, keepsakes, that I've kept at home. That will be enough." She looked like she was about to cry again. She got up quickly, sudden tears streaming down her face. "Please forgive me. I've got to go. Apologize to the gentleman for me." She grabbed up a white bag that had been lying on a table near the sofa and dashed out the front door, off the stoop and into her blue station wagon. David came back into the living room when he heard the sound of her car driving away. Anna explained what had happened.

"Well, the tea is ready anyway. Care for a cup?"

"Yes, I think I'd like that."

They sat in the kitchen, a small and cheery place with a big window that let in the sunlight. It was an ambience at odds with their mood. Anna expressed her sympathy for Paula, verbalizing the thoughts she had had while comforting the woman. David simply listened and sipped his hot tea, appreciating Anna's beauty even now. "This is going to be quite a job," she was saying. "Packing up Jeffrey's belongings. I don't know what I'll do with them."

"Go through them. See what you want to keep. Put the rest in storage until you figure out what to do with it. Even if you don't sell the house you can't just leave everything lying around."

"Yes, I suppose you're right. It will take a while, though."

"You might as well do it while you're up here, Anna. If you think you can handle it. If you want to stay for a day or two that would be all right with me."

"Oh, David, I couldn't impose on you."

"Don't be silly. I wouldn't mind. I'd be with you, right?" He smiled and took her hand, then kissed it. "You might need help, a little moral support."

"There's no hurry. I could come up here again."

"It's up to you. I've got nothing to rush back to the city for. Nothing at all."

She swallowed half of the tea in her cup and licked her lips. "I couldn't ask you to stay for such a dreary task, sorting through Jeffrey's things with me. That's something I wouldn't wish on anyone."

"I said I don't mind."

Anna thought it over for a minute. "Well, maybe we'll stay overnight. Go out and get something to eat. But we won't stay here," she said determinedly. "We'll get a hotel room. I brought all my credit cards so there's no problem with the expenses."

David kept silent, wondering when the humilation of letting her pay for everything would end. "All right," Anna concluded. "We'll stay overnight. But I won't have you stuck in here digging through my brother's effects. I can do that myself. Why don't you go for a drive, go into town, see a movie? No need for you to be as depressed as I am."

A chill went up his spine at the thought of driving her car, driving *any* car, even that short distance into town. He just wasn't ready for it. He had thought that he would have been by the time they'd arrived in Milbourne, but the old icy fear still gripped him and he was positive that he would freeze behind the wheel. Maybe if she went with him? But no, she wanted to stay and go through Jeffrey's things. She had used a polite excuse before, but the fact was that she wanted—needed—to be alone.

"Maybe I'll walk into town," David said. "I could use the exercise." Immediately he thought about the distance and wondered how his gimpy leg would fare. That was a factor he'd have to worry about later. Aside from the pain, he seemed able to get around and walk for blocks without problems in the city. He saw no reason to think things would be different out here.

He kissed her goodbye, both of them holding back, as if too strong or deep a kiss would be improper in such a somber atmosphere, an affront to Jeffrey's memory.

He walked across the ragged front lawn with its brown patches and tire treads and started on the long lonely walk towards town.

Chief Walters was nothing if not a creature of impulse.

He was out at the campsite where the four teenagers had disappeared, when he found himself thinking again of the morning meeting with Anna Braddon and her boyfriend. After all—there was nothing more he could do about those youngsters. The search parties were still out, combing the woods in ever-widening circles, still concentrating on the southeastern end of the forest. Nothing had turned up. A few more people had set up halfheartedly through the mountain on the path undertaken earlier by Sam Withers and his group, believing that if the kids were anywhere, they were there, but they'd come back before completing the journey. Withers and Co. were still on the mountain. The general feeling was still the same: The kids had hitchhiked or walked to another town, leaving the cars to throw off the scent. Walters was fast losing interest with it all. The patrolmen could handle matters. He was more concerned with Jeffrey Braddon's death.

He drove back to the office and once there started to pace. He ignored Old Tony and Cecelia as they pleaded with him to get a copy of Anna Braddon's autograph. He felt impotent, tied down, stuck at the station while Jeff Braddon's body was prodded and probed by the coroner. Something funny was going on. He had always wondered about their coroner's credentials—virtually *anyone* could get appointed to the office—and the way he stalled over the Braddon boy made him wonder if he knew what he was doing? How many autopsies would it take to find out why he died? He thought again of that half-eaten body and grimaced.

He had been planning to take his men and have a good look in those tunnels and find out where they led—he might pick up a clue or two—but those teenagers' disappearance, and other matters, had gotten in the way. They'd only had time to bring the body to the surface. Boy—had *that* been unpleasant!

Something had gnawed away half of Braddon's body. He told himself that it must have been rats or some other cave creatures that would probably leave you alone unless you were already injured or dead. In that case, there was nothing to fear underground except the occasional resurgence of his nagging, but controllable claustrophobia.

His reverie was interrupted by the arrival of Patrolman Stevens, a young freckle-faced pup who'd turned out to be more dependable than men twice his age. He took off his cap as he walked over to Walters' desk and scratched his shiny red hair.

"What's happened?" Walters asked.

"Ain't found nobody," Stevens said, sitting on the edge of the desk, Walters grimaced as usual, but said nothing. He didn't want to come off as stuffy or unreasonable, but he hated the sight of buttocks on his desktop. "We searched the whole area five times over. Hanson has taken a bunch of 'em over to the other side of the mountain. The only thing we can do is look over the whole fuckin' mountain, and personally, I think it's a waste of time. Everybody thinks so, but nobody'll admit it—not in front of the parents, at least. If we call off the whole thing the parents will turn the whole town against us, you bet." He brushed his hair with his fingers and put his cap back on. "I'm going to take over from Hanson in four hours, though by that time it'll be too damn dark to see anything."

"We call it off in two hours, unless something comes up. Think you can handle it?"

"Yeah sure, but—"

The Chief put on his jacket and his hat and started for the storeroom in the back. "I'm going to take another look down where Jeff Braddon's body was found, while I've got the chance."

"Now? But what for? There ain't nothin' down there. You said so yourself."

"Maybe I just didn't look far enough."

"You shouldn't go alone. You need a whole bunch of men to go into all those tunnels you talked about."

"Maybe, but I haven't got a whole bunch of men, and I want you to stay here and hold down the fort. If anything else comes up, Cecelia will have someone to send out on it."

Walters got himself a large lantern, a heavy duty flashlight, several yards of coiled-up hemp rope, a collapsible ladder and a spare backpack full of first-aid and other provisions which was always left ready for

158

immediate use. Walters wondered why he was doing this. It was clear that the key to whatever had killed Braddon would be found on an autopsy table by a crackerjack pathologist, and not in the empty catacombs below the street. Or was it? They hadn't come up with anything, had they?

He knew why he was doing it. He told himself that he felt helpless as far as those four kids were concerned; he was in no shape to trudge around the woods, and if they hadn't found anything yet, they probably never would. He told himself that he had liked Jeffrey Braddon, and had liked his sister, that he hated incomplete investigations and unsolved deaths. He told himself that he had intended all along to eventually make an exhaustive search of the cavern for anything that might explain what had happened to the deceased, to the Forester Building, to the storeroom floor of London Hardware. Yes, all these things were true.

He had also told himself that since it was always nighttime underground, he might as well go now, even though daylight was fast fading and the sun was slowly scraping against the tops of the trees.

But the real reason he went, and he knew it and accepted it, was that there was something he simply had to prove to himself. He could think of nothing more frightening than being beneath the earth in an enclosed space, with dusk fast approaching overhead. The whole picture was macabre and eerie, the stuff of childhood nightmares. He was no longer a child, but a grown man gone to fat at a job that had long since been without challenge or opportunity.

Something about the abyss underneath the town compelled him to come, called him, beckoned him to fathom its unholy secrets. To learn once and for all how and why Jeffrey Braddon died.

He would face the unknown. He was going down into

that hole to find out what he could. And he was going to do it *now*.

Because if he didn't, he might never again work up the nerve.

Chapter Eight

Forty-five minutes after he'd left Anna to go through her brother's possessions, David arrived in Milbourne proper. The town seemed slightly bigger on foot than it had when viewed through a passing car window. His limp more pronounced than usual, David walked slowly up the main street, looking in shop windows and stopping in front of the movie theater. They weren't showing anything that particularly appealed to him, so there went one chance to kill a couple of hours.

In these small towns the drugstores also functioned as magazine stands and stationery stores—they had books and periodicals and things not always found in the typical city pharmacy. He saw one about a block away and decided to investigate. Perhaps he could pick up one or two paperbacks, then sit in the restaurant across the street and read for a while.

David, oh, David, he asked himself, what are you doing here in the middle of nowhere with a beautiful, famous—and married—young woman? Answer: *I don't know, but I'm not complaining.*

The block he was on seemed familiar. He realized he was near the London Hardware store. He was suddenly anxious to see this mysterious Forester Building that Harry London had referred to earlier; the one under which Jeffrey Braddon's body had been found. He saw the building looming up beyond the hardware store, looking ancient and out of place among the more modern buildings on the street. This was it, all right. He saw the same in raised bronze letters above the door.

He stood on the sidewalk in front of the building looking up at it, his eyes ascending to the higher stories, wondering if the building were connected to Jeffrey's horrible death in more than one way. During the time it had taken to walk from Jeffrey's house, he'd been thinking about many different things: his future with Anna, his leg, the accident, about Janice and her tragic death. Now he found himself caught up in the same spell that had enveloped Police Chief Walters and Harry London, as well as others in the town who were curious about the strange death of one of their own number. What *had* killed Jeffrey Braddon? He, too, was wondering. He would like to find out, if only to bring Anna peace of mind. Or might he only unlease unwittingly a barrage of even more horrible facts and memories, creating more agony for Anna? He had no answer.

The door to the Forester Building opened abruptly and out walked Harry London and two solemn-looking men—one portly, the other thin and bald—who seemed deep in conversation with each other. Harry nearly collided with David before he saw him. Startled by the presence of someone else in front of him, London did a neat sidestep and continued on his way, until he recognized David and turned back to greet him. "Hello, Mr. . . . ." He tapped his head as if to bring David's name to the surface.

"Hammond," David told him. There was no need for him to remind London of who he was, for Harry had not forgotten his talk with David and Anna earlier in the day. Of course, David realized that when people first made Anna Braddon's acquaintance, they probably failed to notice whomever she might be with, let alone recall them afterwards.

London placed his hand on David's shoulder, as if to assure him that he would not be forgotten, and turned to the two men who had accompanied him out of the building. "Gentlemen. I thank you for coming. I'll be in touch with you if anything new develops." After shaking hands with each of them, he dismissed them by turning back to David. The two fellows walked off towards a parking lot just across the street.

"Would you care to have a cup of coffee with me?" Harry asked. Before David could answer, he added: "Is Anna with you?" He looked around.

"No, she's still at her brother's place. I think she needed some time to be by herself."

"Understandable. Well, how about some coffee?"

David let himself be led to the coffeeshop across the street, while Harry made small talk about the place, its zip-zip service and its tasty food. They found an empty table in the back—most of the tables were empty, but the counter was full—and made themselves comfortable. David was wondering what to say next when Harry surprised him.

"Acid," London stated. Just that one simple word: acid. David didn't know if the man was referring to the condition of the coffee they served, or was making a reference to a stomach ailment. He cocked his head and said, "Pardon me?"

"Remember I told you and Anna about the building next to my shop, the one I came out of just now?"

"Yes. That's why I was looking at it," David replied. "Hasn't been used in a long time, has it?"

"Nope. Anyway, you'll recall what I said about the big hole in the place, the one that runs all the way from the top of the building to the bottom, or vice versa if you prefer."

"What about it?"

"Those men I was with are experts in building collapse. You know what *they* say did it?"

163

The waitress came and they both ordered coffee. "Have a cheese danish too," Harry urged. "I recommend them highly." David acquiesced.

"What did it?" David prompted.

"Acid. Corrosive acid. We thought it had been an explosive, or something worse. But some kind of incredibly powerful acid just spilled down from the top floor straight to the bottom, eating away all of the wood. Probably left that awful stench, too. They say that whatever it was probably seeped next door into my place, traveling from the foundation of the Forester Building to mine. It passed harmlessly through the dirt until it got to the wooden floor in my basement. *Voila*—the floor was weakened."

"Why didn't it dissolve entirely?"

"Because the acid was too weak, too diluted, by then. They looked into my storage room earlier and suggested that it was the wood itself that had weakened—not that something had necessarily smashed through it."

"Acid? Do you think that's what happened to Jeffrey Braddon's body?"

"It's one explanation. But I think the coroner's initial report would have found something along those lines. Chief Walters has been good about letting me in on what they've found. Which, so far, is nothing. If Jeffrey Braddon was—" he stumbled on the word, "attacked—by animals, it wasn't animals that anybody's ever seen before."

"That's impossible."

"Not only that. Those two fellas weren't able to explain the oddest thing about that floor in my storage room."

David felt chills running through his body, felt a strong desire to be safely back in his apartment in Manhattan where there was nothing more threatening than roaches. "What was that?" he asked, not sure he wanted to know.

164

"They never explained why the cracked boards of the floor were pointing *upwards*." He leaned in towards David as the waitress approached with their coffee and pastry. "*Something* tried to get into that storage room. Something from below the cellar.

"Something big."

Sam Withers and the five townspeople he'd taken with him reached the end of the main mountain trail at just about the same time David and Harry London were drinking coffee in the Main Street Cafe. There was still a way to go, but for all intents and purposes, they were finally off the mountain. So far they had not found a thing.

Sam Withers had stormed along the trail in much the same way that his son's friend Jack had the day before, leading the "troops" into enemy territory. He was always a few feet ahead of them, which was fine with them, as they were able to whisper among themselves about the damn foolishness of it, able to grab beers and consume them without calling undue attention to themselves. It had been a long day and a pointless one as far as they were concerned. For all they knew, someone might have been trying to get in touch with them even now, to tell them that the kids were safe and sound at home, their mamas too relieved to even scold them for their thoughtless behavior. We're even bigger fools than they are, thought beefy Chet Bannon, taking another swig of a once-cold, now-warm bottle of piss-poor bottled beer that he'd been carrying in a small plastic cooler for the past few hours. He was looking forward to going home.

"Say, we're near those old caves now, aren't we?" some mother-fuckin' son of an asshole had the misfortune to say. "Maybe we should check them out, too?"

Chet, now well on his way to insobriety, looked, took aim, and hurled the half-empty bottle at the younger

165

man who'd pronounced those irritating syllables. "Shit! Haven't we spent enough time looking for those brats? Enough is enough!"

Al Barton, the younger man, easily dodged the bottle, although some of the beer spritzed onto his shirt. He advanced on the drunkard with a rage in his eyes that came as much from the thought of a wasted day as it did from the beer in Chet's bottle.

"Keep quiet," Herb Lloyd said testily, fearing Chet's words would carry up the trail to Doug's father. "It won't take long to poke into those stupid holes anyway."

Suddenly Chet wasn't standing next to Herbert any longer—Al Barton was! Chet was lying at Al's feet, his one hand already covering an eye that was red and rapidly swelling. "I don't need none of your crummy beer on my shirt, you jerk!" Barton bellowed.

Herbert pushed himself between the two men, fearing reprisals. Chet had had the fight taken out of him, which was just as well, as Al Barton could have easily torn him to pieces. Herb helped Chet to his feet and dusted him off. "Get home and get something on that eye," Herb instructed.

By this time, the men had completely forgotten about Doug Withers up ahead, and as far as they were concerned, the search was over and done with. None of them particularly cared if any of those good-for-nuthin' youngsters ever came back home anyway.

They were passing by the caves now, whooping and hollering, singing old campfire songs and guzzling luke-warm beer, convinced that there was nothing whatsoever hiding in the woods, and not caring if there was. It was getting rather dark now and they hastened their steps. Any second they expected to bump into Sam Withers, and the more sober among them hoped he had not been offended.

Sam Withers, meanwhile, was at the entrance to the

166

largest of the caves, desperately calling out the name of his son. Sam looked a great deal like his offspring, only he had a receding hairline, and his forehead was permanently creased with lines of fatigue and tension and disappointment. If there was one word to describe his personality, his essence, his very soul, it was *taut*. He seemed constantly on the edge of anxious hysteria, his eyes squinting in constant mental anguish, always afraid of something unknown, something intangible, waiting around that bend comprised of family responsibility and job advancement and financial strain. He was not a happy man. Only one thing really gave him joy—the thought that he was building a better life for his son, a boy he firmly believed would do great things in the world and make *his* very reason for being worthwhile.

He heard the other men of the so-called search party singing and fighting and cursing behind him, and he couldn't understand how they could be so callous about something—someone—who mattered so much to him. He made up his mind then and there not to have anything to do with any of them ever again.

Then he saw something caught in the glare of his flashlight.

Something appeared to be—bending, if that was the word—over the remains of a human body. He saw other figures lying in there, too, just on the edges of the circle of light, their bloodied and mutilated forms covered by shadows. The lips of the things—if you could say it had lips—were eating something: a piece of meat, a morsel, no longer recognizable as part of a leg or arm. Blood dripped down from the chewing orifice. Sam stepped back, too shocked to scream, and his light shined over the other bodies which had been formerly hidden by the dark. His eyes widened in pain and disbelief, his worst fears realized.

One of them was Douglas.

And when the creature's companions came for him,

Sam did not even try to run or escape. He had no will any longer, no will to live or to survive. He dropped sobbing to his knees, and let them crawl all over him.

It was only when one small part of his mind realized what was happening to him that he at last cried out.

The men in the woods were not without their more decent impulses. When they heard Sam Withers' ear-shattering, bloodcurdling outburst, they ran pell mell as one to the caves.

None of them ever returned.

Harry and David were driving up Petemont Road to a spot near the base of the mountain's northeastern side to see a man named Hank Danielson. The man used to be the caretaker of the Forester Building. Harry's old Chevy bounced up and down over the rutted dirt lane through the thick forest which hemmed them in on either side, the sky overhead darkening ominously. "There. I think I see the old man's cabin now."

Directly after finishing their coffee, Harry had taken David over to the courthouse. "I'm glad that you and Miss Braddon showed up today," he had said, his face aglow with fortitude and determination. "You've galvanized me into action. I'm a great procrastinator, even about important things like this. Guess I figured Jeff was beyond help. But that's no excuse, is it?"

They had entered the courthouse and walked down a hall to the room where the records were kept. "I would have put off getting men to look at that floor, at the Forester Building, for days. Weeks! God knows when I would have gotten around to this. Chief Walters said he'd take care of it, but he's got his hands full, I bet; especially with those four missing kids." He'd explained to David about the disappearance of the youngsters. Harry seemed to share the viewpoint that they'd be coming home out of the hills any hour now. "They're gonna catch it but good," he said.

Harry had gone through various files with the aid of a fortyish, mousy-looking brunette who wore a plain print dress that seemed too large for her. The green eye shadow she wore was out of place on her face, but was obviously a small stab at glamour. With her help he soon found what he was looking for: information on the last tenant of the Forester Building, the Barrows Corporation (although said information consisted only of a main corporate address and the president's name), and the address of the now-retired janitor and caretaker who'd been put on a pension when the town decided to shut the building up for good. This was the man they were going to see.

"Might as well do it now, though I don't know what Danielson can tell us," Harry had said as they got into his car. "But you got a couple of hours to kill, and business is slow today. If my staff can't handle things—" He paused. "Well, they have to learn sometime."

David told him about running into Paula Widdoes. "Yes, that's the woman who works for me," Harry said. "She took Jeffrey's death awfully hard. I hope she'll come out of it, though. Not for the sake of the store, mind you. It's just that—well, she's a good friend."

The car bounced over an especially deep rut and David's head nearly brushed against the roof. This drive had been particularly unpleasant, although conditions couldn't have been more different than what they had been during the time of his accident. He tried to ignore his feelings of apprehension.

Harry parked in front of a ramshackle cabin that looked as if it had been deserted and left to die at least ten years before. The windows on the side facing them were cracked and full of holes. The grounds had not been kept up, and the lawn—if you could call it that— was merely an ugly carpet of weeds. Even the trees around here were bare and spindly.

They got out of the car and approached the cabin.

Harry knocked on the door with his knuckles. There was no reply.

"I think the door's open," David told him.

Harry bent his head and he too saw that the door seemed to be ajar a few millimeters. He knocked a few more times, paused out of consideration, then pushed the door open with his hand. He motioned David to follow. They soon found themselves inside a one-room structure that was so dark, so dirty, and smelled so badly, that it was all David could do to keep from running back outside.

It took only a moment for them to see that the house was unoccupied.

"Wonder where he went?" Harry said.

"If you were him," David replied, "would you stay here?"

"I see your point."

"Hmmm . . . no toilet facilities that I can see."

"What do you think . . . he's out taking a crap?"

David laughed. "Well, I suppose this place has an outhouse. Must have been built during the Civil War."

"Or before." Harry chuckled, and rubbed his cheek. "Anyway, we'll have to go back to the courthouse and see if we can dig up Danielson's current whereabouts. I'd like to find out if he could tell us anything about what went on in that building a few months ago. He was there while the Barrows Corporation was leasing it. It's the only lead we have." He smiled. "Listen to me. I sound like some kind of amateur detective."

David and Harry got in the Chevy and drove back to town, completely unaware that the object of their search was indeed out back in the crap-house. The body had long since started to decompose, and wouldn't be found until the postmaster wondered why old Danielson had failed to take his last monthly check from the mailbox. He would find Danielson sitting on the white toilet seat in the crude wooden outhouse, his pants down, flies and bugs swarming all over his legs and eyes, and dabs of blood and spattered brain tissue on the walls and on his clothing. He would see the one, neat, clean bullet hole in the middle of his forehead. And he would wonder—who'd kill a harmless old man like that?

But it would become just another mystery in the series of mysteries surrounding the town of Milbourne that year.

At the picnic grounds at the base of Hunter's Mountain, most of the search parties had already reported back to Patrolman Hanson, who was the head organizer of the various expeditions. Most of the tired and discouraged—not to mention indignant—towns-people were getting into their cars and driving back to their respective homes for dinner. No one had reported a sign of the four missing youngsters, either in the woods surrounding the picnic area or in the other small areas surrounding Milbourne. No one but the parents believed anything evil had befallen them. Everyone believed that that no-good Jack Potter had talked his three pliable friends into running off somewhere for a good time. They'd be back. They always came back. They had their fling and once it was out of their system, they came back dragging their tails behind them. It never failed.

Hanson was inclined to agree with them. All he wanted now was a nice warm bath and a kiss from the sweet lips of his girlfriend Lucy. Patrolman Stevens had called over the radio to tell him to quit at sundown, which it very nearly was. That meant that both of them would be free for the night. Stevens was a schmuck, but he had a nice cache of hard liquor out at his place, and he usually invited Hanson to bring Lucille and her sister over for a few quick ones. Stevens' backroom was better than the back seat of Lucy's convertible. Hanson tightened the belt of his perfect-fitting trousers, and ran a

171

comb through his lacquered, golden locks. Narrow-faced and well-built at thirty-seven, he looked like a man who'd been reluctant to leave the 1960s behind. Tall and good-looking, he enjoyed the added authority his gun and uniform gave him.

Had the missing parties been little children or old folk or beloved citizens of the town, no one would have complained and no one would have gone home until they were positively ready to drop from exhaustion. But this was another story entirely. Although the cars were there, there were no signs of foul play. Nothing to indicate anything out of the ordinary. They had probably run off to another city like everyone had said. The Chief had already alerted adjacent police departments to keep an eye out for them just in case.

Hanson mentally checked off all the search parties and the people in them as they reported back to the encampment. Something nagged at him. Who was missing? Anyone? Nah—who would stay out there anyway? Unless—? Yes, that was it. There was no sign of Doug Withers, no sign of the men who'd gone with him up the mountain. No one had really believed that those lazy teenagers would have done anything as ambitious as climb old Hunter, but Withers had thought it a likely possibility anyway. He and the men accompanying him had planned to walk the trail up and over the mountain, then check the caves at the other side just in case. Unless they decided to walk back along the trail the way they had come, they should have followed the connecting trail around the base of the mountain and arrived at camp thirty minutes ago. He wished that the department had a few more working walkie-talkies available. Two just weren't enough. Everything about the tiny Milbourne police department was second-rate.

Even if the bunch of goons with him had brains in their buttocks, Sam Withers was smart enough not to go *back* over the mountain this close to dark. Even with flashlights it could be treacherous—the trail wasn't very clear in daylight at some points. By themselves, Hanson was sure the other men would have sat down somewhere, drank their sixpacks and got drunk and wandered around God knows where. But Sam would have kept them in line, wouldn't he?

Watching the last of the townspeople depart, Hanson called in to the station and asked if any of the men had showed up in town or at their homes. Ten minutes later, he got his answer. All six of them were missing. Mrs. Withers had been tranquilized and put to bed by neighbors.

Hanson got in his car and drove along Route 28 until he reached the turn-off which would bring him as close as possible to the area where the caves were located. He didn't imagine that there'd been any trouble, but for his own peace of mind he wanted to know what was keeping them. Al Barton had been particularly anxious to look into those caverns. There was no real danger; they'd been thoroughly explored years ago and everyone knew that they didn't run very deep into the mountain.

The night was coming in very quickly. What was responsible for the disappearance of those youngsters? Hanson turned on his headlights and let his imagination run riot. An axe murderer on the loose, as in all those cheap, low-budget horror films, hacking up teenyboppers for dubious motives of revenge? Giant insects, like in some of his favorite old horror films, chomping on luckless campers and backpackers? He laughed, the sound of his own voice giving him reassurance. The woods sure were spooky at night.

If they were found in the caves, Hanson mused, more than likely they'd be caught in a state of disarray, the women naked, the boys an amusing blend of ruffled hair and hickies. He pictured them trapped in the spotlight, hurriedly pulling on panties and underwear, tugging shirts over chests, blouses over breasts. The thought of it pleased Hanson, excited him. He put his free hand on the bulge of his trousers, and thought of the naked girls again. Rubbing his crotch, he imagined all kinds of abandoned, erotic action. The sex had probably been so good they'd stayed out all night and done it over and over again during the day. They were fucking their lives away while everyone was out huntin' for 'em. The scamps. He laughed again and thought of Lucy, waiting for him. Hopefully. She was not a one-man woman and he confessed that was one thing he liked about her. He did not have marriage on his mind.

He parked his car at the side of the road, got out his flashlight—shit, it *was* dark—and started for the cave area half a mile away. He had to trudge through a small field of tall grass and razor-sharp reed-like vegetation until he came to a narrow stream which he crossed without wetting his sneakers, thanks to the many rocks jutting out conveniently from the water. The caves were just a few yards away; he could see them through the collection of sweet gum and rose-of-sharon gathered at the base of the mountain. He stepped through a patch of persimmon and flashed his light through the woods, hollering out the name of Sam Withers and several of the others who'd gone with him. There was no response, save for the fluttering and agitated hoot of an owl on a branch overhead.

Hanson advanced into the forest. Try as hard as he might to conjure up safe and amusing, *comforting* images, it was all he could do to try and muster enough confidence to keep from dashing out of the eerie woods altogether. Childhood fears sprang up like goose pimples. Then he heard strange sounds, familiar sounds, though he couldn't quite place them. They came from the direction of the caves. "Sam! Sam Withers!" he shouted. "Is that you?"

There was no answer. He hoped for a moment that the sounds might be approaching footsteps, but they were

174

like no footsteps he had ever heard before. *Pop Pop Pop Pop.* "Cut out the jokes, fellas," he cried, at the same time knowing without a doubt—although he couldn't say just why—that the "fellas" were not responsible, that now, in fact, there was nothing human in the woods with him at all. Yet there *was* something out there.

Using every ounce of stamina he possessed, he went in further until the yellow glare of his flashlight caught the outline of one of the entrances to the caves. "Sam!" he shouted out again, knowing there'd be no answer. The men must have dawdled along the way, taking their own sweet time, meandering on the trail that led around the base of the mountain back to the open picnic area. He wondered if he should set out on *that* path and try to catch up with them, but realized that if they were too far ahead of him, he might be stranded there at the camp grounds without a car. No, better to go back to the auto now, then have to walk all the way back to it from the picnic area.

Those noises again! *Pop Pop Pop Pop.* They were so weird, so intense, growing louder all the time. He was almost tempted to draw his gun. But what was there to shoot at, to defend himself against? He saw nothing in the beam of the flashlight. Nothing at all.

Until now.

What was that? He'd seen it out of the corner of his eye, darting out of the path of his light into the underbrush. Something big. A bear? No, a bear wouldn't move like that. It *must* have been an animal, though he had no idea what kind it was. There had been something almost reptilian about it. Yet, it hadn't been a reptile. Nothing like that. A snake? Too large. And not tall enough for a deer.

He thought of the way they'd found Jeffrey Braddon's body and his blood ran cold.

There was something unnatural going on, something he had no care to be part of. But he was a patrolman, an officer of the law, and he had no choice in the matter. He walked over to the spot where he'd seen the critter darting back into the covering brush. His light picked up the tops of the tall grass, the bushy overgrowth, the patchy bark of tree trunks, but nothing moved, nothing stirred. There was not a sound.

Then he heard something in back of him, scraping across the ground, slowly dogging his footsteps as it had been doing all along.

He turned, looked down and screamed. He had only a moment to shine the light on it, to see what it was, before it was upon him. His mind reeled and he refused to believe, not wanting to be part of a world that could spawn something as hideous as this. He became aware in his death throes that he was surrounded, that the whole woods was full of them, waiting, watching, starting at last to come closer. He let out a horrible shriek, blood running down his limbs, his body writhing in agony, and finally struggled no more.

They were approaching Jeffrey's house as it started to get really dark, as a cool breeze started whipping up the leaves in the trees and the night birds and crickets began to call. Harry said good night to David, accepting David's thanks for the lift. David stood in the road for a moment watching the car drive away, disappearing around a bend in the distance. He walked over to the front door and knocked. After a few seconds he heard footsteps in the hallway, the door opened, and Anna stood before him, smiling.

It was obvious that she had been crying. Her eyes were puffy, her nose red. She'd needed to be alone to let it all out, to get it out of her system. David hoped that she felt better—or had her tears only deepened her despair? He knew there was nothing that could erase the pain, the sense of loss, but he wanted to help her any way he could, wanted her to need him in some small way.

She needed him more than that, it seemed. Perhaps she'd felt the emptiness of the house the moment he'd stepped outside earlier in the day, and now she rushed to him and pulled him inside, and nestled in his arms and smothered him with kisses. David knew not from where this show of affection came, but it didn't really matter. He clung to her, grateful that she cared enough to show that she *did* care.

They said nothing for a while, until Anna led him over to the couch and they sat down beside each other. She broke the silence by asking him what he'd done all day. He surprised her when he told her what he'd been up to: bumping into Harry, running around, trying to solve the mystery of her brother's death. He could tell that Anna was touched, but she said: "I didn't mean for you to get involved with all of this. I appreciate what you and Mr. London are doing, but it isn't necessary."

"We think it is. Remember, I may not have known your brother, but he was one of Harry's closest friends. He's not just doing it for you."

She sighed and rubbed her eyes. "I guess not. I suppose I should be glad that somebody cares—cares enough . . ." She leaned her head against David's chest and continued. "It's just that I didn't plan for you to get personally involved with my brother's death. It's not your concern, that's all. I have no right to intrude in your life this way, to make my problems your problems. You probably have enough worries without bothering with this, too. I can't thank you enough for coming up here with me. I don't know what I would have done. I'm sorry you had to stay out all afternoon. It's just that . . ."

"I understand."

"I was afraid you'd just be bored and depressed by my mood. I'm not much fun to be with now."

"You don't have to be 'fun' all the time. You're a normal person with normal feelings, and I've very fond of you. Whether you're 'fun' or not."

She smiled and looked up into his eyes as his head leaned down over hers. She looked down again, studying her hands. "There's nothing here to tell me much about my brother. I was hoping to get to know him a little by going through his things. Didn't find out much. He read *People* and *Popular Mechanics*. Watched TV a lot. Had this *TV Guide* with all the programs circled. Kept all the newspapers in a pile down in the cellar. You should see the cellar. A lot of junk that was probably here when he moved in. Don't know what I'll do with it. There's nothing I especially want to keep. Nothing to help me remember him. Nothing . . ."

She began to cry again, weeping unabashedly into David's shirt, grabbing his collar with one of her hands. She kept apologizing, although it was unnecessary. Finally she forced herself up, and said: "Let's get out of here, David. I made reservations at a motel about three miles away. I don't want to stay here any longer."

They locked the place up and went over to the car. David offered to drive, but she said no. He was glad. They drove to the motel in silence.

While Anna and David checked into the Milbourne Motel as Mr. and Mrs. Braddon, Police Chief Walters was finally accepting the fact that he was hopelessly and incontrovertibly lost. He had gone down into the great hole in the floor of the Forester Building hours ago, climbing down the collapsible ladder, touching down on the soft earth under the cellar. He told himself over and over again that he was a fool, that he should never have gone alone, that his strange compulsion to test his manhood had driven him into an act which made him seem more child than man. But he had been so sure that he'd be able to find his way back, so determined to get to the

178

end of the tunnel branching out to the far right at the end of the cavern where they'd found Jeffrey's body, that he'd failed to take precautions any nitwit would have. He'd stupidly left the rope on the floor of the Forester Building, but had blundered on compulsively anyway, positive that he'd not lose track of where he had come from. At one point he tripped and broke the lantern, leaving just the flashlight to light up the way. And the backpack, hot and heavy on his shoulders, was more irritant than blessing.

What was he doing down here, while his men were out searching for four of the town's missing citizens? He should have been up there with them, running the show, giving the orders, charging ahead. Sure, he was being too hard on himself; after all, the kids hadn't even been missing twenty-four hours yet. But he still couldn't shake the feeling that he was shirking his duty, ignoring his responsibility in the face of the town's only "crisis" in years.

But he had to see this through. Had to find out, once and for all, what was down here. Had to discover for himself the uncanny instrument of Jeff Braddon's horrible demise.

What had been *at* the man?

Walters had gone straight to the spot where they'd found the corpse, then quickly chosen the tunnel nearest the right wall of the cavern. There was no doubt that this was a natural underground chamber, and that the tunnels, too, had existed for possible eons. The funny thing was, something had destroyed whatever wall or barrier might have existed between the Forester Building's sub-cellar and the cave without. There was even something funny about the condition of the dirt, so crumbly and squishy in his fingers, as though it had been loosened and moistened by a thousand tiny earthworms. He had noticed an outcropping from either side of the cavern that neither he nor Harry had noticed before.

The edges of the outcropping were torn and jagged as if they were simply the ends of a wall that had somehow been breached by whatever had crawled out from under the Forester Building. He surmised that the break had occurred fairly recently.

He also believed that Harry and he had been wrong in their initial estimate as to the location of the cavern, as well as its depth. He couldn't be sure without instruments, of course, but it seemed as if it sloped down and curved towards the left, taking it deeper beneath the foundations of the buildings above than he'd first imagined it to be. The leftward swing also indicated that he was no longer beneath Main Street, explaining why this section, at least, had never been discovered when the buildings had been erected so many years ago. It was not really located underneath the town.

No more stalling; he had finally decided to enter the forbidding tunnel and bravely stepped inside, having to stoop down so that his head would not scrape against the natural ceiling above. Odd—the very walls seemed to glisten in the glow from the flashlight he carried. He touched them and pulled back. His fingers were coated with a slimy gray substance that had been smeared, as it turned out, all around the entire circumference of the tunnel—walls, floor and ceiling. The sticky stuff felt oily and thick and disgusting. He wiped his fingers on his trousers.

He continued along his way, wondering if his were the first human eyes to set sight upon these walls, the first person to walk within this space. Things seemed to be closing in on him, but he shrugged it off, determined not to let his claustrophobia get the better of him. He had it under control, he told himself; he always had it under control. *Don't let your mild neurosis inhibit you now. Get on with it.*

He walked faster. Still the space seemed to get smaller, tighter, and he wondered if it *had* been in his mind. He reached out. No—the walls *were* closer, there was no doubt of it now. Again he rubbed his greasy fingers on his pants, wondering what kind of slimy creatures passed through here while the township slept. Had Jeffrey taken a peek in here? Had he seen too much and paid the ultimate price for his fatal curiosity? The Chief stopped, then closed his eyes tightly, and summoned up a reserve of strength. He would not think like that. Not here. Not now. He had a job to do. No one else could have been sent in his place, he knew that now. Let them brush through the overgrowth with sticks, searching for four wayward children; the real work, the *man's* work was being done down here.

Then the Chief started seeing things.

Lights at first. Little dots in front of his eyes which he assumed were strictly imaginary, special effects playing off his retinas. Optical illusions. He started—he thought he'd seen a figure in the passage way before him. Then it was gone. No, it too had been an illusion. In a place like this even a sane man could start seeing things that weren't there. He shivered; his mother had always told him he had too active an imagination. It would get him into trouble someday.

And here he was.

The first tunnel had branched out into other tunnels and he'd lost track of how many forks he'd chosen, and before long he'd had no idea where he was. There was nothing familiar, no wonderful landmarks, in any direction. He was lost, lost, lost.

Just as he was about to give up hope, the tunnel he was in broke through into a cavern even larger than the one he'd entered from originally. The odor, which he had gotten used to easily enough before, was stronger than ever. He shone the light up and down, trying to determine exactly how big the place was. A few bats scurried away from the light, flying into sinkholes overhead. Stalactites hung down from the ceiling, and their sisters, stalagmites, pierced upwards from the floor. He saw a lot of multi-colored speleotherms, rock formations frozen in strange and twisted shapes. Spiraling cylindrical helictites grew out of the walls, and murky brown fungi covered the stone drapery hanging from the ceiling. Insects, large spiders with pallid skin, and darting lizards hurried away from his feet into a multitude of holes, pockets and crevices in the walls.

The place had an eerie, ancient look to it, as if it had not been disturbed by a human presence for centuries, as if, in fact, it had not been distrubed by anything save the bats and lizards and bugs throughout history.

But there *was* something else in there with him besides the bats and lizards and bugs. Whatever they were, they had formed an uneasy alliance with the winged creatures nesting above and the insects and others below, as if the bats and spiders tolerated the presence of the enemy because they had no other home and were too weak to evict the invaders, and the invaders tolerated the presence of the spiders and lizards because they used them and the bats for their food supply.

Until now.

First they had eaten each other, feasting on siblings and spouses alike, working their way out from the enclosure, boring and squirming slowly through the many rocks and crevices. They found the cavern at last, and squeezed through the different tunnels, and swarmed out into this, their final home. Then they'd found the bats and insects and consumed them. They lived on next to nothing. One bat was enough for many days. Then one day a few of them had come upon the man, the man who'd fallen down into the area where first they had been kept. (At one point they had crawled up into the building next door, through the floorboards, but the vibrations they had heard had frightened them, disturbed them, so they had gone no further. They had not found anything to eat there anyway.) The man, however, was food. Fine, delicious food. They had subdued him, and taken a quick taste, but that was all. They were too close to the vibrations, so had left some of the delicious food behind. Had they not been so wary and so disoriented, they might have taken the rest with them.

The ones in the cave had also been food. And the ones in the woods. Finally they had ventured out of their dwelling place, had found that in the darkness they could hide and make their way about unseen, though they had never gone far from the caves. The food had come to them. Now it was time, yes nearly time, for them to go to the food.

But not just yet. For they sensed that more food had somehow found its way into their dwelling place.

They waited for the food to come closer. . .

Aiming his flashlight towards the right of the cavern, Walters found to his surprise that it illuminated a rather large body of water—an underground lake. He felt like a primordial man coming upon a stagnant prehistoric sea, a dead sea full of seaweed and the skeletons of Mesozoic creatures. He expected to see giant fish bones sticking out of the water. He stepped closer, ignoring the shrill cries of the bats circling up above, concentrating on the lake before him. Yes, it was huge. Absolutely huge. It stretched out towards the back of the cavern, becoming narrower as it turned into a stream which had run through the earth for God only knows how long, before coming to rest in this monstrous pool near his feet.

The light was reflected by the water, chasing away some of the surrounding shadows. The Chief looked around and saw piles of bones, hundreds of them. Animal bones. And a few that looked . . . human.

Jeffrey, he thought. And then he turned his head back to the underground sea because he sensed movement. Yes, something was rippling the surface of the water, just beneath the tiny bubbles that were rising to burst upon the air. Yes, he could see something. He could see . . .

Oh my God!

The lake . . . the lake was literally alive with hundreds of—there was only one way his mind could describe them—*things,* horrible man-sized *things* with eyes, bright, flashing eyes. And each pair of eyes was focused on him!

The water parted and the things came out. Chief Walters bolted, screaming and running through the pile of ghastly bones, stepping on bits of cartilage, shattering and cracking the pieces beneath his heavy feet. He stumbled and fell to the ground, felt the sharp pain of something jagged caught under his leg. He tried to get up, but couldn't.

These creatures were hungry; some had not been fed in weeks.

Joseph Walters closed his eyes, for he could look no longer. He felt the stabbing pains as needle-like appendages were thrust brutally into his body. Felt his blood dripping out, draining away. Felt teeth—huge, grinding jaws—ripping away chunks of flesh, biting all the way down to the bone. Heard the horrible eating, swallowing noises of the creatures as they consumed him. Heard the soft roar in his ears as death approached, the rush of blood hurtling towards the gaping wounds in his body. He felt the rendering tear of muscle, the popping and wrenching of sinew and bone. Blood was lapped. Cartilage sucked. Flash gnawed away.

Calm and satiated after their gorging frenzy, the wave of hungry creatures subsided. The lake bubbled briefly as they returned to the water; bubbled, billowed and at last settled down.

All was still.

Chapter Nine

The Milbourne Motel was not exactly the lap of luxury, but it would have to do. David felt at home here; he suspected he would feel at home anywhere as long as Anna was with him. He had gotten used to Anna. That was it. He knew it seemed ridiculous—after all, how long had they known each other? A couple of days? They'd spent one night together, then a few hours one evening after that, and all day today. Yet he had seen her in her most vulnerable state, and therefore understood her better. Not only had they been "intimate," but they'd been *personal*, probably the more important of the two. He had tried, in his way, to share her pain.

True, that had not yet come about in reverse. Anna had not yet had a chance to see him vulnerable, to feel his need for her. Or could she sense his loneliness, his desperate need for companionship, his need for love of a certain kind? Did she think he was merely starstruck, or *so* desperate that anyone would do? Did *she* feel the same closeness that he did? Some day he would find out. He had to. He was getting in too deeply. He lay on the bed wrapped in a towel, and waited for her to come out of the shower.

Anna's thoughts were similar as she washed away the dirt and tears of the afternoon, the grime of this most depressing of days. Yet in some ways it had been a happy day, too. Because of David. Because David was there. Not because he was a man, coming to the rescue of a damsel in distress, but because he *was* David, someone she liked and trusted, and maybe—though she told herself again that it was much too soon—even loved a little.

She wanted to make love to him now, and refused to let thoughts of her brother interfere. It would be no crime against Jeffrey to share this man she cared about, knew so little of, this evening. She knew her desire for him, on the carnal level at least, came not just out of a need to be comforted and held, although she needed that, too. No, she felt pure lust for him as, she was sure, he felt for her. They had both enjoyed it that first time. The second time would be even better.

She cried again in the shower, thinking of the beautiful things in life her brother would never feel or hear again, assuming he had ever had a chance to. How deep had his relationship with Paula Widdoes been? Ah yes, it was *she* Anna really cried for. The one left behind, the one suddenly left with nothing to do, no one to turn to in that special way that everyone needed.

She turned off the water, got out of the stall, and toweled herself dry, checking her face in the misty-white mirror. She rubbed it with the palm of her hand. Were her eyes too bloodshot, too puffy? She would have laughed at her vanity, only it was no joking matter for a woman in her profession. Ever the model, checking for the first wrinkle, the first dreaded sign of a cold sore or pimple. The ugly lines of fatigue. Those were her greatest enemies. She could not turn it off, this compulsion to always check her beauty, to make sure it was still there. How she wished at times that she could be like other women, without this fear of growing older, of growing *old*, this lack of purpose, this gap in her sense of self-worth. Was it too late for her to break out of the chain of oppression, the rigid cocoon she'd been imprisoned in? She'd been taught for so many years to be a "lady," to be feminine and proper and subservient, to dress and walk and eat properly, to subordinate herself to a man, any man. Yet, she was not really like that. Not any longer, if she ever had been. She was not subservient to Derek. But Derek was not faithful so there was no need to be. She was so confused, pulled apart by conflicting mores and patterns and social beliefs.

Derek was on the way out of her life—or rather she was on the way out of his. She would have to be the one to pack up and leave, as Derek had lived in that townhouse long before he'd even met her, and she had no desire to stay there and live with old memories, especially since most of them would be unpleasant. She could probably get the house away from him if she tried, but who wanted it? So she was more or less free to pursue her relationship with David Hammond. Or was that the wrong move, a mere flight from independence, a rush to find some other form of masculine security? He seemed to be developing an intense feeling for her—it radiated out of him—or was it merely sexual attraction, a desire to fondle and touch and kiss an object that was held up to the world as a personification of female beauty? Did he see *her*, really see her for what she was, and did he like what he saw? Were his feelings as intense as hers obviously were? Maybe all his concern, his compassion, was just a reaction to her grief over Jeffrey—a natural softness and caring even strangers give to those who are in emotional or physical pain. But that had nothing to do with love, more with "Christian charity." Was that all it was? Oh, how she wished she knew.

She stepped outside of the bathroom, her towel wrapped around her, and saw him smiling at her from the bed. He did not pat the mattress, the space next to him, in that friendly but vulgar manner like so many men did. He just smiled and waited for her to come over to him. When she sat on the bed, he asked her if her shower had been nice. She answered the question as if his words had been profound, sighing yes in a low, clear voice, bending over to place her mouth gently above his. His lips pushed upwards, pursing to meet hers. The tips of their mouths touched gracefully, then blended together, their mouths suddenly opening wide, all lips and tongues and moans of pleasure. David's arms went around her body, pulling her in close to him, enveloping her in a luxurious warmth and sexuality. She responded, wrapping her arms around him, pulling him over, all the way over, on top of her. She squirmed out of her towel, pushed him up momentarily so that she could pull it free and fling it across the room. David's hands went out to the lamp on the night table by the bed. He extinguished it, then removed his own towel. He was stiff and ready, wanting her to feel how much he loved her, feeling definite lust without apology, but something *more* also, something that could not be spoken or communicated in any other way but this.

They seemed to melt into each other, the lights from the window speckling their bodies, creating a white-and-black pattern over the bed, a painted backdrop for their passion. He entered her and she cried out with joy. Her fingers scraped his back, grabbed the edge of the sheet. He covered her lips and face and neck and eyes with gentle kisses. His head went back and he moaned softly.

Her fingers found his face and she drew him in for a lingering kiss that seemed to last for the remainder of their night together.

Back in the Hall of Records—a pretentious designation if ever there were one, as it was only a small, cluttered room—Harry poured over various forms and leaflets, looking for further information on Hank Danielson and the Barrows Corporation. Miss Elden, the mousy creature who was mistress of the record room, waited impatiently at her desk in the corner. It was five minutes to five and she was anxious to get home, shove a TV dinner in the oven, and watch the news while whatever it was in the package baked until ready. Under normal conditions her disposition was nice enough. Now it was strained and irritable.

"Have you found what you're looking for yet, Mr. London? It's almost closing time," she reminded him.

"Uh, yes. Yes. Almost there," he replied. "Just give me a moment more, please. Just a moment more."

He had found the floor plans of the Forester Building, an old tattered copy that had been lying in back of a drawer since the year one. Each floor had been outlined and built to specification. The Corporation had apparently not made any changes in the design. No new rooms or partitions. No walls knocked down. All that had to be explained was that big hole in the northeast corner.

Chief Walters had said that as far as he knew the hole had not been there when the building had been shut down a few months before. Yet, Harry had always wondered why they'd shuttered a perfectly good building, especially when there'd been civic groups and the like clamoring for office space and meeting halls. It didn't make sense—even Walters admitted that. Harry recalled someone on the town council mentioning something about "structural weaknesses"; who had it been? It had happened so long ago; no one had paid that much attention, too concerned at that particular meeting with zoning laws and property taxes and other things of larger concern. Whatever, it indicated that the damage to the building might well have happened before it had been closed down; in fact, might have made it imperative to close it down in the first place. Why had no one been honest about it? He could understand the town not wanting to pay good money to fix the old place up when there were better ways to use the cash. But why all the secrecy? Who'd been bought off to hush the whole thing up? (For that matter, why was there such a hush-hush atmosphere surrounding Jeffrey's autopsy?) He shrugged; there he was—imagining conspiracies and counterplots. He read too many paperback thrillers, that was what was wrong with him.

"Are you about *through*, Mr. London?" came the nasal voice again from the other end of the room.

"Look, might I borrow this for a few days?" He indicated a pile of papers on the table beside him. "And these other documents?"

Miss Elden looked as though he had expressed an intention to set fire to the record room. "Borrow?" she said in disbelief. "No one *borrows* material from the Hall of Records, Mr. London. This is not a library." She let out with an involuntary chuckle, as if he were a child who'd committed a ridiculous but charming faux pas.

"Can't you make exceptions, Miss Elden? This is rather important.'

She started to approach the table, tugging on the edges of her sweater, which she'd placed over her shoulders without pulling her arms through the sleeves. She was so hunched over from the chill in the room it was unlikely the sweater would fall off. "Just what *are* you looking for, Mr. London?"

Harry was in no mood to be cross-examined. Like every worm, Miss Elden had turned. The sweet, quiet mouse apparently changed into a tiger every night at five o'clock. "I'd like to go home," she snapped in response to his silence. He had turned away from watching her advance, and was again studying the floor plans. "What *is* it you're looking for?" she bristled.

Oh, hell—maybe if he took her into his confidence she'd let him stay a little longer. Out in the hall the janitor was moving about, shutting off lights and checking doors. "Look," he said in a conspiratorial tone. He motioned for her to bend down so she could study the document on the table. "*This* one is the floor plan to the

190

basement of the Forester Building. Notice anything unusual?"

She peered intently, studying the diagram. Her eyeshadow stood out garishly on her face. "Nothing," she said. "What's so strange about this?"

He pointed to a spot designating a staircase. "See the arrows. One marked UP, one marked D W N—for down?"

She looked at him as if he had stated the more-than-obvious.

"So it's a staircase. What about it?"

He stood up with a smug look on his face. He always liked knowing more than librarians, and although Miss Elden, as she had pointed out earlier, was not a librarian, she was the closest thing to it in town. "Why would a basement need stairs going *down?*"

"Hmm. I see what you mean." She scratched her nose with a fingertip. The nail was cracked.

"It wouldn't. Unless there was a *sub*-basement. *Voila!*" He slipped another unwieldy piece of paper out from under the one they'd been persuing. "The floor plan for the *sub*-basement. Which, for some reason, was never built. Or should I say, never finished. It was dug out, all right, as I saw for myself the other day. But the walls, the stairs, were never constructed."

Miss Elden was not impressed. "Why didn't you just say that? You could have just showed me the second floor plan. Why did I have to look over the first one and play guessing games with you?" She didn't give him a chance to answer. "This is all very interesting, Mr. London, but it's five past five and I'd like to get home before midnight this evening."

Harry loved having people's undivided attention, something which Miss Elden no longer intended to give him. He sighed, and began to roll up the diagrams. "I do wish I could take these other papers with me, study them overnight."

191

"Now Mr. London," she said, walking towards the coat rack by the door. "Would you want me to get into trouble? Tomorrow is soon enough for all that, I'm sure."

He began putting the material back in the drawer from which it had come. "Why do you suppose they failed to complete the sub-basement?"

"I don't know," the woman replied wearily. "Maybe they just changed their minds. Maybe they decided they didn't need it. Or ran out of money. Does it make that much difference, Mr. London?"

"No. No, I suppose not. Uh, I don't mean to keep you waiting, but it will take a while for me to put all these things back."

"Just leave them in the cardboard box on the table," she said. "I'll put them away in the morning. Or better yet, I'll set them aside for you so there won't be all that fuss and bother getting them out again tomorrow."

He did as she had instructed. "Thank you very much, Miss Elden." He walked out of the room with a jaunty step, and nodded good night. Behind him he heard her flicking out the light and locking up. Out in the street, the town was quiet, the air still. He didn't know if it was the weather giving him the sudden chills, or something else lodged in his subconscious that he could neither explain or, for the moment, understand.

He went into the very next building, the police station. He would tell Walters what he had discovered, although —as Miss Elden had so charmingly suggested—it seemed without significance. At least he knew that the "cavern" under the Forester Building had been man-made, with a purpose in mind. It did not explain why it stretched out far away from the building, nor why it even extended slightly under the foundation of his own hardware store. Something had widened the basement far beyond its original dimensions, but he could not imagine what.

Joe Walters was not in the sub-station, and Cecelia told Harry that Hanson was out and Stevens was taking a nap in the back. He left and decided to go home and take a nap of his own; he was awfully fatigued—all that running around today, he supposed.

He made himself a small supper, watched TV for an hour, and fell fast asleep in his easy chair. When he woke it was nearly ten o'clock.

He felt like driving back to the police station, having a chat with Joe. Besides, he had a sudden craving for a milkshake in the diner. Felt like some company, too. He missed Jeffrey. Ordinarily he would have called him up, invited him out for a beer. But now . . . it sure was lonely. He would have gone to see Paula, but he knew she had to work things out by herself eventually and she might as well start now.

There was little activity in the police station, as was usually the case, although a knot of tension seemed to run through the air, invisibly binding Stevens, standing nervously by a table in the corner, with Cecelia, still behind the switchboard, doing overtime. The woman nearly lived there. Stevens' face was anxious, as if he were waiting for someone or other to walk in or call on the radio.

"Anything wrong?" Harry asked.

"Sure is," Stevens replied. He looked pale and sheepish, as if he'd doomed the town by oversleeping. "Hanson has disappeared. Can't get him on the radio. He called in hours ago and said he was headin' for the old caves to see if he could find a search party that hadn't reported back yet. He should have come back by now." He then told Harry who the missing men were.

"I wouldn't worry," Harry said. He knew both patrolmen well, knew Hanson could take care of himself. "Probably having the time of his life rollin' those old boys back home. Each of 'em must have polished off a six-pack or two. They'll have their heads handed to 'em when their wives get hold of 'em."

"Probably," Stevens said, offering a weak smile. "Their wives, and the parents of those kids, keep calling up, too. Nothing we can do. Too damn dark to search anymore."

"Still haven't come home?" Harry asked.

"Not hide nor hair of 'em out there," Stevens replied. "And now I don't even know what Chief Walters is doin'. Don't know why he's sticking his nose underground when things are hoppin' up here."

"Where did Joe go?" Harry queried, sitting down on the nearest desktop.

"Down into the hole in the Forester Building. Said he wanted to investigate it some more. That was a hell of a long time ago. He set out of here like a bear on fire headin' for water. Don't know why he had to go runnin' off like that. Something seemed to be on his mind."

"He went down alone?"

"He told me to stay in the office in case something came up. Said somebody's gotta be here. With Hanson up and gone that someone's gotta be me."

"How long has Joe been gone?"

"A few hours. Right, Cecelia?" The lady nodded in agreement. She kept trying to raise Hanson on the radio without success.

"Hell. I don't know whether I should go down after the Chief or ride out and see what happened to Hanson. To make matters worse, there was a big explosion over in Boonton. They got the state police, the county sheriff, the Jactaw police pickin' up the pieces. Literally. They can't spare a single man until tomorrow. They said half the cops are out huntin' down an arsonist."

"Oh boy." Harry felt very afraid all of a sudden, frightened for himself and all of them. He was bothered by the fact that Walters had gone down there, where they'd found the body—alone—and had not come back yet. He made a hasty decision.

"Hank." He placed his hand on the young man's shoulder. "Go over to the diner and round up a few fellows. Bud. Charlie. They're all over there now, I bet. Take them out to the woods just to see what's up. Hell, at least a couple of them can go with you. They got nothing better to do. While you're out looking for Hanson, I'm going after the Chief."

"Wait a minute, Mr. London. If the Chief went down there—armed—and hasn't come back after all this time, do you think it's wise for you to go down there by yourself?"

"Lend me a gun then."

"Better than that. I'll go with you."

"Hank, someone's gotta keep those old-timers in line. Besides, you might have to give Hanson some help if you find him."

The boy bit his lip with indecision, wondering what to do. The kid hadn't even had this job that long. Harry knew what he was thinking: *What would the chief want me to do? Go with a gang of old sots after another member of the department? Or go look for him?*

Harry could tell that Hank was troubled at the idea of sending another "old man" down alone into an abyss that might have already trapped one person, as well as claimed the life of Jeffrey Braddon. "You stay here, Harry," the patrolman said. "You're trustworthy. Something's happened to Chief Walters and I've got to find out what. No need for you to get involved."

"Remember your own words, son," Harry reminded him. "The Chief had a gun. Didn't do him any good, if the worst has happened. Let me go with you. Cecelia can hold down the fort." Though with that explosion in Boonton, it was unlikely the woman would be able to call for help if an emergency arose.

"That's right, Hank," the dispatcher said, putting on a brave front.

"All right, Harry," Hank said. "You can come with

195

me." He grabbed two rifles from the supply closet, shouting over his shoulder, "Know how to use one of these?"

"Yes, I know how to use one of those."

"Just in case," Hank said grimly.

"Just in case."

Harry waited at the entrance of the Forester Building while Stevens organized a bunch of civilian "deputies" at the diner and sent them out to the caves at Hunter's Mountain. Hank arrived fifteen minutes later, his face tense with worry.

Each of them, in their own way, had faced more clearly dangerous and frightening situations than the one awaiting them below; or so they thought. Harry had been in combat during the Korean War. Hank had disarmed a liquor-besotted townsman who had been threatening to murder his cowering wife and children. They did not know if anything, aside from rats and bats, was down there to give them the slightest alarm.

But Jeffrey Braddon *had* died.

And Joe Walters *was* missing.

And both Hank Stevens and Harry London were more afraid than they'd care to admit.

David didn't know what had awakened him, but suddenly his eyes were open and he was rubbing them, trying to adjust to the darkness, trying to clear his head. He felt Anna's soft body lying next to his, her long hair spilling onto the pillow, his chest, the blanket. He bent down and touched her forehead lightly with his lips. He felt very glad to be alive.

This is the scene, he thought, where the lover wakes up all contemplative and anxious for a cigarette. Only he didn't feel like smoking so he was stuck with contemplation. He was still too tired to think in lucid sentences; he simply lay back and let the images and thoughts float through his head, bits and pieces of memory here, fragments of conversation there, pictures of the past. He let the remembrances wash over him: their lovemaking; her warmth, her tears; the lonely house where her brother had lived; the deserted shack at the outskirts of town where the old man should have been, but wasn't; the restaurant, coffee with Harry. Everything came rushing, rushing through him, without chronology or focus. The pictures and thoughts turned around in midstream, in mid-sentence, jumbling together in strange patterns. Everything seemed distant, yet intense. He reached down and touched the top of his sex, longing for her in that way once again.

He was becoming sleepy again, drifting off slowly, listening to the sounds of her breathing, when he was jarred awake by the telephone. He tried to reach it before the ringing disturbed Anna's sleep—luckily the phone was on the night table by his side of the bed—but he could hear her stirring under the sheets, sighing in that perplexed manner that the half-awake have. His fingers found, caught, the receiver. As he lifted it to his ear and the ringing stopped, he saw the luminous dial of the wristwatch he had taken off and left on the night table. Two a.m. Who was calling at this hour? Who knew they were here?

"Hello?" he said.

"Hello. David, is that you?"

"Yes."

"Thank Goodness. I was hoping you'd stayed the night. Luckily this is the only motel in town."

David knew who it was before the man confirmed it: Harry London. There was a strange quality to his voice. He was gasping out his sentences, speaking abnormally fast.

"Are you out of breath?"

Harry didn't answer, but said, "Listen. I found something . . . something under the building. I know what killed Jeffrey. You must come. I've been calling everyone and no one will believe me. We need more men."

David struggled to clear his head, to understand what the man was raving about. And he *was* raving, of that there was no doubt. There was a manic, almost hysterical edge to his voice; it had climbed to the upper register, a pitch of panicky fear, as if London were on the verge of losing his mind and were fighting desperately for his sanity.

"What are you talking about?" David asked. Had the man gone crazy? It was two a.m.! Was he drunk?

"They got Officer Stevens. Killed him. Hanson's disappeared. And the Police Chief is gone. *Will you come?*" He almost screamed the last few words. David was sure that Anna, struggling under the blankets at the rim of consciousness, could have heard it where she was.

"Come *where?* You said you knew what killed Jeffrey. Can you tell me?" It was hopeless. The even-tempered Mr. London had turned into a lunatic within the space of several hours. He simply would not answer the questions put to him.

"You won't believe," London cried. "You must see. See with your own eyes. WE NEED MORE MEN!"

David wasn't used to having veritable strangers talk to him that way, not at this hour, not without proper explanation. Helplessly he said: "Listen. Would you care to talk to Anna about all this? I don't know what—"

"No! Someone must help me destroy them! You must come! *Will you come?*"

The man sounded as if he were about to split a blood vessel. To placate him, David said, "Yes, I'll come."

"Good. Hurry. You must hurry."

And then the line went dead.

"The fool!" David said aloud. "He hung up!" London had pleaded with him "to come," but had neglected to tell him *where* he was supposed to go! The idiot! It was just as well, David thought, as he replaced the receiver. He had no desire to crawl out of bed in the middle of the night only to put himself at the mercy of a man who—for some reason—was out of his head. Lord only knows what London, in his condition, might have done to him. It was nice and warm and comfortable here in bed with Anna beside him. She was half-awake now. "Who was that?" she murmured. Should he tell her? No, she'd only be upset for nothing. There was nothing they could do now. David told her to go back to sleep, and cuddled up beside her.

The urgency in the man's voice came back to haunt him. London had seemed like a nice, quiet, rational man. What could have affected him so but something of major importance? He must have found out *something*. David couldn't simply shrug this off. For Anna's sake, he had to see it through. He sat up again, wondering what to do.

Could the man have meant for him to come to his home? That could be it. Or the Forester Building? Perhaps his hardware store. David picked up the phone again and asked for the operator. "Can I help you?" a woman's voice replied. David asked to be connected to Harry London's place of residence. No, he did not know the address. A few moments later the line was ringing. There was no answer. David then tried the number of London's store. Again there was no answer.

He wrestled with his conscience, wondering if he should wake Anna and ask her what to do. He was not about to wander around the town at this time of night looking high and low for Harry London. Perhaps the man would realize his omission and call him back. Yes, of course. When David didn't show, London would call again.

The phone call and its implications kept nagging at him while he tried to get back to sleep. Anna stirred and he kissed her. His arms about her, he felt wearier and wearier. Sleep was only seconds away.

But the memory of London's voice troubled him to the last.

The Main Street Diner, open twenty-four hours, had always been a gold mine. Just as the footsteps of the giggling kids and late-night revelers faded away down the steps, the dawn would break and in would walk the truckers and farmers. Harry London hung up the phone in the booth in back, and rubbed his forehead with two pinching fingertips. He leaned back and relived the experience of the past few hours, and wondered if somehow the world had gone crazy.

He and Stevens had gone down there, down into that hell-hole, down into the sub-basement. Through the cavern, into one of the tunnels. Like Chief Walters before them, they'd even found that ghastly living pool.

Harry was shivering so badly from the memory of it all that he was hardly able to stand. The waitress on duty, a middle-aged redhead named Sarah, saw him stagger out of the phone booth and stumble to the nearest counter seat. "Are you all right, Harry?" she asked. He threw her a reassuring look and asked for a cup of coffee. While he drank, he reviewed the evening's terrible occurrences.

First he had gone to the police station. He had been so incoherent, had been stuttering so badly, that Cecilia had taken one look at him and practically ordered him home and into bed. He had tried to make her understand, but it had been a losing battle. She had told him that none of the men sent to look for Patrolmen Hanson had come back, so she'd already called the State Police again. Only they were still so busy with the Boonton explosion and its after-effects that it would be some time before anyone would be free to come to Milbourne. She'd been worried, plenty worried, but she'd not been able to make head or tail out of what he was yammering about. "Go home. Go home and wait," she'd said. She'd asked again and again what happened to Hank and the Chief, but Harry just wasn't able to get the words out. He ran out of there with her hollering after him, telling him to come back, to give her some news of the man she'd worked with for nearly seventeen years.

Harry had run through the empty streets, trying to calm himself down, to stop his teeth, his tongue, his lips from quivering, his arms and legs and knees from shaking. He had stood in front of Cecelia blabbering away, realizing that she hadn't been able to understand one word—not one word—of what he was saying. *God— make the shaking stop. Why can't I stop shaking?* he had thought. Did it have something to do with the puncture wound in his leg? The whole limb was throbbing from the knee to the ankle. He'd been injured and he could feel an alien substance spreading like cancer through his veins.

He ran to his store, but realized with a shock that his key ring had fallen out of his pocket sometime during the night, that there was no way he could get inside short of shattering a window. He had calls to make, important calls. He needed silence, privacy, to make them, to compose himself. Cecelia would not have let him near the phone, let alone given him the peace and quiet he needed to think straight, to put his thoughts in order. He had to get inside, get to a phone. He thought of running to his car, driving home, but even if he had been in any condition to drive—and he wasn't—both door keys and ignition keys were now lost below the earth.

He ran around in circles on the sidewalk in front of his store. Had anyone seen him they would have thought him drunk or bereft of his senses, and they would not have been entirely wrong. He dashed around, whining like an animal, wishing he could think clearly, talk lucidly, know instinctively just what to do. God—he had a raging fever. Again he thought that the injury he'd sustained must have been responsible.

He could not wait, the town itself could not wait for the State Police to arrive. They were going to be tied up for hours, might be stuck there at the scene of the explosion all night, as Stevens had said. Even if he had successfully communicated the danger, the incredible circumstances, to Cecelia, no one would have believed him. Not Cecelia, not the Police. Who could he call? He tried as hard as possible to organize his thoughts, to shut out the horrid sounds and grisly sights he had seen beneath the ground. Dwelling on what he'd seen—even for an instant—would surely drive him into madness. Already he was on the edge, gibbering away like a gibbon, his speech a mindless babble.

Something had to be done. Something had to be done *now*.

Only one place in town was open at that hour. The restaurant. He ran to the diner, nearly falling to the ground in his haste, and dashed inside the comforting lighted interior. He could not stand to think of the dark, let alone be in it. Bright lights, like these—that's what he needed. It was a slow night at the diner, and much to his dismay the few patrons inside looked too young, too tired or too drunk to be of service. He ignored the waitress and stormed into the telephones in back. Tugging out what little change had not already fallen from his pocket, he started calling people, strong, reliable people. Those who lived nearby, who could and would help him.

He had a great deal of difficulty making himself understood. But by that time he had at least calmed down enough to be able to make his words reasonably intelligible. A couple of men were very old friends, and were worried about the state he was in. They promised to come posthaste. One of these was Bill Spooner, who owned the gas station. Ignoring Bill's protestations—Bill didn't think Harry sounded capable of speaking, let alone walking—London insisted that he meet him at the station. He told the other men he called to meet him there, too, although most of them thought he was drunk or nuts or playing a practical joke they wanted no part of at that hour in the morning. He didn't call the parents of the missing teenagers. He was sure the youngsters were dead, and he simply could not bring himself to tell their families. Not now, certainly. He called David Hammond as a last resort.

The sound of Sarah's voice interrupted his ruminations. "I think you oughta get on home and sleep it off," she smiled, giving him a wink. "I think you were out with your friends tonight, eh?"

His friends? Would they come? He didn't even want to think about doing what needed to be done by *himself*. He drained his coffee cup and left a dollar bill on the counter. He pulled himself off the stool, rising to his feet with stops and starts until he stood as straight as he could manage.

"*Harry,*" Sarah scolded. "Are you all right? Want me to call a doctor?"

Harry ignored her and hobbled to the door, stepping out hastily into the night. The waitress saw him run down the street towards the gas station as if the hounds of hell were nipping at his heels. "Drink sure makes some people spry," she said, then went back to cleaning the counter.

Harry stood in the chilly air waiting for the men to gather, wondering if any of them had taken his garbled pleas seriously. He was counting on years of friendship and mutual respect to pull him through. How would he get them *down* there, he thought, once they got here, if they got here? How would he ever convince them to follow him back to that fetid underground, that horrible pool? What would he say to them?

He stood there by the pumps, the seeds of the plan that had grown in his mind while on the telephone sprouting out now into something that, to his fevered mind at least, made perfect sense. He tried to keep his mind off the past few hours. He tried not to think of him and young Stevens wandering for what seemed like days through tunnels and passages, in and out of rocky chambers covered with slime, breathing foul air, recoiling from the stench. And then finding that voluminous cavern, with its horrid lake and the things inside it. The bones, the horrible bones, and that one repulsive shape lying in a heap near the water, with bits of flesh still on the ribs, what was left of the ribs, and the pieces of clothing, parts of the uniform, and young Stevens had screamed, had gagged at the realization of just *what* that was revealed in the light from his hand. And Harry had nearly passed out then and there, as when he'd discovered Jeffrey's body.

Then they heard the movement in the water, and only quick thinking and the blasts from Stevens' gun had saved them. They backed away, using the flashlight only now and then, afraid to reveal their position to the creatures sliding slowly out of the lake. Just once, just *once*, Harry wanted to dare to turn on the light full strength, and shine it onto the water, to get one good clear look at what they were. He had seen so little before, but enough to know that nothing of their kind had swum in the seas or walked on the lands of earth before. He had seen that they had had long bodies, thick like sausages, and heads of some kind, separate from the trunk, but he had not caught a glimpse of arms or legs, if they had any. There appeared to be appendages of some kind sticking out of the back and . . . even if he'd had the time and opportunity to look, he wondered if he really would have. He knew only that he might have paid the price for his curiosity. One good look might have frozen him to the spot in horror, making him fit game for the monsters as they advanced. He realized that at some point he had dropped and lost his rifle.

Then Hank had stumbled, and they were separated. Harry had heard an outcry, and suddenly the boy's flashlight had come on full, and there in the glow was a terrifying sight. They were all over him, several it seemed, only the outline of their shapes visible in the light. Blood seemed to be gushing from torn limbs and neck wounds. Then the boy was covered completely and the flashlight was crunched under the weight of one of the things, and all was darkness again. But not before Harry had glimpsed the way out. The boy was beyond help; all Harry could do was run back through the tunnel to safety. Before he could get away cleanly, he felt a painful jab in his leg, and knew that one of those awful creatures had bitten or stabbed him somehow. He screamed and pulled away, afraid to suffer the same fate as Stevens.

So he had run and run and run, not ever looking back, stumbling along the corridors etched in stone, through the greasy, slimy rock, over boulders and down dark tunnels, until he'd reached the Forester Building sub-basement, and then the outside at last.

He heard a noise now. Footsteps. He turned and saw Bill Spooner—the first one to arrive. Bill was a big man, loud and malevolent to strangers, but warm and boisterous with friends. Harry London was in the latter category, and had been for nearly three decades. The big, bear-like man came over to Harry on short, rapid steps that belied his heavyset appearance.

"What is it, Harry?" he called as he approached. "What's the matter, pal?"

Harry gesticulated wildly, trying to make himself understood. The fever had infested his entire system by now. "Gas. Get your gas cans out. We must set fire to them, to the whole cavern. The pool."

"What are you talking about?"

"I believe the viscous liquid will prove flammable; we'll set the very slime they're covered in on fire." What

205

Bill Spooner heard roughly translated as: *I beve viki kid vepor flabble.*

"Harry, you're not making any sense!"

Harry, as unsteady on his feet as he was with his tongue, told him the whole story, described what he had seen as best he could. By enunciating very carefully and speaking at a crawl, he was able to form recognizable syllables with his lips. He could tell from the look on his face that Bill Spooner didn't quite believe him, though.

"Don't you see?" he pleaded. "The cavern with the pool must connect somehow with the caves at the base of the Hunter's Mountain. That explains what happened to the children and all the others.

"You must believe me!"

Only one thing made Bill decide to check out Harry's incredible story. The mention of the missing kids. Spooner was Sam Withers' closest friend. He had spent half the night remembering Dora Withers' tears, wondering if he should have gone out again in the woods to look for both her husband and her boy. He was sure Sam was still out there, wandering around in the darkness, but knew that he would just have to sit tight until the sun came up and the search parties could see their way around. He wondered if he should call up the woman now, tell her Harry's story. But no, it would be cruel to bother and frighten her at this hour with such a cockamamie tale. That was why he didn't rouse any of his other friends. If this turned out to be something Harry's mind had created out of the depths of his imagination, the fewer people bothered by it the better. But if there was any chance it was true, it had to be looked into, that much was certain.

Only two other men answered Harry's desperate summons, only two out of all the people he'd called. They arrived to see Spooner and Harry carrying several cans of gasoline to the back of Bill's battered pickup trunk.

Bill went over to the two new arrivals. "Harry thinks he's found out what happened to those kids. And to Sam Withers."

"What's with the gasoline?" one of them inquired, not unreasonably.

"If what he says is true, we're gonna need it."

"Shouldn't the police take care of this?" the other asked.

Bill explained why that was impossible. Harry had told him about the Boonton explosion. "Let's just humor him and see what the story is. Trust me, fellas," he whispered. "If I told you what he told me, you'd think we were both nuts."

"Well, where are we going? You can at least tell us that much."

"The Forester Building. We'll drive the trunk there, then each of us will carry a can of gasoline. Harry," he called. "I think we have too much already. Only be the four of us, I guess."

The Forester Building, Bill thought. Can't be very dangerous if all we're gonna do is go in there. "What are we going to do, Harry? Burn the darn thing down?"

Then he remembered why the Forester Building had been on everybody's mind these past couple of days. Jeffrey Braddon's corpse had been found under there.

Suddenly Bill wished that he had never answered his phone.

The things in the woods were looking for food. The soft, chewy flesh. The thick, tasty blood. The muscle. The bone. Their appetites had not yet been satisfied. They had fed on the body of the one who had come alone. As they had fed on the bodies of the young ones, and the man who had come in search, and the other men who had responded to his screams. Then they had waited in the dark, some searching, moving through the underbrush, exploring this strange new world, accustoming themselves to its sights and smells. Despite the fact that the woods were pitch black at this hour, they could see everything quite clearly.

They heard the men arriving before they saw them. **Hanson! Where the hell are you?** they had cried, over and over again. The sounds made no sense to them. All they cared was that the creatures were approaching, the creatures who walked upright on two legs and who seemed so vulnerable, so defenseless—all that mattered was that those creatures were warm-blooded and fleshy and edible.

So the things attacked. And ate.

For hours they picked the bones clean, swallowing every piece of sweet, delicious meat, then finally set upon the bones themselves. Some limbs, and the head of one of the men, were saved to be dragged back later into the cave and then fed to the young ones in the pool. The young ones had to have their food brought back to them. At least for now. But the food was so good that it was difficult for the things in the woods not to consume it all at once. They had never tasted anything quite so good before. They were bolder now, unbothered by the vibrations, the presence of the food. All that mattered was their hunger.

They could go for long periods without eating. They had been bred for that. But inside, the hunger still grew and the appetite remained, and when they finally came upon something edible—and they could eat virtually anything organic—there was nothing that could stand between them and their prey. They sucked the blood, warm, thick blood, in through their mouths; sharp mandibles gnawed on bone and muscle, tearing into tendons with violence born of weeks-old hunger.

It was still very dark in the woods. They preferred the dark and would not step out of the caves during daytime. They were nocturnal in nature. They would stay there waiting almost until the dawn, then they would make their way back to their habitat, and the young ones. Hopefully, more prey would arrive before the morning. Perhaps tomorrow they would be brave enough to move out in search of the prey, instead of waiting for it to come to them. Had that first one, that young female, not walked into the edge of their lair, one of the many tunnels they had bored into, one of several openings into the outside world, they might never had tasted this delicious food again after that first time, when some of their number had come upon that man. The desire for this food was so strong that it had prompted them to leave the pool, to seek out more prey, to taste the delicious flesh and blood again. it was all they lived for now.

But they would bide their time, for safety's sake. Tomorrow would be soon enough to leave the woods. In search of more of the food.

Then something strange happened. An unusual fragrance, an odd aroma permeated the air. Smoke. A haze developed over the woods as more of the gray fog poured out of the cave openings. The young ones.

The babies were on fire!

As quickly as they could they made their way back to the caves. The smoke did not bother them as much as the heat. A scorching wind blew through the tunnels. Some came close to collapsing, but finally all of them managed to make their way back to the pool. Not one was left in the woods.

They saw more of the food, three men—no, four—

standing by the pool. One of them was hurling a strange liquid from a container onto the water. The other three seemed to cower in the background; they too, held containers, empty containers. It was clear that the fourth one, screaming like a madman, pouring the liquid with frenzied thrusts onto the water, had emptied all of the containers himself. One end of the lake was already on fire. He had thrown matches onto the liquid, which floated above the water level and gave off a smell almost powerful enough to overwhelm their own, natural odor. Though most of the smoke had been carried up through the caves or sucked up through sinkholes to the outside, that which remained made the men cough and cry and rub their eyes. "**Harry. We've got to get out of here,**" one of them yelled. He was ignored.

The one called Harry continued pouring the gasoline onto the surface of the water. He lit another match and threw it onto the bubbling, frothing lake alive with living creatures. The things from the woods were frightened of the fire, but could not ignore the agonized cries of their young. They dove into the fiery pool, determined to save their offspring; but it was too late. Each of them burst into flames on contact with the water, the slime covering their bodies instantly igniting. The cavern echoed with their death screams, the eerie light from the flames casting bizarre and horrible shapes and shadows over the rocky walls. The "children" squealed, and struggled, shocked senseless by the terrible heat.

Harry moved backwards, his eyes caught and held by the incredible sight, unable to tear himself away from the maddened throes of the beasts inside the flames. The container he carried was held downwards in his hand, the opening pointing towards the ground. As he moved back to join the others with him in the cavern, a steady stream of gasoline dripped along the dirt below his feet. He did not see this. A stray spark, a tongue of flame, flicked onto that stream of flammable liquid, and set it on fire. Harry had just reached the men when he saw the fire hurtling towards him in a straight line, following the fallen gas. He dropped the gas can in a panic, and hurled himself away from it. The three men were too slow. The stream of fire hit the can and it burst apart, igniting the other cans they held, and hence their clothes. The three agonized men darted about the cavern, beating their shirts and pants and jackets, their arms flailing, while Harry watched in horror. There was nothing he could do. He stood there, at the entrance to the tunnel which led back to the Forester Building, watching the bodies of his three close friends turn to ash before his eyes. Before long, their blackened shapes bore little resemblance to the men he had once known, looking more like the twisting, writhing *things*—some of whom still struggled —burning alive in the lake.

Harry's fragile consciousness ceased to function clearly at that point, awe-struck as he was by the horror he had seen and had innocently perpetrated on his friends. They would not have died had they not come here, had he not begged them to come, had he waited until morning when the proper authorities might have arrived. But he had seen the things moving towards the holes in the opposite wall, holes that he'd assumed led to the surface; and had surmised that there had been no time to lose. They might have devoured the entire town while everyone was sleeping.

There had been no choice, he told himself over and over again. No choice at all.

The heat was unbearable. He was sure that he had burned them all, including those who'd come rushing back in to defend the first victims. He had won. *Won!*

Then he saw the blackened husks of Spooner and the others, and the tears began streaming down his face. He turned and re-entered the tunnel they had come through. What would he tell them? What would he say to their children and their families? Would anyone believe him?

They would come down here and they would have to believe. They would come and see all the dark, burned, unrecognizable shapes floating on the water, and they would wonder for the rest of their days why such hell-spawn had ever chosen to inflict itself upon the quiet town of Milbourne.

David and Anna were up at nine a.m., sitting in a little coffee shop connected to the motel. They had ordered coffee and eggs and juice, and everything else that came with the two-dollar-and-fifty-cent special. David was telling her about the mysterious two a.m. phonecall. He had not been eager to mention it, afraid she'd admonish him for not waking her, for not going to the store or to Harry's house to find him, but knew if she heard it from Harry's lips first it would not go well for him. Luckily, she felt he had done the right thing.

"That's the oddest thing I ever heard," she said. "I think we should drop into his store this morning and find out what it was all about."

"Good idea. I hope he's speaking to me."

"I think he'll understand. No one would have expected you to go running off on a wild-goose chase at that time of night. He must have been drunk. Why else would he have forgotten to tell you where he was?"

David had told himself that over and over again, but

212

the sound of the man's voice, the manic urgency, ran through his mind almost constantly. He had heard it while he'd washed up, brushed his teeth, while they'd walked to the restaurant, ordered breakfast. Even now, he heard it. Had he done it again, ignored someone who'd needed assistance, as he had practically dismissed George Bartley? *No,* he told himself. *Stop doing this to yourself!* In both cases, he had done everything he could have been reasonably expected to do. More than anyone would have expected him to do. *Stop feeling this guilt.*

Anna was talking, asking him something. " . . . feel this morning."

"Excuse me?"

"I asked how you were feeling."

"Fine. What about you?"

"Better."

"That's good." They were too tired and too preoccupied to speak very much. It didn't matter. There'd be plenty of time later for meaningful conversation.

They left the restaurant and got into her car. Their first stop was the hardware store. Roger told them that Harry had not yet "reported to work," an odd term for an underling to use in reference to his boss. He told them where the man lived, but warned them that he often liked to sleep late. "And with Paula out," he rolled his eyes unfeelingly, "that means twice as much work for me." He got little sympathy.

They drove out to his house, located on an off street near the edge of the town, right next to the river. The smell was refreshing, but somehow unpleasant. The clear, fresh scent of water mingled with the mild aftersmell of pollution. The river was not very wide. Across it they could see vegetation, grass, the beginnings of a forest. No one lived over there.

They walked up the steps to the house, set apart from others on the block by a driveway and some hedges, and rang the bell. Both noticed that the door was half open.

After a few moments, they heard a grizzled voice cry out, "C'min. C'min." David was nervous; Harry's voice sounded as tense and frazzled as it had the night before.

Harry London sat in a chair in his living room. It was a pleasantly decorated room with two large chairs, a sofa, and lots of bric-a-brac on the bookcases, along with one or two actual books. But they were hardly able to notice the surroundings when confronted with the man himself. He was still dressed in the clothes he had worn the night before, the coat blackened and singed at the edges. He seemed to have grown ten years older than the last time they'd seen him. Gone was the respectable, level-headed businessman and store owner. In its place was a grim changeling, hollow-eyed and sunken-cheeked, unshaven, spittle dripping out of his lips and onto his chin. He saw them, but did not see. There was no real sign of recognition in his eyes.

Kneeling next to him, tears in her eyes, was Paula Widdoes. She looked much the same as they had last seen her. She looked up at their arrival, and said: "I found him like this. This morning. I came over to tell him I felt well enough to go to work. I was going to make him breakfast. He won't talk to me. Won't say anything. He barely acknowledged me when I arrived. The door was open. He just sits here, muttering to himself. I was surprised when he told you to come in. The doorbell must have startled him."

At that point, something in Harry's brain clicked again, and he turned to look at Paula. He did not seem aware of David's or Anna's presence. "I killed them, you see," he said. "I killed them." He started shivering again, violently, remembering what he had seen and done. "It was me. I killed them."

David came over and leaned down, his face very close to Harry's. God, it was true. Harry had gone mad. The phone call had only hinted at the degree of mental deterioration. Something had put him into a temporary—

hopefully—state of near-dementia. "Who did you kill, Harry? What were you talking about last night? We don't understand. Help us understand, Harry."

"*You.*" Harry looked straight into David's eyes, a terrible knowledge reflected in his own. "You didn't come." His voice rose in intensity, as his hands lifted up off his lap. "I called you. But you didn't come. You might have helped us. If you'd been there, maybe I might have saved them. YOU DIDN'T COME!"

Suddenly Harry sprang out of the chair and wrapped his hands around David's neck, as if David were to blame for everything. Anna screamed and tried to push him away. David's hands tugged at his assailant's, but the man was too strong in his fury to be defeated so easily. His grip was like a death hug. Paula pulled at his shoulders from behind, crying for him to stop. Anna raised her fists and beat at the man, hitting him everywhere: the head, the arms, the neck. The fierce look in her eyes indicated that had she a knife in her possession she would have used it without hesitation.

Finally, as suddenly full of fatigue as he had been of energy, Harry released David's throat, wheezed, and dropped back into the chair. "I'm sorry," he said, still in a fog over the whole incident. He looked up. "God help me. I didn't mean—" He dropped his head into his hands and openly wept. "I'm sorry."

David went over to the sofa, rubbing his throat, which was reddened with the marks of the man's nails and fingers. He could deal with the pain, the quiet shock that comes after a close brush with eternity, the throbbing soreness on his throat. But he could not deal with the horrible accusation in the man's tormented eyes. He would not forget that glare—it accused him of betrayal, of cowardice. It was as if Harry knew that he would not have come even if he had told him where he was. Was that true? Had he committed an unpardonable sin—in this man's eyes, at least? Perhaps in his own, too? He had tried, he told himself, to find out where Harry was. Should he have pulled on his clothes last night, gone to the store, to Harry's home, looked everywhere he could, walked all over the town? David suddenly felt low and weak and pathetic. Why, he couldn't even stand the thought of getting behind the wheel of an automobile. He had never felt so helpless and vulnerable before, so wretched.

"Are you all right?" Anna asked, sitting down beside him. He could sense her genuine concern and wondered if he were worthy of it.

"Yes. Yes, I'm okay. Gave me a scare, didn't he?"

Anna looked over at Paula, who was leaning over Harry, holding him tenderly in her arms. "Have you called a doctor?" Anna asked. "I think he needs a doctor."

Paula seemed to start for a moment, as if she had really only awakened just that second. "Oh, of course. I had better do that." She pulled away from Harry, and put one hand to her forehead, her expression still perplexed. It was as if she were having trouble accepting that there was something really wrong with Harry. He had been her strength these last few days, her rock. Someone to lean on, to talk to. She was clearly not prepared for the situation to reverse itself so soon, so suddenly. All at once came this great responsibility, and even the thought of it was probably enough to throw her into a panic. She went to the phone in the kitchen. The could hear her dialing, talking to someone.

David sat on the couch, still wrapped up in his own thoughts. Anna touched him, her fingers rubbing the hair at the nape of his neck, silently communicating her concern.

Harry London sat in his easy chair, staring out into space, images of the night before locked inside his eyes, caught for all times, never-ending. The wound in his leg, hidden by his trousers, was infected and festering, its

216

poison spreading through his system, setting fire to his mind, burning out his brain. Again and again he relived the evening's horror, one part of his mind wanting to tell them about it, the other refusing to accept that it had ever happened, refusing to acknowledge any of the memories which came uninvited. Torn this way, his mind simply sank into a semi-comatose state, where no sound or smell, voice or touch, could ever reach him.

David and Anna left Milbourne, Connecticut the following day. They would have been surprised to know what was to happen to the town in the weeks to come.

Bill Spooner's family, and the families of the other men who'd died with him that night, and the families of the youngsters who'd disappeared, and of the men who'd vanished on the mountaintop while searching for them, would live in mortal fear of late-night phone calls, wondering who would be the next of their kin to walk out at night and never come back. Over the following months, they would tell themselves a hundred different stories to explain the disappearances, but none would ever really satisfy them or ease the chill in their hearts.

Everyone would suspect that Harry London was the key to all the mysteries, that Harry knew the answers, and could tell the town where everyone had gone. But Harry would be silent, entombed by his own fragile mind, unable to tell a soul what had happened. Two weeks after that horrible night, he would walk out of the hospital and disappear from Milbourne without a trace, a note, or a backward glance. Months later, a body would wash up on the beach at a small lake in upstate New York, and dental records would confirm the dead man's identity. The identity of the virulent chemical or biological agent that had raged through his system, however, would never be determined.

Paula Widdoes would not be able to stand the loss of two friends, two loved ones, coming so soon together.

217

She would stay home from work one day, and while the telephone rang incessantly in her ears, and the TV played at top volume, she would take the gun her father had left her for protection out of the night table drawer and blow her brains right out of her head.

The Coroner of Milbourne, Connecticut finally released the body of Jeffrey Braddon two days after his sister went back to Manhattan, his final report full of insubstantial gobbledygook and double talk. The verdict: death by misadventure. Cause: unknown. The Coroner, finding himself with extra, unreported income, would decide to take his wife and family on a trip to Europe. Unfortunately, they would be killed in a mysterious "accident" on the way to the airport.

The Forester Building would eventually be torn down, and a large chain supermarket put up in its place to compete with the grocery on the other side of town. The sub-basement would be completely filled in, and before long the residents would forget all about what had happened under the market's shiny tile floors.

Representatives of the State Police, who took over the law enforcement of Milbourne during the interim between the disappearance of the entire police force and the appointment of new law officers, would instigate an exhaustive search for the missing parties, particularly the Chief and his patrolmen. They, too, would go through the hole in the floor of the Forester Building, would go through the tunnels and discover the cavern, with its burned human bodies, and the lake full of charred black things, unrecognizable to the eyes of those who found them. There would be much speculation as to the nature of the beasts, and the circumstances that led to their demise, as well as the deaths of the men—not to mention the origin of the many bones lying about the cavern, including the skeletal pieces of the former Chief of Police.

But further speculation, inquiry and investigation

218

would be abruptly curtailed by a visit from the mayor and several other town and county officials, who in turn had been visited (not only this time but several times in the past) by representatives of the Barrows Corporation, a huge conglomerate that owned whole towns and thousands of officials, as well as prominent senators and influential lawyers. Money would change hands. Voices would speak in hushed tones. Pressure would be exerted in sensitive areas. And before long, even those who had seen the pool and lived to tell the story, would be suitably convinced that it was not worth the trouble to tell anyone else. An "official" story explaining the disappearances would circulate. The missing parties had been caught in a freak fire in the woods, their bodies completely destroyed. People would remember the smoke they had smelled that fateful night. But they would notice: *None of the trees were charred*. And they would shake their heads and wonder.

But in another town, several hundred miles away, events were already in motion that even the mighty and all-powerful Barrows Corporation might have trouble controlling . . .

Or would they?

True, the *first* test had been a dismal failure.

But the *second?*

That was another story.

Part Three

Outbreak

Chapter Ten

Hillsboro, Vermont—Summer, 1983

David Hammond woke up at three in the afternoon, quickly responding to the alarm clock buzzing on the dresser two feet from his bed. He got up, stepped across the space between bed and bureau, and pushed in the notch on the clock, shutting off the sound. He sat back down on the bed, and rubbed his eyes. Bright sunlight came in through the window on the opposite wall from the dresser. A clear, sunny, mild Vermont morning.

He was glad that yesterday's hot weather had abated for the present, although it was by no means chilly. He looked around the room. His clothes were lying in a little pile on the floor, and his suitcase sat on the lap of the hardbacked wooden chair over in the corner, still unpacked for the most part. The dresser top was piled up with paperbacks and library books he'd brought up to read in the quiet hours. Only he doubted he'd have time to read any of them. Today was the day Anna was arriving.

The thought of it made him feel fantastic. In just two short hours her bus would be here, pulling up to the parking lot of the Hillsboro diner. The lonely weekend would finally be over. Today was Sunday, the day she had promised she would join him.

He'd come up here on Friday afternoon to get the

223

house ready before her arrival. At that time, Anna hadn't known for sure when she might be able to get enough time off to come up and spend a week or two with him. But then Saturday morning he got the call. She had made arrangements, juggled an appointment or two, used all her connections, and now had two full weeks of free time—and she was coming up by bus on Sunday!

All during the rest of the weekend he had waited anxiously, afraid that the phone would ring and Anna would be calling, canceling her trip due to unexpected business. But that had never happened. Now here it was, Sunday, and Anna was already on her way.

He had called his father the week before, asking permission—though he knew he would not need it—to use the house for most of the summer. He could work up here in peace, out of the city heat and smog, able to swim and sunbathe whenever the mood struck him. He could mail the free-lance assignments he did directly to the Belmont Company back in Manhattan. (They'd already bought a couple of things, so he had a little money, and in September, he had learned, a full-time position on their art staff was waiting.) It had been easy to persuade Anna to come up and join him at the earliest opportunity.

Two whole weeks! It was wonderful! And it was only the beginning. If luck was with him, perhaps Anna might get even more time off later on.

Upon returning to Manhattan from Milbourne, Anna and David had continued to spend a great deal of time together, while Anna's problems mounted and David's life got better. He was finally on the verge of a new career, new prestige, away from the humiliating combination of unemployment and poverty. Anna, on the other hand, faced the debilitating prospects of a divorce, in addition to the emotional upset she had already been dealt by the death of her brother. They had left Milbourne with more questions than they'd had when they'd arrived. Jeffrey's body had finally been released, and there had been a funeral—which David attended, although Derek did not—and a proper burial. In a sense, David thought, the impending breakup of her marriage was the best thing for Anna at that time. It had so filled her days and nights, kept her wondering about her future, that she had had less time than she would have had to wonder what on earth had happened in Milbourne. It had become clear that Jeffrey's death had not been a random incident; the disappearance of those backpackers, the policemen, Chief Walters and others indicated that something very strange and horrible had happened. But if the authorities could not find out what it was, she pointed out to David, what chance would she have? Although there had been a few minor news stories about the incidents, after a week or two it was all but forgotten.

Anna had gone to Milbourne determined to learn the truth. She had come back tired and drained, knowing that whether or not she knew the truth, it would make no difference to Jeffrey. When his body had been lowered into the ground one rainy Sunday morning, she had done her best to shut out all thoughts of him—except for the pleasant memories from her youth. He was dead. That was that. It was final. David hoped Anna would continue to cope with it so well.

So here they were. Starting out on a new life together. They'd had time to get to know each other better in the days since Milbourne. Anna had turned to David. David had turned to Anna. Nothing else seemed to matter very much.

David went into the small kitchen in the back of the house and made himself a pot of fresh coffee. The aroma was energizing. He drank two cups, with cream, no sugar, and planned the evening's itinerary. No, Anna would probably be tired from the bus trip—why did sitting in a moving vehicle doing nothing for hours make people tired?—and would not be in the mood for much activity. He'd make her supper then, and she could rest. Later on, drinks in front of the fireplace—it was a shame it was summer, a fireplace without fire seemed rather unromantic—then they'd make love. And then the next day, he would show her the sights of Hillsboro, his home town.

He had called his father Saturday afternoon, but the nurse had said that he was sleeping soundly, so David had left a message saying he had arrived and would drop by for a visit on Monday, leaving Sunday free for Anna. He could spend an hour or two with Dad, and still have plenty of time left over to drive Anna around in his father's Chrysler. He had also called George Bartley's parents, but when that same voice came on the phone, the voice of the French woman he'd spoken to weeks before, he had hung up without saying a word. When things were a bit more settled he'd find out where the Bartleys were living now and go see them in person.

He had some cereal with his coffee, then took a cool, brisk shower. He tugged a pair of dungarees on over his underwear, which was all he wore in bed all year round, and put on a light blue shirt. He checked the clock. He still had an hour before Anna's bus arrived, and it only took a few minutes to drive into town. Anna had decided against driving up in the car they'd taken to Milbourne, because it actually belonged to Derek and she wanted nothing to remind her of him, nothing he could cause a fuss about later.

David sat down on the sofa in the living room and read a mystery to pass the time. At a quarter to five he went outside and got into his father's car. He pulled away from the property, drove down a narrow country lane which connected with the main highway and turned left. He drove past the Hillsboro grange, the old firehouse, a motel that never seemed to have any business,

226

and a collection of cabins that was never without business. Within five minutes he was in the main part of town; its commercial district.

It stretched along Route 30—a connecting road running perpendicular to the main highway—for about three blocks. On one side of the street there was a gas station, a very tiny shopping mall and a post office. Along the other side, there was a French restaurant (which charged prices as high as big-city equivalents), a barber shop and adjacent liquor store owned by the same family and a small, rustic library. The commercial area was entirely on David's right as he waited at the intersection for the light to change. On his left the road continued on to the next town. The main highway continued on to the state line, passing in front of the Hillsboro Diner. The major residential district, where resided all the inhabitants who didn't live on farms, estates or in houses in the outlaying areas, was just one block beyond the main thoroughfare.

When the light turned red, David pulled across the main street and over into the diner's parking area. The place had always been a greasy spoon, with good service and adequate food, its customers consisting of road-happy truckers and teenagers with nothing better to do but hang out in the back booths nibbling catchuppy hamburgers and ice-cold French fries. David had not sampled their fare in many years; it had probably not changed very much in spite of the sign—UNDER NEW MANAGEMENT—in the window.

He checked his wristwatch. The bus should arrive any minute. He had parked in a spot with a good vantage point and would be able to see the bus a good while before it reached the diner. The land in this area was flat and smooth, courtesy of the farm which bordered the restaurant. The road sliced down through the flat surface of the ground, level for about thirty yards, then inclined downwards, a panorama of grass and

227

gravel and sky.

He settled back in his seat and waited.

Anna Braddon sat in one of the back seats of the Trailways bus, watching the wild colors along the roadside, the trees and flowers and gaudy signs blending into one never-ending blur of country beauty. She was reminded, uncomfortably so, of the type of scenery she had seen in Milbourne, the quaint little antique shops, the ice cream stands and tiny "bar and grilles" along the roads, and she felt ill at ease, although she told herself that she was going to a completely different town, with completely different people, and that no one there had heard of or met her brother, or Harry London, or any of the people in that other, more ominous suburb.

During the bus ride she had time to reflect on the events of the past few weeks, weeks that were troubled and yet happy, full of woe, and yet carefree. It was David who made the difference. So much had happened to her, to everyone around her. Derek and the divorce. Jeffrey and the inexplicable events and disappearances in Milbourne. Nothing made sense anymore. While even David, or anyone for that matter, might have been incapable of dealing with such situations, incapable of taking away the hurt, the tension, his presence and his friendship had helped to get her through these times more easily than she might have.

On top of everything else, she had been assuming that her contract with Exclusiva cosmetics would be renewed for another year, but now there was talk that they wanted a new face, a new look. Over the hill already, and not even thirty-five. Of course, there would be other offers, new campaigns and magazine covers, but none would be as lucrative, none would offer the type of security that Exclusiva did. Being dropped from a campaign as big as Exclusiva, one could practically hear the death knell. She was not poor—and she told herself over and over again that her troubles were as nothing compared to the kinds of torment afflicting people without money, without basic sustenance—but she was still bothered and worried about the future. None of the "big deals" she'd hoped for had ever materialized and probably never would.

She'd seen Derek only two times since her return from Milbourne. Once he surprised her by coming into her bedroom drunk at three o'clock in the morning, alternately shouting filthy words at her, then making clumsy advances. She rebuffed him and he left in a huff. The second time had been at a party given by a mutual acquaintance, a woman who was starting her own agency. Derek spent most of the evening in a corner necking with a petite blonde, waving on occasion to old friends and would-be conquests. Anna tried not to watch, knowing if she did that the good times would come rushing back, and she'd feel that certain something for him again, that strange mixture of affection and lust. She did speak to him at one point, having bumped into him on the way to the john. Their conversation was friendly, but guarded, and ended with him saying jovially, "I'll tell my lawyer to say hello to yours." She didn't hate him. She couldn't hate him. Maybe they'd still be friends. But even if she had not met somebody special, somebody better like David Hammond, she would have wanted out. Everything about the marriage, and about Derek, had become predictable and exasperating. Enough was enough.

She wondered if she were doing the right thing, just dropping everything and running up to some one-horse town in New England. But she had no choice. She wanted to be near David. And David was in Vermont. Had she asked him to stay in New York, he probably would have. But he looked so happy describing his old home, and the town, and what they would do together, so happy and full of almost child-like anticipation. She could not have disappointed him. Besides, it all sounded very nice. Different. He was different. Refreshingly so.

Anna felt a little dizzy, probably a result of the vibrations of the bus, and stumbled to the cramped little toilet in the back and relieved herself, feeling somewhat better afterwards. Tension. Tension and anxiety, she thought. Who wouldn't feel upset, bewildered by life? Her brother dead, killed mysteriously. Getting a divorce from a man she's been married to for years. Her career at a crossroads. Falling in love—and yes, she now believed she was—with another man she knew relatively little about. Who wouldn't feel strange, anxious, excited, even a little frightened?

Her mood soon changed. The driver announced over the loudspeaker that they were entering the town of Hillsboro. As Anna began pulling her belongings together, a middle-aged woman turned around in her seat and said: "I just wanted to say that I see you on TV all the time, and you're even more beautiful in person."

Anna blushed, of all things, and thanked her, returning the smile. The woman was in her late forties, overweight, a blotchy, pale complexion on her pleasantly homely face. A little girl who looked just like her, her daughter probably, sat in the seat next to her looking thrilled. Perhaps they both dreamed of the glamor and excitement Anna's life symbolized. Maybe they thought if they were like her they would have no problems, that their husbands would be faithful and true and never leave them feeling adrift and unwanted, that all their loved ones would live good, long lives and grow to a ripe old age, and that they themselves would stay young and beautiful and in the public's favor forever and ever. And suddenly Anna wanted to cry, right there in the aisle, while she struggled with her suitcase to the exit, cry for them and for herself and for any poor fool who thought that there was any sure formula for happiness.

And then she looked past the driver and out the giant windshield, and saw David sitting in a car, looking up with surprise, and she didn't feel sad any longer, only terriby, *terribly* glad that she had come.

The house was not quite what she had expected. They had turned into the cutoff and were approaching the grounds, and Anna saw this rather large two-story house in the distance. She had expected some kind of cabin, or cottage, a small intimate little thing (although David had never described the place in that manner), and was instead confronted with a large, rectangular house with a porch and second story, and an attic. She wasn't disappointed, just surprised.

"Why David, it's huge."

He laughed. "Not really. Just three bedrooms, a living room, kitchen, den, with a fireplace, and the usual bathroom facilities. Out back."

She grimaced. "You're kidding."

"Yes," he snickered. "Relax, we do have the usual modern conveniences, even way up here in Vermont." She gave him a playful poke in the ribs. "Remember, this was our *home*," he continued. "Not just a summer place."

They got out of the car, and David took her luggage out of the trunk. There was no lawn to speak of. It had long ago gone to seed after his father had been hospitalized, and there were only a few meager patches of grass. The house was surrounded on all four sides by forest. The woods were set back a way, beyond an overgrown field which seemed to have crept up to the building as close as possible on the sides and in the back, although the area in the front of the house was free of vegetation, as if the lawn had taken everything with it when it had died, draining the soil of its life-sustaining properties. If anyone needed proof that things had not been disturbed for quite some time, the tire tracks in the dirt outside the front porch, so rugged and ancient that they seemed carved in permanent concrete, gave silent

231

testimony, as did the yard-high weeds, and the crumbling chimney which seemed to defy the elements as time progressed. Anna felt a pall of dread pass through her. What must the place be like inside? Suddenly her husband's townhouse seemed very inviting in comparison. She was reminded of Jeffrey's house; though different in appearance and smaller, it, too, had had that unmistakable look of loneliness and encroaching decay.

David reacted to her hesitation, sensing that something was amiss. "It's not as bad as it looks," he reassured her. "The place is old and unkempt, but clean. I saw to that."

The woods around the house should have been pretty and full of birds and brightly colored foliage. Instead the trees held only pale green leaves, if any, and were packed closely together, making the forest appear impenetrable. She didn't want to say anything, but she couldn't help but think it: The property was not attractive. The dirt on the ground where grass should have been. The encompassing weeds. The prickly gray forest. Everything seemed to depressing and dead.

David did his best to dispel that atmosphere. He gave her a hug and a moist, passionate kiss and picked her up in his arms. "I know we're not exactly married, but I've always wanted to see if I could do it."

"David, oh, David," she squealed appreciatively as she was carried bodily over the threshold. "Put me down. Put me down." The door was opened and suddenly everything changed: The inside of the house was charming and quaint, every bit the kind of ambience she had been hoping for. They were in a living room with a big lumpy sofa and tables full of attractive glass figurines—his mother's—and even a grandfather clock in the corner. Two overstuffed chairs had been placed near the sofa, and there was an old-fashioned reading lamp next to each of them. A circular, patterned rug covered the floor.

He put her down gently. David's face showed a strain, and she wondered if she had been too heavy for him. She realized he might have hurt his leg carrying her. She had long ago noticed his limp.

He showed her the kitchen. Small but functional—how odd it would feel to cook with gas again—with well-stocked cupboard ("I've been shopping," he confessed) and a 1940s toaster and coffee mugs with Daffy Duck and Porky Pig painted on them. The den had a real brick fireplace and more glass figurines on the mantel. The furniture in here was more modern, but no less attractive. There were two rocking chairs that she simply had to try out later on.

There was one small bedroom on the first floor, next to the den, where David had been sleeping the past two nights. David took Anna's suitcase up to the master bedroom on the second floor, holding her hand with his free one. His parents' bedroom had a big canopied double bed with a headboard with sliding doors, behind which could be stored books or bedtime snacks. Lace curtains, which had unfortunately yellowed a bit with time, hung daintily over the windows. There was a small round table in the corner with an old clock sitting on it, and a gray upholstered chair with jagged tears in its cushion that had been placed near the closet. He showed her the other bedroom, which was similar to the one downstairs, and the second-floor bathroom. Obviously, it had been the original bathroom, that was indicated by the old tub with its clawed feet and the sink with two faucets. The toilet downstairs, next to the lower bedroom, was modern in comparison, with a shower stall and chrome fixtures. David told her that the den and the downstairs bedroom had been added to the house long after it had been originally built.

"I love it," Anna said, sitting down on the mattress in the master bedroom. "Is this where we'll sleep?"

David seemed to breath a sigh of relief. Anna had automatically assumed that they'd sleep together each evening like married couples or lovers. She couldn't see the point of him being downstairs while she was up here, and luckily, neither did he. "Yes," he said. "I better bring my stuff up."

"Umm," she said bouncing up and down. "The mattress is hard, but not too hard. Just the way I like it."

He chuckled and went out into the hall. Anna looked out the window and stared down into the weeds and the forest beyond them. Perhaps it was just the day, she thought, that made it seem so ominous. The sun wasn't shining, and the grayness of the sky permeated everything beneath it. Perhaps that was it. Maybe she'd get used to the outside of the house as she had the inside, given time.

David's car pulled into the parking lot of the Hillsboro Rest Home and he drove into a space at the back. A few moments later, David was in front of the receptionist's desk, asking for the green visitor's card that would gain him admittance into the building. He was looking forward to seeing his father, although not anxious to see how much his condition had worsened. The little woman who handed him the large square card offered no clue.

He followed her directions and walked down a corridor painted pale gray, as if they were determined to make the place look as stereotypically grim as possible. Through open doors David saw old people crippled far worse than he, lying in bed, struggling about with those special "walkers," sitting up playing solitaire with gnarled and bent fingers. David steeled himself; his father's room was just ahead. He stepped in the open doorway quickly and heard the sound of television. The room smelled of antiseptic—didn't they always—and David felt momentarily ill, remembering his long recent stay in a sickbed, how he'd wondered if he would ever walk properly again, would live or die, how he'd survive once he was out. Well, he had survived. And so, it seemed, had his father.

He was sitting up in bed watching the TV, which had been placed on a stand at the foot of the bed, its long, thin antennae reaching towards the ceiling. The place was sparkling clean and new—David recalled that the home had not been built until a few years ago—with no visible signs of decay. The same could not be said of his father. It was not so much that he looked older than his sixty-odd years, but that those sixty-odd years did not look good on him. His jowls were more pronounced, his face redder, his nose bulbous, with enflamed pores, as if he were a drinker, which he had never been, and certainly could not have been in here. He had lost weight, and looked strangely naked without one of the ever-present cigars he had puffed on for most of his life.

He was very glad to see David. He brushed his white crewcut with his left hand, a nervous habit he'd always had, and held out his right one to his son. Shaking hands —it seemed peculiar, but they were not the hugging, affectionate sort, neither one of them. David spoke first. "How ya doin', Dad?"

"I'm okay," John Hammond replied, lowering the volume on the set with a twist of a knob on the black gadget lying by his arm. "Is the house all right?"

"Fine. I spent the last couple of days cleaning it up."

"Maybe you'll find time to do something about the lawn. Must be a mess."

"Worse than that." David sat on a stool near the window and looked outside the wide pane glass for a second. All he could see was dark forest. The sky was getting gray again, too. "I'll have to hack my way through the weeds with a machete."

John laughed, and David was reminded of how warm and funny he could be. "Maybe we oughta just burn it all out," his father suggested.

"The house will go with it if I'm in charge." David smiled. "I'll see what I can do about it." The room was quite different from the one he'd been in back in New York. Smaller. Brighter. But it had the usual night table, and the bathroom in a corner, and the radiators under the window, not in use now, of course. The room had an air-conditioner, but it was turned off. It was not that hot today and his father had never liked air-conditioning anyway.

They talked for a while about the nursing home, David's new job, and his new girlfriend. John had seen Anna on TV and David said he might bring her for a visit later in the week. His father seemed pleased she was staying with him, almost excited.

"Did you go see George's folks?" John asked suddenly.

David had told his father about George Bartley and the mystery surrounding his appearance over the phone not long ago. "I will," he said. "Probably this afternoon. I hope they have some news of him."

"Strange business," John said. "But there's a lot of strange business going on around here lately." David remembered that his father had said something along those lines during their first phone conversation after his release from the hospital. "Things are going kinda funny," he had said. David remembered he had never received a full explanation from his father. For a second time he asked, "What do you mean?"

"Well, stuck here in this bed I only hear things indirectly," he explained. "Don't see any of these things myself. But I hear stories."

"What kind of stories?"

"Well, earlier this year, while you were in the hospital, I heard there was a big shakeup out at the plant. Lots of heads rolled."

"Housecleaning at Porter Pharmaceuticals?" David said, referring to the company his father had worked for. "I thought that was strictly a family outfit." The plant had been there since before his birth, and had provided the small town with many employment opportunities. Some said Hillsboro would have gone and died had it never been built. It was on the outskirts of town, not too far from the abandoned quarry.

"The 'family' sold out," his father said. "And there were a lot of hard feelings about it. A whole new power structure moved in. New supervisors were appointed, and a lot of men got fired. I'm glad I was gone before it all started; they might have given me the axe, too."

"Why did it happen?"

"The firm was bought out by another one, that's all. Or the pharmaceutical company was incorporated into something else. The whole thing was real mysterious, which is what ticked everyone off. No one seems to have the right story. Anyway, a bunch of guys were so angry at being fired or demoted that they got drunk and raised hell in town one night, tore Joe's place apart. Bartley didn't help matters." He spoke his former friend's name with disdain. "He was promoted. Real bigshot now. Couldn't pass the time of day with his old friends. Naturally some of them kissed his ass, hopin' he'd take their part, do them favors. It turned friend against friend—those kissin' up to Bartley on one hand, those who hated his guts on the other. A lot of families aren't speakin' to each other anymore. Of course, everyone who came to see me expected me to choose sides. It sounded like Bartley was getting too big for his britches, but how did I know? Man gets a promotion, what is he supposed to do—turn it down? Give up an opportunity like that because some other fellows got laid off? I don't know. I just told everyone I wasn't *around* to see all the fireworks so I didn't know who was wrong or who was

237

right, and was too old and tired to care anyhow. So, everybody got mad at me 'cause I wouldn't take their part. It's a cold place, this town, now. Real cold. Spend the summer and then get out, David. I'm glad you found work. If you'd tried to get it up here you could have used my connections before. Hell, *now* I'm not sure who's with me or agin me anymore."

"Sounds crazy to me," David said. "Don't let it get you down. When people come to their senses, they'll still be your friends."

"Don't give a shit anymore," he said. "It's all beyond me. Behind me, too."

"What else has been going on?"

"We have a new county sheriff, though I've yet to meet him. People say he's okay. Watson is his name, I think."

"What happened to Sheriff Oakes? He was around for years."

"Too many years, I guess. They put him to pasture and folks say he's mad as hell and runs around trashing the mayors and the councils of the county and everyone else he can think of. People say he was replaced by a man sympathetic to the new owners of the plant. Some corporation or other. I don't remember right now and I don't care."

David fiddled with the buttons on his shirt. "Everything's gotta change, I guess."

"For the worse." Almost dispassionately, he added: "And then there were the murders."

David sat up straight on the stool, almost toppling off it. "The MURDERS? *Here?* What the hell happened?"

"A whole family was wiped out. The Harpers. Found dead in their beds. All four of them. Little kids, too. Two of 'em. They said it was burglars. But a nurse here went to the funeral and said all the coffins were closed."

"Did they catch the guys who did it?"

"Not that anyone knows of. Happened a few days

ago. They lived up near Sumner Road, about a quarter mile from the quarry. Kept to themselves mostly. They were awfully isolated up there anyway. Killers just came in the night and murdered them while they slept. 'In Cold Blood' kind of thing. Shocked the hell out of everyone. Who would think something like that could happen in Hillsboro?"

Who would indeed?

In the Bartley residence on Old Steward Road, the maid pushed the cart into the center of the library and exited quickly. There were two men in the room. One was tall and lean, oozing confidence; he looked like the kind of rich, successful businessman who had kept his college figure due to a strict regimen of exercise and diet, and not because he couldn't afford three meals a day. He was dressed in a stylish suit that was a perfect fit but seemed somewhat out of place on him, too youthful for a man in his late fifties. His hair was graying at the sides attractively, but was thick and black everywhere else. His head was round, with features that would have been handsome had the nose not been so broad, almost bulbous, had the lips not been so thick, the eyes so small.

The other man was even taller, over six feet, and he, too, was slim and powerfully built. One sensed his frame was composed of big strong bones, and only illness would ever make him look weak or undernourished. He did not need special diets or strenuous exercise. He looked like a practical man who could not be bothered with foolish luxuries like gourmet food and sumptuous repasts. Energy and intensity practically bristled, crackling, along his eyebrows. His calories were consumed from within. His eyes were big and brown— wide, wet pools of flaring passion—flaming now with anger. His nose was long and straight, with large nostrils. Perfect teeth could be seen when he opened his full lips, lifted his determined jaw. He had a high fore-

239

head and his hair was swept back, a mane of black. He had prominent cheekbones and muttonchops. He, too, wore a suit. He was more traditional.

The men had been arguing, stopping briefly while the maid had brought in the coffee. The first man, the owner of the house, poured from an electric pot, filling two cups to the rim. The fresh aroma filled the room. Polished bookcases reflected the light from the fixture set high in the middle of the ceiling. The room was large, bookcases full of thousands of novels and scientific tomes on all four walls. There was a large desk, a table in one corner, several comfortable chairs, and no windows.

Both men stood up while they talked and sipped their coffee. The larger of the two, the guest, put his cup back down on the serving tray for a moment, and said: "As I was saying before the interruption, it seems unfair that I am blamed for matters which are beyond my control. Besides, it would appear to me that we should welcome the possibility of another testing site."

"This is my hometown, damn it!" said the other vehemently. "I live here. My family lives here. This is entirely different from before, Anton, and you know it."

Anton shrugged and picked up his cup again. He started pacing the room, deep in thought. He stopped abruptly, turned to his host and said, "You're letting your personal feelings, your personal life, get in the way of your job, Bartley. Can't you see that?"

Bartley took a beat to fully absorb what the man was saying. "If what you're saying is true I'd be the first to recognize it and admit it. To myself, at least. But it isn't. I just can't see what purpose can be served—"

"The company found a purpose once before."

"What choice did they have? After you played all your games and tricks on us? Fooling around until it was too late to take any kind of positive action."

"They didn't want 'action.' They wanted to see what

would happen."

"I don't believe that. I can't believe it. People . . . people *died* there. It could have been much worse . . ."

"We found their vulnerability, didn't we? And I'm taking steps to correct it. We need another test site. Why not here? You can always get out, send your family away. If it comes to that."

Bartley went over to his desk, stood before it, fiddling with paper clips in a glass bowl. "What if it gets out of hand, then what? What do we do then?"

"It won't get out of hand."

"Can you be absolutely certain of that? There may not be any heroes in this town."

"We'll step in. We'll stop things from going too far."

"And then?"

"And then we'll cover up like before. Only it will be easier this time. The company already owns anyone of power in this forsaken little burg. Including you."

Bartley was getting more upset by the second. "Cover-ups, coverups, coverups. Where does it end? I still can't believe they're taking your side in all this—"

"On the contrary. I'm taking *their* side. It was all their idea. They suggested we sit back and do nothing. Both there, and in Hillsboro. They wanted to see the power of what I'd created. Only they didn't get enough of a demonstration. This time, they will. That's what they want, Ted. You might as well accept it. Go along with them. It will be so much easier."

"It's against . . . It's—"

"—against everything you believe in? Is that what you were going to say? What a hypocrite. You sold out your own son. You wanted this position. The money, the power. You were moving upwards fast, but not fast enough. Your son knew the truth before you did. Your son could see it quite clearly. So you had to go and shut him up—"

"Stop it! STOP IT!" Bartley screamed. He almost

241

lunged at the man. He crashed his cup down onto the desk, cracking it. Coffee spilled all over a stack of papers. Ted Bartley did not seem to notice. "You're twisting the facts. I will not have you implying—"

"It's not an implication," Anton said softly, calmly. "It's a fact. I will not be made to pay for your mistakes, your reticence. Your lack of foresight. I will not be blamed for the death of that family, or for the others. I am only doing what I have been told.

"Poor Ted. A hard-working family man. Only wants what's best, what every man wants. Only you had to pay a price, and it's much too steep. You can't accept that the firm you've worked for all these years, the company you've given your life to, can be as crass and commercial and as cold-blooded as every other one is. No, not your employer. Not them. But they are, Ted, just as bad. At least, in your eyes. I wouldn't use a word like 'bad' to describe them. Only competitive. Aggressive. Or more to the point: *realistic.*"

He went over to the desk and put his hand down gently on Bartley's shoulder. He held it there a second, then took it away. The touch of his fingers had been far less comforting than intended. "You've got to face it, Ted. Life is changing. New things are being developed, hence being exploited. That's the way it is. You can't change it. Science has an obligation to fulfill. And industry will use the products of that fulfillment just as they always have. You think this is the first time some new creation has been tested on human beings, unaware that they were being tested? You think towns and villages, and whole cities for that matter, haven't been used as testing grounds before? This isn't new, what we're doing. Not new at all."

"What's next?" Bartley asked, his voice too tired to sound bitter anymore. "Are you going to tell me how it's for the good of the country, how it will benefit the many by using a few? How it's just another example of

242

progress and that you either go along with it or get ground under? How I have to be open-minded and modern?"

Anton answered with his silence.

"Well, I'm not buying," Bartley continued. "As far as I'm concerned, murder is still murder."

"How pious and self-righteous you sound," Anton replied. *"Now."*

Bartley ignored him but the remark had hit home. His voice was more feeble as he said, "I'm calling the others this afternoon. I have to know the truth about this. I still can't believe we would be a party to what you're suggesting."

"You already know what the truth is," Anton snapped. "Open your eyes, man!"

Bartley went behind his desk and sat there, assuming a posture he obviously hoped would indicate dismissal. Anton showed no signs of leaving. He walked up to the desk and said: "Call for all the meetings you want. The only result will be your eventual resignation. It's only a matter of time." Anton's mouth pulled upwards in a nasty grimace. "And how far do you think they'd let you get with what *you* know? I'm warning you, Bartley. Give it up. Just sit back and let matters take their course. It will be much healthier that way."

Bartley's hand flew towards the phone as his face registered disgust. "Who are you to threaten me, Anton? I'm sick of your questionable morals, your lousy ethics, and your—your Frankenstein sadism. You just want to sit back and see what your monsters will do. Well, I say if we must engage in such projects at all there are better ways to test the capabilities of your products than the ways we've apparently used so far." He finished dialing. "And I think I'll let everyone know that I feel this way."

Anton bristled. "You're a fool, Bartley. A contemptible idiot."

"Whatever. Just get out of here, Frederick. I've had

243

enough of you for one day."

They both heard the busy signal. Anton looked victorious for the moment. Still surprisingly calm, Bartley put the phone down and began dialing another number. "They say there's a thin line between genius and insanity, Anton, and you must cross that line twenty times a day."

At that Anton rushed out of the library in a huff. Bartley couldn't help but chuckle. His mood changed, however, at the second busy signal. And the third. Maybe they were all on the phone together, having their own secret meeting without him, hooked up to that special conference line. Why was he left out? Anton couldn't be right, he couldn't be. Stop being paranoid, he told himself. But his meeting with Anton had cast a pall over the whole afternoon that nothing would dissipate.

His mood became even worse when the maid knocked on the door and came in upon his request. He could tell from the harried look on her small, hawk-like face that something was wrong. "What is it, Mimi?"

The old woman stepped into the room, and closed the door behind her. "There is a man here. He insists on speaking to you. He says his name is David Hammond."

Ted Bartley's eyes glittered with recognition, then dulled with worry.

"He is here about George," she said with finality. "I did not know what to tell him. You instructed me to say nothing, but he was so insistent. He was the one who called a few weeks ago, I believe, while you and Mrs. Bartley were away. What would you have me do?"

Bartley steeled himself and stood up. If he didn't see the boy—boy? He must be in his thirties now—it would seem suspicious. He got up from behind the desk. "Let me talk to him. Bring him into the living room."

He walked down the outside hall behind her until they reached another corridor running perpendicular to the first. There they parted company. Mimi went back to the front door and Bartley turned right and walked towards the living room, a large square chamber situated in the northwest corner of the house.

He was over at the bar fixing himself a drink when David came in. He turned to look at the young man. He hadn't changed that much, not fat or bald or anything like that. Instantly recognizable. He wondered if that was true in his case as far as David was concerned.

"Hello," David said, his hand outthrust in greeting as he walked across the room. Bartley took his hand, and shook it warmly, smiling. "It's good to see you again, David," he said.

They talked for a moment or two about the usual things. How times had flown, how David had grown, Mr. Bartley grown older, and so on. Small talk. Finally, Bartley offered David a drink. David took a dry martini and sat down on the luxurious white sofa near the picture windows. They afforded a view of the whole outlying area behind the house. It was on top of a small hill, overlooking the woods and a picturesque garden that seemed very carefully tended and rather expensive to keep up.

The room itself was very attractive and large, decorated in light, subdued shades of white and tan and blue. The rug was thick and slightly off-white; the furniture literally glowed with the light from the chandelier above. Yes, Ted Bartley had come up in the world. David took a seat across from him, a blue-cushioned chair, and fixed his gaze upon the older man.

"Well, you said there was something specific you wanted to see me about?" Bartley asked, leaning back comfortably in his seat. He looked very calm, almost cunning, ready for anything David might say. David, too, looked in control, considering he was the intruder. He complimented Bartley on the drink, then told him about his son's sudden appearance at his apartment in New York, as well as his abrupt departure. He also mentioned the phone conversations with the maid, George's story about being experimented on somewhere, held against his will. At that point Bartley started to look a little uncomfortable. He recovered nicely, and launched into a pre-arranged explanation even before David was through.

"So it *was* you, wasn't it?" Bartley said, slapping his knee with joviality, looking suddenly humble with apology. "I'm so sorry, David. Mimi told me about your call, but we assumed it had to be a prank. You were always a responsible lad; I couldn't imagine you actually calling up with such a preposterous story when George was right with us in Lancaster all the time. Why, he was right there in my hotel room waiting for his mother to get ready to go out for lunch when Mimi phoned and told us about the call. Now, David, I know you're not the type to play practical jokes. Your father and I go way back. So, obviously, the person you thought was George had to be somebody else, playing a joke on *you*. Experiments. Breakouts. *Really*, David." The young man did not look convinced. He was going to be more trouble than he had imagined.

David looked down at his drink, his expression disappointed, maybe even a trifle angry. "I don't know. If you say George was with you, then of course, he must have been with you. It's just that the man who came to my apartment not only looked like George—I could tell that despite the clothes and the hair—he sounded like George, he had George's memories. He—"

Again Bartley interrupted. "George had a stint in the army, you know. He met a lot of wild characters. Real crazy guys. Probably one of them got it in his mind to pretend he was George. Who knows? Some of his friends were real wackos."

"But *why* would they do that?"

"Who knows when you're dealing with lunatics? It has me stumped. George probably mentioned you to some nut he served with, and when the nut was on his last legs in New York, he decided to give you some grief, maybe get some money. All I know is, I know my own son, and George was with us in Lancaster all that time. One full week."

David looked as if he were about to say something, but stopped. A second later he asked: "Do you have any idea who this amazing impersonater was?"

"Not the slightest. And I don't care. I'm sorry if he caused you any trouble. But if I were to worry about every Tom, Dick and Harry who tries to fatten off the good Bartley name, I'd never get any sleep at all. No, David. It was all just an unfortunate misunderstanding."

"Where is George now? I'd like to see him." Probably noticing the look in Bartley's eyes, he quickly added, "Not to check up on you, Mr. Bartley. Just to say hello."

"Of course. I'm sure George would like to see you. He'll be sorry he missed you, but he's out of town now. Running a little errand for me. Won't be back for a couple of weeks probably."

Had he heard right? Had David just muttered *how convenient* under his breath? The younger man shrugged and drank down the last sip in the martini glass, then popped the olive in his mouth. "Well, I'll be here all summer probably. So, when he gets back, I'd appreciate it if you asked him to call on me. I'm staying at the house."

"Ah, good. Always liked that place. Too bad about your father. I hope he'll be coming home one of these days."

"Me, too." He got up and again shook hands with Bartley. Bartley gave him another warm smile, but one that was forced, tension nipping away at the corners of his mouth. "Well, thanks for talking to me," David said. "Say hello to Mrs. Bartley. And I hope I'll soon be

247

seeing George one of these days."

"Certainly," Bartley said, releasing his hand. "I'll have Mimi show you to the door."

"I can find my way out," David said plesantly. The atmosphere was getting more precious every second.

But Mimi was there, anyway, just outside the door, as if she had been hovering all the while, waiting for her cue. As she walked down the corridor with David following, Bartley realized how ridiculous it looked. It would have been rather difficult for someone to make a wrong turn unless they wanted to. Obviously, that's what he was afraid of. He chuckled. He had a vision of Mimi wrestling David to the floor to keep him from going in the wrong direction. Somehow he couldn't see her in that role.

Bartley went back to the bar and made himself a double. It hurt at times like this, it really hurt. Every time he saw an old friend of George's, every time he had to lie and manipulate and cover up the truth, every time he had to face the fact that his son would never be normal like them again. David was strong and handsome. He'd noticed the limp and had almost asked about it, but it seemed minor when stacked against young Hammond's assets. David was everything George could never be. Not now. Damn! He put down the glass and lifted his hands to his eyes, which were already tearing. Just one mistake. Just one lousy miscalculation, and your whole world crumbled. Had he really sacrificed his own son on the altar of ambition? There had been no love lost between the two of them, true, but whose fault had that been? Had he even *tried* to understand the boy, tried to love him? He would have to live with the results of his anger, his actions, for the rest of his life.

Which might not be too long if Anton had his way. Was Anton correct in his assessment of the situation? Were things that bad, was life really that rotten, people that miserable? Ha, he should know the answer to that.

Look at you, he thought bitterly, and ask yourself that question. Are people miserable? They sure are.

He threw the glass across the room where it shattered against the opposite wall, spattering liquid and ice over the painted surface and onto the rug. He shook violently, then wiped his face free of all traces of remorse. Mimi came in to investigate the noise. He could only stammer, his eyes looking away from her direction. "P—Please clean up. It was an accident." He pointed to the corner where the glass still lay.

Then he turned on his heel and dashed out of the room.

Chapter Eleven

Randall Thorp woke up suddenly, smelling smoke. The children. The children were up to something. "Martin? Gladys?" He pulled himself out of bed, surprised that he was fully dressed in evening clothes instead of pajamas. Then he remembered: the party at the Evanses' the night before. Ah yes. He'd come home quite late, paid off the babysitter—little bitch—and gone straight to bed, too tired to undress.

Or to brush his teeth. His mouth tasted dreadful. He called out again—"Theodore!"—but there was no answer. Time enough for the children; he would brush his teeth, wash his face first. Take a couple of aspirins, too. His headache was killing him. Where *were* the children? He saw the pile of cigarette butts in the ashtray on the night table, and knew where the smoke smell was coming from. Good thing he hadn't fallen asleep with one in his hand.

Randall Thorp blundered into the bathroom sleepily, the way he blundered from day to day hoping his life would change, afraid it would get worse—as if it could get any worse. Forty-four years old and he felt ninety. An old divorced man out of work struggling to retain a little dignity, taking care of three brats for almost as many weeks while their mother got some rest. Why did they call it visiting *privileges*? The whole thing was absurd, a scenario for a Hollywood screenwriter, something Cary Grant could have pulled laughs from. But in reality, his situation was about as funny as a tubercular baby.

He heard laughter, childish giggles from afar. Were they out in the yard? He went to the window, toothbrush still in hand, gobs of bubbly toothpaste dripping down his chin. "Teddy? Is that you? Gladys? Martin?" No answer. He must have only thought he'd heard laughter; it probably had only been the water in the faucet, tricking him. Everyone seemed to delight in playing tricks on him.

He went back to the sink and stared dolefully into the mirror. His face seemed to be crumbling into itself; was it the liquor doing that, or merely age? The marks of failure? The weakness of his chin was more pronounced by his shrunken cheeks, the heavy stubble on his face. His forehead seemed to stretch up endlessly before it met his receding hairline. He combed the hair straight back; it looked better that way. More appropriate for a man his age. His small eyes, so close together, peered at the reflection, and back at him, without mercy. Hazel in color, some might say they were penetrating; others, beady.

He turned off the faucet and listened carefully, trying to detect some kind of aural clue as to the children's whereabouts. Nothing. Were they all right? That would be fitting, the perfect way to cap his life's pathetic demeanor—having his kids die when they visited their daddy. Now and then he thought of the burglary—massacre actually—at the Harper house down the highway.

Worried in spite of himself, he went into the kitchen, scouting for traces. They had assembled some sort of breakfast, that much was obvious, but it was now nearly evening. He saw lunch's residue, too. They liked to have sandwiches, and most of the bread was gone. Where the hell had they gone off to?

He looked into the backyard. Except for some toys scattered here and there, there was no sign they'd ever been there. He told them never to go off without him, to stay within sight of the house. He would be blamed, he knew. Blamed for this. He had been asleep upstairs, drunk, a shiftless no-account bum of a father. They'd never take into consideration that he had gone to the party at the Evanses' because Mimsy Evans had told him that several producers would be there, people he ought to get to know. He was just trying to make a living for himself, to better his pathetic life, but no—they wouldn't see that. All they'd see would be a contemptible, middle-aged man running off to get bombed at cocktail parties, living it up while his children stayed home with babysitters, sleeping to all hours while the children went off God-knows-where by themselves. They wouldn't see his side of it, just the way his wife, Patricia, had never seen his side of it. He would be to blame, always be to blame.

Then he heard the voices, the laughs. Were they laughing at him, the little brats? He'd teach them. He was not to be laughed at, especially not by *her* children. He'd teach them but good.

They had been in the garage all the time, too busy talking and playing to bother answering his calls. He found them in there, huddled behind the car, playing jacks or some such foolish inanity. When he'd been their age he'd had far less frivolous things on his mind, things like hunger, and weeping, hard-working mother, and an alcoholic father who beat his children mercilessly for the slightest offense.

Knowing, but not caring, whose crimes he was re-enacting, he menacingly removed his belt from his pants and advanced steadily upon them.

Anna and David got up at the crack of dawn, it

seemed. Actually it was later than that, but David had been used to getting up so late (and even Anna had had times in the past few weeks when she'd been able to sleep past noon), that the hour of their awakening seemed positively wholesome in comparison. They'd gone to bed, if not to sleep, quite early the night before. Anna had spent the morning and early afternoon resting up from her bus trip and capturing some badly needed sleep. David had seen his father and Mr. Bartley. Then during the late afternoon, David had taken them for a leisurely drive around the town in the Chrysler. There wasn't much to see in the way of landmarks—the quarry, the apple orchards, Bannon Mountain Drive— but Anna enjoyed it just the same, breathing deeply of the fresh country air, enjoying the solitude and quiet to its fullest. And all the time, she and David got to know each other better, to feel more secure and comfortable beside one another. They had decided that today they would go back to the quarry for a swim. Lots of towns-people used it, although the wealthier ones had built their own pools and some used the pool in the motel for a small fee. (Since it had so few customers, the management figured it was a way of bringing in some added revenue.)

David had so far refrained from discussing the whole George Bartley incident with Anna; it was not a part of her life, nothing to concern her with. But *she* was becoming part of his life, and if he couldn't share things with her, then who could he share them with? He brought the whole business up while he was making an early morning omelet, filled with mushrooms, tomatoes and peppers.

After listening to him relate the story behind George's appearance in New York, and his father's explanation for the kiss-off attitude when David phoned, Anna said, "Sounds like he's trying to cover something up. All you can do is wait until George gets in touch with you in a

253

few weeks."

"If he ever does. I wish there were some way of getting in touch with him. I don't buy his father's impersonator story for one minute."

She giggled. "Perhaps the man at your apartment was a *clone* of George Bartley."

He handed her a plate full of omelet, a look of mock dismay on his face. "Shut up and eat. That's all I need. Clones. Mad scientists. I'm still recovering from that business in Milbourne—" He stopped short and put his plate down on the kitchen table. "I'm sorry." They had agreed some time ago not to discuss what happened in Milbourne; it was too strange, too upsetting. Anna reached out and touched him. She said softly, "It's all right. I think about it myself sometimes. Those men disappearing. Harry London going into shock over something that he couldn't verbalize to anyone. It haunts me. But there's nothing I can do about it." She straightened up, pulled her hand away, managing a bright expression. "Ummm. This is quite good. Now why don't we forget about old mysteries, and see if we can solve this new one."

He didn't remind her that the mystery over George predated the death of her brother. "I keep thinking. Why would Mr. Bartley lie? If he had disowned his son and didn't care about him, why didn't he simply say so, why didn't he say, 'The affairs of my son are no longer my concern; a good day, David.'? Why cover up the way he did?"

"Maybe he's ashamed. What father would want to admit that he knew his own son was penniless and unbathed bumming around New York in dirty clothes, and that he wouldn't do anything to help? I think that George must have done something to anger his father, to really infuriate him. When you called, and the maid relayed your message, he was still angry. How did he know George was that badly off? How did he know that

254

his son hadn't *fed* you your lines—y'know, the old sympathy routine? Now, weeks later, he and George are back together and Dad is ashamed of what happened, ashamed of the message he had the maid relay to you: in effect, 'Get lost.' So, he says it wasn't George. Some crazy army buddy. Nothing to worry about. If George is a good little boy he'll go along with the deception, you wait and see."

"Not George. He wouldn't do that. He's too honest, too independent."

"Ah, but think how embarrassed he'll be when he sees you. He'll be remembering what he looked like, how desperate he was, the humiliation of it all. Who would want to admit that they'd once been a tramp cluttering up your living room? Uh, the mere thought of it! I would have had the place fumigated."

David was about to tell her that fumigation cost money and that a friend was a friend, after all, but stopped himself in time. No use nitpicking. "Still, George would *know* that I know the truth. He might come clean, no pun intended, because of that. Then again, I also know how poverty can affect a person, how it can change their whole character around."

Anna smirked. " 'Let him go,' said the judge, 'he hacked the old woman up because he was underprivileged!' "

"No, that's not quite what I mean," David said, annoyed, rushing out the words too quickly. He paused, recovering lost ground, not wanting to offend her. "I mean, if his father offered George a good job—and I assume he's in the position to now—as much as George might have once hated the idea of working for the man, the thought of being penniless would still be fresh in his mind. So if his father said, 'Don't shame me, son. Tell no one about your desperate life as a bum in New York or I'll cut you off without a penny,' would anyone blame George if he kept his mouth shut?"

Anna seemed to be preoccupied and he wondered if she had heard him. He sensed she was inwardly reacting to something he had just said. He was about to repeat himself when she looked at him again, acknowledgement in her eyes.

"Uh, yes," she said, wiping her mouth with a napkin. "I suppose no one would blame him. I guess you'll find out what the story is when you see him."

"If I see him. His father may not give him my message, which would be understandable if what we've surmised is true. And George may not particularly feel like facing me again anyway. I guess I should forget about it. According to Mr. Bartley, George is alive and well and running his errands and probably wants to forget about New York. I'd only remind him of it, of his humiliation, like you said."

He lifted a glass of tomato juice. "Here's to George Bartley, wherever he may be. May we never meet again." He drank the juice down, wiped his lips and smiled.

But the thought of George stayed with him.

The quarry was deserted except for Anna and David. The day was not very hot, true, but still they had expected to see a few teenagers, at least. It seemed so much more desolate than ever before. Sometimes when David was a boy the kids used to come here at night and it had been so spooky and eerie that none had dared stay there alone. Now even in daylight and years later, that ominous quality remained. David looked down at the water and wondered what might be beneath the surface.

"How long has this place been abandoned?" Anna asked, while they took a few towels and accessories out of the car. She looked around for a good spot to lay claim to. Not that she'd have to fight for one.

"Decades, I guess." For emphasis he pointed over to an area a few yards distant, where the empty remains of old buildings stood out against the grass. The spot where they had parked the car was gray and packed with gravel, but woods surrounded the quarry on the other three sides. Trees had been cleared for about three yards all around the water, and weeds and bushes sprang up everywhere. Anna carried a picnic basket over to a patch that seemed relatively flat and brush-free. "This looks good," she shouted to him as he locked the car; an unnecessary gesture—no one was around and they could easily see the auto from any point around the quarry.

"Kids have been swimming here for as long as I can remember," David continued. "This operation was shut down even before I was born."

She had placed a blanket over the grass and was stretching out on it. "Ummm, the sun feels good." She sat up and grabbed for a sweater. "It is a little chilly, though. In fact, I feel kind of silly in a bathing suit."

"You may feel silly, but you look terrific. I never knew a one-piece could be so voluptuous." It was light blue, and showed off her figure to maximum advantage.

She laughed appreciatively. "Bikinis are going out of style, haven't you heard? The latest fad is designer one-pieces. The designers got sick of putting their names on everyone's ass, so they switched from jeans to bathing suits. Next it'll be designer bras. Too bad. I burned mine long ago."

David eased down next to her. "Maybe it'll get hotter later on."

"Was that a proposition?"

"Entirely innocent, unless you decide to take it otherwise."

"Speaking of bathing suits, you fill yours out nicely too, young man."

David felt self-conscious. "I'm skinny," he said, fiddling with some grass at his feet. Anna was being kind. He'd lost a lot of weight and muscle tone while in the hospital, and his body was awkward and scrawny.

He knew he had to gain a few pounds in the right places. He'd have to start on a new exercise routine, too.

Anna laughed. "Not where it counts, you're not." She turned around and lay down on her stomach. "It's so lovely here. So peaceful. I could just fall asleep right now."

"Better not. I'll be lonely."

"Just let me know when you go in the water and I'll join you."

"I took a dip the other day. It was too cold. Didn't stay in long. It made my leg feel strong again, though.

"Your leg?"

He suddenly realized that he had broken new ground absentmindedly, that he'd blindly dived into uncharted territory. He was so sensitive about his leg, how could he have just brought it up like that? Well, there was no backing out now. Surely she had noticed his limp anyway, even seen the leg itself. God, maybe she found it unsightly, hideous. He swallowed his embarrassment, steeled himself, glad she was facing away from him now. "Yeah, my right leg. The one I limp on. I hurt it in an accident awhile ago. Before I met you." As if she hadn't realized that, fool!

"It's not that noticeable," she said, trying to make light of it without sounding unsympathetic, not an easy trick. "Want to talk about it?"

"Nah," he said, in a similar tone. His face must have been bright red. He felt it burning. The silence stretched out between them and for the first time he felt discomfort. He wondered what was going through her head. What a relief that they could not see each other's faces! He hoped he had not offended her. He searched in his mind for something to say. Only by saying something could he dispel any impression she might have that he was hurt or angry. "Feel like eating yet?" he asked finally. "I make great tuna sandwiches."

"Maybe later, honey."

Honey. She hadn't called him that before. Was it an expression of endearment or one of sympathy, of pity? He looked at his leg. He knew there was really nothing there to see. No obvious disfigurement, although he could swear it seemed patchy and red in places. Did the bone stick out at a funny angle? Was he a freak? He knew he was going on about nothing, dangerously close to a jag of debilitating self-pity. He got up and walked over to the water.

The ground inclined sharply before meeting the water's edge, and the surface of the lake was still and silent. Mosquitoes buzzed nearby in the bushes. A fly went passed, darting over to some rocks jutting out of the water a few feet away. The whole scene somehow chilled him. Or was it only that awkward moment with Anna a few minutes ago? The thought of unease rising up between them filled him with dread. He had hoped she'd feel at home here, at home with him.

He felt movement behind him. He felt Anna's hand on the back of his neck. Turning, his arms went around her waist almost involuntarily, as hers went up around his neck at the same time. She pulled down, he pulled upwards, their mouths met. Warm, moist, clinging tenderly, yet forcefully, to each other.

One of Anna's hands explored the corded muscles of his throat, his adam's apple, then swept down towards his chest, the curly mounds of hair laying like a blanket between and around his breasts. Her fingers centered on a nipple, delicately rubbing, the fingernails scratching the flesh ever so faintly.

His right hand had moved down to her beautiful, curving buttocks, firm and fleshy, wonderful to the touch. His left hand came up and moved towards her breasts; she sighed. As one they began to descend, their arms and legs positioned for balance as they tumbled with surprising grace onto the grass.

And then some damn fool decided to turn onto the

259

road up to the quarry. They heard the car clearly, although it couldn't yet be seen. Quickly they disentangled themselves, frustration and amusement stamped equally on their faces.

The car, a battered blue station wagon with a dented front fender and a cracked tail light, drove up and parked several yards from their own. Although they could see children inside, they could not hear them. David had never seen such submissive and quiet youngsters before. So far.

Anna smiled. "So much for peace and quiet."

"Do you want to leave?"

"Of course not. They won't bother me. I like children. Other people's children."

David felt the same way. He was discovering new areas of compatibility all the time. Kids needed time and attention. Something a busy fashion model and a struggling commercial artist might not be able to give them. *Slow down,* he told himself, *who's been talking about marriage?* He realized with a slight shock that it was time for him to consider most carefully how much of a commitment he was willing to make. He'd also better be prepared to accept that Anna might not want to jump from one bad marriage into another, although he had every reason to believe he would make a better husband than Derek had.

The driver of the car was busy carrying blankets and containers over to an area which the children had picked out, some distance away from David and Anna. The children were still strangely subdued. Aside from a few unintelligible comments to each other, they said very little, and expressed no enthusiasm or interest in their surroundings whatsoever. Except for the littlest one, a boy, who seemed somewhat intrigued by the water, and who ran down to the edge to peer into it. The other two children, a boy and a girl, watched him but showed no signs of joining. David and Anna walked back up to their blanket.

"Cute kids," David said. Anna agreed that they were adorable.

"It is getting hotter," she noticed. "I suppose the whole town will come out now."

"Maybe. But somehow I think the citizens of Hillsboro have discovered better places to swim in the years since I left home. I'll have to ask around. I wonder if anyone goes to that old pond George and I used to splash around in."

"Your father would know."

"Maybe."

They watched the man who they assumed was the father trudge over to join his children. He looked like a disagreeable sort: tall, thin, a cold malice in his eyes, a begrudging attitude in his walk. David wondered why the man had bothered to come out here, as neither he nor his children seemed particularly glad to be there.

The children boldly moved away from their spot— where they had placed their towels along with a rubber raft—as soon as the man approached. He didn't seem to notice or care. He laid his own towel down over the grass and slowly sat down. He was unshaven, his thinning hair all tangled. He was fully dressed, too, in brown pants and a wrinkled white shirt. He stared at the water.

Anna felt uneasy; there was something ghostly about those zombie children and their glaring, silent father. "Not very spirited, are they?" she asked.

"Father must have scolded them or something," David whispered. "The calm *after* the storm."

"Were you a good child?"

"Disgustingly good. Never got in trouble. Had a permanent halo over my head. How about you?"

She poked two fingers up behind her head. "Devil's horns. I was precocious and nasty."

"But cute and lovable in spite of it, I bet."

"I suppose so. I seemed to get away with everything. Well—look who's here."

David turned and saw that the younger boy was coming toward them as he circulated the quarry, stopping now and then to investigate a bug or wildflower. He had big eyes and a tousled thatch of blond hair. He wore red shorts, sneakers and a white T shirt. David studied the face more carefully and mentally recoiled. He could tell that Anna had noticed it, too: The child's face was bruised and marked as if he'd been in a fall or accident. Or worse.

"Hello," Anna said as the boy passed near them.

"H'lo," he replied, looking up at them impishly for a second. They failed to hold his interest, and he continued on his way, a midget explorer circling the globe. "He looks like he's been beaten," Anna said.

"Just what I was thinking."

"What a shame. He's such a beautiful child."

"We may be jumping to conclusions. He might have gotten in a fight with one of his little friends."

Anna looked mildly perplexed. "Well naturally. What did you think I meant?" She realized before he had time to answer. "You don't mean the *father*? Is that what you . . .?"

"That's what I thought you meant, yes. But there's no reason to assume that. Anything could have happened."

"To one child, maybe," Anna said, her voice deepening with anger and dismay. "But not to all three. Look."

The girl and older boy were slowly following in the younger boy's footsteps. As they approached, David could see what Anna had been referring to. Their faces were also damaged, cruelly, the red slashes on their cheeks contrasting vividly with the milky whiteness of the otherwise unblemished skin. "Looks like somebody took a whip to them," David said.

"Oh Davey, I hate people like that."

The father still sat on the towel, watching the water, lost in his own universe. "We don't know for sure that he did anything," David said. "There's nothing we could do about it anyway. We didn't see it happen."

"Can you imagine what it must be like to be a child and to feel unloved?"

David thought for a second, then said: "All children feel that way from time to time, especially when they're punished. But no, I guess I always knew deep down that I was loved."

"So did I. First by my parents. Then my aunt and uncle. It must be so lonely. So desolate."

He followed the children's progress. The older two had caught up with their brother. He was showing them something on the ground. "At least they have each other," David said.

"Oh, David," she said with reproach, "they're just *children.*"

There was silence for a moment or two. David suggested they leave. "It's still too chilly to swim. I think this place is just depressing you."

"Let's at least eat some of the lunch you made."

"All right." He got up and pulled the picnic basket closer. As he handed her a sandwich, he heard the childrens' voices rise. They were more animated now over something, acting more the way youngsters should act. Full of curiosity and spirit. "Daddy. Daddy. Come see what we found," the youngest called.

It was always the youngest ones who forgave first. David could see the boy's sister *ssshing* him quickly, turning to confirm her hope that their father had not heard and was not coming over to look at their acquisition. Although the boy's voice had carried across the quarry with clarity, the father sat looking at the water as if deaf and dumb.

The boy started running back towards them, and for a

moment David thought the child might confront his father with the prize, and David wondered if the man would react and what that reaction might be. Instead the boy stopped at their blanket, showing what he'd found to them. "What do you think it is, Mister?"

David took it and laughed. "I wasn't much of a biologist, but let's have a look. What do you think, Anna?"

"Ugh," she exclaimed. "Whatever it is, it's awful."

She was right. It appeared to be a long piece of almost perfectly smooth bone, thick at one end, tapering off to a needlelike sharpness at the other. "Looks like a walrus must have dropped it," David said. It was over a foot long.

The older children had come up to reclaim their brother. "You don't think it's a *tusk*, do you?" the girl said somewhat petulantly. David was reminded of those pitiable plain girls in junior high who wore glasses and were said to be brainy.

"Well, what do *you* think it is?" David asked. It was smooth to the touch, so smooth that it almost felt wet. Though bent like a tusk, it was clearly something different. The thick end appeared to have broken off of something, and it was honeycombed with round hollow vessels made of some kind of sticky, fleshy material. It *couldn't* have come off an animal. David didn't want to hold it any longer. He handed it up to the girl.

"I don't know," the girl admitted, and David liked her better for her ignorance. He hated smart-alecky kids. "It might be part of a rock," she guessed, "or maybe a tree."

"How come it's so yucchy?" the older boy asked.

Anna stopped chewing her sandwich long enough to say, "Why don't you take that—that thing, whatever it is—back to where you found it. It might have a mother and I wouldn't care to meet her."

"This isn't alive," the youngest boy protested. "It's *dead*."

264

"It's not even an animal," the girl remarked, that adults-are-dumb tone back in her voice. "Maybe it's part of an animal, but I doubt it."

"Give the National Geographic a call, darling. Now let us eat in peace!"

"*Sorry.*" The kids moved off en masse, taking their trophy with them. Anna had spoken a bit too harshly, and she apparently regretted it. "Don't know what got into me. I guess it was the way they were surrounding us, asking all kinds of questions we can't answer."

They finished their sandwiches and carried the stuff back to the car. "It's early yet. How about a walk through the woods? There's a nice path near here."

Anna consented. "If we're not swimming we'll have to get our exercise some other way." She kissed him on the cheek. "Don't get ideas. That was just in appreciation for some wonderful tuna."

"It was low calorie, too. How about another kiss?" She gave it to him. They put their clothes back on over their suits and locked up the car. He took her hand and led her towards the broken-down buildings in the distance. "The path begins over there," he explained.

They looked around the quarry before leaving. The children were back to circling the water, voices raised, their sudden energy dispelling much of the worry David and Anna had felt at the sight of their bruises. Anything could have happened. Perhaps someone else had hit them, and that was why their father was deep in thought. Planning revenge.

Although the man who sat staring into the water was the most perfect illustration of self-loathing either of them had ever seen.

They had been walking for about half an hour, traveling along a pathway through the woods that had been beaten down and etched into the earth by thousands of backpackers and boy scouts and junior-grade explorers.

The trees were very close together, and the summer brush filled up all the spaces between them with all manner and shape of flora, from long thin weeds to color-dappled honeysuckle. Anna imagined that this was what the inside of the forest near David's home would look like. It wasn't so bad. But of course, she was not alone, and that made all the difference.

"Where exactly are we now? In regards to the quarry?" she asked. The path had cut through thickets of oak and pine and black maple, past prickly brambles of violent red raspberry.

David stopped, studied the sky, and got his bearings. "Well, let's see. The quarry is back there," he pointed in an southeasterly direction. "I can tell because the front of Bannon Mountain is before us. The quarry is on the eastern slope, and this path loops along the side of the mountain at the base. The pharmaceutical plant where my father used to work is at the very end of the path, on the other side of the mountain. That's how I found *this*. I was out in the parking lot one day, waiting for Dad to finish work. I discovered this passageway through the bushes at the end of tarmac, and set off to conquer the land. I finally got too tired to go any farther, and headed back. Dad was frantic. I got my little behind slapped but good."

"What about your halo?"

"I left it at home that day." They started walking again. "Want to see the plant?"

"Why not? Maybe I can fill a few prescriptions while I'm at it."

The path turned towards the left and went upwards. Stones were lying everywhere, and they had to traverse here carefully.

"Watch your ankles," David said. "Rock slide." They continued upwards and David took Anna's hand again. She imagined what this scene would have been like with Derek, who was about as romantic as a case of botulism. He would have been bored half an hour ago, sick of trees and greenery; no sense of mystery or adventure. She squeezed David's hand, grateful to be with him.

"I used to bicycle out to the plant when I was a kid every day at quitting time," David said. "My father would drive back home slowly while I rode behind him on the bike. On some days, he'd put it in the trunk and I'd ride up front with him. I stayed away for a while after that time I found this path. Finally when I got older I made up my mind to follow it to the end. I'm not sure if I was pleasantly surprised or a little disappointed when it turned out to be the same path that ran off from the quarry. I'd followed that one for a while too, but had always come back before I got in too deep. I was hoping to find something unusual, I guess. Something exciting I could take back to my friends. Instead, I found the same old quarry."

"Aww," she said in commiseration.

"We're about halfway there now. To the plant, that is."

"Sounds a lot closer," she said. "Listen." They both came to a halt. They could hear people talking, a dog barking, the cries of children. A car horn honked. A screen door slammed and a woman called, "Johnny. Oh, Johnny." It sounded like there was an encampment just around the bend.

"It can't be," David said. "There's nothing in here but trees."

"I think you've found something to tell the kids about," she teased. "Isn't that nice? It may take a while, but some dreams do come true."

"I guess so. Seriously, I wonder what *is* up ahead."

They continued up the hillside trying to see through the trees, the voices and noises getting louder with each step. "Are you sure we didn't take a wrong turn?"

"Positive. There *are* no turns." They reached the top

of the hill, turned left and stared into the enclosure beyond.

"Don't look now, Livingstone, but I think we've just found Brigadoon."

David looked around in puzzlement. "No. This must be where old TV commercials come to die."

Nestled in a large clearing in the woods before them was a short street with houses on either side, as if a suburban block had been somehow teleported into the middle of the forest. The street ended abruptly at their feet, and stretched out into the opposite woods, until it reached a curve and vanished. The houses went on for only about the length of the block, then were replaced with lots where, presumably, new houses would be built for about another half a block. Then the woods crowded in again on either side of the road.

The houses were not unusual. They were all square and one-storied, with brick stoops, bay windows and a side entrance, as well as a front door. They each had driveways and hedges to separate them. All of the houses had backyards, and one or two had screened-in porches, where they could see people sitting through a gray and hazy gauze. The whole village, if that was what it was, had an unfinished look to it, as if it had been assembled in a hurry. Not all of the houses—there were about twelve—were completely painted, and the lawns in front looked freshly-seeded and sparse. There were some kids playing ball in the street. In the backyard of the nearest house, a man was cooking steaks on a barbecue grill. A woman sat on the front lawn two houses down, doing needlepoint in a lawnchair.

"This must have sprung up in the past couple of months," David said. "This road here must go out and join the main highway."

"David, look." Anna pointed to a sign that was nearly level with the spot where they stood, a few feet to the left. They walked over to get a better look. It read: FELICITY VILLAGE home development, a project of

268

Clarence Realty.

"Poor David," Anna said, "the woods aren't your own anymore."

"It's spooky," he agreed, "this thing springing up in the middle of nowwhere."

"People have to live somewhere, I suppose," Anna continued. "Although I don't know why anyone would want to live here. You might as well live in Queens. Why move to the country when your next-door neighbor is still two feet away? The houses are awfully ugly, too. No imagination at all. Remember Pete Seeger's song 'Little Boxes'? 'They're all made of ticky-tack, and they all look just the—' David. What *is* the matter?"

He was still staring at the sign, his eyes glued to the small print. He had not moved, had not acknowledged anything Anna had been saying.

"David, what's wrong?"

"Oh my God."

"David!"

He was hoping it meant nothing, that it was just a funny coincidence, but nothing he could do or say to himself would dispel the creepy feeling in the center of his gut. He was foolish to assume that there was anything wrong, anything to worry about, but his mind still raced off in dizzying, morbid directions. He thought of a two a.m. phone call, and whispered, frantic words, a call for help. He thought of missing men, and another man driven insane. He thought of Jeffrey. And he thought of Anna. Should he remind her of the significance of these words, which might mean nothing, which might mean everything.

"David, please tell me what's the matter."

Involuntarily he pointed to the bottom of the sign where it read:

CLARENCE REALTY—A DIVISION OF THE
BARROWS CORPORATION.

Chapter Twelve

Joey's Bar and Grille hadn't been this busy on a week-night in months. The Hillsboro ladies' club had had a special night meeting to plan their annual September auction and flea market, and some of the members had come to the bar for a nightcap. In addition to the ladies' club women, Joey's was also playing host to a large group of teenagers who had just come out of the early show at the moviehouse, a bunch of business men from New York passing through town on their way to a convention in Rutland, and David Hammond and Anna Braddon.

Ordinarily respectable women stayed away from Joey's, as it was predominantly the hang-out of the plant men and other male blue-collar workers, and they disliked trespassers of either sex. Still, even they couldn't stop the tide of customers coming in sometimes, and owner Joey wouldn't have wanted them to, for he cleaned up on those nights. They made up for the slow ones during the winter.

David and Anna had eaten dinner at the fancy French restaurant across the street, then come to Joey's for another drink or two. David had suggested they do so for nostalgic reasons: His first real drunk had been in Joey's —hardly a memorable occasion, but unforgettable none-theless. He'd had a lot of good times in here. Anna welcomed the chance to sample some quaint country night-life.

Joey's had been built in 1950 as a private residence, and was located just within the Hillsboro border. A few years after his family had moved in, as the town became more and more inhabited, Joey thought there might be a definite need for a tavern. The kitchen was enlarged so that they could serve sandwiches and easy meals, and the whole living and dining room scooped out to make way for a circular bar counter and lots of tables. Recently they'd put in a small stage where local bands could perform, and they pushed some of the tables up against the wall when they needed a dance floor. The family itself was moved up to the second story and the attic; one of the unused bedrooms was turned into a lounge where guests could be received.

The lights were kept low in the place, most of the illumination coming from candles in small red goblets on every table, as well as from lights over the bar. The wood counter and square wooden tables, decorated with red and white checkered tableclothes that deliberately covered only about half of the tabletop for contrast, were smooth and brilliantly polished. The paneled walls were attractively decorated with pictures and plaques. Some of the customers considered the place's most attractive addition, however, to be Jeanine, the bar maid, who went from table to table balancing trays and taking orders clad in a white apron, a tight-fitting top and a short, creased skirt. Other cusomters preferred Bobby, the handsome twenty-seven-year-old bartender, with his crisp white shirt and black tie. Counted among his admirers were Wilma Waters, Eleanor Morrison, and Clair Bartley, Ted Bartley's wife. They sat at one table talking, the heavyset Wilma unable to refrain from making politely lewd remarks. Though Clair blushed a lot, she enjoyed the conversation and the direction it was taking; things were always so polite and stuffy at the ladies' club meetings—it was nice to let your hair down afterwards. Eleanor agreed that the young man was handsome indeed, and laughed at Wilma's comments, although she herself had long since stopped thinking of herself as a sexual being. She hoped Wilma would not become too vulgar or crude from the liquor she had consumed; Eleanor was so frightened of being home alone at night that she'd probably have put up with the coarsest remarks just so she'd have company. Jeanine came over in answer to Wilma's gesturing, and the women ordered another round of gimlets.

David and Anna sat a few tables away, conversing quietly over background music and amiable chatter. David had been the one to suggest they eat out; he did not want to sit at home and brood, although Anna had assured him that he was letting coincidence go to his head. (She had bullied him into letting her pay for the dinner. More accurately, he had *allowed* her to.) Every now and then the subject of Felicity Village came up again, and this was one of those times.

"For one thing," she was saying, clutching a martini in her right hand, "we don't know if the Corporation— what was it? Winnoes?"

"Barrows," he corrected.

"We don't know for sure if it had anything to do with my brother's death. They rented the building next door to the hardware store, and something funny happened there, but that's all we know. There's no reason for us to jump to conclusions."

"I know. But it's just so odd. First I find out they've built a development in my home town, and then my father tells me that they were also the ones who took over the pharmaceutical company." He had called his father to inquire about the housing development out by the plant, and his father had recalled the name, and made the connection. "Maybe there *is* nothing to worry about," he continued. "But the Barrows Corporation *was* somehow mixed up in the trouble in Milbourne; there's no way around that. There's no proof, of course. All they did was rent a building for a while. But I feel it in my bones."

"I know, David. But I'm sure that they must be a pretty huge conglomerate. Nowadays these corporations own just about everything: movie production companies, publishing houses, real estate firms. Everything. And they get blamed for everything, too. Even if they were involved in some funny business in Milbourne, that's no reason to assume anything odd is going on here."

"I guess so. There's nothing I can do about it anyway."

"Maybe you could talk to Mr. Bartley about it. You said he was supposed to be a big shot in the firm now."

"Only in the pharmaceutical division. He might not know anything of importance. It might be worth a try, though. But would he talk to me?"

"He did before."

"He had no choice then. I was asking about his son. This is different. He can't give out company information just like that."

"If only there *were* some connection. I've done a good job of putting Milbourne and Jeffrey's death out of my mind—"

David interjected. "And here I am bringing it all up again."

"Now don't blame yourself, I would have badgered you until dawn if you hadn't told me why that sign was upsetting you. I can handle it, really I can. Anyway, what I was saying—if only Bartley *did* know something about Milbourne, something to finally clear up the mystery of Jeffrey's death and everything else once and for all. Oh, David, what if there's a chance?"

"Are you sure you want to know?"

"Yes. No matter what. I have to know."

"All right. I'll pay another call to Bartley. Although

the chances he would know what had gone on in the Forester Building are pretty remote.''

"But he might know someone who does know. Look David, you don't have to do this. I don't mean to put you on the spot. If you think the man lied to you about his own son, I'm sure he'll probably deny everything about Milbourne, assuming the corporation *was* somehow involved. It's just that—''

"I understand. I'll give it a shot. Tomorrow. How's about that?''

"Great.'' She leaned over and kissed him on the side of the mouth.

He was peering over her shoulder, his attention focusing elsewhere. "Say, I wonder if that's—? It's been quite a few years, but . . .''

"What are you talking about?''

"George's mother. Mrs. Bartley. I think that's her. She's with some women over there. She's put on a little weight, but she's still a good-looking lady.''

"Oh, do you like older woman? Perhaps I should check out the competition.''

"Be my guest. But I doubt if you'll be jealous.''

Mrs. Bartley turned out to be an attractive middle-aged woman with fading brown hair set in a wavy permanent that curled over her forehead. She had bright green eyes and a nice smile. Her mouth was small and her nose slightly long for her face. She was wearing a plain green dress, and was smoking a cigarette in a thin white holder. Her face was somewhat puffy, probably from an excess of calories, constant grief, or both. The woman on her right was fat but pretty, with curly brown hair worn down to the shoulders, and a slash of red lipstick on her mouth. The other woman was thin and gray-haired, in her fifties, all tucked in on the chair, as if fighting off cold or fear. The three of them seemed to run the gamut for excessive ebullience to almost neurotic repression, with Mrs. Bartley stuck squarely in the middle. At least she seemed to be enjoying the rather loud banter of her chubby companion more than her skinny friend was.

"Too bad, David. All three of them seem to be paying unseemly attention to the bartender, who, by the way, is not bad-looking at all."

"Oops." David joked. "I can't compete with a hunk like that." He laughed, but inside he was far from amused. He really couldn't compete with those Derek types. He suddenly felt quite ugly and gnome-like sitting at the same table with Anna Braddon. Since Anna seemed off somewhere by herself now, a grim expression on her face suggesting that she was pondering the horrors of the past, the both of them sat in quiet, morbid contemplation for a while. Anna broke out of it first.

"Say, why are we so solemn all of a sudden?"

"Hmmm? Oh, I don't know."

"Silly. I'm not interested in the bartender."

"I'm not interested in Mrs. Bartley." They both burst out laughing at themselves. "Shall we have our next drink here or at home?" David asked.

"I have this urge to be in that lovely bedroom of yours," Anna purred, "with one hand on a cool, icy drink, and the other hand on your big, thick—"

The waitress was hovering over them, a smile on her lips that she tried to subdue but found hard to fight. "Will you have anything else?" she asked.

"No," Anna said. "We were just leaving."

The waitress handed them the check. "Good night, and I hope we see you again." They got up and David helped Anna on with her coat. They could pay at the door. Initially David had been afraid that they might have been mobbed by customers who would recognize the Exclusiva girl, but now that they'd been left alone all evening, he was somewhat disappointed that he hadn't gotten a chance to show her off. "I've got an idea," David said. "Let's stop at Mrs. Bartley's table so I can say hello. She might have news of George. In any case, it might help ingratiate me with her husband."

They could hear some of the conversation at the other table as they approached. "What is Jeremy up to tonight?" Eleanor was asking.

Wilma shrugged, her eyes slightly aglow with alcohol. "Who knows? I can't keep up with that kid. It seems he's barely finished one project when he's starting up another."

"I hear he's a talented sculptor," Clair remarked.

"Oh, he is," Eleanor said. "I've seen some of his work. You should encourage him with that, Wilma. You never know. You might have an artist on—" She stopped short as the attractive young couple came up to the table. All three ladies took them in, obviously marveling at the woman's beauty, probably noticing that her date was nice-looking, if a bit underfed. Before David could speak, Wilma said in her best flirtatious tone: "I'm not as beautiful as your girlfriend, sonny, but there's more of me to love."

Eleanor put her hand to her mouth and giggled with embarrassment. Clair blushed again, unsuccessful in stifling a laugh. Wilma was quite in love with her own wit.

David couldn't think of a good comeback, so offered her what he hoped was his most charming and most polite smile. It seemed to please her. Then he turned his attention to Clair and said, "Mrs. Bartley, I don't know if you remember me. I was speaking to your husband the other day—"

"David! David Hammond. Of course I remember you. My, you're all grown up now."

"I'd like you to meet Anna Braddon."

Wilma looked as if she had been wondering why the girl was so familiar. She opened up her mouth wide, gasped for a second or two, then screamed: "Of *course!* Ladies, it's Anna Braddon. I've seen her on TV. The

276

Exclusiva girl."

Clair and Eleanor recognized her then, and also started to gush. David realized that now there was little chance for him to ask about George, or to make an appointment with Clair's husband. At least Anna didn't seem discomforted by all the attention.

"Oh, you're even more beautiful in person," Wilma said. "I love those ads you do. They're so—so liberating." Wilma was clearly taken with Anna's outfit, too, a bright white pants suit worn with a gold belt and necklace.

"I'm glad you enjoy the ads," Anna replied. "I have fun doing them."

David waited for a few minutes until there was a break in the conversation, after Anna had assured the women that her life was as exciting and glamorous as it seemed to be. He dove in during the pause. "Have you heard from George, Mrs. Bartley?"

There was silence for some time, while everyone waited for Clair to respond, to compose herself. The question seemed to have upset her, and she seemed confused and unsure of what to say. "George? Oh, he's out West now. Visiting friends. He doesn't come to Hillsboro very often."

"But—" David stopped himself. He could tell that the woman was reacting a preplanned story, and he had no wish to embarrass her. He began to realize that Anna's theory had been the correct one. It *had* been George in his apartment. Now the shame of the Bartley family, George had been packed away and sent off to an institution, a sanitarium. The Clair Bartley he remembered from his youth would have been mortified had such a thing become common knowledge. Not because she was snobbish, or stiffened by uppercrust superiority, but because she had always seemed to genuinely love her son. What mother likes to tell people that her child has come to a bad end? David would spare her further humiliation; perhaps even these friends of hers didn't know the full extent of the story.

"George has always wanted to travel," Clair continued. "Even as a boy he had the wanderlust." David looked down at the other two women; they were looking away awkwardly, staring down at their hands or at the drinks on the table. Obviously they knew that the subject of her son was a touchy one with Clair. David wished he had never brought it up. Mr. Bartley had said George was "away" on an errand. His errand *could* have taken him "out West." But somehow David thought things were not as simple as that.

"Well," he said. "If you talk to him, tell him I said hello."

"Of course, David."

Anna saved the day. "We have to be going now."

"Sure you can't join us?" Wilma looked quite disappointed by their abrupt departure. "We could pull up two more chairs."

"No. We have a busy day tomorrow."

Wilma smiled almost lewdly and giggled. "Well, have a nice time."

David and Anna said goodbye to the other women and started for the exit.

Clair Bartley stared dully into her gimlet, idly stirring it with the little plastic swizzle stick. Then she put her head down in her hands and started sobbing. Wilma and Eleanor looked at each other for a moment, then began to console their friend. "There, there, dear," Wilma said, stroking her hair tenderly. "Everything will be all right. Just wait and see."

After a moment, Clair lifted her head proudly, dug into her purse and started dabbing at the wet spots near her eyes with a handkerchief. "I'll be all right," she said. Eleanor and Wilma exchanged looks again, looks full both of pity and relief.

Clair lifted her arm and caught Jeanine's attention. "Another round, please," she said.

Jeremy Waters at fifteen was a melancholic figure. He sat on his bed, surrounded by plastic kits and clay statues which he had either built or created himself. His mother was fond of saying that he had magic fingers, and that someday his work would grace the finest parks, the exhibit rooms in the best museums. "Maybe they'll hire you to sculpt another big thing of Lincoln, like they got in Washington, someday. That one just be getting old and wrinkled by now."

He didn't argue with her. His mother, Wilma Waters, was a plump and lovable figure of fifty-three, who managed to stay solvent, balanced and chipper in spite of the increasing bills, the hard work she had to do each day, and the trial of raising a son without a husband to help her. Jeremy tried hard not to think about his father, who had died when Jeremy was seven.

Some deaths are so brutal and so shocking that news of them can only incite numbness in the listener's ears, only the worst possible kind of chill, a truly piercing horror that cuts right through the bone marrow. Jeremy's father had had that kind of death. There had been an explosion out at the plant. The best anyone could reconstruct it was that the force of the blast lifted Jim Waters—who was a bulky, but well-constructed man—right off his feet, and blew him with hurricane force against the brick wall, smashing him to pulp.

They'd had to scrape him off the wall.

Jeremy had always been somewhat shy and reserved, but the loss of his father had made him even worse in those respects, and his mother—in spite of her natural survival instincts and ebullience—was not able to draw him entirely out of his self-imposed, self-restricting shell. She simply loved him as best and as much as she could, and hoped that all would turn out right in the end.

Jeremy and his mother lived in a two-story house on the outskirts of town. Besides the garage, they had a small toolshed out back, a tree house that had been neglected since Jeremy's eleventh birthday, and two acres of not-very-well-tended ground. The upper rooms in the house were unused except for when relatives came to stay. They had a rickety old picket fence surrounding the front half of the property, and a long clothesline which was always full of wet, flapping things like sheets and towels.

In his bedroom Jeremy scrunched down further in his pillow, messing his longish, wavy brown hair. He had an innocent, sweet-looking face and was built along slender lines. Whatever muscles he had came from swimming alone in a pond three-quarters of a mile down the road which his mother's friends owned. He was tall for his age, almost gangly.

Jeremy never talked about much besides his models and sculptures, so his mother would have been surprised at the content of the book he was reading. It was a study of astral projection, otherwise known as out-of-the-body experiences, when a person's intangible astral body could detach itself from the physical body and float around in the astral plane, meeting other live astral travelers as well as the "spirits" of dead people. He had first heard of it in a movie or a comic book, then had found a few books on the subject at the local library. He found it all quite fascinating.

It was said that people had out-of-the-body experiences while they were asleep, and that part of their dreams were actually memories from their travels. It was much harder to travel on the astral plane while *conscious*, however, and this is what Jeremy was hoping to achieve—the ability to step out of his own body while fully awake. There were certain techniques, practices one could develop, to make the transition easier.

It wasn't so much that he hoped to find his father in

the astral plane, to communicate with him, to feel his love from that lost land that lay beyond death; perhaps it was more than he might finally be able to deal with the facts of his father's death if he knew, without a doubt, that there *was* something else after this mortal life was finished. Not a heaven or hell, not something measured in religious terms, but rather in scientific ones. It was not necessarily his soul that would separate from his body, but a non-physical form, an aura perhaps, that could travel anywhere freely, through all barriers, without restrictions of distance or place. He could find death so much more acceptable, so much less frightening, if he knew that there was *more* to existence afterwards. How much nicer his world would seem, this world where people were shot and stabbed and blown apart, decapitated in auto crashes and bus accidents—so many truly horrible ways to die—how much nicer it would seem if he knew that the people who died (especially those who died in *that* way, that bloody, terrible manner like his father had), if they had a place to go after it was through, a place without pain, without suffering, where one's body—if that was what you could call it—would be whole again and without imperfection or flaw.

So he read and he studied and he read and he studied. It was near ten when he gave it his first shot. First he had to lie still, very still, on the bed. Oh, he hoped it worked. He hoped he wouldn't fall asleep. He had to be awake, had to be conscious, and then he would know. Then he would really know.

Yes, yes, he was tingling. Did that mean anything, or was he fooling himself? Was he just getting sleepy, or actually preparing to pass over? Would it happen. *Still,* lie *still!*

He opened his eyes, hoping to see himself a foot away from the ceiling, with his body lying on the bed far below. He realized instead that his astral body hadn't budged an inch.

Perhaps the problem was mental. Perhaps he really didn't want to travel into the astral plane as a disembodied bit of ectoplasm. All the books he'd read on the subject had said that it could be a pretty scary experience when fully awake. It was said that our distorted dreams were deliberately cryptic, because if we ever clearly remembered what we saw in the astral plane while sleeping, we would go mad. Maybe Jeremy was too subconsciously scared to *allow* himself to float unchaperoned through the ether. Maybe this subconscious dread was what was preventing him from leaving.

He tried to remove all traces of fear from his mind, but it wasn't easy. He reminded himself that one really couldn't receive injury in the astral plane, and that it was very easy to *think* your way back to your physical body without incurring damaging side effects from the experience. Everyone always said that ghosts couldn't hurt you. But they were *scary*. If only he could rid himself of that parochial, irrational fear he had of spirits. If only he would accept that once he'd passed over—even though he was still alive—he would, in effect, become a spirit himself. What was there to be frightened of?

So he lay there and concentrated and did all the things the books had told him to do. The mental exercises. The physical preparation and conditioning. And most of all, he tried to develop the proper frame of mind. That was the most important thing. He had to truly *believe*, or else all was lost.

And then, at quarter of ten, something finally happened.

Jeremy fell asleep.

In his sleep he dreamed. He dreamed that he was floating, floating, lifting free of the bed, drifting down to the end of the mattress, and out onto the empty air, flowing past the bureau upon which his latest sculptures had been placed, floating, floating towards the door, through the door, which had been closed, and down the hall. He passed through solid objects, moving so fast now that he could not tell what they were; it seemed that he was in the kitchen briefly, floating, still floating, then he went through the wall of the house and was outside. He had no control over where he was going.

Suddenly he was high in the air, moving at a rapid rate, the tops of the trees racing by just beneath him, scraping against his body although he could not feel them. No pain, no sensation whatsoever. Just a dull, nagging throb of mounting fear. He tried to fight it now, afraid of what would come after he reached his destination. On the bed, Jeremy's body twisted and shuddered, his lips formed low and anguished groans as he tried to wake himself up from within, his dream rapidly turning into a nightmare.

And still he floated, floated. Over the trees, up high in the air, far, far away from the house, traveling toward Bannon Mountain. It seemed as if he was heading for the quarry. No—not there! Only the bravest children went there after dark. Tormented ghosts hung out in the shattered derelict buildings, the ghosts of those who had died while the quarry was in operation, the ghosts of children who had drowned in the water rising up at midnight from the bottom of the quarry to pounce upon those unsuspecting ones who came to witness their arrival. Not *there!* He fought and squirmed, his mind and body fighting to regain consciousness, terrified of his journey's end.

Part of his mind thought he was having an out-of-body experience, although he also knew that he was asleep. Perhaps his experiment had only partially succeeded. He was half-conscious at any rate, aware of what was happening, of the voyaging sensation, but not entirely sure that it was not just a dream of the ordinary kind. He had been hoping so much to enter the astral plane that it would only be natural for him to dream that he had done so. Which was it? He was afraid to find out.

He was approaching the mountain. Although he seemed to be facing the sky, somehow he could see underneath himself, too, could see the houses and their lights receding in the distance. There were few homes out this far from town. He was traveling up the mountain road, past the home of his mother's friend, Eleanor, not far from where the whole family had been slaughtered. He hadn't known them very well.

He was going up the road, traveling at a dizzying speed, swishing over the trees, racing through the air. This road ended at a cleared-out lookout post where kids sometimes went when they were in a romantic mood. The quarry was about a mile away, but still too close as far as he was concerned. God, this had to be a dream, just a terrible dream. Why couldn't he wake up?

On the bed, the trunk of Jeremy's body wiggled and squirmed. His arms and legs were paralyzed, the body's defense against thrashing out and hurting oneself during sleep. His mind struggled to wake up, to pull himself out of sleep. His cries were louder now.

He had arrived at the lookout point. Everything seemed so intense, so clear. The wind flapping the leaves of the trees. The warm, summer night air. He saw a car parked over near the edge of the clearing. Suddenly everything was foggy again. But he felt a strange presence and hard horrible screams. Someone, someone in the car, was screaming. A shrill panicky scream of utter horror, of shuddering revulsion. A scream high-pitched and fierce with agony.

His blood turning cold, his mind on fire, Jeremy finally awakened.

Someone was dying up there on Bannon Mountain, and *only he knew!*

Or had it only been a dream?

He was lying there wondering what to do when he

heard his mother coming in the front door, humming to herself, causing more fuss and bother in the opening of one simple lock than most people did moving furniture. He steeled himself. As much as he loved her, she had a habit of intruding at the damnedest moments.

"Jeremy! Mother's home!"

But the sound of her voice reminded him how good it was to have someone else near him now, in the house, especially after his frightening ordeal or nightmare or whatever it had been. He could feel her warmth radiating down the corridor, entering his room before she herself did. This time he did not scold her for not knocking.

"How's it going?" she asked, smiling. She had been drinking, that much was obvious. He sort of liked her in these pixilated moods, although it frightened him a bit. She was still head of the household and it scared him when he was more in control than she was. He felt he was not quite ready to assume command.

"Hi Mom. Did you have a nice time?"

"Oh, yes. You'll never guess who I met." She came over and sat beside him on his bed. He listened while she told the story of meeting "that girl on TV" but he was only mildly interested and could not place the woman anyway. He sat there quietly and politely while his mind replayed the images he had seen in his dream, heard the screams again, felt that unseen presence in the dark.

When she finally left to pass out in bed, he kissed her on the cheek and said, "Goodbye."

" 'Goodbye'?" she laughed. "You mean 'good night,' little pumpkin. Never say 'goodbye.' "

It had been a slip. He had made up his mind to sneak out that very night and go up to the top of Bannon Mountain. He did not know why, only that he *had* to. The thought of it made him shiver with horror, but he had to confront whatever it was, had to find out if he really had traveled up there in his sleep. He had to know if there really was some kind of special plane, the existence of which would increase the chances of some sort of life after death. Maybe up there in the dark, he would at last come face to face with his father again.

He had told his mother "goodbye."

He hoped his words had not been prophetic.

Clair Bartley used her key to enter the house, not sure if her husband or Mimi were still up at that hour. It was only a little after ten—she and the girls had stayed out much later than they had intended to—but Ted often retired early, and Mimi had been taking to her bed more and more often these days; work she had once breezed through five years ago was suddenly giving her fits of exhaustion. The woman was ill with something, but Mimi was not the type to discuss her private affairs with her employers.

Clair entered the foyer quietly and walked down the hall to the living room. She had had quite a bit to drink this evening, but now she found herself wanting yet another one to steady her nerves. That crying exhibition in the bar had been terrible. Normally she was such a composed, calm and clear-headed woman. But seeing that old friend of her son's like that, his innocent question . . . Everything had come rushing back at her and she'd felt confused and dizzy, disoriented. It had all been too much for her. She tried her best to keep herself in control when it came to the subject of her son, but sometimes . . . sometimes it was difficult. Yes, she did need another drink.

First it had been a couple just to be sociable with her friends; she had never been crazy about Joey's Bar and Grille. But then she'd needed another to recover from her impropriety, crying in public for God's sake. Wilma and Eleanor had been so understanding. They knew something was wrong with George, only they didn't know what and did not press her. Still, she knew she had someone to talk to when the time came, if ever; if her husband ever said it was all right.

Then all three of them had been feeling so good, having such a good time—and how often did she, did *any* of them have good times, really?—that they'd had another and another and it was a wonder they had managed to get up from the table. Eleanor had wisely ordered two cups of strong, black coffee. She had a good distance to drive on the night-swept highway. Although the traffic was thin at this hour, there was no sense taking chances.

Clair froze in her tracks. There were voices in the living room; someone was in there. More than one. She listened. She recognized her husband's voice. And a woman's. The nurse. The nurse he'd hired to take care of George. She felt ashamed, but she had to listen, had to find out of there were any foundation to her insane, hysterical suspicions. Although she could not quite make out what they were saying—only a word here and there, a phrase—she was relieved by the tone of their voices, still denoting an employee—employer relationship, *his* deep and authoritative, *hers* submissive and quieter. They must have been talking about George.

Clair crept up carefully. From this new vantage point she could see their reflections in the living room window, although they themselves were still out of view, as she was out of theirs. The nurse had a drink in her hand! It was hard to tell, but it looked as if she had been crying. She seemed quite upset. Ted, always in control, was sitting in an easy chair, holding a scotch and soda, using his resonant voice as a mainstay to calm the woman down, to soothe her.

" . . . never seen anything . . . like . . ." the nurse said. She was a pretty woman in her late twenties. Efficient, or so Bartley claimed. Good figure. Always neat and clean. She slept in a room adjacent to the one where George was kept. She was on hand most of the time, although she had her off-hours, loosely defined.

" . . . will never give up hope . . ." Bartley said, holding his feelings in as usual. God, Clair wanted to scream, to bellow, anything to break his composure. He had brought all of this upon them, and she was the one who wept.

" . . . I'm not sure how much longer . . . take . . ." the nurse said, rubbing her arm with her free hand.

" . . . know it's trying, but we must . . . we can do."

Clair wanted to know what had happened. She strode into the room and startled the both of them, nearly causing the nurse to spill her drink.

"Clair. I didn't hear you come in."

"Mrs. Bartley. You frightened me."

"A drink during working hours? Isn't that risky?" Clair said testily, directing her question to her husband instead of the nurse.

"Miss Hamilton has had quite a fright, Clair," Bartley said slowly. "I thought a drink might do her some good. Besides, she's entitled to some relaxation now and then. There's usually no trouble at this time of night anyway. George is sleeping quite soundly."

Next he'll have her in here in an evening gown and mascara, she thought. "Well, I can use a drink myself." She hoped it was not apparent that she'd already had a few. She did not go near Ted or kiss him, not wanting to betray the alcohol on her breath. He got up and made her a gimlet, as she instructed. "What happened?" she asked Miss Hamilton.

The nurse looked at Ted before answering. This annoyed Clair a great deal. Was she not the boy's mother? Didn't she have a right to know everything that went on? Did she need her husband's permission for even this?

Ted nodded, almost imperceptibly. Clair waited patiently, then said: *"Well?"*

"George gave me a scare." Miss Hamilton had bright

288

yellow hair pulled up on top of her head, although a few strands hung down stylishly by her cheeks. She wore little makeup, and had a naturally creamy complexion. She was a tall woman, and a strong one, with muscular, but feminine, arms that played a great deal of tennis and were capable of lifting the heaviest private patients. Ted had told Clair that he had hired her from a very reputable agency. "At around nine o'clock, he just—stopped breathing. Oh, it was nothing serious. He started breathing again of his own accord a few moments later. No damage."

"Then why aren't you with him now? It could happen again!"

"Darling, please stay calm," Bartley chastened. "It was just an initial reaction to his new medicine. He's over the hurdle now. Jean sat with him for some time afterwards, and there were no repercussions. She's carrying the beeper with her. If there is any change in his vital signs, the machine will beep and his room is just down the hall." The specialized beeper had been expensive, but it was worth it. Unlike most doctors' beepers, which alerted them to phone calls, this one—developed by the firm Ted worked for—notified a doctor or nurse any time the machines the patient was hooked up to registered the slightest change. "So you see, there's nothing to worry about. Here, take your drink. It will help you."

She took it gratefully. "Where were you so late?" Ted asked.

She decided to tell the truth; any lie could be easily uncovered. "I went with some of the ladies to Joey's for a nightcap. I ran into David Hammond there—"

"What did you say to him?"

"I only had a chance to say hello and goodbye," she lied. "His date for the evening turned out to be Anna Braddon. You know, the TV model."

"She's beautiful," Nurse Hamilton said.

"And everyone was so eager at seeing her that I'm

afraid I didn't get a chance to say much to David. She's staying with him at his father's house. I didn't get a chance to ask about Jonathan, either. I must call David tomorrow."

"Is that wise, Clair?" He looked at her pointedly.

"Oh. All right then. I won't." She remembered that they'd told Mimi to tell David what amounted to a bold and outrageous lie when George had turned up at his apartment earlier that year. That was when his father had still been furious with George, unaware of how serious his condition had been. He'd sent down men to look for him in the city and they'd found him and brought him back—and he had gotten progressively worse ever since. She could hardly bear to look at him now. Still, he was her son. And she loved him. She did not understand what had happened to him or why, but she loved him.

She put down her drink and moved towards the exit from the room. "Where are you going?" her husband demanded.

"To see George. I want to see my son before I go to sleep."

"There's no need for that. He's fine."

"Ted. He's my *son.*"

"There's no need to disturb him. Besides, you know how it always upsets you to see him the way he is."

"I don't care."

"Please, Mrs. Bartley." Nurse Hamilton moved towards her, her hands both free now. She was tensing her body.

"What's the matter with you two? Why can't I go in to see my own son? I'm going, and that's all there is to it." She moved again, starting for the corridor.

"Miss Hamilton," Bartley said. "Stop her."

Suddenly the nurse grabbed her from behind, pinioning her arms. "Damn you! Damn you!" Clair struggled and snarled at the nurse. "Leave me alone! You may have taken my husband from me but I won't let you take my son!"

Startled by the woman's unfounded accusation, the nurse released her and stepped back, looking towards her employer for guidance. That was fatal. Clair slapped her savagely in the face and ran down the hall towards George's room before she could be stopped again.

"Clair! Don't! Don't go in there! Please listen to me!" Bartley ran down the hall after her, brushing the nurse aside, desperately trying to reach his wife before she reached their son's room. "For God's sake—*Don't open that door!*"

But it was too late. She had it open already, and was looking inside. She was gasping for breath, her eyes widened in disbelief. Her fingers shook, then her arms, and her entire body. She lifted her hands to her mouth. And she screamed. She screamed so loud that it resounded through every room of the house.

And then she plummeted to the ground in a dead faint.

The moon was out tonight, and though it was not full, its light nonetheless bathed the earth in a gray glow, casting deep dark shadows where creatures could hide and wait. Eleanor Morrison concentrated on the road ahead of her, too frightened to think about what might be watching and waiting in the woods on either side of the highway. She was a good way out of town now, so isolated and vulnerable. She had been hoping that the liquor would have affected her in such a way that everything would have had an air of unreality about it, like a movie or a play viewed from afar. Nothing would seem menacing then. How could it? She would be safe in a gentle, protective haze of booze.

But the closer she got to her house, the more she realized that such peace and safety was not to be. The coffee she had drunk had sobered her up enough to enable her to drive. She had thought that she would not have cared whether she got home in one piece of not, that this terrible fear she lived with would have made her welcome death. But instinct had prevailed, and she found herself fighting her intoxication every inch of the way, sobering more each mile, so that she could traverse this lonely stretch of highway with the greatest of care. She didn't know why she was being so cautious; there was nothing waiting for her at home but more unending terror until the dawn broke through; and even then, there was the loneliness. She would have stayed alone longer in Joey's Bar and Grille had her sense of propriety not balked at the very idea. She'd stayed for almost two hours after Clair and Eleanor had left, pretending that she wanted to "catch her breath" before embarking. She'd watched the TV set over the bar, nursed the cups of coffee, and listened to the coarse, vulgar voices of the men drinking beer. A lady did not do such things. That was for drunks and teenagers.

She saw the lights of her house—she always left a few on, not so much to scare off burglars, but to light up the way—as she turned onto the side road leading up the mountain. She thought for a moment that she'd seen something in the light of her car as the auto swerved around the corner; a person, a boy really. She hadn't gotten a very good look. But no, what would a boy be doing out here at this time of night? It could have been a trick, thieves waiting to ambush her on the road. *Or perhaps the ghost of the boy who died in the Harper home that horrible night.* Only he had been much younger.

She turned into her driveway, which was well-lit, and parked the car outside the garage. She could not bear the thought of driving it in there at this hour. Of leaving an entrance to her home wide open for the few minutes it would take for her to drive in, get out and pull down the heavy door. No, she would leave the car out here tonight. She disembarked and ran for the front door.

The noise of the crickets seemed unnaturally loud. A warm breeze rustled the leaves of the trees, and a distant howl of an unseen animal sent a chill through her body.

The house was a large, rectangularly shaped structure, the front higher than the back, constructed of brick and wood and glass. The living room was almost entirely enclosed by huge windows which looked out onto the forests stretching down into the valley. Although it was not really that high up on the mountain, the view was still quite breathtaking, particularly on clear, sunny days. A terrace ran around three sides of the house, hanging over the undergrowth below them. A stone fireplace was set in the middle of the wall, between glass doors leading out to the terrace.

The house was closer to the Harpers'—now an empty, ugly death house—than anyone else's in Hillsboro. It was just as isolated—the woods around it just as thick and as capable of masking the approach of a hundred careful and clever killers—as the Harpers had been.

And there was no one—absolutely no one—nearby.

Eleanor got the key in the lock in one swift stroke, turned it, and pushed the door open, shutting herself safely inside.

She stood there for a moment, letting out her breath, trying to relax. Her small nose, large brown eyes, tiny mouth all turned as one as her head darted around the foyer, looking for something, someone, some *sign*. She could feel the effects of the liquor again, warm and tempting, but she kept little booze in the house and did not intend to have any more. It might put her to sleep, true, but she wanted to be in possession of all her faculties, in case . . . in case a sound in the night woke her up and she had to prepare herself for them, prepare herself for the intruders when they came up the stairs to kill her the way they had killed the Harper family. She was living on borrowed time, and she knew it. Everyone said their murderers were far away from town by now, but she knew that criminals always returned, they waited until everyone's guard was down, and then they returned, to plunder once more, to get the same "easy pickings" that had led them to the neighborhood in the first place. It was only a matter of time.

She walked into the living room, which was already well-lighted, and sat down on the couch. She wondered about retiring early, or about reading a book, or making herself a cup of hot tea. Or more coffee. She wanted to sleep tonight, but did not feel like sleeping. Perhaps it *would* be better if she slept through it all, if she never woke to hear them approaching, to see them enter her bedroom, to feel them as they butchered her. Better to sleep through it all, to never wake up, if she was doomed to die anyway. But what if there was a chance, a small chance of escape? She asked herself why she clung to the idea of life so doggedly—was it mere instinct—or did she still feel there was yet a chance for happiness, to get something further out of life? If only she could think, could see things clearly. Ever since the murders she had come unglued, caught in a depression that refused to yield or budge an inch, refused to allow her the luxury of rational, unemotional thought. She had not been this bad off since her husband's death. This was worse. Fear for the future was bad enough even when one was well-provided for; but fear of losing life itself, coldly, brutally, was far, far worse. And in one's own home, too. She just couldn't deal with it.

She was giving herself the creeps again. She felt naked and vulnerable there in the living room with the lights on and those huge windows reflecting herself and her surroundings, but not permitting a glimpse into whatever might be waiting out there for her to put out the light. It seemed as if images of herself were spying on her, invading her privacy, entreating her to come join them in their ghostly mirror land. How she hated this horrible room. What had possessed them to put in such huge windows?

They were too big for blinds and they had never bought curtains or drapes. "There's no one way out here to spy on us," her husband had said. During the day they had that wonderful view, and at night the moonlight, or the pitch blackness, had contrasted nicely with the warm glow of the room. They had never considered ruining the effect by covering up the windows. Now Eleanor realized she should have done something long ago, certainly after the murders. Drapes, curtains, blinds—anything would have been better than this. Even so, she would still be aware of how easy it would be for someone to look in, even with the drapes up, and how much easier it would be for them to creep up next to the house unnoticed. Perhaps with the windows uncovered like this and the lights on, the criminals might be deterred? No, they would realize that the reflection prevented her from seeing outside.

She had made up her mind to go to bed when she heard the first noise. It had come from outside, near the end of the driveway. Like something falling and hitting the ground. Then she did something remarkable, something she never thought she would have done.

She turned out the living room lights.

She had felt too exposed under their glare, and though being in darkness had always been one of her greatest fears, she now found it preferable to standing out in the surrounding blackness as if she'd been holding a beacon. Now she had the advantage. They could no longer see in. She went close to the window which formed the left wall and peered outside, trying to distinguish something moving or standing near the trees where the sound had come from. There!—What was that? She thought she'd seen something moving slowly through the grass towards the terrace. What could it have been—a man crawling on his hands and knees perhaps?

Her hand went up to her mouth and she stifled a cry. It was happening, finally happening. *Stay calm, try to stay calm*. She must get something to protect herself with. She must call the police. Maybe they would get here in time. She must do something!

There was a scratching sound at the front door. Whatever she had seen was not alone. Someone else was trying to get in. Had she locked the door? My God, had she locked it when she'd come in, or had she been too drunk, too damn drunk to remember? She wanted desperately to check, but the scratching had become more furious and she was afraid to go near there. *Force yourself, force yourself; it will get in.* Why wasn't it trying the doorknob, testing the lock? Why was it scratching like that?

She ran to the door and checked it, relieved to see that she had locked it and put the chain in place. Yet it seemed so flimsy. Then she heard something crack under her feet. She looked downwards. A jagged mark had appeared in the door frame, loose slivers of wood fell onto the floor by her shoes. Something protruded from a hole in the door. She screamed out loud, stepped back, then came to a halt. *Now they would know someone was inside.* The same tools they had used to enter could be employed to murder her. She turned and started for the kitchen, for the precious phone she would use to call for help.

Before she had moved two feet there was a burst of activity behind her and she felt musty air on her back. She was covered with sharp splinters of wood. She turned and saw that the door had practically been torn from its hinges. Something was crawling into the foyer. She wondered if she would see the face of her killer before he destroyed her.

It was then that she realized that whatever was coming into her house that moment was definitely not a man; there was nothing human about it. It pulled itself towards her, and though she tried to run, she was caught, held tightly by fear and fascination; death did not seem important. She had to see what this thing was! She had to see!

But as it came closer, she realized that there were others just like it following in the rear. All of them looked alike, except that a few of them—very few—had pale white appendages at their very front tips, instead of the darker, bulkier growths that the others had. They all emitted the same disgusting noise, a sort of *pop pop pop*, a kind of repulsive clicking sound. There were about a dozen of them clustered outside her door. They had some kind of short limbs, and spiny sharp outgrowths grew out of their backs, and their bodies were long and narrow, tapering at the far end. Perhaps the most horrible thing about them was their odor.

She collapsed onto the carpeted floor of the hallway as they advanced upon her. One of them was near her leg. She did not even bother to pull the limb out of reach. There was nothing to be done. She knew what they wanted with her, and even if she had reached the phone, no one would have come in time, no one would have believed her. She shook and sobbed, but did not scream. It would have done no good. She was too shocked to do a thing to save herself.

As the first and second of them started gnawing on her leg, she noticed what the white appendages were that some had instead of the dark, knob-like heads. They were like *faces*. Human faces. Yes, some of these monstrosities had human faces, although nothing else about them was at all related to the human species. She recognized some of the faces, too. They all looked familiar, like people she had once known, people she still knew. But it wasn't possible. These things weren't human!

It was not clear exactly when her mind snapped for good, when she was mercifully consigned to an oblivion in which she was incapable of taking notice of the things as they tore away her garments, feasted on the flesh and bone, and sucked up blood with their oddly shaped mouth-parts. It might have been when she saw that one of the creatures had a face that looked just like her late husband's, like Frank's. But most certainly the final moment of her sanity came when the creature with her *own* features stared directly into her eyes, opened its mouth—and dripping viscous fluid—began nibbling on her face.

Chapter Thirteen

They sat in the den, sipping a sweet liqueur, telling each other stories from their past. David occasionally brushed a hand through his tousled hair and gave his lovely Anna an affectionate squeeze. Both of them had lost track of time. They pulled apart from a particularly lengthy clinch and David asked Anna if she were hungry.

"We just had dinner. Didn't we?"

"That was hours ago."

She studied him. "You know I bet you'll still be cute even when you're fat."

He laughed, and rubbed his lip lingeringly with an upraised thumb. "Cute and jolly. A winning combination."

"I haven't had this much fun since I went necking with Eddie Pester in the Runlake drive-in when I was seventeen."

"Who did Eddie pester? You?"

She groaned. "If that's what hunger does to your sense of humor, you better have something to eat. I'll settle for another glass of this liqueur."

He grabbed the bottle from the table in front of them and poured some of its contents into her tiny glass. He took some more himself, then settled back into his seat. Mugging, he affected a Brooklyn accent and said,

"Hows about another kiss, babe?"

She gave him one.

David and Anna almost spoke their lines automatically, reliving scenes from their youth, their early days of heavy petting—or rather what they imagined those days would have been like had they had the active social lives their teenage friends had had. David had not been much of a Lothario, and Anna—although she'd been rather attractive even in those early developing years—had not been hot stuff with the boys. Each of them felt as if they were finally catching up with what they'd missed, getting a "steady" to go with at last, a date for senior prom. Derek had not given Anna, and Janice had not given David, what they had really needed. Passion. Romance. *Excitement.*

Both of them wondered if there were any more to their relationship other than the fact that they both desperately needed one at this point in their lives. Sure, they were comfortable together—but was there anything else? Anna knew that with David she felt much more than mere physical attraction—that had been the mainstay of her feelings for Derek, that and the fact that he had radiated the kind of casual glamor she had always found attractive in others and desirous in herself. There was no glamor in David, and she found herself equally excited by that. Or was it just a reaction to her lousy marriage—a compensation?

David clinked his glass against hers. "A toast."

"A toast to what?"

"To you and me."

"To you and me." They drank. David drained his glass and poured himself some more. Anna watched him, trying to see him objectively, trying to understand just what he represented to her. Propelled by the buzz of liquor in her head, she said, "What about you and me, David? What's happening with us?"

He said it very quickly and very simply. "I love you."

Pause. "But I don't know anything other than that. I'm content with the way things are. I'm in no hurry to tie you down, to make you rush into something when you're not ready. I'm not even sure there's anything to rush into. Or that I'd be good for you. I certainly wouldn't make a great provider. You'd be the breadwinner in this pair, that's for sure. And my 'masculine ego' could deal with that quite nicely—to a point." Another pause. "What about you?"

She didn't need to think about it. "Maybe I love you too, but I'm not sure I'm *in* love with you. Yet. And neither are you sure. It takes time for that kind of feeling to develop, and you're right, it can't be rushed. It has to come about slowly and naturally. So I guess I feel the same way you do. Content. Unhurried. And while you might become more of a success than you think you will, I am not anxious to have someone support me. Yet." She sipped her liqueur. "Hmm. That was easy, wasn't it?"

"Yes. And a little disappointing."

"How so?"

"I guess I *wanted* to be the object of some kind of grand passion as much as I was afraid of it. Does that make any sense?"

"Perfect sense. We all feel that way. We want to be wanted—even if we don't want the people who want us." She laughed, and dipped her head onto his shoulder. "Not very eloquent, am I?" She pointed to the liqueur. "I've got to stop drinking this stuff."

In a way both of them were relieved. They had each confessed strong feelings for the other—but with reservations. There was no danger of desertion, no fear of unrequited love that one or the other couldn't handle. Putting it all out of her mind, Anna suddenly said, "This is a grim little town, isn't it?"

"Why do you say that?"

"I don't know. It just slipped out."

"We have no discos, if that's what you mean."

301

Perhaps he had said it a bit more harshly than he'd intended, she thought. Perhaps he'd been offended by her remark, as if by insulting his home town she had insulted his character. "Now David, don't listen to the gossip columnists so much. I do not spend my every waking hour dancing up a storm and snorting cocaine. I'm just a victim of bad press like everyone else."

He reacted to the slightly hostile tone in her voice. "That's the price of fame, I guess. You can't expect riches and notoriety if you don't make your private life public to all the little people who put you up there in the first place."

"It was no 'little people' that put me where I am. I worked hard. Real hard."

"Anna, darling, no offense, but all you had to do was look beautiful. Your fame and fortune are the results of an accident of birth. Besides with all you've got, why worry about a little bad press?"

Anna was infuriated by his condescending tone, and had to work hard to control her temper. "David, you're not being fair. I've paid my dues, I assure you. Sure I had help, but not because I came from a rich family or had an uncle in a modeling agency. I know my looks certainly didn't work against me, but it takes more than looks to get ahead. I suffered through a lot of setbacks, had to deal with male chauvinism and bitchy jealousy. I missed out on contracts and opportunities, spent years living off cereal while I waited for a big break. It takes drive and ambition to make it in this world." Before she could stop herself she added: "Maybe you'd get someplace if you had some."

Anna could tell she'd offended David, which is what she'd been hoping for. How dare he say such things to her? She was not some untalented movie star's niece, living off a famous name. She had done it all by herself. She steeled herself for his rejoinder.

"Look, what do you know about it?" David exploded,

making no attempt to hide his anger. "You're not an artist, you're just a slab of cheesecake people dress and glob makeup on and take pictures of. What do you know about waiting for a big break? I've been waiting ten years. I've worked hard, too, and I didn't get big contracts and 100,000 dollars a year, either. Just a lot of rejection slips . . . until this chance with Belmont Cards came up. Do you know what it's like to have talent that goes ignored, to watch yourself sink into failure more and more each year? Maybe I was a failure, and I recognize that. But don't tell me I don't have ambition. All I *have* is ambition. I tried and tried and tried to get someplace and . . ."

"Is that why you're jealous of me, because you haven't gotten anywhere? I wish you would get somewhere! I'm getting a little tired of paying for our dinners all the time."

David looked away from her, obviously humiliated and embarrassed by his outburst, but still very angry. A moment ago they'd been professing love for each other, now they were practically tearing at each other's throats. "You don't have to rub it in," he said. "All along I've wondered why you bothered with me. I'm not in the social register, after all." His face was scrunched up in a show of sulkiness.

"Neither am I," Anna replied, trying to sort out her feelings. Did she want to savage him or show affection? Or both?

"I don't make much money. Even when this job starts in September I won't be able to compete with you moneywise."

Anna threw her head back and slapped her legs with her hands. "Who says you have to compete with me? Your 'male ego'?" Before he could respond, she added: "What started all this? My innocent remark about how grim this town is?" She was suddenly out for blood and loving it. "Well, it *is*. It is grim. That awful man and his

303

scarred children out at the quarry. Those pathetic, gushing women at the bar. The awful cluttering weeds all over this ugly house. Grim, grim, grim."

She got up, her mind racing, wondering how she could get out of there quickly. She started crying, hating the thought of breaking down in front of him, but unable to stop herself. "I am not a slab of cheesecake. I'm a human being. I'm sick of defending myself and my way of life. All of you 'little people' talk about how you hate those of us with fame and money, yet you idolize us, you read all about us, buying those dirty little rags they sell in supermarkets, the ones with disgusting, slanderous stories about this one or so and so. You resent us as much as you adore us, because we have what you want. Do you think any of you would act any differently than we did if *you* had the money, if *you* had the fame? I know there's a lot that's shallow and frivolous about the so-called beautiful people, but I thought you knew me better than that. What would you have me do? Scar myself, scratch up my face so that no one will want me anymore? Give up my contracts and my money? Oh no, not me. Because I know you're *nothing* when you're not wanted, and you're *nothing* without money, and I know the day will come when no one will want to look at me and no one will offer me contracts, and I damn well want to be protected when that day comes. I'm not Mother Teresa ministering to the Indians. I can't fool myself into thinking I am. But I won't apologize for wanting— and having—what *everyone else wants*. I want a good life, David, the same way you do. And I can't help that." She turned away from him, her hand pressed to her lips.

"I'm scared, David. I'm *scared*."

He got up and stood beside her, his hands on her shoulders, trying to calm her, trying to apologize. "I'm sorry, Anna. It's just that . . ." He sighed and exhaled, all artifice crumbling. "Maybe I do resent you. I know blanket condemnations of people aren't right, but . . . it's just that I've felt so humiliated sometimes, so *poor* compared to you. So damned unsuccessful. I'm sorry. It wasn't nice to take it out on you."

"Oh David."

"When you said this town was grim, well—this 'grim' house is about all that I own. And it's not even mine yet. Hey—maybe you can help me clear the 'awful weeds' away tomorrow."

"Me and my big mouth," she said between sniffles. "I'll regret it for the rest of my vacation."

"What's the matter? Don't like garden work, huh?" He kissed her eyes, her tears melting on his lips.

"Some garden."

They sat down again. David hugged her and kissed her and said, "I guess it was building up in me for quite some time. Resentment. Of your money, your prestige. Something had to give. I'm sorry for the terrible things I said. You were right, what you said was right. Will you forgive me, honey?"

"I forgive you." For the first few minutes they cooed and kissed and murmured heart-felt apologies and behaved for the most part like gooey schoolkids. When things had settled down and returned to normal, David made them both a cold, economy-sized ginger ale and vodka and they got pleasantly plastered. They had survived their "first fight" with flying colors. When they finished their drinks Anna wiggled her finger suggestively through his chest hair and said, "If we're going to make love tonight, David, we'd better do it soon. Or we're both going to pass out."

"That would be a tragedy."

"Then what should we do about it, hmmm?"

"I know what to do. Get up."

She looked puzzled, but did as he said, nearly tumbling over on top of him as the liquor started rushing to her head. He stood up beside her and held out his arms. "You're not going to carry me again, are you?" She asked hesitantly.

"I'm going to try. I've always wanted to carry a woman into my bedroom."

"You brute, you." She leaned over so that he could grab her. "Let's go," she directed breezily.

He had made it only one step when he suddenly cried out in pain, dropping Anna ungracefully onto the floor. She had not been hurt by the fall, but David was collapsing in agony onto the couch. "David, what is it? Did you sprain your ankle?"

"No," he said between gasps. "I should have known better than to press my luck with that stunt a second time. It's my fuckin' gimpy leg, that's all."

"Do you need a doctor?"

"No. I'll be all right. I'll just have to wait a minute until the pain stops." He sucked in air through puckered lips. "There, it's getting better already."

"I didn't know I was that heavy."

"No, it's just my bum leg." There was a moment of silence while they waited for him to recover. David took advantage of the situation. They'd already told enough truths that evening, so why not another? "Anna, you asked about my leg earlier today, but I didn't want to talk about it. I think I'll tell you what happened now, and then let's just forget about it, okay? The memory is more painful than the leg is."

"All right, David." The look of concern on her face was as strong and genuine as her anger had been earlier. She sat down beside him and listened.

"A few months ago I was in a bad car wreck. I was in the hospital for some time recovering. Everything's all right with me now, except that I'll have a permanent limp. Some days it's worse than others. But I was lucky compared to Janice. Janice Foster. She was a good friend of mine, maybe my only friend. *Real* friend, at least. She was kinda hung up on me. I know that sounds egotistical of me to say it. Let's just say she cared about me, although I never really did anything to deserve it. I could never really return her feelings.

"One afternoon she came by and we decided to drive out to the country, just to relax, breathe some clean air for a change. She had this sporty little foreign job that she'd saved up for. She was a private secretary. She was a real good driver, but—but something went wrong that afternoon. I don't think she had ever accepted that I thought of us only as good friends, not as lovers. I said something—I don't remember what, I'm not even sure I want to remember—that made that fact brutally clear to her for the first time. I had said it casually, always striving to keep things relaxed and platonic between us, despite our occasional sexual interludes. She had always been a very calm and controlled individual, always keeping her deepest feelings bottled up for the most part.

"Something snapped that afternoon on the highway. Oh, she didn't rant and rave or anything like that. It was her *silence*. The whole atmosphere in the car abruptly altered, and I could feel the tension in the air. We kept talking as usual, only her answers were shorter, almost curt in a subtle way. I've never been able to exactly reconstruct what happened then. I was sort of drifting into my own reverie, wondering how I could recoup lost ground. I need her friendship, you see. I think she'd felt that I'd been using her, and maybe I had been. I could not give her in return what she needed the most. Real commitment.

"Anyway, she passed the car ahead of us on a double yellow line. I remember seeing another car coming towards us. She didn't scream. I think I did. She swerved the car into the right lane a second too late. The car went out of control and we hit a tree. I survived because I was thrown through the windshield and out onto the embankment. Her side of the car was completely smashed and she was killed instantly.

"I didn't regain consciousness until I was in the hospital." His voice got very low and started to crack. His breathing got louder and more forced. "I read the details of the accident in the paper. They even had a picture. The reporter said that she had . . . had been . . . decapitated, and I think I found that the hardest thing to deal with. Anyway, I've alive and she's dead, and I can only think that had I spoken with some tact and delicacy, instead of that simple-minded cavalier attitude, maybe she'd still be alive. I've often wondered if she'd meant to kill us both, but I don't think she did. Her judgment had been impaired, that's all. I guess."

Anna wrapped her arms around him and held him tightly. She did not bother to say: "You mustn't blame yourself." She knew that David knew it was wrong for him to blame himself, but she also knew no amount of rationalizing could ever erase the guilt he felt—and that he simply had to accept.

"I'm sorry," he said. "I'm afraid I've not put you in a very romantic mood."

"We'll work it out," she said. He had told her to forget about the accident once he told her the story, and that was what she intended to do. Janice Foster's death, tragic as it had been, was over and done with and no amount of soul-searching would ever bring her back. Anna intended to offer David comfort, the kind of comfort that would be satisfying to her as well.

They walked up to the bedroom together.

There seemed to be no light at all in the room. Yet they could see one another. Perhaps they were so familiar to each other's touch that their minds made up the difference, casting substance where there was only shadow. There were whispers floating over and around the bed; the words were unintelligible, although their meaning was clear. The bed moaned—what might have been an obscene sound was instead warm and sensual and perfectly fitting.

Arm touched arm. Leg touched leg. Anna sighed, lifting her head until her lips met his. She seemed to see him above her, could trace his outline, though she could actually only guess where he ended and the blackness began. His presence was enough. It was above her, around her, inside her, everywhere.

He could see her too, beneath him. Felt her soft breath on his face, the brush of her hair, even the scrape of an eyelid now and then, the moist caress of parted lips. He wanted to be gentle. God, how he wanted to be gentle. Wasn't that what everyone wanted these days? *No.* Anna did not want that, not just now, not that way. She clenched his shoulders with a sudden frenzy of desire, and David felt glad that her lust easily matched his own, that he did not have to hold back, secure in the knowledge that they were not so much using one another, as gaining from each other, expressing a need and love that now, at least, seemed sturdy and enduring.

Neither of them could hold back any longer.

Jeremy had been momentarily caught in the glare from Eleanor Morrison's headlights as he began to bicycle up to the top of Bannon Mountain. For a moment he wondered if she had seen him clearly, if she would stop—or worse—call up his mother when she got home. But he couldn't worry about such things for long. He had a job to do.

He had sneaked out as soon as he heard his mother's snores issuing from her bedroom down the hall. He pulled on sneakers, grabbed his jacket to guard against the summer night's chill, and got his bicycle out from the garage. It was an old bike, but a reliable one, with speed shifts and even a headlamp which, unfortunately, was running out of juice and emitted a very weak light. But it was better than nothing.

It took him half an hour to reach the turn-off. There was a breeze blowing against him, but still he was grateful for it. Burning calories as much as he was, his body heat had soared and he was sweating profusely. It would be even worse once he started the climb. Once he was safely past Mrs. Morrison's house he pulled over to the side of the road and rested for a moment.

He was not as scared as he had thought he would be. Then again, he was still a good distance away from his destination. He was sure that he would be terror-stricken once he actually reached the lookout. Already dark strains of fear tugged at his heart and his pulse quickened. This was really an isolated area out here; except for the Morrison place, the mountain was completely deserted. What was he trying to prove? he asked himself —but he knew he could not turn back now. His warm bed and safe quarters beckoned longingly, but the mountaintop beckoned even more. He had to find out if somehow his unconscious mind had been up there earlier this night, if he had really seen what he'd witnessed in his nightmare. But Lord, if there *were* a car up there, and somebody in it, he would go stark, raving mad with terror. And if the car's occupants had been screaming almost ninety minutes ago, what sort of condition would they be in *now?*

He started up again after a few minutes, the road steadily progressing at an increasing slant. Forget about the fear, the sheer drudgery of it all was beginning to dissuade him. This was a road made for cars and trucks, not people walking or bicycling. He found that he had to rest every few minutes. Finally, he just gave up and hopped off the bike and walked along with it. He would make better time that way.

Like Eleanor Morrison before him, he looked straight into the portion of the road illuminated by his headlamp, trying *not* to think about the darkness beyond it, and what might lie inside it, but thinking about it nonetheless. He had to be brave. He had to prove what he could do. He was reaching an age where he would soon have to support his mother—both financially and emotionally—and not the other way around. He had to begin taking responsibility, had to carve out a niche for himself, and to do that he had to face up to his fears and confront them. He had developed a sense of deja vu while climbing the mountain, and he realized with an icy start that he had walked up this road many times in his dreams. Not just tonight, but often. Remembrances of these past dreams or unconscious astral journeys—if that was what they were—came rushing back to him.

And here he was, walking into the very sum and substance of his nightmare, entering his dream world of his own accord. What a fool he was. But he couldn't stop himself. He had to know. He had to know if what he had seen was real. He had to know that there was *something* beyond the mortal ken and consciousness. He had to know that somewhere his father was alive, somehow still living, as if that knowledge would erase the horror of his death, its sheer futility, and all the pain he and his mother had suffered because of it.

He heard a fluttering in the branches over his head. Don't worry—only a bird. Nothing to harm you. Ghosts can't hurt you. What would he do if he saw a ghost? Stop thinking like that! *Ghosts can't hurt you.* Your father's ghost would never hurt you! Your father loved you, didn't he?

Didn't he?

The wind had grown calmer, and the air was still and there were no birds crying out in the night. Nothing moved, except for Jeremy, wheeling his bicycle to a strange, forbidding destination. In his dreams, he had come here many times; had traveled often to his lookout he was even now approaching. He had been up there and looked down on the valley below, at the buildings, at the roads, curving like strings through the green and yellow patches of the earth. He had not been alone then.

He would not be alone now.

At last he reached the final bend in the mountain road, beyond which lay the observation point. His heart was pumping wildly; he could hear it, and he wondered if everything in the woods could hear it too. He took each step separately, slowing to a snail's pace, inching around that last tantalizing, mesmerizing curve. What would he find there? He prayed the little light on his bicycle wouldn't go out; the batteries were so old and run-down. The moon was not nearly bright enough. He would scream if it went out, scream right out loud, like a child, like a baby, not caring who heard. He knew in the last second before he rounded the bend that this lookout point had always symbolized for him the most oppressive and lonely terror he could ever face at night. His light must stay on. He could not stand the darkness!

To reach the observation post he had to first walk through a natural tunnel which cut through the trees and underbrush and emerged in the clearing on the other side. Little white pebbles, long reeds of narrow green grass, and the rutted marks of countless automobiles crunched beneath his feet. Overhead, the branches of the trees, their gnarled outgrowths tangled together like witches' fingers, formed an impenetrable natural ceiling. The forest on either side looked impassable.

And then he was there at the clearing. He held his breath. *There was the car!* The car he had seen in his dream! It was gray and dirty, windows glinting with moonlight. Perhaps it was an abandoned vehicle. Perhaps it had been there for months. Yes, yes, that was it. It was an *old* car, had been here for years. Exhaling with relief at the thought, he made a cautious approach.

This was no abandoned car, he realized upon closer inspection. He recognized it for one thing. It belonged to Tommy Bradley, an older boy who had just graduated high school. Tommy was bumming around town during the summer before leaving for college in the fall. He always hung out with his girlfriend, Shelly Spencer.

Just about to look in the back window, Jeremy stopped in his tracks, thinking of Tommy and Shelly. What if they were in there? They would kill him, think he was some kind of Peeping Tom or pervert. They'd never believe that he'd come to save them, to warn them of inpending danger. And they'd tell his mother, too.

No, they wouldn't dare snitch on him. It was awfully late and he bet they'd told their respective parents some kind of phony story to cover up their actual whereabouts. Still, it was not his place or desire to spy upon people, especially people engaged in *that* kind of stuff.

So he stood and listened, hoping he had not been seen, waiting to hear some noise, some sign, a whisper, anything to indicate that they were both safe and sound inside, alive and breathing.

But there was nothing. He felt cold and lonely again. Wait! There was a noise. An odd sound. Only it didn't come from the car. It came from the woods all around him. He wondered if the sound had traveled up from the valley. He could see a few lights way down below, but was sure that the cause of the noise was closer to him than that. He looked around the clearing, but saw nothing.

Then he heard a rustle in the grass near his feet.

He looked down, saw it, and quickly backed up with a start. The thing crawled into the light shining from his bicycle. Jeremy saw what it was but could not believe it. There was no name for it, no word; it was like nothing he'd ever seen before. And it wasn't alone—there were others with it, too. His mind too perplexed to be shocked, wondering if perhaps a joke, a grisly trick, had been played upon him, he stepped over to the car door and put his hand on the knob. Pressing inwards with his thumb, he pulled the door open and got inside.

His mind was working now on a purely instinctual level, not stopping to dwell on the nature of the creatures that were even now surrounding the auto. He shimmied over onto the front seat, his body smeared with a viscous liquid that was all over the vinyl covers. Blood. A great deal of blood. *It had already happened*, what he'd seen in his "dream." Somehow he had seen it, those two people murdered. People he knew. Fearing incapacitation from a morbid reverie, he snapped out of it and focused his attention on the dashboard in front of him. He had not yet learned to drive, and had never been particularly interested in acquiring the skill. Now he wished he had learned early like some kids did, anticipating their first license at sixteen. If only he could turn on the headlights, if might frighten the animals off.

Again he told himself not to think too much about the things outside the car. Time enough to do that once he was safe and sound. While he experimented with the various knobs and dials on the dashboard, his mind acknowledged the fact that the windows on the right hand side of the car had been smashed inwards; he had not noticed before. Furthermore, the front door on the right side was slightly ajar. Tom and Shelly must have been attacked while in the car, must have somehow gotten out and ran off into the woods. Had they escaped? Somehow he didn't think so. He *knew* that they were still in the woods, past concern, horribly dead. And he was next!

The headlights came on suddenly, but it only made matters worse. The whole clearing was alive with the horrors, squirming and wiggling and crawling every which way, darting out of the path of the light, still intent upon reaching him in the car. The keys? Where were the keys? If only he could have started the ignition, somehow he would have found a way to drive out of there.

His worst fears had come true. He had known all along that something horrible waited for him at the top of the mountain, but he had never expected anything like this. His mind still reeled at the sight before his eyes, unable to comprehend or explain, or even accept, what he was seeing. A dream. It had to be a dream.

They were swarming all over the car now, some entering in through the broken windows like they had before, others preferring to crack through the panes on the other side. The sound they made hurt his ears, and the sight of them as they came at him was more than he could bear. But he could not cover both his eyes and his ears at the same time. Shutting his eyes was not good enough: he wanted to *protect* them. His flimsy eyelids would rip apart easily under the creatures' attack; they would be shredded like paper, leaving the succulent, tender eyeballs vulnerable to assault. Not his eyes. Anything but that. They must not take his eyes.

They were all over him. He could feel them tugging at his skin, biting into his chest through the clothing. His final thought, surprisingly, was how much he hated his father. Jeremy had spent so many years mourning him, had come up here tonight *because* of him, and now he was suffering a death that was a hundred times more horrible than the one which had claimed his father.

In the last seconds, a reflex action, he sat back and relaxed while they fed on him, determined to at last set free his astral spirit as he had been trying to do all week. *That* they could not take from him; his flesh and blood, perhaps, but not his astral body, not his "soul."

Mercifully, Jeremy died before he had time to wonder: *But what if there's no such thing as a soul?*

Randall Thorp had spent a good part of the early evening trying to make up with his children. He had taken them to the quarry, hoping that their delight with the place and with the water would help to soften their attitude towards him, but they'd stayed away from him all afternoon. Little Martin had come closest to weakening, but the others—especially Gladys—made sure he stayed well away from his father. Gladys hated him; he

315

was sure of it. And who could blame her?

He didn't know why he had done what he had done. Looking back on it, it was the act of an insane man, a barbarian, someone worthy only of contempt. And he had never thought of himself as that kind of person. Not until now. No matter how hard he tried to make excuses for his behavior, his conscience was having none of it.

He had lifted that cruel black strap and slashed it across their faces, their skinny arms and bare, shorts-clad legs, as if they were wild dogs threatening to tear him asunder. Thank God he had stopped himself before it had gone too far. Already their lovely faces were marked. He desperately hoped all traces of the wounds and strokes would disappear before they went back to their mother, or else. Or else she could take legal action against him. No one in this world was more despised than a child-beater. And what had they done to deserve it? Surely nothing so severe that such punishment was just or fitting. Maybe a spell in jail was what he needed to atone; a sacrificial offering before he would even begin to forgive himself.

Sitting in the kitchen with his bottle, however, his thoughts began to lose focus; he veered back and forth between self-contempt and self-congratulations. The kids had asked for it, he told himself, not answering him when he called, hiding in the garage. *But they had only been playing,* his other voice said, *maybe they hadn't heard you. Stop being paranoid.* I Am Not Paranoid! Let's have another drink to celebrate!

He had come out of his self-induced trance by the time they'd returned home from the quarry. The kids had found it too cool to go in the water, and they had left not long after that couple had gone off into the woods. He didn't know who the woman had been, but he sure envied the man she was with. A woman like that, what was it like to make love to a woman like that?

After dinner—he'd served three TV dinners to three

unsmiling children—he'd given them ice cream, and patted them on the heads, and let them watch what they wanted to see on TV. But at bedtime, there had been no good-night kiss from any of them, no hug. He had never cared before; not he could think of nothing more precious. Little Martin had come that close to giving in, but a harsh look from his sister had deterred him. He had tucked them into their cots in the room down the hall, turned out the light, and gone straight to the kitchen to have, he had told himself, only one tiny little nightcap. Half a bottle later, he was still in the kitchen, still wallowing in self-pity.

He felt suddenly fatigued. He hadn't realized how tired he was. Better get to bed. He would try even harder to win those kids over tomorrow and he *would* succeed. He had to. Why, if they ever told their mother what had transpired . . . *There you go again*, he admonished himself, *worrying about yourself again*. Well damn it, said the other voice. If I don't, who will?

He went into his bedroom, so exhausted and intoxicated that he could not be bothered with removing his clothes. Sleep, sleep was all he wanted. His bedroom was large and looked even larger because he had nothing in it but a narrow old bed with metal railings at either end, a small night table and a tall black wardrobe in the corner. His socks and underwear were simply thrown onto the floor of the wardrobe in disarray, as he could not be bothered separating things or buying a dresser to keep them in. Clothes were scattered all over the bed and on top of the tattered straw circular rug that covered the space in front of it.

He lifted an arm that felt like lead and turned off the lamp on the night table, nearly knocking it over in the process. Within moments he was fast asleep and snoring.

He had terrible dreams, so vivid and intense that he could have sworn they were actually happening. Screams were coming from the children's room, and in

317

his dreams he tried to get up from his bed, but he couldn't move, and the floor seemed fifty feet away and the door to the hall at least 500 yards. The screams grew louder and louder, and he thought, "The children—something's hurting the children," but try as hard as he could, he was simply not able to get up off the bed.

He woke, bathed in sweat, his body odor and whiskey breath mingled together disagreeably. The house was silent. It had been a dream. The children were all right. Thank God for that. Patricia would have killed him if he had let anything happen to them.

He became aware that something was in the bed with him. One of the children, of course. They had forgiven him at last! Which one was it? Martin? Yes, little Martin, who frequently had nightmares and called out in his sleep. He had been crying before, and when his father had not come, he had forced himself down the hall and into the safety of his father's bed. Randall did not stop to think how odd it would be for a frightened child to walk down a dark corridor alone, but he was glad his son had come to him at last. Or *was* it Martin? Maybe it was Teddy, or even Gladys. He seemed to feel pressure way down on his leg, and Martin was not too tall yet. He put his arm around the child and pulled him closer. He was full of fatherly love and affection. God, he wanted the children with him always and he would never, ever, hurt them again.

But it wasn't Martin, or Gladys or Ted. He pulled back his arm, which was covered with filth. Beneath his own bodily and breathly odors, there was another smell, a stench really, that was nearly indescribable in its foulness. They had played a trick on him, the little beasts, a nasty, revolting trick which he would never forgive them for. Now, when he needed them so badly, they had dared to do this, to put—filth—in his bed, his own bed, while he was sleeping. How dare they do this to him!

318

But then the filth *moved*, and he knew it was not a mound of earth from the yard, or wet leaves, or a sack of potato peels or a pile of refuse. It was something *alive*. It was fat and thin all at the same time, for it wiggled under his embrace, and seemed to undulate. It made terrible sounds. Grease came off its body and stuck to Randall's arm and clothes and face.

Randall felt hot breath at his neck. A bite. No, the children could not be doing this. Not *this*. He felt a sharp pinch on his arm. Blood. Blood from both wounds. And those horrible noises.

His eyes had adjusted somewhat to the lack of light. He had to maneuver so that he could turn on the night table lamp, see what was in bed with him. It seemed not much bigger than one of the children, and there was a white head above its oddly shaped body. Were those arms or legs? He fought off his revulsion, reached up and over the thing, and turned on the light.

A face stared into his own. It was no one he had seen before; it was not human at all. It was as if someone had grafted a human head onto—onto a *thing*.

Randall froze and pushed backwards, for the face was coming in closer, and already there was blood—his blood—smeared all over it. Randall sunk into his pillow, too shocked to scream. He could not take his eyes off the thing's most horrible feature. The face did not have a normal mouth. When it opened its "lips," there was no tongue, no teeth. Instead, there was a strange collection of oddly shaped hooks and tubes, pincers and mandibles made for biting, grasping and sucking. What was worse, they were constantly in motion, the mouthparts darting up and down like the legs of a fly. The effect of seeing such an assemblage of biological equipment in the middle of a human face where the mouth should have been, only inches from his own head, was enough to make Randall succumb almost eagerly to unconsciousness.

And while he lay there in a faint, the animal pulled itself up and over him, its companions clambering up from the floor and onto the bed. They struggled for position, eager to feast, piling on top of one another, not satisfied with the meal that the children had made. Still, they had traveled far tonight and they were sluggish.

And Randall Thorp was eaten alive.

Slowly.

Chapter Fourteen

The following morning, Ted Bartley sat at the breakfast table with his wife while Mimi served the coffee and eggs. It was a sunny day and the temperature had risen nearly ten degrees. Despite the nice weather and the clean air coming in through the open window behind the table, neither the Bartleys looked in the peak of health. Mr. Bartley wore a grim expression and the bags which had lately developed beneath his eyes were more pronounced and bluish than ever. Mrs. Bartley simply sat in her chair and picked at her food, her face a blank mask that seemed to mirror no emotion at all, as if everything had been drained out of her the night before. As usual, Mimi asked no questions and offered no sympathy. She simply did as she was told, and answered any questions put to her. When everything had been put on the table, the woman went back to her dusting, and left her odd employers to their own devices.

The Bartleys made an effort to snap out of their moods, but it wasn't easy. They both knew that their marriage was over, even though it was unlikely they'd separate or get a divorce or anything messy like that. They had stopped having sex with one another seven years before, simply lost the interest as time went by, and one could say they were *accustomed* to each other instead of being in love. Neither of them wanted out of the relationship entirely. Where would they go? What would they do? They would stay together, each blaming the other for the tragedy that had befallen their son. Mrs. Bartley would feel that her husband had betrayed his own son for the rest of her life, and Mr. Bartley would rationalize that, had his wife not been forever nagging him to get ahead in life, he would never have taken the drastic steps he had.

Eating his toast, Mr. Bartley sat mulling over a phone call he had received from the Corporation early that morning. They had done what Anton had told him they would do. They had not yet determined the death toll, although they insisted it wouldn't be that high, as only the isolated homes on the outskirts of town had been hit. Still, it would nag at his conscience forever.

Mrs. Bartley had started to make idle chatter. It was such a trial listening to her go on and on about her ladies' clubs all the time, such an effort to listen. He let her talk, hoping it would take her mind off what she had seen last night. That would have been enough to drive anyone insane. He'd had no idea that things would get that bad.

"She looked just like she does on television," Mrs. Bartley was saying. Her face held none of its usual animation and she spoke without feeling. Bartley wondered if she even bothered to pay attention to herself.

"What's that, dear?"

"Anna Braddon. The woman David Hammond was with last night. Such a beautiful creature. Wish I looked like that."

"You're perfectly lovely darling, and you know it." He wiped his lips with a napkin.

She kept droning on, Bartley's attention wandering. He finished his breakfast and excused himself. He had a phonecall to make. Clair seemed not to notice. She was still talking as he left the kitchen. "I must call David's father. Must have them over for dinner some night. I'm

322

sure David would love to see George again. And I haven't seen Laura Hammond in ages."

Bartley was worried about his wife's sanity. David Hammond's mother had been dead for years. This whole thing with George was slowly driving her over the edge. Something would have to be done. When he reached his study, he put her out of his mind and turned his attention to other, more immediate concerns.

Anton answered on the first ring.

"I've been told about last night," Bartley said. "What's going to happen when they find the bodies? The police—"

"Poor Ted. Don't you realize that we *own* the police? There won't be anything *left* to find in any case. Our men went out at the crack of dawn, when it was safe, and took care of things in their own inimitable fashion. A burglary here, a fire there. People will be suspicious, but what can they do? Really, Ted, what can they do?"

"But it's murder! Cold-blooded murder! What will we do, wipe out the whole town? That would be one way of squelching curiosity."

"We have already worked out a solution, dear boy. We have the perfect testing ground."

"What do you mean?"

"The *clearing*, Ted. The clearing in the woods."

"You don't mean Felicity Village? But there are families living there. A dozen or more. Bunched together. Isolated. You can't do that. Besides, some of those people must have developed friendships, connections, with people in town. You won't get away with it this time."

"Nonsense. It makes more sense than destroying all of Hillsboro. The village has fewer victims, which should please you, and is also self-contained. There's less danger of things getting out of control, of the creatures getting so far away from their lair that they'll set up a new one. Besides, it would be so easy for, say, a 'fire' to

323

sweep through the woods, destroying everyone and everything in the village overnight. No one would be the wiser. No one would ever know. We would have done it last night, but we wanted to see again how capable the creatures were of hunting out victims on their own. We simply neglected to supply them with food, and once more they went out under their own initiative. Some of them went quite a long distance in a relatively short time."

The whole conversation was taking a sickening turn. Bartley was reminded again of how much he wished he weren't a part of it. "I still think about that poor Harper family."

"They would have been honored, had they known what hit them. A noble sacrifice for science."

"Stop it, Frederick."

"Anyway, tonight we shall again neglect to feed our little pets. Instead we shall release special attractive scents into the air near Felicity Village, drawing them to the clearing like flies. The results should prove most interesting. Would you care to drive up with me tomorrow to see?"

"I can't believe the Corporation is approving this. I can't believe they would sacrifice an entire village!"

"You fool! The Corporation *owns* that village. The Corporation *built* it!" Anton's voice thundered into the phone. *"What do you think they built it for,* you idiot?"

Ted Bartley was too dumbstruck by the realization to answer. He simply put the phone down, severing the connection. The man was a monster! They were all monsters! It had gone too far. No one was on his side in this, no one cared about the immorality of it. All that concerned them was profits, and scientific progress, no matter at whose expense, no matter how grotesque their actions were. There was no one to turn to, either. His wife was losing her faculties, and in any case would be

324

completely useless in a situation like this. None of his friends could help. And the police, as Anton had reminded him, were merely Barrows pawns who'd been placed in their positions in order to serve the Corporation and no one else. Even if there were those at the plant who were sympathetic to his viewpoint, they'd be too frightened to admit it, and certainly too concerned with self-preservation to come to his aid.

His mind raced wildly wondering what to do, who to contact. Would they let him leave the town alive? Could he take Clair and run? But what about George, connected to life-sustaining tubes and instruments? No, he had to stay, had to stick it out. Could he write or phone some out-of-state newspaper or TV show? They'd think he was mad. He'd need to get proof, and before he did that he would be killed in the night, his house set afire, or "burgled" by killers who came in the night to do away with him. He had to get that proof first, had to pretend that he was going along with everyone else. Or was it too late for that? Would they really believe that he had come around to seeing their way? No, it *couldn't* be too late for him to save himself. All he needed was time. God, he wished he had never known about this project, that he had stayed with his own lower administrative position instead of being promoted so that he knew about and was implicated in every one of the Corporation's dirty and horrible schemes. But he had wanted so much to get ahead. Now look where he was.

But, he thought, better to know what they were up to, or else he might have become a victim of one of those—things—those horrible things, himself. He picked up the phone and dialed Anton's number; it was time to give the performance of a lifetime. And while he dialed he thought of someone he could contact.

David Hammond had been so anxious to know where George was. David Hammond had actually *seen* George, in the earlier stages, of course, before his son's condition had gotten as bad as it was today. David Hammond was sleeping with Anna Braddon, a famous model and personality who would surely have contacts, high-powered contacts, in the media. Yes, he would have to get in touch with David. He couldn't handle this himself.

Anton answered again. "Hello, Anton. Bartley. Listen, I've been thinking . . ."

Five minutes later, when the phone call had ended, the phone rang immediately in another part of the house, the bedroom Nurse Hamilton occupied while she watched over George. She had been lying in bed, thumbing through a fan magazine. She, too, lifted the receiver after only one ring.

"Hello," she said. "Yes, Frederick. What is it you want me to do?"

Early that evening, all was quiet at the Hammond house. David and Anna had spent most of the day in bed, resting up from the exertion—both physical and emotional—of the night before. When David woke, Anna was sitting up sneezing violently, a worried look on her face.

"Oh, God," she moaned, looking at him for commiseration. "I think I'm getting a cold. I *can't* be getting a cold. I've got twelve more days before I have to go home. I must not get a cold."

"You didn't get it from me," David said, "unless you caught a chill from somewhere. Was it too cold in here last night?"

"A bit. Summer nights can be deceptive. You think you're going to smother, and instead . . ."

"Where did my socks go?"

"They're underneath the pillow. Don't ask me how they got there."

They pulled themselves out of bed, Anna still sniffling, David stretching. He looked at her and

326

laughed. "Poor thing, you look so miserable. Is the cold that bad?"

She sneezed in reply. "I think it's just one of my accursed allergies, if you want to get technical. Hay fever." She went over to a chair in the corner of the room and started digging through her bag. "I have some medicine in here. I'm sure I brought it with me. I'll be back to normal in a few hours."

Anna took her pills, which made her terribly drowsy again, and went back to bed while David prepared dinner, an easy blend of tuna and tomatoes served on a bed of lettuce. He called her to the table in half an hour and she forced herself to get up. "Damn medication makes me feel like Rip Van Winkle."

"Just as long as you stay off the highways."

She bit into a stalk of celery and tried to concentrate on the plate in front of her. At least she had stopped sneezing, although her face had become a bit puffy, and her eyes were watering. "You don't know how much of my income goes to the allergist," she sighed. "Poor man doesn't seem to be able to do a thing for me."

They were nearly finished when the doorbell rang. "Who would that be?" David wondered aloud. Anna shrugged, busy picking at a mound of tuna, too tired to summon up any interest. "Keep your mitts off my plate while I'm gone," he told her.

She threw a piece of lettuce at him playfully as he walked down the hall to the front door. He reached out and turned the knob; a warm breeze came into the hall as the door swung open.

Standing at the door was the last person David had expected to see: Ted Bartley. He was dressed in a casual outfit—slacks, yellow short-sleeved shirt, his rayon jacket folded over his arm. David realized he had never seen him when he had not been dressed to the nines. His face wore an agitated expression, and his movements seemed nervous and jerky. "May I come in, David? For

327

a moment?"

"Of course. Come on in, Mr. Bartley. What can I do for you?" He stepped back to allow him entrance, then closed the door behind them. Bartley stepped into the living room, and peeked out through the curtains as if looking for someone. He seemed satisfied.

He turned to face David as the younger man came over to him, a puzzled expression playing on David's face.

"David," Ted Bartley said, his voice quivering with desperation. "I must speak to you."

After listening to Ted Bartley in the living room, David had gone back into the kitchen to get Anna. He wanted her to hear this. But she had already left the table and gone back to bed. She was sleeping soundly and David thought it best not to wake her; perhaps she could sleep off this attack and would feel better in the morning. Bartley was disappointed that Anna could not come with them; but he did not press it.

Now David drove across town with Bartley in the other's Chevrolet. "It's actually my wife's car," the older man explained. "I didn't dare take the limousine I usually use, in case anyone wondered where I was going, or spotted the car. Things have gone too far, much too far. You say you've suspected all along that I was lying about George?"

David could tell from the older man's demeanor that all facades were to be dropped, leaving a raw, exposed truth to be dissected. "Yes. I *knew* I had seen him in New York," David replied, not sure if he really wanted to finally learn the answers behind the mystery. Now that he had consented to go with Bartley to "see George," to be "convinced of the danger" they were all in, he wondered if the man was even sane.

"I couldn't tell you the truth," Bartley explained. "I should have made up a better story, I suppose, but your appearance at the house was so unexpected. I had no idea you'd be spending the summer here. So few of the youngsters ever come back." There was pain in his voice, deep pain, as if each desertion took away a little part of himself. David suspected, however, that his anguish came from another source entirely.

"Just what did happen to George? Why is he isolated in your house?"

"You'll see. You'll see what they've done to him. What I allowed them to do. I don't think I'll ever forgive myself. My wife has become—unhinged—because of it. I've let the Corporation destroy my family. Well, I've finally awakened to the truth. I'll stop them from doing any more harm if it's the last thing I do." His voice quivered with fury and frustration.

"You're implicated in all this, aren't you?" David asked. Seeing the sudden alarm spread across Bartley's face, he wished he had kept his mouth shut.

"I suppose I am. My ambition got the best of me. But that doesn't matter anymore. My only ambition now is to do my part to undo the forces I myself have helped to set into motion."

"Just what are those forces?" David asked, full of questions, dying to know if the condition, as yet unrevealed, of Bartley's son had anything to do with the death of Anna's brother, the strange disappearance in Milbourne. He wanted to scrape away every last bit of information this man was carrying inside him.

"You won't believe me until you have proof. And you *will* have proof, that I can promise you."

"Can't you tell me anything else while we're driving? Anything at all?"

Bartley hesitated, took a deep breath, then plunged in. "Have you ever heard about recombinant DNA experiments?"

"Yes, I believe so. That's when a new life form is created by genetically combining two species that wouldn't mate normally."

"Exactly. They use an enzyme to sever the genetic material from two different sources, hook the pieces together to form a *plasmid*, then move them into a host cell where this new plasmid is duplicated. They started out by working with lower-class life forms, like bacteria. But they've progressed far beyond that point. Way beyond it. Because of the controversy, they've had TV specials and news reports about it all.

"Well, when the Barrows Corporation took over Porter Pharmaceuticals, they developed a new department whose purpose would be to create and experiment with new life forms. Frederick Anton is the head of the department, and he's a brilliant man, years ahead of any other researchers in the field, most of whom are dedicated and responsible scientists. Frederick, unfortunately, is also quite amoral, almost the stereotype of the kind of mad scientist who would stop at nothing to prove his theories and to create new life forms. But everything he does he does with the full cooperation and approval of the Corporation itself. It took me a long time to accept that, to realize that he was only one monster among many. People in these large corporations—I can know this because I was one of them—are fond of passing the buck, doing their part to build up profits, hoping to be rewarded with promotions, more money, more responsibility. More power. So they close their eyes to what's really going on. They tell themselves, 'If I don't take this job, somebody else will.'

"So that's why people get poisoned with lousy food, and why wastes are dumped in riverbeds, and why killing mists escape from labs to wipe out whole herds of cattle. Nobody cares. Or if they do care, they keep their mouths shut. They want their paycheck, and although the corporate structure is simply made up of individuals, as a *body* they want their paychecks and profits, too. So they all play along with the game. 'For the good of the company.' And the men and women at the top are the worst of all. They might have the best chance of doing something about the dirty stuff they're involved in, but the profits would drop, and besides—everybody else is doing the same thing they are. Who gives a hoot? It's the way of the world.''

Bartley stopped talking while a car behind them speeded up and passed them, and did not resume until the other auto was well ahead of them. "My son was never the sort of person to stick up for causes," he continued. "No peacenik, no 'anti-nuke' demonstrator, was he. But sometime last year he started going with this girl, and he got in with a crowd of activists. Radicals, you might say. It changed his way of thinking a lot."

George? An activist? David would sooner have imagined the sky falling down. George had always been an old-fashioned, meat-and-potatoes, God-and-country kind of guy. That was one reason they'd drifted part. David *had* been an activist of sorts, for a while. George and he had disagreed violently on just about everything.

"He and I used to have lots of fights," Bartley continued. " 'This is something different,' he would say to me. 'This has nothing to do with new energy sources, or defending one's country. This has to do with changing the fabric of life, of nature.' He had no objection on religious grounds, he just felt we were tampering with things that should better be left alone. Y'know, the usual story with these opponents of recombinant research. I didn't see his side of it until now.

"I paid a visit on his little girlfriend and paid her to leave my son alone. He was shocked, disillusioned with both of us, with what I'd done, when he found out. He came to my study, infuriated, and physically assaulted me. He threatened to alert the entire town to what was going on out at the plant, to alert recombinant DNA opponents across the country. There'd be pickets, all kinds of fuss and bother. And I'd be the one they'd blame for it. I cursed myself for having ever told him. But you see, I had been hoping to interest him in the work being done. I thought he'd find it fascinating, would be inspired to work there as an assistant. I was thinking of his future, afraid he'd turn into just another bum like all those friends he used to hang out with. God help me. I was crazed with anger, furious at him for hitting me, for threatening me.

"After George stormed out of the house, I called Anton and told him about it. Anton told me he would go and talk to him, explain our side of things. I can still hear myself saying, 'I don't care what you do to him, that ungrateful bastard. Use him for one of your experiments if you want. I don't care.' " Bartley's shoulders dropped visibly. He seemed to be deflating even as he drove.

" 'It *would* keep him from talking,' Anton said. 'We'll hold him out at the plant for a while, until he calms down, sees reason. We *will* use him in our experiments' —harmless ones, he assured me—'so that he feels like he's part of our little group'. Anton said he'd take care of everything.

"What they did—and I blame myself for it—was force his car off the road, and drag him bodily to the plant to be imprisoned. They injected him with—stuff—that they'd never tried before. I don't know what they thought it would do. Before it had taken too much effect, George managed to escape, managed to get all the way to New York. Probably he dropped in on you as a desperate measure. When you called my home, Mimi contacted me in Lancaster and I instructed her to tell you a lie, while I called Anton. I was still angry with my son. Anton sent men to search for him. They found him, brought him back. Already horrible changes had occurred to his body."

David shivered, remembering how George's shoulders had just—squeezed in—as if there was nothing to him.

332

"It was getting worse and worse, his condition, and Anton didn't know what he could do aside from keeping him alive. I insisted they return him to the house, and set up a special room and installed a nurse. I think they went along with me because they were afraid I'd explode. My anger at George had turned to guilt and regret. Every day his condition got worse and worse, more and more horrible. Wait until you see! Wait until you see what kind of things they're capable of!"

More than ever David questioned his willingness to find out, but knew he couldn't turn back now. "How exactly do you fit in with this experimentation?" he asked. "What is your position in the Corporation?"

"I was one of the few who argued in favor of merging with Barrows, of shifting our emphasis from drugs and pills to recombinant DNA research. It caused quite a furor at the time, as most of the employees—men who were unskilled in such research, and even opposed to it in some cases—had to be let go, and new ones hired. I had been an administrator before, but afterwards was promoted to vice-president of the pharmaceutical firm in charge of public relations, as well as receiving a minor, but powerful appointment within the Corporation's administrative body itself. My salary increased tenfold. I thought that life was going to be beautiful.

"It's not beautiful, David," he said as they pulled into his driveway. "It's rather ugly, I'm afraid."

David didn't argue. They got out of the car and stole into the front hall. "George's nurse was asleep when I left. I don't entirely trust the woman. She's a bit too friendly, and I've long since stopped thinking I had enough sex appeal to attract a much younger woman. I think Clair thinks there's something going on between us. Sometimes I wish it were true."

They reached the inner hall, which ran perpendicularly to the one they were in and led down to George's room. Bartley still spoke in a whisper. "First I'll show

333

you what they did to my son. Then we'll go out to the plant. It's risky, but we'll have to take that chance. They plan on committing wholesale murder this evening, but I need proof—charts, diagrams and such—before I can go to the authorities. In some other town, where hopefully, the Corporation has no influence."

"Murder? How do they propose to do that?"

"You'll have to see when we get there. Otherwise . . ." He let his words trail off. "Remember, you've promised to get Miss Braddon to use her influence on any media people she knows. I want to blow this all sky high."

"I'll do my best. I'm not sure who she 'knows,' if anyone."

"She can get to them through her contacts, if nothing else. And a beautiful woman *always* has contacts."

Bartley put his ear to the outer door of the nurse's chamber. Hearing nothing, he assumed she was asleep. They sneaked quietly into George's sickroom. It was painted crabapple green and its one window had been boarded shut. In the exact center of the room was a regulation hospital bed around which partitions had been placed. A bank of complicated machinery stood off to one side, monitoring his functions. Through the gap between to partitions, David could see a huddled form in the bed, covered with sheets, a tube from an intravenous bottle going into his arm.

"Prepare yourself," Ted Bartley said, drawing aside the curtains. "I guarantee you've never seen anything like this before."

The figure in the bed was finally revealed. David stepped back, gasping. Never had he imagined anything so *horrible*.

"They can't put bandages on him. They are immediately absorbed into his skin." Bartley leaned over the body, familiarity with it not entirely disguising his revulsion, and pulled down the bedcovers. David felt waves of nausea overwhelming him. He tried to stay steady on his

334

feet, tried to recover from the shock.

The man on the bed resembled a skeleton, encased by a gelatinous sheath of some transparent substance, which fully revealed all the internal organs, gray and undulating, inside the hideously transformed body. The bones were barely holding it all together. The face had no recognizable features, only a see-through head revealing a pale white skull thin as eggshell and a messy, pinkish brain. The eyes bulged out from sunken eye sockets; they stared unseeing straight ahead. There were no eyelids, no hair, no flesh, anywhere. Veins and capillaries stood our red within the grayish mass that George's skin and bones had converted to.

"He is alive. Barely," Ted said. "The bones are too weak, too rubbery to support him, so he cannot move or get out of bed or be transported anywhere. Besides, what could a hospital do that isn't being done here? He is not conscious. He is not in pain, physical or mental. He is not even human anymore.

"First the bones start converting, so that he could not sit or stand or walk. That was why they had no trouble capturing him in the city, he could not possibly run away. It must have already started by the time he saw you. He has been in bed, wasting away, all this time. Then the other night, the final transformation. The flesh completely changed, the skin as we know it disappeared within the space of a few hours. Clair ran in here, saw what had happened, and went quietly mad.

"Now do you know why I want to destroy the Corporation and everyone behind it?"

"Is George's condition related to this Frederick Anton's plan to commit 'wholesale murder'?" David asked.

"No," Bartley replied. "Not at all. It was just a sideline. They introduced mutated, contaminated genetic material into his—"

David put his hand out and silenced the man, soundlessly telling him to stand stock still. "Listen," he whispered. "I hear something moving. It's coming from behind that door."

The connecting door to the nurse's quarters appeared to be closed, but both of them could hear low noises, short clicks, coming from behind it. Bartley realized that the door was slightly ajar. "The phone. She's on the phone. The bitch must have been spying on us. Even now she's calling for help."

He stepped over to the door and swung it open with a violent thrust, marching angrily into the next chamber. David saw a pretty, slender young woman standing by a bed, holding onto the telephone. She knew what Bartley was up to, what he planned to do.

"PUT THAT PHONE DOWN!" Bartley dashed to her side and knocked her onto the bed. She emitted a tiny scream as he put the receiver to his ear and listened. "Good. It's still ringing. She didn't get through." He slammed the phone down and turned his full attention on the nurse. "Listen to me, you little bitch. You are not to call anyone. You are not to contact anyone. Or I'll make you regret it, I assure you."

"What are you talking about, Mr. Bartley? I was only going to order a sandwich."

"Bullshit. That door was closed when we came in; now it's ajar. You were listening to us. You work for them, and I don't trust you. Besides," he looked down at the tray sitting on the bed, a plate with smears of gravy, a few pieces of fatty meat. "I see you already had your dinner just now. Mimi would never leave a tray lying around for long, and she could have made you your 'sandwich.'"

The submissive expression left Nurse Hamilton's face. "I have my orders," she said. "I'm not to let you out of this house, and I'm not going to. You're already opened your mouth too much. Go ahead and threaten me. If I don't call in, they'll send someone here to check on me."

Bartley's hand lashed out, slapping her across the face. Her cheek was blazing red. Furious at his action, she picked a fork up off the tray and stabbed at his face as he hovered above her. Bartley managed to swing his hand up in front of his eye before the implement could plunge into it, but the prongs sunk into the hand just above the knuckles. He cried out, pulling back, as the fork fell to onto the floor. "BITCH!" He slapped her again. Thin rivulets of blood ran down his arm.

David had been watching from the doorway. "Your hand—?"

"It's all right. I'm going to have to tie her up."

"Go ahead! Tie me up!" Hamilton screamed. Suddenly she got up and ran past Bartley and David before either one could stop her. "I'll murder this thing you call your son," she shouted. She reached out and knocked over the intravenous stand, the bottle crashing to the ground and shattering into a hundred pieces, spilling clear fluid all over the floor.

"NO! NO! *Stop her!*" Bartley screeched.

David grabbed the nurse from behind, but she was too strong, too determined. As if sensing his weak spot, she kicked him in the leg, and he doubled over in pain. The machinery began to beep, signaling that something was wrong with the patient in the bed. "He's dying!" Bartley rushed over to the nurse as she started pulling tubes and wires off of his son, parts of George coming with them, slapping disgustingly against the walls, the nurse's white uniform, the curtains. Still she pulled, the beeping growing louder, Bartley's voice more hysterical. Beyond reason, he started battering her, his arms and fists flailing out, hitting her in the back, the neck, the head. David tried to ignore his pain, not sure of who to help, who was most in danger of dying at the other's hands. It would not do Bartley any good to commit murder.

He shouted for them to stop but they were beyond

hearing. The nurse took the metal stand which had held the intravenous bottle, lying against the bed at an angle, and began beating at George's body with it, ignoring his father's blows. There were horrible *glopping* sounds as the rod left indentations wherever it hit, picking up parts of the body with each downward thrust. "STOP IT!" Ted Bartley rammed his fist directly into the woman's open mouth. She bit down with all her strength, but he kept jamming it in. Teeth and blood poured out of the orifice. Sensing an opening, a temporary lull in her concentration, Bartley thrust out his other hand and started pulling at the side of her mouth with his fingers, pulling the lips over as they formed a grotesque, unnatural grin. The flesh started tearing, and more blood poured out. His hand was in her throat up to the wrist, and above the sounds of her agonized whimpering came the noise of ripping membrane.

Fighting back unconsciousness, the nurse reached back to the small night table beside George's bed. She had carelessly left her cigarette lighter there, although she had been prohibited from smoking even when next door. She grasped the lighter in her fingers, and managed to produce a flame. Lifting up the fiery lighter, she held it to Bartley's back, setting fire to his shirt.

It didn't have the desired effect. Even with his flesh burning, he would not remove his hands from her face. Blood drenched down over the woman's uniform, spattering onto the skirt, Bartley's clothes, and the floor. Seeing the flame cascading over Bartley's back, David was at last shocked out of his benumbed inactivity, and ran over to him, beating out the fire with his fists and a handkerchief. "Let her go," he screamed. "It won't help any! Let her go!"

"They didn't even try to cure my son," Bartley hollered above the woman's death rattle. "They just let him turn into this—this horrible thing. They didn't even try! And she's one of them. We can't let her tell them this. They mustn't know I plan to betray them until we have time to get away."

The woman's struggles were weakening. David was sickened by all the blood. Bartley's hand was in almost halfway up to the elbow joint now. Vomit and mucous coated his fingers, the woman choked and heaved. David wondered if he could keep down the contents of his own stomach. "You don't have to kill her. She's incapacitated now. We'll tie her up as you suggested."

Bartley hesitated, but saw the wisdom in what David said. He removed his arm, and stopped pulling at the ragged, bloody remains of her mouth. But as soon as he released his grip, she came back to life again, and began scratching wildly at his eyes. "My God!" David grabbed the rod she had dropped before and jammed it into her stomach, too sickened by the brutality of his actions to do it hard enough to have effect. He saw blood seeping out from under her fingers, which were clamped to Bartley's face. God, she was gouging his eyes out! He hit her with as much force as he could muster, closing his eyes at the moment of impact.

There was a scream, then a *plop*, and a muffled, horrible yelling. He opened his eyes. Her nails had town at the skin below them, but Bartley's eyes themselves had been untouched. Thank God. Then David looked down on the bed and wished he hadn't.

Nurse Hamilton had fallen onto George's body. It was now in the process of absorbing her. She had simply *sunk* into the sticky, translucent miasma of organs and bones, and kept on sinking, the stuff oozing into her mouth, cutting off her cries of horror and outrage. Her legs, which were sticking out of the bed, and hence were free of the substance which made up George's form, kicked out and kept on kicking for moments until they finally stopped. David finally tried to pull her free, grabbing an arm which dangled from the bed. She would not budge. She had been suffocated inside George's re-

mains. David was in shock—*he had just killed someone!*
Bartley seemed to sense what he was thinking and put
his hand on David's shoulder. "You saved my life,
David. Keep reminding yourself of that. You saved *our*
lives. And maybe many more."

The machinery on the wall registered no life signs.
George, too, was dead.

Bartley stood there a moment, staring down at his son
and the woman George had virtually engulfed. There
was nothing to do now but continue. David wondered if
either of them could retain their sanity after this terrible
episode. David also knew that if the Corporation could
do *this* to a human being, they were fully capable, as
Bartley had implied, of unleashing God-knows-what
horrors on the unsuspecting town of Hillsboro.

"I'm sorry," David said. "I'm standing here, and I
can scarcely believe what I've seen."

"I know. That's all that lies between you and madness. Take my word for it." The man seemed to lift
himself up, full of vitality and renewed enthusiasm,
turning away from the bed. "He's dead. Perhaps it's
better this way. But we still have work to do. I will not
think of this again until we're through. Put what
happened here tonight out of your mind, David. Put it
out, banish it from your mind until later." He leaned
against the wall for a moment, suddenly fatigued. "I
want to cry, I want to rail, I want to—" He lifted his fist
and shook it, banging it into the wall. He stopped just as
suddenly and composed himself. "But there's . . . there's
no time for that. You're committed now, David. Will
you help me? Please?"

David was doing his best to keep from thowing up.
Finally he ran into the bathroom and emptied the
contents of his stomach into the toilet. His mind was
racing wildly. Murders. Corpses. Torn flesh and
internal organs. What was he getting into? How was
that hideous scene in the outer room going to affect his

340

future life, his life with Anna? Bartley knew that he had done what he had done to save the older man's life, but how would the police—the corrupt, *pro*-Corporation police—interpret his actions? He washed his face and re-joined Mr. Bartley. "I'll do what I can to help you."

"Wait until we get to the plant. I'll show you things there that will make your hair stand on end."

What could possibly be worse than *this*? "Why don't we get help?" He said. "We can't handle this all by ourselves. I know you can't go to the police, but surely you must have friends, associates . . ."

"Like I told you, I alienated a great many former friends and co-workers when I was promoted. Besides, it would take too long to round them up, to convince them to come with us. No, we'll go directly to the plant and hope that no one tries to call Nurse Hamilton."

"She implied that she was supposed to call in at pre-arranged times. When she doesn't call . . ."

"By then it will be too late. Besides, she may have been bluffing. We can't worry about that. I'm hoping no one will suspect what I plan to do. No one in security will question my presence there at night, as I often stay late."

"How will you explain *me*?"

"If anyone asks, I'll tell them you're a research assis-tant from New York who's planning to join our little group. No one will doubt me. Now let's get out of here."

"Wait a minute," David said. "Your back. You have to do something about it. The pain must be killing you."

Bartley tore off the blackened remains of his shirt and grimaced. "My shirt bore the brunt of the damage. I can't stop to worry about it now. I'll get a new shirt and we'll be off."

They stepped out into the corridor and began walking to the other hall that led to the front door. David wondered if he was doing the right thing, allowing him-self to be dragged along on some nightmarish quest for

341

"evidence." He had only Bartley's word on everything, and Bartley had been known to lie before. Yet, he had seen what had transpired in the bedroom, seen the man's righteous fury, seen what had happened to the thing on that bed—with his own eyes. He had heard the nurse's threats. There had to be some truth to the man's story. He had thought of breaking away from him once they'd stepped outside, running to someplace with a phone so he could tell Anna and have her pick him up. But he remembered that he had let someone down once before— Harry London in Milbourne—and had never seen the man *sane* again. His presence that night could have made the difference. Perhaps he would have just disappeared along with all the others. Or perhaps he might have offered just enough assistance to *save* the rest of them. He would never know. He decided that he would help Ted Bartley as best he could. He did not care for a second dose of guilt. Anyway, as Bartley had pointed out, he was already committed. His complicity in the death of the nurse saw to that.

"Mr. Bartley," he said. "Does the town of Milbourne in Connecticut mean anything to you?"

Bartley stopped dead in his tracks. "How did you know about that?"

"Then it does have significance?"

"Yes. Our Corporation had set up similar operations there for a time. Anton had a laboratory there."

"In the *Forester* Building?"

"What? How could you possibly—"

So there was a connection. David's mind reeled with the implications. He could not stay behind now, no matter what. Ted Bartley was going to lead him to Jeffrey Braddon's murderers. "I want you to tell me all about Milbourne while we drive to the plant," David said. "Or I won't go with you."

Ted quickly acquiesced. "All right. Wait here! I must get another shirt before we go."

Bartley was back in five minutes. David could tell that the man had been crying, at last giving in to his grief over the death of his son. David realized that he himself felt nothing. He could still not bring himself to accept that the mess on the bed had been a human being, let alone George Bartley.

They continued on they way. Just as they went by the living room, they heard an odd, musical sound drifting down the hall. They looked inside the room where only a couple of days earlier they'd sat and drunk martinis and told each other lies. Now the living room was occupied only by Clair Bartley. She was singing softly to herself, a drink in her hand, its liquid splashing out unnoticed onto the carpet. She danced to and fro against the rhythm of the music, and it was clear to both David and her husband that if it were not an alcoholic stupor that dictated such behavior, then the woman was quite insane.

Bartley hesitated for a moment, on the brink of stepping inside to go to his wife. "No," he said sadly, "there's no point."

They continued down the hall, the sound of Clair Bartley's madness following them until it was cut off abruptly by the hollow slamming of the heavy front door.

The Chevrolet sped through town, turning onto Route 30, heading out to the plant. "You don't see anyone following us, do you?" Bartley asked.

David checked, but he didn't see anything. "No one else is on the road."

"It's starting to get dark. It will be pitch-black by nine o'clock. We don't have much time. I *think* I can stop what's going to happen. If only I could be sure."

"Just what *is* going to happen? And while you're at it, what is it that happened in Milbourne? I'm more than curious about that."

343

"What's going to happen in Hillsboro is what *should* have happened in Milbourne. The town is going to be used as a test site—or at least part of the town. Tonight. God knows what they'll pull tomorrow if we don't stop them."

"Slow down," David complained. "You're not making any sense."

The speed of the car seemed to increase as Bartley's words issued from his mouth at a reduced rate, as if he had to make up for the decreased vocal pace by physically barreling down the highway. "All right. I've already mentioned that the Barrows Corporation is engaged in recombinant DNA experiments. I didn't tell you that they had succeeded in creating a new and extremely dangerous life form."

"Like oil-eating bacteria?"

Bartley almost laughed. "We're far beyond such primitive stages," he said. "We moved past bacteria a long time ago. Our scientists, under Anton's direction, have been capable of working with much more advanced life forms. They have actually succeeded in creating a horrible *chimera*, more horrible than anything out of a nightmare."

"Chimera?"

"Named after the mythological beast which was part lion, part goat, part dragon and so on. *Genetic* chimeras are creatures made up of different animals, their DNA blended together to form completely new, hybrid life forms."

"For what purpose? Just because it can be done?"

"No. The reasons are much more practical than that. You've heard of the 'super soldier,' a human trained to be absolutely perfect and invincible in combat? Well, the Barrows Corporation worked along those lines, and literally made a creature that could function in that manner. Not human, but a blend of various life forms. They used techniques that other scientists haven't even

344

thought of yet. Believe me, what the public and some journalists know about recombinant research just scratches the surface of what's actually being done."

"Let me guess: The Corporation hopes to sell these things to the military. Or to foreign countries perhaps."

"I wouldn't put it past them. But first they must test the capabilities of these creatures, these chimeras. In order to do that, they planned to simply let them loose on a large, if isolated populace."

It finally dawned on David, the true horror of what they were up against. "I can't believe it. That would be mass murder, for Christ's sake!"

"You're as naive as I used to be. You think this would be the first time that instruments of death have been tested on an unsuspecting populace? *Before* it was bacteriological agents, or chemicals, nothing that could be seen by the naked eye, nothing that could be suspected by the general public. This is different. The risks are greater. And the Corporation can't afford for anyone who sees or knows of these creatures to survive. That makes them ten times more deadly than anything ever used before."

"What exactly are these creatures?"

"I've never gotten a clear look at them. Haven't wanted to—until now. Even I'm not sure of all their components. I hope to find out tonight."

"They were set loose in Milbourne?"

"Not exactly. They were destroyed before that could happen. They had been contained in the Forester Building, in a sub-cellar that had never been completed. The Corporation chose a building in the heart of town because they felt no one would suspect that such a place, in the middle of a populated area, would house such experiments. They were afraid of security leaks. It was all insane as far as I'm concerned, which should tell you the type of people we're dealing with. Anyway, some of the things escaped from the cellar, burrowing under the town, until they reached an underground cavern in the outskirts and made it their home. It took them quite some time to multiply and to nurture, and Anton convinced his superiors that what had been a mistake— the escape of the animals from the lab—could easily be turned into a lucky accident. Instead of trying to contain the creatures again, or destroying them, why not test them in the field, why not just sit back and see exactly how devastating their killing capabilities could be? Anton was very clever."

"What about that tremendous hole in the Forester Building I've heard about? Did that have anything to do with the creatures' escape?"

"No. Before he got his 'brainstorm,' Anton panicked. He deliberately poured an incredibly strong acid through the floors, and claimed it was an unavoidable accident. He asked for a new location in which to continue his work, as the Forester Building had been made uninhabitable. He still had many of the creatures alive in the basement, and transferred them to the plant up here, hoping he could track down and destroy the ones who'd escaped before news of it got out. Unfortunately, one of his assistants talked. Anton convinced the Corporation to leave things as they were. They had to vacate the building, not only because of the damage he'd done, but because they wanted all traces of the Corporation gone by the time the killings started. Anton also knew how deadly his hybrids were, and he had no intention of staying in a town where they were literally running around loose and out of his control. Of course he kept someone in Milbourne to keep tabs on things, to step in and cover up later on at his direction."

"So he continued his work in Hillsboro," David said.

"Yes. Now tell me how you knew about the goings-on in Milbourne."

"Just one more thing first. Are these chimeras—are they flesh eaters?"

Bartley paused before answering, God only knows what thoughts running through his head. "Yes. Yes, they are."

David shuddered. Now he knew what had been at the body of Jeffrey Braddon. And where all those others had disappeared to. If the car had been at a standstill at that point, there was a good chance he might have dashed out of it and run screaming back to the relative safety of his home.

David then told Bartley about his end of things, about Anna's brother. Bartley seemed pleased with the information. "Then she'll be *sure* to help us, to aid us in exposing these people. What a lucky coincidence."

"Not for her brother," David said. "What about you, Bartley? You knew what was going on?"

"No. No, I swear. I didn't know about all this until much, much later. Only recently did I realize what they had planned to do. You must believe me."

"What happened to those hybrids in Milbourne?"

"They were apparently destroyed by a great fire in the night. Someone must have been responsible, but I don't know who."

David put two and two together and knew who had been responsible. *Harry London!* Harry had sacrificed his sanity to do it, too. He had been an unsung hero. The man had saved his town from terrible destruction. Could David do any less?

"The Corporation stopped at nothing to safeguard the existence of the chimeras," Bartley said. "Paid off people. Or killed them. They even murdered some poor old man who'd been superintendent in the Forester Building because he *might* have seen something." He shivered. "And these are the people I work for."

Finally they reached the turn-off to the plant and drove up to the guard-house by the gate. Bartley pulled out his identification card; he didn't need to, as the guard recognized him immediately and greeted him respectfully. He didn't inquire as to David's identity. They drove past the gate and on to the plant itself.

"So far so good," Bartley said. David exhaled with relief.

They parked the car and walked to the wide glass double-doors leading into the inside of the plant. It was a formidable modern structure made of stone and glass, with marble walls near the entranceway and in the lobby. At least four stories high—although it was hard to tell as there was no windows in front—it also had several sub-levels below ground. David had seen part of the inside as a boy when his father had worked there. He imagined great changes must have been made in some sections to accommodate all the new equipment needed for their special research.

Bartley and his guest went past the reception area without a hitch. They walked down a wide, brightly lit corridor towards Bartley's office. Bartley closed the door and turned on the light, revealing a large, attractive room with red carpeting and wood furnishings. A massive desk had been placed against the far wall. "I run my administrative duties from here," he said wearily. David surmised that the man was reminding himself that this was probably the last time he would ever see his office, this beautiful room which he had worked so hard and sacrificed so much for. It had symbolized a great deal in his life, and now the dream had turned into a nightmare. They had taken everything from him. Everything he had.

Bartley went to the desk and picked up the phone. He punched three numbers. "Hello. Is Anton there? Thank you." He hung up the phone. "He's out of the building for the moment. That makes things easier. We can go directly to his lab."

"Won't that cause suspicion?"

"Not immediately. I often go there to confer with him. As public relations man I must know what's actually

348

going on—if only so I will know exactly what to *deny*."
He smiled at the irony of it. "I'm not privy to everything, of course. But it's always been my job to escort visiting VIPs and company men throughout the labs, so gradually I've pieced together most of what's going on down there. I keep my eyes open."

They left the office and headed for the nearest elevator bank. Bartley was carrying a briefcase he'd picked up off his desk. "If anyone asks who you are, remember our story. And let me do all the talking. I can't tell you how much I appreciate your coming along, David. I haven't much strength left. You were George's friend. Perhaps you can help avenge him for me. You'll have to lend me your strength 'cause I haven't got much left."

The elevator came and they stepped inside. The ominous constriction in David's stomach had worsened. He felt like a fly traveling into the spider's web, a high-rise worker deliberately stepping off a girder into empty space. This was all so crazy. And yet he sensed every word was true.

They went down three levels until the car came to a stop. They stepped out into a narrow green corridor. The lights were almost significantly darker down here, and the atmosphere was most oppressive. David wondered if it was all just in his mind.

"Follow me. And remember: I do the talking."

Several yards down the hall they came to another glass door with a security guard. The guard was an older man with a granite jaw, a mean-looking mouth, gray hair, lots of muscles and a nasty-looking gun secured inside a holster. David wouldn't have wanted to grapple with the man in broad daylight.

"Hello, Mr. Bartley," the guard said pleasantly. "Go right inside." Although David felt the guard's eyes boring into his back, he kept on walking. He expected to be stopped at any second, but nothing happened. Then he heard the door close and lock automatically behind him with a hydraulic wheeze, and the feeling of being trapped and oppressed was even worse, despite the initial sense of relief at having gotten this far without mishap.

The halls were wider and brighter, but somehow more sinister. There were no sounds, although David could see movement behind the glass windows in the doors they passed. Were those people really planning on committing wholesale murder tonight? Could they all be that callous? Or were only a select few aware of what was going to happen? Yes, that was it. Others might have suspected, but like Bartley—until now—they knew it was better to keep silent. They knew the Corporation would not hesitate to deal with them if they didn't.

Bartley opened a door at the end of the hall and admitted David into a large laboratory full of long, green tables. Large metal equipment had been placed against the walls, and there were sinks and shelves full of vials and bottles. There was nothing of the "mad scientist" about it, however. Rather it had the even more chilling appearance of the ultra-cold, ultra-clinical modern lab. He saw a few people in white smocks situated around the room. Bartley ignored them as much as they did him. He must have been a familiar figure to all of them. He put his hand on the knob of a door to his left, which apparently led into an adjacent office. Before they could step through, a woman's voice called out. "Anton isn't here right now."

She had startled them. "Then I'll wait for him," Bartley said, recovering nicely. "I have someone here he must meet."

The woman smiled and turned back to her work.

Bartley closed the door behind them, then locked it. The room was small and cluttered. Magazines and piles of paper were everywhere, tumbling in different directions. The furniture consisted of a small wooden desk, and two large gray tables pushed up against the wall.

There were also several folding chairs in another corner, opened and laid out as if there had recently been a meeting. A large file cabinet stood directly behind them. Bartley was already poring through it. "Thank God he doesn't lock this."

"Do all those people know? Those people outside."

"Most of them. Even if they don't like it they know better than to say so. One of the research assistants disappeared without a trace last week."

David digested that information, unpleasant as it was, and asked, "Is there anything I can do now to help?"

"Sit tight. I can only take *some* of these notes and documents with me. I'm not a scientist, I'm not sure which is most significant, but I'll have to hope that I steal something of worth."

"Where are the creatures kept?"

"Relax. They allowed them to burrow out of their containment and reach their own natural lair like before. They now reside in the caverns beneath and beside the old quarry. We built underground tunnels which lead there." The quarry! But David and Anna had just been out there the other day! He sat down hard on one of the open metal chairs. Bartley continued pulling out different file folders, shuffling through papers with his fingers. "I'm going to take the tunnels and try to destroy them from below. Meanwhile, I want you to get out of here and drive to Felicity Village. Do you know where that is?"

"Yes. I could even reach it on foot."

"No. That wouldn't be safe. The things are going to attack the village tonight. That is the first testing ground. So far some of the creatures have gone out on their own hunting food. Several deaths have already resulted. They've been covered up, of course. That includes the deaths of the Harper family, which you've probably heard about. Tonight the creatures are going to be *deliberately* directed to the clearing for the express

351

purpose of testing their lethal tendencies."

"What chance do the residents have against them?"

"Very little. These monsters are—wait a minute." He studied one sheet more carefully. "This is it. The composition! The various animal chromosomes that were used in forming the chimera. God, it's incredible!"

"You said you've never seen these things?"

"Not up close, no. No one but those working with them directly are ever allowed . . ." He continued reading. "Lord! What sort of monstrosities have they let loose on us! According to this, the creatures are comprised of—"

There was the sound of a key gliding into the lock. Suddenly the door was opened and a tall, slender man dashed into the room, slamming the door behind him. He turned to confront Bartley and David, his face twisted with rage. He quickly stepped toward Bartley and grabbed the paper out of his hand. "Give that to me!" He then turned to David. "Who are *you* and what are you doing here?"

"Anton. Anton, please—"

"Shut up, Ted. Why are you going through my files? I should never have trusted you. I should have known you would try to betray us. I had faith in you, Bartley, and you have destroyed that faith." He moved towards the phone on his desk. "I'm going to call security."

"No, you're not." Bartley had extracted a gun from his pocket. The man was full of surprises. He must have gotten it when he'd changed his shirt back at the house. "I'll kill you if I have to, Anton. So don't make a move. Just sit down in your chair slowly, like a good boy. I warn you, I won't think twice about putting a bullet in your brain. Tell me, Anton, is it true? About the hybrids? Their composition? Is it true? Tell me, God damn it!"

"Which hybrids are you referring to? The ones in Milbourne, or the ones out at the quarry? There is a difference. By the way, 'hybrids' is a misnomer of sorts, as they have more than two *original* parents. You might say our animals were created by combining one hybrid with another hybrid and so on. A slow process, but a rewarding one."

Bartley was losing patience. "What is that 'difference' you mentioned?"

Anton smiled. "Why, many of the ones here in Hillsboro have a *human* component."

"Human! My God!"

"Surprised? There is nothing unusual about combining human cells with those of other animals. It has often been done before. The results this time were most gratifying. We did it to add a unique psychological factor to our chimeras. They are supposed to be the ultimate killing machines. Their appearance induces extreme shock, which in turn retards defensive action against them until it's much too late. But we added this other, human factor. Some of them have actually developed a kind of *human* head, with an actual face. And the most fascinating thing is where we *got* those human cells. For the past several years, even before Barrows took over Porter Pharmaceuticals, the Corporation has been collecting cells from virtually all of the inhabitants of this lovely little town, along with cells from many towns across the country, storing them for future use."

"How?" Bartley asked. "And *why,* for God's sake?"

"Simple. We contacted the country doctor here one day—as we also contacted doctors in similar towns—and made him a satisfying and lucrative offer. He had no idea what we planned to use the cells for—neither did we, back then—which amounts to a variation of cloning. That is the ironic, delicious touch. The creatures that shall march out to eventually destroy this *entire town,* after our initial test tonight, will have the faces of the loved ones, both living and dead, of the very people they are slaughtering and consuming. Some will even have

353

the faces of their victims. Isn't it marvelous?"

David wanted to go somewhere to throw up again.

Bartley's face had turned a stark white, but he showed no signs of cracking. "Why do you have to destroy the entire town? Won't the village satisfy your bloodlust?" he pleaded.

"This is not bloodlust, but commercialization, Bartley. If all goes well tonight, we shall go ahead with our plans to fly in several representatives of firms, armies, even nations, who would like to have exclusive use of our chimeras. They shall see, from a safe vantage point, of course, how effective our hybrids are as they wipe out an entire town and all its population within the course of an evening. We shall start the bidding at, say, ten million. And there's nothing you can do to stop it. The forces have already been set in motion."

Bartley seemed to be stalling for time. "Tell me again how you propose to get the creatures to attack the village and then the town."

"Simple." Anton leaned back in his chair and smiled, only too happy to comply. "This afternoon the area surrounding Felicity Village was sprayed with a highly concentrated gaseous pheremone which will serve to attract the creatures unerringly. Tomorrow we will have a crop-dusting plane fly over the town itself with that same compound. Do you see how easy it will be?" He leaned forward and stared venemously into Bartley's eyes. "Go ahead. Kill me. *There's nothing you can do to stop it!*"

David had heard enough; he was close to going crazy from this horrible conversation and everything it meant. "Just *what are* these things? I want to know and I want to know now. I want to know what we're up against."

Before Bartley could reply, Anton spoke, his voice calm, his words almost soothing despite their repulsive content. "They are primarily a combination of vertebrate and invertebrate, as incredible as that may sound, a blending of different species who never could and

354

never would mate with each other through normal sexual channels. The body is somewhat mammalian in nature; in some individuals more elongated than in others. It also has the peculiarities of certain insects which were also blended into the final product."

"Insects? What insects?"

"Various types. Most predominantly, the earwig."

"*Earwig!*" Bartley's eyes widened with disgust. David could barely compose himself.

"I assure you," Anton sneered. "The old wive's tale about earwigs slipping into people's ears while they're sleeping is entirely unfounded. Besides," he laughed, "our chimeras are capable of far worse things than that. The earwig is carnivorous and nocturnal, and can find all sorts of hiding places in the dark. It has a wonderful protuberance jutting from its stomach, which has been duplicated in our animals, except of course it is proportionately larger and protrudes from the tapered far end of the creature."

"These things are big insects?" David asked, recoiling.

"*No!*" Anton thundered. "Not at all! Despite a hundred horror films to the contrary, outsized insects could never exist because their respiratory systems would not function at an increased size, among other reasons. Our chimeras are not insects. Nor are they mammals. They are not invertebrates. They are not verterbrates, either. They are like nothing that has ever existed before. That is why they are so special. Why people will pay such a high price for the privilege of owning them, of using them. They are a brand new life form, a *new* species made up of parts of *old* species."

In spite of his revulsion, David could not help but find the man's story fascinating. In another time, another place, he would have wanted to know how all this had been accomplished. Now, he had only one thing in his mind: "How can they be destroyed?"

"They can't be."

"You're lying," David countered. "Something destroyed them in Milbourne."

Anton's eyes shot over to Bartley, who was still holding the gun on him. "My, you do have a wagging little tongue, don't you? You've told him everything."

Bartley ignored him. Not daring to turn his gaze from Anton, he told David: "You must get out of here now. They saw you enter with me. As long as I prevent Anton from calling security, you can get out without any problem. Take my car. Smash through the gate if you have to, but get out! Go directly to Felicity Village and warm the people there. You must convince them to leave the area immediately. Tell them anything, make up any story. Just as long as you get them to leave!"

"What about you?"

"I have work to do. Trust me!"

David hesitated, wondering if he was taking the best course of action, but unsure of what alternative he had. He said goodbye, wished Bartley good luck, and stepped out into the lab.

"They'll never listen to him," Anton said, that disgusting chesire cat grin still plastered on his face. "He's going to die. They're all going to die!"

Bartley said nothing, his hatred of the man before him sustaining him as nothing in his life had ever sustained him, his need for revenge preventing him from falling to the floor with fear and fatigue. He knew that Anton was probably right. He could only hope he had enough inner fortitude to put his own plan into action.

Or else it would be too late for all of them.

Chapter Fifteen

It had all happened so quickly.

One moment the gun had been leveled at Frederick Anton's head, while Ted used his free hand to shovel papers into the briefcase—incriminating, damaging papers that would give the authorities all the proof they needed to blow the whole nasty business wide open.

But first he wanted to kill Frederick Anton. For murdering his son and turning him into a monster. For helping to create the chimeras, even now slaughtering helpless innocents. For driving his wife beyond sanity. Yes, for all that Frederick Anton must die.

Anton had kept telling him that he was a fool, that he'd never leave the plant alive. He said Nurse Hamilton would mutilate his wife while she slept. Ted told him about the nurse's death. "I was . . . very fond . . . of Nurse Hamilton," Frederick said. "That's something else I'll get you for, Bartley."

Bartley had only smiled, glad that he had hurt the man in some small way.

He had been planning to order Anton into the closet, hoping that if he placed the gun close to the man's forehead, the sound would be muffled enough not to carry out into the lab. But he never got the chance. Two assistants suddenly walked into the office, and Anton—taking advantage of the diversion—jumped for the weapon, nearly wresting it out of Bartley's hand. A shot rang out. The two assistants dove for cover, while Bartley and Anton grappled for the gun.

Possessed of a demoniacal courage, Bartley held onto the weapon, backed Anton into a corner, and shot him. It was only a glancing blow, but the sight of blood seeping out from his shoulder was enough to incapacitate Anton temporarily. Grabbing the briefcase, Bartley had left the office and the lab. He now knew what he had to do.

While the other two in the office rushed to Anton's assistance, Bartley went out into the corridor and headed for the tunnel that led to the caverns beneath the quarry. He was too desperate now to stop for anyone. He saw the security guard standing in front of the steel door marked NO ADMITTANCE. He shot the man in the leg before he could reach for his gun. He had no wish to kill anyone if he could help it. No one except Anton. He prayed for a chance at a second shot.

Bartley opened the door while the guard writhed on the floor, blood pouring out of his wound and wetting the floor. Once inside, he slammed the door and locked it from within. As there was no other entrance, this would slow his pursuers down most effectively.

Inside, a circular tube had been carved out of the earth, receding far back into the distance. Small lightbulbs hung bare every few feet from a metal rod along the rocky surface of the left wall. Bartley ran down the tunnel; the sound of the alarms ringing in the distance drove him on relentlessly. His feet padded over the earth, barely touching the ground.

Within minutes he had reached the end of the tunnel and another steel door. There was no guard here. He twisted the circular hatch and pushed it open, putting all of his back behind it, wishing he were younger and stronger. But he had had to send David to the village. David would not have known what to do down here.

David could not have killed Anton for him, either. That was a privilege Bartley wanted all for himself.

He was inside the cavern now, a huge hollow underground area similar to the one Harry London had discovered back in Milbourne. Bartley had been here only once before, when they had been doing some blasting to make the cavern wider than it had been naturally. There was a wooden shack a few feet away, nestled on the edge of the cliff. That was where they kept the dynamite that had been used in the blasting.

He looked over at the pool, a few yards away and several feet below the ledge he was on. There was a stone incline with a metal guardrail leading down to the pool. The beasts had gravitated here of their own accord, resting during the day—which is why no one swimming in the quarry had ever been attacked. They did not move, he had been told, during the daylight hours, except when they were extremely hungry. The bright lights which had been installed in the cavern helped to keep them docile. Although they were air-breathers, they could stay under water for long periods of time. The scientists had tried to keep everything as "natural" as possible. They had blasted away part of the wall only so that they would have more room to set up equipment. As the population of the hybrid inhabitants increased, they intended to blast even more.

The shack was locked with a heavy chain. Bartley blew it off with one well-aimed bullet. He swung open the door and peered inside. There was enough dynamite in there to blow the whole place sky high. He would wait, hold them all off with the gun if he had to, until the chimeras came back from the woods, until they dove down into the depths of the quarry, entered the underground streams far below, and emerged back in the cavern's pool. He would not have long to wait. They would come back long before dawn arrived.

He grabbed the dynamite and set about placing the

sticks in strategic places. That locked steel door at the other end of the tunnel might keep the opposition out for hours. In any case, they would never suspect him of going this far, not even Anton. They would think he was simply trying to find another way out, trying to make it to the surface so that he could go to the authorities and blow the whistle on them. Well, they were wrong. He was far more dangerous than that.

But he had to accept the fact that he and his precious evidence would probably not survive, no matter what precautions he would take. No matter—David would tell them. The explosion would be investigated, their operations crippled. Maybe this time not even they could cover up what they'd been doing.

He sat and waited. Soon, very soon, it would end.

Anna woke up and was surprised to see how dark it was. What was it that had disturbed her? The phone, that was it. She could hear it downstairs, its persistent ringing calling to her, nagging. David. David will answer it.

But then she remembered that David had left. She had just been barely aware that someone—she had heard David call him "Mr. Bartley," that George's father probably—had come to the house during dinner. Part of her had wondered what was happening. Another part— the part controlled by the debilitating chemicals in her antihistamines—only wanted to go straight back to bed. The antihistamine won.

She had heard a car drive away, heard the silence of the house afterwards, telling her that David had gone off somewhere with the visitor.

So David was not there to answer the phone. It might even have been David himself who was calling. She pulled herself out of bed and walked down the stairs, clinging to the banister. Still the phone rang, over and over, crying to her to answer. She shivered without knowing why; she felt warm enough now.

She managed to get to the phone before the caller could hang up. It was a man's voice on the other end. It kind of gave her the creeps. Perhaps that was because she was still sleepy and all alone in a strange house. Deep in the country woods. Alone.

"Miss Anna Braddon?"

"Yes?"

"I have a message for you from David Hammond."

"David? Where is he?"

"He's been in an accident. A car accident. Him and Ted Bartley. I'm sorry to have to tell you this."

"My God—is he all right?"

"I can't lie and say it isn't serious. But it's not exactly hopeless either. He was able to ask me to call you. The accident occurred right near my home, so they were brought into the house while we waited for help to arrive. The doctor's with them now. They can't be moved just yet. Please try and get here as quickly as possible, Miss Braddon. He keeps asking for you."

"Why haven't they taken him to a hospital?"

"They will later. They can't be moved just yet. If they do move them before you arrive, I'll tell you where to go. Please hurry."

"Yes, yes, of course. Where are you? What's your name?"

"Ernest Dunsinger." He gave her directions to his house. "We're in a small settlement off the main highway. Perhaps you know of it?

"It's called Felicity Village."

Frederick Anton hung up the phone and smiled.

Damn Bartley. Damn them both. Well, he would have the last word. His shoulder, which had been washed and wrapped with bandages, hurt like hell, and his men were having difficulty getting through the door that led to the tunnel—but he'd get one small revenge at least.

He'd called Bartley's wife first. The maid had said she was "indisposed." Well, he could still get even with the other one, that Hammond fellow.

He had realized who David was before Ted had finally told him, sometime before the battle which had ended with him getting shot. Bartley had, after all, told him weeks ago about Hammond's phone call, about his son's visit to the young man's apartment. Anton had sent men down to search the place, to find George. They had found him eventually, lying, *festering*, in an alley. So it wasn't hard to figure out who Bartley had enlisted in his war against the Corporation; one of George's friends. And Bartley had confirmed this for him.

Anton also knew that the fair and lovely Anna Braddon was visiting the fair and lovely town of Hillsboro; he knew where she was staying and *who* she was staying with. Little that went on in this town went unobserved by his multitude of spies. He had got Hammond's number from information, and placed the call, his hands thumbing through a file that listed the names of the various residents of Felicity Village. Ah, yes. "Ernest Dunsinger" would do quite well.

So now Miss Anna Braddon was heading out towards the village, to arrive just in time for the chimeras' attack. Hammond had helped Bartley; they had taken the life of Nurse Hamilton. It would be a fitting revenge to arrange the death of Hammond's woman. And she would die. There was no way Hammond could stop the attack of the hybrids; no way either of them could survive. He closed the book.

And smiled.

Everything was very still and strikingly quiet in the parking lot of Porter Pharmaceuticals, like the tranquility of the sea before a gale. David had made it out of the building without inncident but now came the hard part. How would he explain why he was taking Mr. Bartley's—or more accurately *Mrs.* Bartley's—automobile from the parking lot *without* Mr. Bartley? He crossed his fingers mentally, thinking up all kinds of plausible explanations. He *could* have the security guard at the gate ring Anton's office, but what if Bartley didn't answer, or what if he had left by that time? Even worse, what if he had been disarmed and apprehended? It was too risky.

Luckily Bartley had remembered to leave the car unlocked, keys in the ignition, or it would have all been over already. David had just started to climb behind the wheel when he saw a shadow looming over him, felt a presence staring downwards.

It was another security guard, one he hadn't seen before. A younger fellow with short-cropped hair evident under the sides of his cap, and a trim, muscular body that looked more than capable of subduing unwanted visitors. "All right. Just hold it," he barked. "Can I ask what your business is here?"

David prepared himself for trouble. "Mr. Ted Bartley was showing me around the facilities this evening," he explained, "and had to stay late for a conference with—uh—Frederick Anton. As it was getting quite late, he gave me permission to drive back to town in his wife's car. I believe *Mrs.* Bartley will call for him later on this evening."

David had thought quickly. The guard seemed convinced that he was not a simple car thief; the name-dropping had seen to that. But what about the rest?

"I'll have to check with Mr. Bartley if you don't mind. Why don't you come with me?"

A shiver shot up and down David's spine. If he went along with him, he thought, he'd never walk out of there alive. Somehow he knew that as well as he knew his own name and birthdate. He looked to the right through the windshield and got an idea. That path was there, the one through the woods, the one that led right to the village, and then on to the quarry. Yes, that was it. He got out of the car slowly, acting friendly and submissive to keep the watchman off his guard. He closed the door, wondering if the man would take a shot at him if he ran. He would have to take that chance. Then he got another brainstorm.

As they started back to the lobby, David looked up and over towards the woods. He raised his arm, shouted "Hey you! Stop that!" and ran off towards the path—pretending to be in pursuit of someone else! He knew what he was doing had to be the dumbest ploy this side of the Keystone Kops—if that guard wanted to kill him, no games would prevent it—but it startled the man just enough so that David was in the woods before a shot could ring out. As he dodged through the brush and onto the path, he realized that there had been no shots at all, as if the man didn't care where he went and knew better than to follow him at that time of night. And he was not following him, or David would have heard him. He was glad for that, at least. Perhaps the watchman didn't know about this path, and figured David would wind up hopelessly lost. And if he knew about the chimeras—which was unlikely, but not impossible—he wouldn't follow David even if he *did* know where he was going. More likely, the watchman wasn't allowed to wander far from his post; it was too easy to be suckered by decoy action that way.

And then it hit David. He was in the woods alone at night, approaching the clearing where the hybrids were even now about to mass. He must have been crazy to dart into the forest like that! At least in an automobile he would have had some protection, some means of escape. But now?

Fortunately, there was enough moonlight coming

from the trees so that he could see where he was going. Just barely.

The most horrible thing was, even though he had been told what the creatures were made up of, he still didn't know *exactly* what they looked like. Except that some had human heads.

Of course, he would know what they looked like when he saw them.

But by then it might be too late.

"I'm sorry, Miss, but you're obviously mistaken. Is it possible that someone was playing a joke on you?"

Anna was trying very hard not to cry. She had ran out of the house, panic-stricken, filled with dread and fear, so anxiety-ridden that she had nearly cracked up David's car more than once getting over here. The thought that David was badly injured, that she might lose him, had been too awful to even contemplate. Now here she was in Felicity Village, standing in the foyer of Ernest Dunsinger's house, and they were telling her that there had been no accident, that no one in the house had called her.

"Pretty sick joke, if you ask me," Dunsinger's wife Madeline said sympathetically. "Maybe you got the name wrong. Or the address. We would have heard the sirens if an ambulance had driven into the village. Not much excitement in here, let me tell you."

"I don't know anyone in Hillsboro," Anna protested. "Who would do such a thing? I just can't imagine."

And then she thought: *Derek?* Is he jealous enough, nasty enough, to engineer a sick joke like this? But no, how would Derek have known that David had driven off with Mr. Bartley? Besides, she had never even discussed David with Derek. Maybe it was Bartley's son George who was behind it. But why? *Had* there been an accident; if so, where was David and what was his condition?

Anna had felt sure that she was at the right place when she'd first walked in and seen the doctor in the living room, which was just off to one side of the foyer. A heavy set, elderly woman was lying on the couch looking pained and uncomfortable. It was Mrs. Dunsinger's mother, who had been having chest pains ever since dinner time.

The portly middle-aged doctor was just leaving as the Dunsingers and Anna stood awkwardly in the foyer, trying to come to some resolution over David's strange disappearance and the phone call that the Dunsingers had not made.

"Indigestion," the doctor said. "That's all it is. Your mother has a vivid imagination, I'm afraid. One burp and she thinks she's having a heart attack. I've given her a sedative and she'll be fast asleep shortly." It seemed that the doctor lived next door and was friendly enough with the Dunsingers to make an occasional house call. He worked in the hospital in the nearby town of Wallingford, and when he heard of Anna's predicament, suggested that she call there for information. "If your friend was in an accident, he would have been taken there. Why don't you call the emergency room?"

"Yes, that's a good idea," Mrs. Dunsinger agreed. "You can use our phone. It's right down the hall in the—" She was interrupted by her mother calling out from the living room. "Excuse me just a second." She went in to see what the elderly woman wanted, leaving her husband and the doctor standing in the foyer giving Anna admiring glances. Anna was beginning to think the whole thing had been a mistake, a joke, and she felt relieved. She hoped that the call to the Wallingford Hospital would not shatter her newly found composure.

"She wanted some tea," Madeline said, returning from the living room. "But I'm afraid the poor dear will be asleep before I can bring it in to her."

"Just see that she gets lots of rest," the doctor reminded her. "A lot of your mother's trouble is tension. Lack of sleep. She'll feel better all around if she relaxes some more."

"I'll see that she does," Madeline assured him.

The doctor excused himself, and Mrs. Dunsinger turned to Anna. "You look like you could use a little rest yourself. Come and have some coffee with us. You can use the phone in the kitchen."

Anna appreciated the gesture. "Thank you so much. I'm sorry to be such trouble."

"You're no trouble," the husband said, already smitten. There wasn't a soul in the village who wouldn't want to entertain *the* Anna Braddon for an hour or two.

They went into the kitchen and Anna had her first good look at her hosts. Mrs. Dunsinger was an attractive woman, thirtyish, with blond hair cut short and a rather pretty face and clothes; she knew how to make herself look good on a limited expense account. Her husband was kind of plain, but nonetheless appealing, with a rugged, unshaven face and a masculine build.

Madeline dialed the number of the emergency room while Anna stood by her side on tenterhooks. While it rang, Madeline called out to a little boy who was playing on the back porch. "Our son Steven," she explained. "It's past his bedtime, but it's his father's birthday today." Anna smiled quickly at Ernest. "We went out to dinner and the movies. Oh, here we are—"

Madeline handed the phone to Anna; a lump had formed in Anna's throat. She felt nervous and prickly all over. She asked the woman on the other end about David. Not only had he not been brought to the hospital, but there had been no accidents so far that evening, and the woman would have known if there had been, unless it had happened within the past half hour or so. It had been longer than that. Anna hung up, relieved, but terribly confused.

"Have some coffee, dear," Madeline insisted. "Then

you can drive back home and wait for your friend. I'm sure they'll be a good explanation for all this."

"Thank you for being so nice," Anna said. Madeline *pshawed*. She put the water on the stove, while Ernest sat in the chair next to Anna, grinning away at her. Anna couldn't help but smile.

Suddenly the phone rang, startling them all. Ernest started to rise from his chair in response, but Madeline made a grab for it. He sank back down again, wondering what to say to his glamorous guest.

"Hello. Who is this? Oh, *Viv!* How are you?"

Ernie chuckled. "Her friend. Lives two houses down. Don't know why she bothers using the phone all the time."

Madeline listened carefully, then turned to her husband. "Ernie. This is *weird*. Viv says there's some kind of crazy man running around the village telling everyone to get out. Says we're going to be attacked or something."

"What?"

What *now*, Anna mused.

"Ernie, go get your rifle. Just in case. Viv is scaring me."

Ernie excused himself and did as he was told. "If he comes to this house," he muttered, "I'll blow his goddamn brains to kingdom come."

Madeline was speaking again and it took Anna a few seconds to realize that the housewife was addressing her. " . . . probably someone who wants us all to leave so that they can rob all of our houses. And we left Yonkers for this?"

Anna smiled, almost too tired to wonder what it was all about. She hoped she could get out of this lovely house before too long. Guns and looters made her nervous.

The doorbell rang. Madeline gasped. Anna sat up straighter in her chair, suddenly wishing she had simply driven straight to the hospital instead of calling from here. Someone was banging on the door now. The knocking had an ominous quality to it, although Anna assured herself that in her tense state she was merely imagining things. She watched her hostess step out into the hallway, calling her husband's name, then got up herself and stood by the exit from the kitchen, hoping the visitor was only a harmless neighbor coming by for a cup of sugar.

Ernest marched heavily past his wife as she approached the door, a rifle held rigidly in his hands. "Let me get it," he told her. "Go look after Steven." He advanced on the door, pulling it open with a rugged wrench. "What do you want?" he said to the figure outside. Neither Anna nor Madeline—whose curiosity had prompted her to stay there rather than follow her husband's instructions—could see who it was. The figure was bathed in a bright glow of light from the fixture above the door, and was surrounded by a blackness punctuated here and there by glows of illumination from the other houses in the area.

"I know this is going to sound strange," the person in the doorway began, "but I must insist that you evacuate. Your family is in terrible danger."

Dunsinger was having none of it. "So *you're* the nut who's been going around spreading that cockamamie story! Our neighbors warned me about you. Why don't you get the hell out of here before I blow your goddamn brains out with my rifle!" He lifted the weapon and aimed it, shifting his body to a more strategic position. In that instant, Anna saw who it was at the door. She ran down the hall shouting: "No! No! Please don't shoot! I know him. He's a friend of mine!"

David was as startled to see her as she was to see him. "Anna! I *wondered* if that was my car parked outside, but it didn't seem possible."

His face reflecting caution and wariness, Ernest put

down the gun and let David come in, whereupon David and Anna quickly embraced. "Oh, David, thank God you're all right. What's going on?" Before he could reply, she rapidly explained how she had come to be there. She told the Dunsingers who David was. "What is this all about?" she asked him. "Are you the one who's telling everyone to leave their houses?"

"Yes, I am. But no one will listen to me. Not that I blame them." He looked helplessly at Mr. Dunsinger. "Look, Mister. I know you have no reason to trust me. But if you have any influence over your neighbors I suggest you use it." As with the last few families, he didn't bother Dunsinger with the details, knowing it was unlikely anyone would believe him. Instead he said: "There was a—a mishap—at the plant. There's a cloud of poisonous gas heading this way. It's extremely dangerous to human life. You must get out of here. All of you."

Madeline stepped forward, her once-friendly demeanor replaced by a nervous hostility. "Then why haven't the *police* come to get us out?" She turned to her husband. "Viv told me she called the police, and they told her that this man must be a crackpot." She looked back at David and sneered defiantly. "There hasn't been any trouble out at the plant."

"The police are *in* on it," David pleaded. "It's a coverup. Can't you understand? This whole village is going to be wiped out just to test the poison gas. Please—"

Ernest cut him short. "Listen. I've never seen you before in my life, but I've met the sheriff on several occasions. Why should I take your word over his? I've put a lot of money in this house and in the furnishings and in everything we own. If you think I'm just gonna walk off and leave it, you're crazy."

"What good will it do you when you're dead?"

Ernest ignored him. "Madeline! Go check on Steven.

No telling how many nuts are out tonight."

"Please," Anna said. "I know this man. He wouldn't lie to you. He isn't a burglar or a crook. There must be some truth to his story."

"I've heard enough," Dunsinger glared. "Take your boyfriend and go. You celebrities may have a different house in every city, but this is the only one I got and I intend to protect it."

There was no reasoning with the man. Anna led David into the hallway, moving slowly. Dunsinger made a move to follow them, but was held back by his wife.

"Is this *true*, David?" Anna whispered.

"No, Anna. It's even worse. It isn't poison gas that's coming, it's creatures—horrible creatures that are being freed from a laboratory. Monsters."

"Are you *serious*?"

"Believe me, I am." He hurriedly told her what he had learned from Mr. Bartley and from Anton, but could tell that it was simply too incredible, too much for her to absorb. He couldn't expect her to believe it. He wasn't sure *he* did. She would just have to trust him. "It must have been Anton who called you with that phony message. That *bastard!*"

Back in the kitchen they could hear the Dunsingers conferring. It sounded as if Madeline was weakening. "What if he's *right*?" they heard her say. The rest of the conversation was lost amid a lot of oaths and mutterings.

On the screened-in back porch, the Dunsingers' young son sat in a garden chair and played with a plastic replica of a robot cartoon character. His attention wandered frequently, and he often turned up to stare at a smattering of mosquitoes which hovered daintily by the porch light, their tiny bodies having squeezed easily through the holes in the screen. His mother had just come out to check on him, knowing it was way past his bedtime, but was too frightened and upset by David's unnerving pronouncement to put him to bed. Steven, a

371

little freckle-faced eight-year-old with tousled blond hair, sat in his chair and idly worked the arms and legs of the toy. He heard raised voices inside, accompanied by angry whispers, and somehow he sensed that there was trouble, and he was glad that he was not part of it and that he had not yet been put to bed.

Barely a mile away they were stirring in the caverns, rising up from the depths of the watery quarry, coming to the surface, their bodies making ripples on the moonlit water. Most of them were still leery of leaving the lair, but had no choice, as their hunger drove them onwards. They had already consumed everything in the caverns. Some of them had gone out hunting and had tasted human flesh for the first time. They were creatures of appetite and instinct, whatever human qualities they might have had were overwhelmed by the laws of nature, by the thirsts of the non-human breasts they had been blended with. They pulled themselves out of the water with their arm-like appendages, and crawled, hopped and scurried away from the quarry.

There was an odor in the air. A distant fragrance, which they found impossible to resist. Before, the braver ones among them had gone in the opposite direction, down towards where the lights were, feeding on those they had found in the isolated homes lying along the bottom of the mountain. They had sensed the large concentration of meat in the area towards which they were now heading, but had not gone there in the past because they had still been too insecure in this new environment to want to confront a great many other life forms all at once; even if they were food. But now, driven on by the pheromones in the air, they could not possibly stop themselves. They were no longer afraid—only hungry. Their insatiable appetites had to be satisfied. The ones with pale faces, those who seemed slightly more intelligent than their faceless companions, opened their eyes wide and plunged into the forest as the others followed behind them.

Before long the ones in front could see the lights from the clearing. The smell of flesh and blood was even stronger than that of the sex smells which had driven them here. They would wait until later for the other, but now—now they would feed . . .

David had decided that the only course of action he could take would be to do his best to save himself and Anna. He had done his utmost to warn the community— this was the last house he'd have to notify—and if no one wanted to leave, there was nothing more he could do about it. Still, the thought of what was going to happen to the residents chilled and sickened him. He stood before the front door, reluctant to leave without first convincing the Dunsingers of the danger.

"I still can't believe what you told me," Anna said. "If it *is* true, wouldn't we be safer right where we are, locked inside, then out unprotected on the highway?"

"Not according to what I heard tonight, and I'm not taking any chances. Besides, if we hurry we'll be gone before they get here."

"What are they, David? You still haven't told me."

"Chimeras, hybrids—look, what difference does it make? We're all going to be killed if we don't get the hell out of here! I tried to convince everybody to leave, but I don't think I got through to them. Maybe I did. Some of them looked scared enough to go, but most were pretty stubborn."

Suddenly they heard a shrill, high-pitched voice coming from the back of the house. A child's voice. "Mommy, mommy. Come see, come see. There's a funny-lookin' dog in the bushes."

David froze. *This was it.* He knew that it was too late. None of them were going to get out of there alive.

The Dunsingers had ended their conference in the kitchen, and it was clear that they had no intention of leaving, in spite of Madeline's doubts. Now the parents went out onto the porch to see what their son was yelling about.

David looked at Anna. "Stay here!" he ordered, running after the Dunsingers. Anna sensed that something was wrong. If these animals he spoke of actually existed she wanted to see them. Otherwise she'd have trouble convincing herself that her new lover had not taken leave of his senses. She ran after David.

Anna went out onto the porch through the door from the kitchen. She looked out into the yard and saw that the Dunsingers' little boy had gone out through the screen door, and was approaching a dark form sitting or squatting at the edge of the light, back where the lawn met the weeds and the overgrowth of the surrounding forest.

"Get the child back!" David was screaming. He brushed past the parents—who were slowly making their way to the child, admonishing him for leaving the porch —and ran up to the boy, sweeping him up into his arms. Too late. Just as the child was picked up off the ground, the thing in front of him reared up and David saw two spikes, like the ends of a wishbone, only sharper, stabbing into the boys' stomach. He pulled the boy off the spikes and ran back onto the porch, ignoring the child's screams. "Close the door!" he cried. Madeline quickly complied, her husband rushing over and taking the boy from David's arms. Thick streams of tears ran down

Steven's cheeks. Anna felt a pang of horror and sympathy for the boy. While his father held him, David lifted off the child's tiny T shirt to reveal two nasty red puncture wounds which were starting to bleed. "I'll take him over to Dr. Ferguson," Ernie said. "What the hell *is* that thing?"

"No!" David ordered. "Don't go outside. Lock the doors and windows and whatever you do—*don't go outside!*"

"But the boy!" Dunsinger protested.

All arguments were then cut off by a hard, *twanging* sound as the thing in the backyard abruptly jumped out from the concealing bushes and attached itself to the screen covering the porch. The four adults could only stare at it in abject horror, as it clawed at the screen, trying to tear its way into the enclosure. They heard screams shattering the night, and David knew that even now people in the other houses were witnessing the same thing they were. The chimeras had invaded the village.

Ernest moved quickly and turned on a pair of brighter lights that lit up the whole backyard and illuminated the thing on the screen even further. It was a nightmare, some deadly spawn of a sick creator, a horror that had no place on earth. Although the sight of it was more horrible than anything they had ever seen before, the four of them could hardly take their eyes away.

It was about four or five feet long from head to tip, with a thick seal-like body covered in slime which shone under the lights. From the end of the body was a pincer-like protrusion—the "wishbone" David had seen—with which the creature could stab its victims. The squirming body on the screen seemed capable of twisting in much the same way as a scorpion, so as to impale victims on the twin needle-sharp spikes of the peculiar appendage. David realized that the odd object the children had found at the quarry must have cracked off one of these creatures' pincers.

From either side of the body were two more long, slimy appendages which functioned as both arms and legs, and ended in pointed, three-fingered claws. The muscles in these limbs were so strong that the animal was capable of pulling along its larger body on the ground as the arms grabbed the earth underneath. The arms also gave the creature enough spring and momentum to jump a few feet up in the air.

The head—a grayish, rounded knob about one-fifth the size of the trunk—had two very large black eyes that bulged outwards from the flat surfaces around them. The skin was leathery and wrinkled; there was no hair. The only other feature on the head—besides two small holes which apparently served as the nose—was the mouth; it resembled that of an insect, except that it was a ghoulish conglomeration with parts for sucking, grasping *and* chewing. That mouth, always working, constantly moving, emitting a ghastly buzzing sound, was the worst thing of all about the monstrosity.

But then, David had not yet seen the ones with a *human* component.

The claws of the creature began to shred the screening as the four of them stood there staring. Already more than a dozen others were coming from the woods, moving slowly because of the lights, but steadily advancing just the same. Madeline let out a screech of revulsion and shock, and Anna stood there trying to control her quivering body. David, at least, had been somewhat prepared, but even he was having trouble keeping himself together. Ernest gave the boy over to his wife, and though his arms and legs shook with terror, lifted his gun and aimed at the thing on the screen. He never had time to shoot.

Anna pulled Madeline protesting into the kitchen, trying to shield both her and the child from what surely was to happen next. The creature had ripped through the flimsy metal barrier, and hurled itself onto Dunsinger's neck. David looked about for some kind of weapon. Even as the thing reared back, and sunk its mouth into his neck, Ernest still held onto the gun. David got a good look at that mouth up close. Pincers on either side of the lip-like structures in the center of the "face" held onto Dunsinger firmly as a long tube-like needle came out from the mouth and pierced the nape of his neck. Blood began pouring out from either side of the needle, although most of it was sucked up into the tube. Meanwhile, the creature bit eagerly into the flesh with "teeth" located on either side of the tube, and chewed away morsels while the dying man screamed. David tried to keep from passing out, wanting to forget all that was happening. He forced himself to lift up a folded garden chair and slad it hard against the hybrid, hoping to dislodge it from Dunsinger's body. Though he hit it time and time again, the creature would not relinquish its hold of the man. Finally both man and monster collapsed onto the concrete floor of the porch, while several other chimeras began coming in through the jagged hole in the screen made by the first hybrid attacker. David tried to bend down and grab the gun, but Dunsinger's fingers had locked around it as if they were frozen by rigor mortis. The man was either paralyzed or already dead.

David knew there was nothing more he could do. He managed to get safely behind the kitchen door just before another of the things could pounce upon him. Within seconds, the entire porch was alive with chimeras, all of them greedily swarming over the body of Ernest Dunsinger.

Firsthand, David had seen the same thing that had happened to Anna's brother, and the sight was more than he could stand. He staggered on shaky legs out of the kitchen, wondering where Anna had gone. He heard sounds coming from the upstair's bedroom: running water, the crying child, Madeline's shrieks. He ran up the stairs, not knowing what he would say or do. He saw the two women hovering over the child who was huddled on the tiled floor of the bathroom, his body already swollen, his face red and mishapen with fright and fever.

"He's unconscious," Madeline cried. "I've called the doctor's house. But there's no answer."

David knew that Anna did not need to ask where Dunsinger was. She could tell from the look on his face. He only hoped Madeline wouldn't ask for her husband for at least a few moments longer. She was hysterical enough as it was.

"I'm going to see if we can get out of here," David said. He went into the nearest bedroom and looked out into the night. The hybrids were everywhere judging from the screaming he heard. He could see other people down below, racing over someone's lawn, running for their lives. One of the fleeing strangers tripped on a stone and went down, and was soon completely covered by slimy bodies. Another nearly made it to the door, but was struck down from behind. His flailing arms were quickly stilled.

The people who'd been outdoors didn't have a chance. David looked to the right, towards the end of the road where they had first spotted the Corporation's sign, and couldn't help gasping out loud. The chimeras were swarming from the woods. *Hundreds*. There must have been hundreds of them, spewing from the forest in wave after wave, an obscene regurgitation of hunger personified. And God—was it possible after all? Even from this distance he could tell that some of them had hairless *human heads*. In every other regard they were exactly the same as the others, right down to the insect mouthparts. But the heads. *Lord*, the *faces* . . .

He looked straight down and thought that if he and the others in the house were to leave right now, they might make it into the car parked out in front. This house was the nearest one to the road leading out to the highway, and as the hybrids were all attacking from the opposite end of the clearing—except for the ones on the back porch—they were concentrating on the other homes first. If they hurried, if they dashed immediately down the stairs and straight out the door, they might just have a chance of getting away. Anything would be better than staying here, completely vulnerable, counting the seconds until they, too, were devoured.

He went back into the hall and saw that Mrs. Dunsinger, carrying her unconscious child, was going down the stairs. He looked over at Anna, who stood helplessly by the bathroom door. "She insists on running next door to the doctor," Anna said, tears filling up her eyes. "She wants to check with her . . . with her husband first."

"We mustn't let her go out there," David said. He wished he had time to give Anna a glance of reassurance, of love and concern, but there was no time for that now. He wondered if he'd ever get the chance. He tumbled down the stairs in a fury, trying to reach the woman before she got to the kitchen door.

It was too late. She had opened the door and let the chimeras in.

Two of them had climbed over her and pushed her and the boy down onto the linoleum floor. Madeline was screaming, trying to protect her son with her arms. David grabbed a kitchen knife off a rack by the sink and plunged in several times into the body of the nearest creature; it was busy chewing on the woman's now dangling and broken limb. With each blow a milky white fluid gushed out and spurted onto his clothes and face, but the animal seemed not to take notice. David got up and dodged just in time as the body wiggled to one side, and the "wishbone" in the back stabbed upwards, narrowly missing his chest and thigh. The clawed limbs scratched at the floor, leaving deep irregular wedges. The child rolled free of his mother's bosom, and fell to the floor. David made a grab for the boy.

But something horrible got to him first.

David looked up and stared into the eyes of Hell. A face looked back into his own. Intelligent, cunning, crazed eyes in a humanoid head. This was one of *them*, one with the human cells. He did not recognize the face, thank God, but it shocked him nonetheless. Nature had never meant for anything like the hybrid in front of him to exist. The human head on the hybrid body gave the creature an evil cast that none of its companions could match. To see a human face chewing on human flesh was unbearable. The sheer grotesqueness of the animal made David nearly vomit and almost release his bowels. He held on, desperately fighting back the waves of nausea, the threatening unconsciousness that barrelled through his system. To faint now would be to die. The insect mouthparts where the mouth should have been, buzzing, hissing, always moving, drained away whatever humanity the face might once have possessed.

The hybrid's "lips," the *labium* and *labrum* contributed by the insect cells, opened suddenly in a mock sneer, the hissing sounds got louder. Suddenly the hybrid shot forward and grabbed the boy's arm in its mouth. David tried to rise, tried to fight, tried to save the child, but could barely keep himself conscious as Steven was pulled away, back back back into the throng of squirming horrors even now squeezing in through the back door. More of them had human heads. In seconds the child had disappeared, lost somewhere among and under the slug-like monstrosities that were rapidly filling up the room.

David finally rose to his feet, wondering where he had dropped the knife, still determined to save the mother and child, not willing to admit that they were now beyond saving. Something crashed through the window above the sink, and knocked him back into the hall. The strength of the hybrids was amazing. The force of the impact of the body as it came through the glass had served to push David temporarily out of danger. More chimeras wiggled through the cracked panes above the sink, dropping like lice to the floor. David turned his back on the unholy mess in there and ran down the hall, knowing they'd be following any second.

Anna was at the foot of the stairs, her hand to her mouth, her eyes and body rigid with horror, staring in the opposite direction. David's eyes followed her gaze. The hybrids were clinging to the windows of the living room! David saw Madeline's mother fast asleep on the sofa, completely oblivious to the impending danger. He ran in there and tried to pull her off the couch. The old woman woke up, but was still dazed from the sedative. She squealed and fought as he grabbed her arm, trying to dig his one hand under her so that he could more easily lift and carry her.

"Leave me! Leave me be!" the woman screamed. "Why are you manhandling me? Leave me alone!"

"Please. I'm not trying to hurt—"

"Madeline!" the old woman yelled. "Why won't he leave me alone?"

Anna placed one foot into the room, but held back, obviously horror-stricken by the sight of the things on the windows. Although their slimy bodies stuck at first to the smooth glass, they soon started sliding down the panes, unable to keep a firm grip. It wouldn't be long before one of them—particularly one of the smarter, part-*human* hybrids—got the idea of jumping through the window, as one had done in the kitchen. David ignored the woman's protestations and kept right on pulling. Anna started forward to help.

Then what David had feared came to pass. Together, several of the creatures jumped through the living room windows. Pieces of glass flew in every direction. As the chimeras smashed through, David dropped the old woman's arm, and shielded his eyes against the flying shards spitting out from the wall. One piece cut into his arm, leaving a jagged gash dripping blood. One of the monsters landed flat on the old lady's stomach, shoving her back down onto the couch, and started burrowing into her chest. Anna hung back by the hallway, screeching at the top of her lungs. David had nothing to fight with but his hands. He curled up his fingers, preparing to dig into the monster's back, to pull it off the old woman's bosom. But as he looked down at its squirming and undulating mass, he found that he simply couldn't touch the thing. He closed his eyes for a second, knowing that every moment he delayed brought the woman closer to eternity. He forced his hands down until his fingertips were immersed in odorous grease. He opened his eyes again, adjusting to the feel of the beast. He could not get a grip on the thing. He knew that whether they had been put together by careful design or by astonishing fluke, they were incredible creatures, so swift and adaptable, capable of killing in any number of ways, almost impossible to hold onto or to capture, virtually impervious to harm. The perfect things to fight wars with, he thought. Easily dispensable, as they were, after all, only "things"—without rights, without moral constrictions, without fear.

His fingers slid helplessly down the back of the animal as the old woman cried out in pain. Then he felt something prick at his shirt. One of the hybrids was behind him, twisting its body so that the spikes in back poked upwards in David's direction. He stepped away, feeling his shirt tear. Sensing her weakness, more of the animals climbed onto the couch and fed on the old woman, whose struggles and cries had finally ceased. David jumped over another one lying in his path, and reached out for Anna. She had grabbed up a chair. As soon as David was out of the way, she threw it at the things on the couch consuming Madeline's mother. It was a useless gesture, as nothing would move them now. David saw that more of the things were inching their way carefully down the hall from the kitchen. As savage as they were, they moved slowly, as if unsure of their footing, not entirely trusting the area they were in. Once they realized that humans were no threat to them at all, they would move forward swiftly, utterly unstoppable, completely assured of their own invincible power.

Desperately, David's eyes looked around for an avenue of escape and spotted another door halfway down the hall. He and Anna were caught between two groups of hybrids, and that door was the only possible exit, if they managed to reach it in time. He grabbed Anna's hand and pulled her down the corridor. She struggled to get free. She hadn't yet noticed the door in the wall, and thought David was blindly taking her towards the kitchen. Had she seen the hybrids at the top of the stairs—some had obviously climbed up to the second story—she would have realized why that route was off limits. Luckily David reached the exit and got the door open before she could wiggle free.

He pushed her into a darkened garage and slammed the door behind them. It was only when they were behind the wall, the sounds from within rather muffled, that they realized how loud the hybrids had been, how intense and nerve-wracking were the noises they made. On every level they were the perfect weapon. The sight, the sound, the feel of them was repellent to their victims, giving them a psychological edge. If the villagers had guns, weapons of some sort, they might have fought back, but David wasn't sure how much damage they could have done against the invaders even then.

He found a switch hidden in the shadows and turned on the light. He would have to find a weapon. Even now the tips of their back pincers were cutting into the wood of the door from the hall. Cracks strarted to appear, forming outwardly spreading lines that deepened and grew as Anna watched. The only thing that kept them from smashing through the door directly was the fact that the hall they were in was too narrow for them to achieve enough momentum or leverage.

David looked around frantically. The light he had turned on was yellowish and weak, illuminating only the front part of the garage, the area near the wide door through which the car would exit. The back part, where there was a workbench and shelves full of paint cans, was still in shadows. Assorted implements hung from hooks on the walls.

He noticed a shovel leaning against the nearby wall and handed it to Anna. "Here. Start beating back anything that protrudes from that door. I'm going to see if I can start this car." Anna took the shovel, her fear-filled eyes already fastened on the cracks, waiting for something hideous to emerge from the wood. From the look on her face, David couldn't tell how far gone she might be. She seemed to be functioning on the most minimal level.

The sight of these things drove Harry London insane, David thought. Why am *I* still functioning? David could not have known that Harry had felt himself responsible for the deaths of his friends, that Harry had had no idea of what the chimeras were nor where they came from, that Harry's blood had been pumped full of a debilitating enzyme. Harry London had been figuratively blind in every way that mattered.

David was just about to open the car door when he heard a rustling sound in the back, coming from under the tool shed. He reached out and lifted an axe off its hook on the wall, holding it steadily, although everything in him wanted to cry out and run back into the light, wanted to stand by and with Anna. If it was one of the hybrids, how did it get in here? Then he saw. Windows in back. Over the worktable. Shattered. Clouds drifted, moon light came in. From under the table, one of the monsters slid out and approached the

384

spot where David was standing. It was one of the part-human hybrids.

It stopped a few feet away, inching carefully closer, sizing up its victim. What was it waiting for? David asked himself, knowing that even with an axe his chances for survival were limited against such a foe. What would become of Anna if anything happened to him? His fingers found a better grip on the axe and began to raise it slowly.

The chimera inched forward, lifting its head.

David could not believe his eyes. That face! *It was not possible.* Not *that* face! *Anything* but that face!

It was his father's visage that looked up at him, waiting, just waiting for a false move, a sign of weakness.

That's *not* your father, David told himself wildly. It isn't human! Look at its body, like a seal, like a sea lion, for pete's sake! It doesn't even have a human brain. *Instinct. Survival of the fittest. Hunger.* That's all it is. Destroy it. *Destroy it!* What are you waiting for?

That is not your father. It just borrowed his face, used some of the cells from your father's body. It has no mind, no memories, no capacity for love or human emotion of any kind.

Destroy it!

He thrust out furiously with the axe. The blade came down with a terrible force, severing the head from the slimy and hideous body. The head plopped down onto the floor. David felt as if he had decapitated his own father. Only the unnatural mouthparts kept the dismembered head from appearing entirely human.

David had not idea how the Corporation could have accomplished it. He knew very little about cloning, recombinant DNA, gene splicing and all the other terms that had been bandied about this evening. He only knew that they had progressed, as Bartley had suggested, far beyond where the public, and other scientists, could ever have expected. And he hated them with a deadly, all-encompassing hatred. He hated them for murdering innocents. He especially despised them for using the face of *his father*. He could never look on his real father's face again without being reminded, without staring at the old man's lips, wondering if they would open and instead of teeth he would see . . .

God, would any of them ever recover from this? No wonder London had lost his mind!

David looked in the car and saw that the keys were in the ignition. Good!—they still had a chance. He looked over at Anna. Pieces of wood were flying away from the door. She was beating at the needles sticking through, but her blows only served to damage the door even further. She was gasping, out of breath, crying, screaming, all at once. Others would have long since lost their grip on reality, but Anna had sunk deep into the soul lying underneath the pampered veneer, and had found a well of strength and courage to sustain her. So, too, had David.

And both of them wanted revenge. A terrible revenge.

The door exploded in a frenzy of wood chips, collapsing onto the floor of the garage. David grabbed Anna and pulled her back, away from the things coming in from the hallway. The chimeras flopped into the garage one by one, too disoriented to attack just yet.

"Get in the car!"

She did as she was told, while he ran to the front of the garage and pulled up the overhead door, heedless of whatever might lie on the other side. It was their only way out.

The door was fully opened. One chimera was clinging to it and hung soundlessly above David's head, about to drop onto the floor. He still held the axe, and swung it in front of him from side to side as he moved backwards to the vehicle behind him. Anna had turned on the engine and driven the car forward to meet him. She leaned over and pushed open the passenger door, urging him to get inside. The chimeras from the hall were almost upon him. He got in quickly. From all over came the hybrids —through the shattered window. From the door to the hallway. From outside. Dozens began creeping over from the other houses, their grisly missions there fulfilled, their hunger still unsatiated.

Anna smashed down on the gas petal, and the car shot out of the garage, horribly crushing three of the creatures lying in its path. She turned the wheel and pointed the car towards the path out to the main highway. Not sure of what was happening, several of the hybrids that had jumped onto the car at the last minute dropped off onto safer, steadier ground. Others were flung off helplessly by the speed and twisting motion of the car, splattering against the trees.

Anna's tears were renewed as they neared the highway. "All those people dead," she sobbed. "Those things killed Jeffrey, too, didn't they?"

"Things very much like them, yes."

"It was easy to figure out," Anna said bitterly. "What do we do now?"

"Drive on to the Wallingford Hospital. I want to get this arm looked at." The gash on his forearm was still bleeding and throbbing. "We have to get their police force out here, too, just in case some of the villagers were able to hold off the chimeras." He realized that tears were pouring unbidden from his eyes. Stop, he told himself. *Later!* Time enough to mourn later. There was still work to do.

Both of them concentrated on trying to keep away the memories of what they'd seen and heard, the deaths they'd witnessed. But David kept seeing the severed head, the uplifted face of his father. They both stared at the monotonous white line of the road ahead of them.

And behind them in the back seat something stirred.

* * *

David and Anna were a mile away from the Walling-ford Hospital, both fighting to keep hold of their sanity, to exorcise the nightmare images etched permanently it seemed on their respective retinas, as the sides of the road began to fill with the small shops and service stations that sprung up on the outskirts of a city. They felt a bit more at ease, at last approaching civilization, the horror permanently behind them. Anna broke the silence first.

"I didn't believe you," she said. "I'm not sure if I believe it even now. I've never seen anything like that!" She paused and added softly, as if afraid the very act of saying the words would bring an affirmative reply, "Do you suppose everyone was killed?"

"I don't know," he said, although he knew it was un-likely anyone other than themselves had managed to get away. His mind kept going back to the child, the little Dunsinger boy, the terrible way he had died. Mercifully Steven had been unconscious through most of it, unable to see or hear what was happening to himself and to his mother. How many other children had they sacrificed? And tomorrow, how many more again, when they released the chimeras on the town itself? It must not happen!

He hoped and prayed that Bartley had done what he had threatened and promised to do. Otherwise . . .

There were no other cars on the road in either direc-tion. The stores and hot dog stands they saw were all closed. Even in summertime, when school was out and the children needed entertainment, the towns up here seemed to pull up their rugs and fold up their tents after dark.

Anna slowed down as they neared the town's border. Behind them on the back seat, a head began to rise from out of the darkness. The lips worked, the mouthparts moved, but the noises were too soft to be heard over the sound of the engine. Anna might have seen it had she glanced just then in the rear-view mirror, but she was concentrating only on the road ahead, on reaching the hospital, on getting to the police. They had passed no houses, no phonebooths, nothing that looked either open or hospitable. Anna did not want to stop until they were far away, surrounded by bright lights and brick buildings and people, instead of dark forests teeming with monsters. No, she would not stop for anything.

David was completely oblivious to the head as it lifted itself upwards and opened its thick, foul lips. The long, stiletto-like labium shot out as the mandibles grasped David's shoulder. He wrenched around in his seat, caught tight by the seatbelt and the harness. Anna turned to see what had startled him and screamed; the car wobbled as it sped down the road, as Anna tried to steer without taking her eyes off the struggle going on beside her.

David's face was only inches from the face of the animal in the back seat. It was a woman's face—despite its lack of hair he could see the femininity of the features. His finger pressed the release button on the seatbelt, and he tore away from the head just before the sucking tube could insert itself into his shoulder. The creature grimaced and hissed, angered by the defensive movements of its prey.

Anna moved the wheel back and forth, back and forth, hoping that the jerking sideways movements of the automobile would jar the creature onto the floor. The maneuver didn't work. The thing got one of its claws firmly entrenched in the upholstery of her seat; she had to lean forward to avoid it, and her view of the road was diminished by the suddenly constricted vantage point. She was not even sure where they were going now. Her foot pressed down on the brake pedal.

"Keep going!" David screamed. "We're helpless out here! We've got to get to town!" He was right. They had no weapons at all to use against the hybrid. Even if they were to stop the car and get out, what would prevent the chimera from coming after them, killing one or both? They had to get to Wallingford, but would they make it in time?

The creature lashed out with its other limb, claws scraping into David's cheek. Blood dripped down over the webbed, finger-like appendages. He began to beat at the head with his hands, feeling bones under the slimy skin. The chimera loosened its grip on David's face. One hand kept hitting the creature, while David used his other to open and explore the glove compartment, searching desperately for any kind of weapon. His fingers found and grasped a flashlight. He pulled it out and turned it on, shining the light into the monster's eyes. The thing backed off a bit, but showed no sign of giving up the assault.

David swung the flashlight at its head, but it ducked and turned its body over, sticking the deadly pincers up in the air. The light was useless against them. David didn't dare flail out with it, for fear that one of the needles might pierce his wrist. The monster flipped over again and aimed the pincers at Anna, who was completely defenseless. She pressed closer to the wheel and the car shot completely out of control, smashing into a picket fence surrounding a country store, careening through the front yard, knocking a pile of empty boxes and trash-filled garbage cans every which way before returning back to the road as it curved around to meet them.

The pincers were a fraction of an inch from Anna's body. The creature was almost in the front seat with her. The noises from its mouth were louder now, louder than the engine, louder than their screams, than the squeal of the tires against the road. David leaned over and tried to steer the car with one hand, batting at the deadly spears with the flashlight in the other. If only they would crack, break off! Although the head was down in the back seat now, almost touching the floor, its loathsome hissing and nauseating odor filled the car. The clawed hands were on the back seat now, giving the monster's body support as it thrust upwards with the pincers; that was one less thing to worry about.

David looked out the windshield and saw that they were veering straight towards a bank of pumps in a gas station! That was one way of slaying the animal. Unfortunately they would die along with it, and he had no intention of giving up his—or Anna's life—to kill it. He swung the wheel and the car swerved out of danger just seconds before impact. They were back on the road again.

"Anna. Trust me. Take the wheel again. I have an idea."

Flattened up against the wheel, whimpering in mindless terror, she mustered enough self-control to steer while David leaned over and pushed himself between her and the seat cushion behind. He let the flashlight drop, and reached out both his hands. The creature was thrashing about in the dark, hoping to pierce the woman's body, unable to see exactly what was going on in front. David managed to grab hold of the pincers, one in each hand, and held on as tightly as he could. They were very thin at the end where he had grabbed them, and unlike true pincers, they were incapable of motion independent of the body. They simply stuck out rigidly from the tapered end, guided by the movements of the trunk. By holding them this way, David effectively kept the body from moving, too, although it squirmed in every direction in order to free itself. Unable to do more than twist around in such a way so that the head was facing upwards, it glared into David's eyes and hissed.

David pushed with all his might, trying to throw the thing completely over into the back seat. Anna was steering with great difficulty, as she barely had room to move her arms, and was too frightened to think clearly. The car raced past lines of trees, branches scraping against the windows. They narrowly missed colliding with a road sign. A dog darted out of their way just in time. The car swerved from side to side.

The monster seethed with rage, unable to use its pincers, caught between the car floor and David's straining arms. It began to push back. David sucked in all his breath and heaved, wishing it had a neck to break, a spine to shatter. The only resistance he felt was resilient flesh and muscle. If the pincers had been greased as heavily as the body, he would not have been able to even accomplish this much. He leaned back and over so that he was sitting in his own seat, giving Anna more freedom of movement. The pincers were dragged over with him, the body still struggling for release. If only he could pitch it out the window, onto the highway. But it was impossible, the hybrid was much to heavy for that. It seemed to weigh as much as an average size man. If only he could hold it like this until they reached the hospital!

But the chimera's claws dug into the back of the seat, and it began pulling its head and upper trunk upwards, doubling over to meet the end of the body held by David. David looked down and saw what was happening, and didn't know what to do. If he let go of the pincers they were back to square one. If he didn't, his upraised arms would be vulnerable to the mouth's tearing caress. Inch by inch the animal ascended, its two ends coming together, getting closer and closer to the top of the seat.

David pumped up and down furiously on the pincers, hoping to loosen the hybrid's grip, hoping the whole mess would fall down into the backseat. Any second those sharply clawed fingers would reach up and dig into his wrists, breaking his hold. Then the head would come up again and he would be absolutely helpless. There had to be something he could do.

"Anna! Step on the brakes. Quick!"

She did. David let go of the pincers and flew forward in his seat. The hybrid nearly toppled over the seat and into the front, but at the last second, the backwards jolt of the car served to snap it back again. It was lying flat on the seat, stretched out, trying to roll over onto its exposed stomach. Anna stepped on the gas and the car shot forward, entering the town at last. David found the catch on the side that released the upper part of the seat and pulled it, letting the cushion flop backwards. His hands shot out and he grabbed the hybrid's arms with his own. The pincers were trapped beneath the seat, the lower body completely unable to move. Anna drove through the town towards the hospital, only a block away now, standing out recognizably from the buildings around it.

While the chimera squealed and hissed, David used its own natural weapons against it. The thing could not move or turn over with the pressure of both the seat and David's one-hundred-sixty-pound body on top of it. David bent the monster's arms backward and used its claws to scrape at the face, gouging out chunks of flesh, spurts of milky-fluid, puncturing an eyeball. He would not stop, no matter how much his actions disgusted him, not until the thing was dead; completely, totally dead.

The head was a mass of slashed ribbons, covered in the foul white juice that ran freely from its wounds. Still the beast struggled. The fluid poured from its mouth, its nose. Flesh hung down in loose, grisly folds. David reminded himself again that this was not a human being and never had been.

Again and again he lashed out, scratching, scraping, slashing the head, the trunk, bending the limbs back so far he thought they would break. He felt moist breath come out of the two holes of the nose. Foul breath. He wanted it to smother, to suffocate in its own blood.

He pushed down with all his strength as the claws sank deep into the hybrid's flesh. A huge gout of fluid poured out and splashed all over David. A last gasp, a dying breath, rushed from the monster's mouth. The body stopped moving. The head hung down—dead. The car came to a stop just as the creature's struggles ended.

"We're here," Anna gasped. "Is it over?"

"Yes," David whispered, pulling the seat upwards again, collapsing into it as it clicked into place. "It's over. For now."

Anna stood by his side in the emergency room. There had been nothing physically wrong with her, and the doctor had given her a tranquilizer and suggested she get a lot of sleep. David had been worried about the injuries to his face and to his forearm. The doctor assured him that they would heal and leave hardly a trace. They had to put a few stitches in the arm and his nerves were shot, but otherwise he was okay. Luckily the creature's mandibles had not punctured the skin of his shoulder, so there was no risk of infection.

One look at the remains of the thing in the back seat had convinced the authorities that they ought to take a look out at Felicity Village. David knew it was too late—all they would find would be a lot of dead bodies, both human and hybrid—or what was left of them. Still, it would start an investigation. Too many people knew now. It was out in the open. Even if the County Sheriff were called and were tempted to tell the Wallingford Police to "mind their own business"—for the sake of the Corporation—he would shut up fast enough when they told him what they had in their possession. The Sheriff and everyone else would disavow all knowledge of, and association with, the Corporation as soon as the shit hit the fan, that was for sure.

The pathology lab had taken away the dead chimera and lots of people had gotten a look at it already. They couldn't buy *everyone* off, could they? Kill *everyone?* Burn down the pathology lab and bribe the coroner? He didn't want to think about it. He was back in the hospital again, and only Anna's presence, although she was bone-tired and shocked and shaken beyond words, kept him from total despair.

She was staring out the window, watching the approaching dawn. He came and stood beside her.

"Sit down," she commanded. "The doctor's not finished with you yet."

"Just want to stretch my legs."

She turned to him and began to sob. This time he could not help but join her. "All those people! Those children," she said. "That little boy. And Jeffrey. They killed Jeffrey, too. All for what, David? For *what*? I know you've explained to me about genetic engineering, and I'm trying my best to understand, David. But I don't. Why do people want to fool around with stuff like that?"

"I can understand why," he replied. "They want to solve the ultimate mystery of life. Religion tries to explain it, but it can't. Not really. A hundred different philosophies and psychological programs and cults and therapy groups have been created in an effort to solve that mystery—what the fuck are we and why are we here?—and they can't either. But if we could unlock the secrets of the human cell, create life itself, we're one step closer to understanding our true nature. Only I don't think we ever *will* understand. Crazy, greedy psychotics like Anton will muck it all up and pervert the true purpose of the experimentation.

"Or," he added grimly, "we'll just destroy ourselves in the process. Correction: People like Anton will destroy us."

"I feel so helpless against people like that," Anna said. "So weak and tiny and helpless. All those people dead. And nobody cares, David. Nobody really cares."

"We care," he reminded her.

"Yes," she agreed, "but are we enough?"

395

He couldn't answer her.

They came back sooner than Bartley had expected. David must not have gotten through. They must have feasted, gorged themselves on the inhabitants of Felicity Village, as had been planned for them to do. Their bellies full, they had slunk back to mate, and then to sleep, in order of preference. Disgusting slime, multiplying like that! He would put an end to them once and for all.

The dynamite sticks were all in place. As soon as he thought they were all back in the pool, he would light the fuse. Having consumed so much this night, they would probably not bother with him. He was betting his life on it.

Yes, there they were, their evil heads bobbing in the water. Don't look. Don't look too closely or your blood will freeze. Don't let them gaze *Medusa-like* on you, or you'll turn to stone as surely as you would from a look in a gorgon's eyes. Don't look. Whatever you do.

There were frenzied sounds coming from the pool now. Writhing dark bodies, mating, breeding, spilling obscene seed into even more obscene stomachs. Their sexual organs were located on their underbellies, near the protecting pincers sticking out from their back ends. They coupled together, white face with gray knob, human head with insect eyes, mouth parts clicking against similar mouthparts.

Bartley felt as if he were on the edge of the deepest pit of the underworld.

Their cries of ecstasy filled the air, and the water in the pool splashed over the edge. It was a nightmare come to life. Bodies turning, twisting every which way in horrible copulation. Creatures that could not have mated before, when they had been separate species, were now all *one* creature, capable of inbreeding, capable of producing more and more of their kind. The fools—

Anton, all of them! Had they not realized that *they* could become the dominant species, *would* become the dominant species before long? Superior to man, without scruples, with endless appetites, aggressively feeding on their enemies.

And everyone would become their enemy. The manic thoughts filled Bartley's mind, numbing him to the horror around him, the sounds of splashing water, bubbling over as if the water were boiling from sexual heat. They had to be stopped before a new generation came into being. They had to be stopped now!

Bartley had to look. Just once he had to look. My God —he saw the faces they had—faces of people he knew, the entire town, fornicating in a grotesque, inhuman parody of some horrible orgy. The whole town locked together in sexual hysteria.

He lit the fuse. He had connected all the dynamite with an ingenious network of wires. He ducked into the tunnel, knowing it offered little protection, also knowing there was nowhere else to go. He clutched the briefcase to his chest, his arms wrapped about it as if it was a precious child.

He heard the sizzle of the burning wires, saw the sparkling light travel towards the clumsy piles of sticks. Then there was a booming noise, and a sudden glare that singed his eyebrows. The first explosion came, then the second. The pool seemed to lift right out of its basin, creatures and all, as more explosions followed. Pieces of the hybrids flew through the air, bouncing against the rocky walls, leaving smears of foul fluid. Heads, horrid little limbs, those slimy bodies, bursting apart, smashing against the rocks, drowned by sudden towering waves. The walls began to crumble and the ceiling fell in.

As if it had been shot from a cannon, most of the water in the pool was pushed out by the incredible force and hurled down the tunnel at breathtaking speed. Ted Bartley was dragged along with it. He felt so flimsy and small, engulfed in a smothering whirlpool, his body helplessly swung over and over, this way and that. He had no time to feel more than a stab of fear, a clutch of regret and dread. He was spattered against the steel door at the end of the tunnel like a bug against brick.

On the other side they had been working with acetylene torches, cursing the engineer who had insisted on putting a locking mechanism within. They did not panic until they heard the explosions. Bartley's surmise had been astute. No one had thought that he would attempt sabotage, only that he would try to escape with the damaging papers. Why hurry? He had no place to go. Escape was impossible, wasn't it?

Then the blast of water hit the door with hurricane force. The steel barrier—already weakened—flew off its tearing hinges and fell over, smashing the men working on it and Frederick Anton to a pulp. Blood and brain tissue spattered the walls, floor and ceiling. Unchecked, the water continued in its mad rush, down the hall, flattening everyone, smashing through open doors, and coming into contact with the sophisticated electrical equipment that had cost the Corporation at least half a billion dollars.

The resulting explosion blew the very ceiling off the plant and was heard over fifty miles away.

When David and Anna heard the explosion, the hospital shook all the way down to its foundation. In the distance the sky over Bannon Mountain was a miasma of black soot, gray debris and hot, white light. A crimson hue began to dominate as flames shot up in the air, in wildly spreading sheets. Porter Pharmaceuticals no longer existed.

He did it, David thought. Bartley actually did it. He wondered if the man had survived. Probably not. Probably nothing had survived. Probably not even those horrible creatures, unless some were left in the woods. But they'd track them down, kill them, every last one.

The village had been avenged. Anna's brother had been avenged. It was too bad the innocent had to go with the guilty. Perhaps there had been no other way.

He assured Anna, still trembling, that the explosion was not a harbinger of some new terror, but rather that it signified, if anything, the end.